the
Summer
List

the Summer List

a novel

amy mason doan

GRAYDON
HOUSE

GRAYDON HOUSE

Recycling programs for this product may not exist in your area.

ISBN-13: 978-1-525-80425-0

The Summer List

Copyright © 2018 by Amy Mason Doan

For questions and comments about the quality of this book, please contact us at CustomerService@Harlequin.com.

GraydonHouseBooks.com
BookClubbish.com

Printed in U.S.A.

For Mike and Miranda

For Mike and Miranda

the Summer List

California
July
27th day of camp

The others were mad at her again.

They clustered behind her on the sand, watching as she stepped onto the wet ledge of rocks.

"What is she doing?"

"What are you doing?"

Ignoring them, she picked her way across tide pools, careful not to hurt the creatures underfoot—quivering purple anemones that retracted under her shadow, barnacles like blisters of stone.

All she wanted was a few minutes away from them. A few minutes alone to breathe in the cold wind off the ocean before the van delivered them back to the airless cabins, the dark chapel.

There were only ten minutes left in the game, and it would take her almost that long to make her way back across the slippery outcropping. If they didn't return in time it'd be another mark against her.

She spotted something tangled in kelp, lodged between two flat rocks *near the drop-off. So close to the surf. As if it had been carried across the ocean and snugged there, at the jagged edge of the world, just for her.*

Stepping closer, she crouched, then flattened herself onto her belly. Her shirt and jeans drenched, her elbow scraped, she reached out but got only a rubbery handful of kelp.

She shut her eyes. If she looked down at the sea she would fall in like the doomed man on the keep-off sign behind her, a stick figure tumbling into scalloped waves.

Salt spray stinging her face, she fumbled through the squelching mass of kelp. Until her fingers found what they wanted and it gave, escaping its wet nest with a gentle sucking sound.

She knelt on the wet rocks as she examined her prize, brushing away green muck. The driftwood was longer than her hand, curved into a C. One end was pointier than the other, and in the center the wood splintered and cracked. But imperfect as it was, the resemblance was unmistakable, miraculous: a crescent moon.

Cur-di-lune, he'd said. I grew up in a town called Curdilune.

A strange, pretty name.

He'd drawn it for her in the dusty ground behind the craft cabin that morning. His calloused finger had sketched rectangles for the buildings. Houses and a church, shops and a park, nestled together against the inner curve of a crescent-shaped lake.

Curdilune. Cur is heart in French, he'd explained. Lune is moon. So it means Heart of the Moon. Then, with a light touch on her wrist— You miss home, too?

The others had walked by then, before she could answer, and he'd erased his little map, swirling his palm over the shapes in the dirt so quickly she knew it was their secret.

If she ran back to her team now, her find might help them win—a piece of driftwood was Item 7 on the list stuffed into her back pocket.

She glanced over at them and slid the wet treasure down her pocket, untucking her shirt to hide it. She'd give it to him instead.

It was a thank-you, an offering, an invitation. A cry for help after the long, bewildering summer.

1

Mermaid in the Mailbox

June 2016

The invitation came on a Saturday.

I was taking Jett for a walk, and she was frantic with anticipation, nails skittering on the lobby's tile floor, black fur spiking up so she looked more like a little dragon than a Lab.

"If you calm down I can do this faster, lady," I said as I high-stepped to free myself from the leash she'd wrapped around my ankles. "Off."

She retreated, settling under the bank of mailboxes. But right when I got my letters out, she sprang up and butted my wrist with her head. Perfect aim, perfect timing.

"Leave it, Joan Jett. Devious girl." I tried to maintain the stern voice we learned in Practical Skills Training but couldn't help laughing as I collected my mail from the floor. A typical assortment. White, business-sized bills. A Sushi Express menu. A slender donation form for Goodwill.

Then—not typical—a hot-pink envelope.

It had fallen facedown, revealing a sticker centered over the triangular flap: a mermaid. In pearls and sunglasses. Holding a sign saying You're Invited!

I assumed it was for the tween girl who lived in #1. I was #7, so there were sometimes mix-ups. I was halfway down the hall to her family's unit when I flipped the envelope over, preparing to slide it under their door.

It was for me.

Ms. Laura Christie, 7 Pacific View, San Francisco, CA 94115.

No return address.

But I knew who it was from.

I knew because of the mermaid sticker, which now made sense, and from the surge of something close to happiness in my chest.

I ripped the envelope open and pulled out a photo of two grinning 1950s girls in pajamas. Over their rollered heads, in black ballpoint, she had printed *Coeur-de-Lune*. My hometown.

Then dates—*Thurs. June 23–Sun. June 26*. Less than three weeks away.

Below that it said:

Scavenger hunt!
Crank calls!
Manicures!
Trio of cookie dough!
But seriously, please come. We're supposed to be older and
wiser. (35—how did it happen?) I promise it will be ok.
No RSVP necessary.
Casey

Casey Katherine Shepherd. I hadn't seen her since we were eighteen.

When I ran into people from Coeur-de-Lune they inevitably

asked me about Casey, and I always said, "We drifted." They would nod, as if this was the most natural thing in the world. People drifted.

In my case it'd be more accurate to say I'd swum away. As fast as I could, trying my hardest not to look back.

I slid the card into its torn pink envelope and turned it over again, my thumb smoothing the top edge of the sticker, where it had curled up slightly.

I promise it will be ok, she'd written.

(35—how did it happen?)

I held the invitation over the recycling basket, pausing a second before letting it flutter into the mess of junk mail. I waited for the soft rustle it made on landing before I let Jett tug me to the door.

It was cool and sunny, a rare reprieve from San Francisco's usual June Gloom.

Jett headed right on the sidewalk out of habit. Saturdays we always strolled to Lafayette Park, hitting up her favorite leisurely sniff stops on the way. But today I pulled gently on the leash, and she turned, surprised, as I led her to a crosswalk in the opposite direction, charging uphill toward Lyon Street. I needed the steep climb, something to clear my head.

Why now, Casey? After seventeen years?

My childhood home in Coeur-de-Lune was now a vacation rental, managed by efficient strangers. I'd never gone back. But my mother kept a buzzing gossip line into her church women from town, and gave me sporadic updates on Casey's life.

She always brought Casey up when I was lulled into complacency. When we'd had a surprisingly peaceful afternoon together. When we were outside on her balcony, or sharing a piece of her peach pie like other mothers and daughters did.

Only then would she jab, a master fencer going for the unprotected sliver of my heart.

The first update, when I was twenty—*Casey Shepherd dropped out of college. Back living with that mother in town.*

That must be nice for them, I'd said, not meeting her eyes.

A few years later—*Casey Shepherd bought the bookstore. Moronic. Might as well have thrown her money in the lake.*

I was in her kitchen that morning, unloading groceries into her retirement-sized pantry. Macaroni, crackers, mushroom soup. Hands moving smoothly from bag to shelf, making sure the labels faced out.

That'll be interesting, I'd said. My eyes were trained on my mother's well-organized shelves, but they saw Casey's bookcase, crammed with her beloved trashy paperbacks. Fat, dog-eared copies of *Lace* and *Queenie* and *Princess Daisy.*

After the bookstore news I didn't hear anything about Casey for a long time. I had men in my life, a few friends I met for glasses of wine. I was fine. Settled. Lucky. And able to keep my face blank when my mother said, three years ago:

Casey Shepherd has a child. A girl. Adopted, foster child, something. Hmph. Surprised anyone would let a child into that house. That mother's still there, you know.

I was thirty-two then, and after nearly a decade of blessed silence on the topic of the Shepherds, I could meet my mother's eyes and say evenly, *Casey always liked kids.*

It was the first time I'd said her name out loud since high school.

I began to run, an easy jog.

Was it because of our ages? Was thirty-five the number at which a goofy card could fix everything?

(35—How did it happen?), she'd written, in that familiar, nearly illegible penmanship. Her cursive had always been sloppy, with big capitals.

Casey's mother, Alex, had gotten into handwriting analysis one summer. According to Alex's book, Casey was energetic and loyal, I was creative and romantic, and Alex was an aesthete with a passionate nature. If there had been something in how we looped our *L*s or curved our *C*s that hinted at what was to come, at less flattering traits, we'd overlooked it.

Alex would be there, if I went. Spinning around as if everything was the same, raving about her latest obsession. Celtic runes or cooking with grandfather grains. Whatever she happened to be into that week.

I sped up, though the grade was now more than forty-five degrees. One of those legendary San Francisco hills, perilous to skateboarders and parallel-parkers. Jett's leash was slack, not its usual taut water-skiing line dragging me forward. But she pushed on loyally at my side, the plastic bags tied to her leash flapping and whistling.

Why, Casey?

Wind-sprint pace now, sloppier with each stride.

Maybe she was bored and wanted to see what I'd do if she dared me to visit.

At the top of the hill I bent over, hands on my knees. Jett panted, her black coat shiny as obsidian.

Below, the wide grid of streets and houses swept down toward the Marina, to the bright blue bay flecked with white sails, all the way to the hills of Tiburon rising from the opposite shore. To my left, I could just make out the graceful, ruddy lines of the Golden Gate holding it all in, because without it such aching beauty would escape to sea.

The dark little crescent lake where I'd grown up was nothing compared to this.

The Bay could hold thousands of Coeur-de-Lunes.

I headed slowly back downhill toward my building. My back was soaked, my chest tight. I was lucky I hadn't rolled an ankle.

And I hadn't managed to cardio the invite from my head. Casey's words were still in there, burrowing deeper. I could hear her voice now. The voice of an eighteen-year-old girl, plaintive beneath her irony.

But seriously, please come.

I was sure the mermaid would be safely buried by the time we got back.

But when I passed the mailboxes, there she was, staring up at me. Her tail was covered by a Restoration Hardware catalog, the top edge perfectly horizontal across her waistline. Or fin-line. Whatever it was called, it looked as if someone had tucked her in for the night, careful to leave her face uncovered so she could breathe.

I reached down and, in one quick gesture, plucked the pink envelope from the basket.

I couldn't go.

But I also couldn't leave her like that, all alone.

Coeur-de-Lune
Thursday, June 23

That was nineteen days ago. And now I was in Casey's drive-way, trapped. Too nervous to get out of my car, too embarrassed to leave.

I blamed the mermaid.

Once she'd escaped the recycling bin, the pushy little thing had managed to secure a beachhead on my fridge.

For days, she'd perched there, peering over a black-and-white photo of a young 1970s surf god conquering an impossible wave: one of the magnets I'd designed for Sam, my favorite client and owner of Goofy Foot Surf & Coffee Shack out by Ocean Beach.

As the date grew closer, the mermaid started migrating around my apartment. She kept me company in the bathroom when I flossed in the morning, and as I ate lunch at my small kitchen table. When I couldn't sleep at night and passed the time brushing the frilled edges of the envelope back and forth under my chin, rereading Casey's words. Trying to figure out why she'd written them now, after so long.

I still didn't understand.

The invitation had said *No RSVP necessary*, and I'd taken her up on that, so she didn't know I was coming. Until today, I hadn't been sure myself.

But here I was.

I tunneled my hands into the opposite sleeves of my coat, hugging myself. I'd rolled down my window a few inches, and chilly mountain air was starting to seep in. Jett was in her sheepskin bed in the back, curled into a black ball like a giant roly-poly. I was stalling. Rereading the invite as if I hadn't memorized it weeks before.

I leaned over the steering wheel and stared up at the house as if it could provide answers. From the front it resembled one of those skinny birdhouses kids made in camp out of hollow tree branches standing on end: a wooden rectangle with a crude, A-shaped cap.

But from the water it looked more like a boat, with rows of small, high windows—so much like portholes—and a long, skinny dock—pirate's gangplank—to complete the effect. When the place started falling apart in the '70s, some grumbly neighbor called it The Shipwreck, and the name had stuck.

It was a love-it-or-hate-it house, and the Shepherd women had loved it.

So had I. I'd once felt easier here, more myself, than in my own home. The Shipwreck hadn't changed, but today it offered me no welcome.

There was a silver Camry ahead of me in the driveway, so someone was probably home. They could be watching, counting how many minutes I sat inside my car. Trying to gather my courage, and failing. I didn't feel any more courageous than I had when the invitation first arrived.

"Wish me luck," I whispered toward Jett's snores as I got out.

I shut the door a little harder than necessary, hoping the *plunk* would draw Casey and Alex outside. Then they'd have to say something to hurdle us over the awkwardness. "You made it!" Or "Come in, it's getting cold!"

But the front door didn't budge.

I walked slowly toward the house, past the Camry. The section of lake I could see beyond the house was at its most stunning, framed in pines, streaked with red and pink from the sunset. It was so ridiculously beautiful it seemed almost a rebuke, a point made and underlined twice. *This* is how a sunset is done.

As I got closer I noticed something about the colors on the water; most of the red shapes were dancing, but one was still. And I realized why Casey hadn't come outside when I pulled up.

Of course. She was already outside.

I walked past the right side of the house, where the ground became a thick blanket of pine needles. I'd forgotten that spongy feeling, the way it made you bend your knees a little more than you did in the city, the tiny satisfying bounce of each step. There were places where the needles were so deep I had to brush my hand along the rough wood shingles for balance. I hoped the neighbors wouldn't see me and decide I was a prowler. I was even wearing all black. Tailored black pants and my black cowl-neck cashmere coat, but still. I could be a fashion-conscious burglar. It would be something to talk about, at least, showing up in handcuffs.

Casey sat cross-legged on the dock, her crown of sunlit red hair just visible above the red blanket on her shoulders.

It was the same scratchy wool plaid throw we'd used for picnics. The same one we'd sprawled on in our first bikinis as teenagers. In high school I'd hidden mine in my winter boots, one forbidden scrap of nylon stuffed down each toe.

A duck plunged into the water nearby, its flapping energy abruptly turning to calm, and she said something to it that I couldn't make out. Maybe we could do this all night. She'd watch ducks, I'd watch her, and once an hour I'd take a few steps closer.

I walked down the sloping, sandy path in the grass and stepped onto the wooden dock. It was still long and narrow, the boards as old and misaligned as ever. *Cattywampus*, Alex used to call them. Casey's mom was young—sometimes she seemed even younger than us. But her speech was full of old-fashioned expressions like that. "Cattywampus" and "bless my soul" and "dang it all."

The feeling of the uneven boards beneath my feet was so familiar I froze again.

The last time I'd been here I'd been running. Pounding the boards, racing away from the feet pounding behind me.

It was not too late to slip away. Take big, quiet steps backward. I could retreat along the side of the house the way I'd come. Return to the city and let the Shepherds sink back into memory, along with everything else in this town.

But a subtle vibration had already traveled down the wooden planks, and Casey turned her head to the side, revealing a profile that was still strong, a chin that still jutted out in her defiant way. "Is it you?"

"Yes, Case."

I walked slowly to the end of the dock until I stood over her left shoulder, so close I could see the messy part in her hair. It was a darker red now.

The greetings I'd rehearsed, the lines and alternate lines and backup-alternate lines, had abandoned me. They'd sailed away, carried off by the breeze when I wasn't paying attention.

But Casey spoke first, her eyes on the water. "You've been standing back there forever. I thought you were going to leave."

"I almost did."

She tilted her head up to look at me. Scanning, evaluating, and, finally, delivering her report—"You're still you."

Her face was a little thinner, her skin less freckled. There was something behind her eyes, a weariness or skepticism, that hadn't been there when we were girls.

I forced a smile. "And you're still you."

I got, in return, no smile. And silence.

Casey made no move to get up, so I fumbled on. "And the house is still..."

"Weird," she finished.

"I was going to say something like *charming*."

"*Charming?* Laura doesn't say *charming*. Tell me Laura has not grown up into someone who says *charming*."

She wasn't going to make this easy. I'd thought, from the cheerful humility of her invitation, that she'd at least try. When I didn't answer, Casey swiveled her body to look back at the house, as if to evaluate it through fresh eyes the way she'd examined me.

"We haven't done much. That tiny addition on the east side. And I managed to put in a full bath upstairs finally. It's yours this weekend, along with my old bedroom."

"I was going to say. I had to bring my dog. I thought it'd be crowded with all of us, Alex and your little girl and my dog. She's kind of big, and she's sweet with kids, but she could knock a little one down... I don't know how old your girl is but..."

Casey looked up at me but let me stumble on.

"Anyway there wasn't anybody renting our old place this weekend, so I'll sleep there..."

The truth was my place had been booked solid all summer, so I'd bumped out this weekend's renters. Some sweet family that had reserved months ago. Other property owners kicked people out all the time when they wanted to use their houses instead, and my property manager grumbled about it, but I'd never done it before. I'd felt so guilty I'd spent hours finding them another place and paid the $230 difference.

Bullshit, Casey's eyes said.

She knew the truth: I couldn't bear staying with her. Tiptoeing around politely in the familiar rooms where we'd once been careless and easy as sisters. But I went on, elaborating on my story—the sure sign of a lie. "Of course I couldn't put you out…"

"'Put you out,'" she said. "Grown-up Laura says 'put you out'?"

I didn't understand it, the utter disconnect between her warm, silly, lovable letter, the Casey I'd first met, and the person who was sitting here next to me, making everything a hundred times harder than it had to be.

Would the running commentary last all weekend? *Laura eats with her fork and knife European-style, now. Grown-up Laura prefers red wine to white. Laura wears cuff bracelets now. Laura changed her perfume to L'eau D'Issey.* Every little gesture picked over and mocked.

It hit with awful certainty: I shouldn't have come.

Would it get better or worse when Alex joined us? I didn't hate her anymore. Enough time had passed. She couldn't help how she was.

With Alex to fill the silences, and Casey's daughter around as a buffer, and me sleeping at my place, I'd just make it through the weekend. Less than sixty hours if I left Sunday morning instead of Sunday night, blaming traffic and work.

"Where's your mom and your little girl? I'm sorry, I don't know her name."

"Elle. Off on a trip together. Tahoe."

So much for the buffer.

Casey nodded at my old house across the lake. "Now. That one *has* changed, I hear. Modern everything."

"Only the kitchen, really," I said. "The rental company insisted. I've just seen pictures." From across the shining water, I could make out the dark line of the dock, a flash of sunset on a window.

I'd planned to drive there first. Drop off Jett, compose myself, drink a glass of wine (or three, or four) to loosen up for the big reunion. If I had I could have kayaked over to Casey's instead of driving.

And paddled away again the second I realized how she was going to be.

"You haven't gone inside?" she said. "Not once?"

I shook my head. "I can do everything online. It's crazy."

"I thought maybe you were sneaking back at night. Hiding out in the house, staying off the lake, calling your groceries in. To avoid seeing me."

"I wouldn't do that."

She narrowed her eyes. "You didn't sell it, though."

The "why?" was there in her expression, daring me, but I didn't have an answer. I'd always planned to sell the house. My mother didn't care either way, and we got offers. Every year, I considered it. But I never went through with it.

I met her stare for a minute before I had to look away. My eyes landed on a spot in the lake about ten yards from the edge of the dock. I didn't mean to look there. Maybe there was a tiny ripple from a fish, or a point in the sunset's reflection that was a more burnished gold than the surrounding water.

She followed my gaze. And for the first time, her voice softened. "Strange to think it's still there. After so long."

"It's not. It's crumbled into a million pieces or floated away."

Casey shook her head. "No. It's still there."

"How do you know?"

"I just do. I feel it in my bones."

"That sounds like something your mom would say. Used to say."

She tilted her head, thinking. "God. It does."

She pulled her knees close to her body and rested her right cheek on them, then looked up at me with a funny little lopsided smile.

There was enough of the Casey I remembered in that smile that I returned it.

I sat next to her, wrapping my coat tighter, my legs dangling off the edge of the dock. It felt strange, to sit like that with shoes and pants on. I should be in my old cargo shorts, dipping my bare feet in the water.

For a minute we watched the quivering red-and-gold shapes on the lake. Then I felt the gentle weight of her hand on my shoulder.

"Don't mind my flails, grown-up Laura," she said. "Grown-up Casey is doing her best. She's missed you."

The words stuck in my throat, and when they finally came out, they were rough. My eyes on the auburn lake, I reached up to clutch her hand—one quick, fumbling squeeze.

"I've missed you, too, Case."

2

Ariel and Pocahontas

June 1995
Summer before freshman year

The fourth day of summer started exactly like the first three.

A second of dread when I woke up, followed by a rush of relief when I remembered it was vacation. Then the quick, glorious tally—no school for eighty-eight days. And finally the smell of vanilla floating down the hall. Yesterday it had been crumb cake, the day before it was muffins, so today was probably French toast. My favorite.

I got dressed fast, changing from my nightgown into my summer uniform: a big T-shirt and cargo shorts.

The last part of my routine was too important to be rushed. I transferred a small, silvery-gray object from under my pillow to the Ziploc I kept on my nightstand, made sure it was sealed to the last millimeter, then slipped it into my lower-right shorts pocket, the only one with a zipper. Where it always went.

Then I had the entire day free to explore the lake. French toast, and no Pauline Knowland or Suzanne Farina asking me what my bra size was up to in honeyed tones, or calling me Sister Christian just within earshot, and the whole day free. Bliss.

It only lasted the length of the hallway.

"You'll bring that to the new neighbors after breakfast," my mother said when I entered the kitchen. She was scrambling eggs with a rubber spatula, and she paused to point it at a pound cake on the counter. "Good morning."

Chore assignment first, greeting second. This about summed up my mother.

She went back to parting the sea of yellow in the pan.

So not only was the vanilla smell for some other family, I had an assignment. I examined the cake's golden surface. It was perfect, but curiously plain. No nuts, no chocolate chips, no blueberries. Not even drizzled with glaze, and it obviously wouldn't be. My mother always poured the cloudy liquid on when her cakes were still piping hot.

Next to the naked cake she'd set out a paper plate, Saran Wrap, a length of red ribbon, and one of her monogrammed notecards. A complete new-neighbor greeting kit, ready to go before 7:30 a.m. I read the card silently. *Welcome—Christies.*

A stingy sort of note, nothing like the warm introduction she'd written when the Daytons moved in down the shore last year. That had included an invitation to church. Surely my mother could have spared a few more words for the new family, a *the* before our last name. They were right across the narrowest part of the lake from us. If they had binoculars, they could see how much salt we put on our eggs.

It seemed she'd already taken a dislike to the new people, and I set about learning why. "You're not coming with me to meet them?"

"They have a daughter your age, you need to offer to walk

to school together the first day," she said, like this was written in stone somewhere.

Shoot me now. The last thing I needed was more complications at school. My plan was to lie low in September.

I watched the tip of my mother's white spatula make figure eights in the skillet. How could eggs be so nasty on their own when they played a clutch role in French toast? I'd take a tiny spoonful and distribute it artfully around my plate so it would look like more.

As if she'd heard my thoughts, my mother mounded a triple lumberjack serving of scrambled eggs onto a plate and handed it to me.

I carried it to the breakfast nook and sat next to my dad, who was hidden behind his newspaper. I could only see his tuft of white hair. It was sticking up vertically, shot through with sun from the window. "Last one awake is the welcome wagon," he said. "New household rule."

He snapped a corner of the paper down and winked at me. "Morning."

I smiled. "Morning."

I pushed egg clumps around with my fork and stared out the window at the small brown shape in the pines across the lake. The junky-looking old Collier place, the one everybody called The Shipwreck. The Collier name was legend around Coeur-de-Lune, though the actual Colliers were long gone. They'd been rich, and a lot of them had died young. The small building across the lake where the Collier kids slept in summer had been falling apart since before I was born, and my mother always said they should just burn it. The Colliers' main summerhouse, the fancy three-story one that had once been a few hundred yards up the shore, had been torn down when the land was split up decades before.

I'd seen trucks at The Shipwreck since it sold. Pedersen's Hardware and Ready Windows. I loved the funny little house exactly the way it was, and now the new family would fix it up and ruin it.

So because they had a daughter my age my mother was totally blowing off the visit? Something was off. In her world of social niceties, frozen somewhere around 1955, new neighbors required baked goods. Not from a mix—new neighbors called for separating yolks from whites. And they definitely called for a personal appearance.

"Saw their car the other day when they were moving in," my dad said behind his *New York Times*, making it shiver. There was a photo of Bill Clinton on the front page, shaking some dignitary's hand, and when he spoke it looked like they were dancing.

My mother was transferring patty sausages from a skillet onto a plate. At his words, her elbows really got into stabbing the sausages and violently shaking them off the fork.

When she didn't respond he continued, "Saw what was on the back bumper."

That did it.

She dropped the plate between us with a thud and stalked into the dining room to tend to her latest batch of care packages for soldiers. They were arranged in a perfect ten-by-ten grid on the dining room table.

I forked a sausage and took a bite, burning the roof of my mouth with spicy grease.

After I swallowed I whispered, "What was on the car?" Maybe a bumper sticker my mother considered racy. Or *inappropriate*, to use one of her favorite words.

The day wasn't blissfully free anymore, but at least it was getting interesting.

A new girl my age, just across the water, with parents who'd slapped an inappropriate bumper sticker on the family wagon. Maybe one of those *Playboy* women with arched backs and waists as tiny as their ankles, the ones truck drivers liked to keep on their mud flaps.

My dad set his paper down and started working the cross-word. He did the puzzle in the *Times* only after finishing the easier ones in the *Reno Statesman* and the *Tahoe Daily Journal*. I liked to watch his forehead lines jump around when he worked on the *Times* crossword. I could tell when it was going well and when he was stumped, just by how wavy they were in the center.

He tapped on the paper with the tip of his black ballpoint the way he always did when he was struggling. He must have thrown in one or two extra taps because I glanced down. Above the "Across" clues he'd drawn a fish with legs. Ah. That would do it. According to my mother's complicated book of social equations, one of those pro-Darwin anti-Christian fish with legs on your rear bumper meant you got a red ribbon, but only tied around a no-frills pound cake, and you got a duty visit from her daughter, but not from her.

My dad scribbled over the drawing and cleared his throat, then sent me a quick wink. I nudged my scrambled-egg plate closer to him and he took care of them for me in three bites, one eye on the dining room entryway as he chewed.

He went back to his crossword, and I got up to wrap the cake, curling the ribbon to make up for the terrible note. The unwelcome note. But as I was returning the scissors to the drawer I saw the black pen my mother had used. I'd mastered her hand-writing years before. (*Please excuse Laura from Physical Education, her migraines have been simply terrible lately.*)

Quickly, expertly, I revised her words.

Welcome—Christies became *Welcome!!—The Christies. We're so thrilled you're here!*

Okay, maybe I went overboard. It was the kind of note Pauline Knowland's and Suzanne Farina's mothers would write, a message anticipating years of squealing hellos at Back-to-School night.

I tucked the note in my pocket, returned the pen to the

drawer, and by the time my mother bustled in again I was at the table sipping orange juice, innocent as anything.

I dipped my paddle, breaking the glassy surface of the lake. I was the only one out on the water this early—the only human at least. The gentle ploshes and chirps and ticks of the lake felt like solitude; I knew them so well.

It was chilly on the water but warmth spread through my shoulders as I set my short course for The Shipwreck. My dad liked to speak in jaunty nautical terms like this; he always asked when I came home after a day on the lake—*How was your voyage?* Or—*Duel with any pirates?*

He gave me my kayak for my tenth birthday. My mother was just as surprised as me when he led us outside after the German chocolate cake. I'd opened up all my other gifts—two sweaters and six books and a Schumann CD I'd requested and a tin of Violetta dusting powder with a massive puff I'd not only *not* requested, but had absolutely no clue what to do with. My mother and I both thought the birthday was done.

Then he'd said, *Might be one more thing outside.*

He'd covered his surprise with a black tarp, pulling it off to reveal the sleek yellow vessel. *So you can explore*, he'd explained.

To my quietly fuming mother, he had said, his eyes dodging hers, *Because she's in the double digits now.*

If they fought about it later—him writing such a big check without asking or, the more serious offense, the implication that he knew me best—I hadn't heard it, and the heating duct in our small house ran right from their bedroom up to mine. I heard their whispered "discussions" all the time.

Eventually my mother grew to accept the kayak. She told her church friends that she liked me to play outdoors all summer. Sermons in stones and all of that.

The lake was small, a crescent of water only six miles around. At the narrowest, southernmost point, where we were, it was only four hundred feet wide. I could paddle across our end in two minutes without breaking a sweat.

Today I took it easy so I could size up the new neighbors as I crossed. I expected them to be outside commanding an army of painters and fix-it people, but the place seemed as run-down as ever, the gutters overflowing with pine needles, the dull wood shingles fringed in moss, the narrow dock as rickety as a gangplank. Whatever the trucks had been there for, it wasn't visible from the back.

The house hadn't been rented in more than six months. We were too far from the good skiing and stores, and you couldn't take anything motorized on our little lake. Everybody wanted to live in Tahoe, or at least Pinecrest.

But there were signs of life. A rainbow beach towel draped over the dock ladder, bags of mulch stacked by the garden gate. The small square garden, to the left of the house, had been untended for years and used unofficially as a dog run. It was basically an ugly, deer-proof metal fence surrounding weeds, but obviously the new owners had plans.

Something else new—a small red spot on the edge of the dock, right at the center. Paddling closer, I saw that it was a kid's figurine dangling from a nail. A plastic Ariel, from *The Little Mermaid*, her chest puffed out like when she was on the prow of the ship pretending to be a statue. It definitely had not been there the last time I'd snooped around The Shipwreck.

I wondered if the famous "daughter my age" had done it. I hoped not. It was the kind of joke I liked, and I didn't want to like her. There was no way we would be friends, not when she found out what I was at school. The best I could hope for was that she would be what I called a Neutral. Someone I didn't need to think about at all. Someone who didn't make my day better or worse.

"You look exactly like an Indian princess."

I jumped in my seat, almost losing my paddle.

A girl was swimming up to me. Her pale skin had splatters of mud on it and she had threads of green lake gunk in her hair. Red hair. The toy Ariel on the dock had definitely been her idea.

"You know, like Pocahontas or someone, with your dark braid, in your canoe?" she continued, breaststroking close enough that I could see it was freckles on her shoulders, not dirt. I'd never seen so many freckles. There were goose bumps, too, which didn't surprise me. The lake wasn't really comfortable for swimming until after the Fourth of July.

I composed myself enough to correct her. "Kayak."

"Right, canoes are the kneeling ones. You coming to see us?" She tilted her head at the house.

Before I could answer, she closed her eyes and sank down into the water up to her hairline. When she popped back up, she squeezed her nostrils between her thumb and index finger to clear them.

"My mother wanted me to bring you this," I said. I stashed my paddle in the nose of the kayak, yanked my backpack from the front seat, and unzipped it so she could see the cake under its pouf of plastic wrap. "To welcome you and your parents."

"Parent. Singular. So you didn't want to bring it? Your mom made you?"

I still wasn't sure what category she belonged to, but she was definitely not a Neutral.

"I didn't mean that," I said.

I was starting to drift from the dock but she swam close and for a second I worried she would grab the hull and capsize me.

At the thought, I automatically gripped my shorts pocket, squeezing the familiar shape, smaller than a deck of cards, through the worn cotton. The Ziploc was only insurance. My good-luck charm couldn't get wet.

The swimming girl's eyes darted from my face down to the edge of my shorts, where my hand clutched. She cleared water from her ears, repositioned her purple bathing suit straps, and slicked her red hair back with both hands.

The whole time she performed this aquatic grooming routine, her eyes didn't budge from my right hand. I forced myself to let go of my pocket and fidgeted with my braid instead.

But her eyes didn't follow my hand. They stayed right on the zippered compartment of my shorts.

I'd have to invent a new category for this girl. She missed nothing.

I would set the cake on the dock. I'd paddle over to Meriwether Point like I'd planned and have my picnic. Lie in the sun as long as I wanted, with nobody to bug me, on my favorite spot on the big rock that curved perfectly under my back. Later I'd collect pieces of driftwood for a mirror I was making and go swimming in Jade Cove.

I had all kinds of plans for the summer.

"Well, I've got to…" I began.

"Do you want to…" She laughed. "What were you saying?"

"Just that I should go. I told my mom I'd help around the house."

"Where's your place?"

I pointed.

She paddled herself around to face the opposite shore. "Cool. We can swim that, easy. We can go back and forth all the time."

She was so sure we'd be friends. She was sure enough for both of us.

"Come in and we'll eat the whole cake ourselves," she said, completing her circle in the water to face me. "My mom's in Tahoe. She won't be back 'til late."

"I wish I could." *Stop being so nice. I can't afford to like you.*

"Are you going to be in ninth?" she went on, panting a little as she tread water.

"Yeah."

"Me, too. You can say you were telling me about the high school. That's helpful."

"There's not much to tell about the school. It's tiny. It's not very good. The football team is the Astros, because everyone around here is seriously into the moon thing."

"See? I need you. Come on."

I didn't offer the most valuable piece of advice—*If you want to make friends at CDL High, don't hang around with me.*

"Please. Tell your mom I totally forced you to eat a piece of cake and help me unpack." The girl grinned, sure of her charm.

It was a wide grin that stretched out the freckles on her nose, and I couldn't resist it.

Her name was Casey.

"Casey Katherine Shepherd, named after Casey Kasem, that old DJ," she said, sprinting ahead of me up the dock to her house. She wrapped the rainbow beach towel around her bottom half as she ran. "My mom was obsessed with him," she called back, leaping onto the sandy path in the sloping, scrubby patch of lawn behind the house. "She has CD box sets of radio countdowns from 1970 to 1988. What's your name?"

"Laura. Named after a great-great-aunt I never met. But I'm guessing she wasn't a DJ."

Casey turned so I could see she was laughing, but she didn't stop running. She didn't rinse her feet off, though there was a faucet right there by the back door, but pounded up the rotting wood steps, opened the screen door, and walked inside, track-ing muck.

I'd always wanted to go inside The Shipwreck. When I was little, I'd imagined wood walls, hammocks, ropes dangling from the ceiling. Maybe a captain's wheel.

But it was only an ordinary room crammed with moving boxes. The small windows and dark green paint made every-thing gloomy.

"Well, welcome to the neighborhood." I pulled the cake from my backpack and set it on a brown box labeled Stuff!

"I have no clue where the knives are, so here." Casey yanked at the curly ribbon. She broke the cake in two pieces, handed me one, and knocked her hunk against mine. "Cheers."

"Cheers."

"Did you know this used to be a kids' cabin for another house that's not here anymore, and everyone calls it The Shipwreck?" she said, crumbs on her bottom lip.

I nodded, finished chewing. "Who told you, your Realtor?"

"We didn't have a Realtor. My mom bought the house from the owner. The guy who fixed the windows told her. When he realized my mom was the colorful type he wouldn't stop talking about it. Flirting with her." She rolled her eyes. *"A house with real history, he said. Built in the 1920s. One of a kind."*

The colorful type. I was tempted to ask if her colorful mother knew the stir her quadruped bumper-fish had caused. "I noticed the Ariel on the dock. Did you put it there because…"

"Yes. Screw them if they think The Shipwreck is an insult, it's cool the way it is. Look, you can still see the marks from the bunk beds." She shoved boxes around to show me the dark rectangles in the wood floor. "There were five bunks, so I guess ten kids could sleep down here. And one babysitter had to deal with them all summer, I bet."

"My mother grew up in our house. She says the boys who stayed here in the forties and fifties ran wild all summer. But she never told me about the bunk beds." I bent to touch one of the marks. "Cool."

There were no bunk beds now. The only furniture in the room was a saggy, opened-out futon against the long wall. It was unmade, the imprint from a body still visible in the swirl of sheets.

"My mom's sleeping down here for now," she said. "She's using one of the rooms upstairs for her studio because the light's better and the daybed she ordered hasn't come yet. Come see my room."

I followed her up the dark staircase. "So she's an artist?"

"Ultrabizarre stuff, but people pay a ton for it because bizarre is in." She thumped her hand on a closed door as we passed, but didn't offer to show me any of the ultrabizarre art.

"When's your furniture coming?" I followed her down the narrow hall.

"Our last four places were furnished so my mom's off buying stuff."

Last *four* places? As I considered this, Casey disappeared into a wall of gold. At least that's what I thought it was until I got closer and figured out it was yellow candy wrappers stuck together in chains, dangling from her doorjamb to form a crinkly, sunlit curtain.

"I made that for our hallway in San Francisco," she said from the other side of the swaying lengths of plastic. "I was going through a butterscotch phase."

"I like it," I said. Did I? I had no idea. I was just trying to step through the ropes of cellophane without breaking them. "How many wrappers did it take?"

"A hundred and eighty-eight. My mom put my real door on sawhorses in her studio, for a table."

I could only imagine what my mother would say if I tried to replace my bedroom door with candy wrappers. When I was little, she didn't let me take hard candy from the free bowl at the bank, saying it was a scam they had going with the dentist.

But the fact that Casey's mom apparently didn't worry about cavities wasn't the weirdest part. The weirdest part was that this girl had *voluntarily* taken her bedroom door off its hinges, not minding that now her mother could peek in whenever. She could catch her undressed, or interrupt her when she was writing in her journal, or yell at her from downstairs right when she'd reached the best part of her book.

My bedroom not only had a door—the wooden variety—but a lock. I used it twice a day, when I transferred my good-luck charm between my pocket and my pillow.

I stashed other objects in my room, too. I had a Maybelline Raspberry Burst lip gloss tucked into the bottom of my Kleenex box. A *Cosmopolitan* I'd filched from the dentist hidden inside the zippered cushion of my desk chair, with 50 Tips That'll Drive Him Wild in Bed. I had come to know well the thrill of concealing objects in my room, the secret electric charge they emitted from their hiding places. My bedroom was strung in currents only I knew about.

I didn't tell her any of this. I'd known her only twenty minutes.

"Didn't you get sick of all that butterscotch by the end?"

She laughed. "Totally. I threw out the last fifty."

We sat facing each other on her unmade single bed, inside a fortress of brown moving boxes, finishing the cake. She was still wearing her wet bathing suit and towel. I would never wear a thin bathing suit like that, even in the water, and definitely not out of it. But Casey, named after the male DJ, was flat as a boy. And something told me she wouldn't have cared about covering up even if she wasn't.

As we ate, and she talked about San Francisco—the freezing fog, the garlic smell that would drift up the apartment air shaft from the restaurant below—I monitored a damp spot spreading out on her yellow bedspread. It expanded around her hips, like a shadow. My mother would have gone ballistic; she pressed our sheets once a week and had a dedicated rack in the laundry room for used beach towels.

By my last bite of cake I had to admit that I liked this sturdy, confident girl. And I felt bad for her. She said she'd had no idea she was moving until her mom announced it on the last day of middle school.

"We'd only been in San Francisco for a year, and I was all

registered at Union High for September, then all of a sudden
my mom heard about this house, and here we are. Goodbye,
Union. Hello, Coeur-de-Lune High."

"People never say that. They say CDL High."

"Got it."

"Which is kind of dumb since it's exactly the same number
of syllables."

She laughed, and I realized in that second just how much I
wanted her to like me. I couldn't resist going on. "Like I said,
it's not such a great school."

"Go, Astronauts," she said, laughing, shaking her fists as if
she was holding miniature pom-poms.

"Astros."

"Right. Keep the insider tips coming."

"I'm definitely not an insider, I... So why'd your mom want
to move?"

"She's impulsive like that. You'll get it when you meet her.
We lived in a bunch of places before San Francisco. Reno, Oakland, Berkeley. Then suddenly she was all about nature. Fresh
air, peace and quiet so she could work and I could... I don't
know. Suck in all the fresh air."

"Weren't you sad? Leaving your friends in San Francisco?"

"Yeah, but...my mom's my best friend."

I licked crumbs from my fingers. "That must be nice. My
mother is..."

Strict? That wasn't the right word. *Cold* was closer to the truth,
but not quite fair. My mother took my temperature when I was
sick, and remembered that I liked German chocolate cake, and
once said I played the piano like an angel. She asked me for my
Christmas list the day after Thanksgiving. *Rigid? Overly efficient?
Judgmental?* None of them added up to a good answer.

"She's what?"

"She's older than most mothers."

"Grandma old?"

"Sixty-two. I'm adopted. And my dad's almost sixty-four. But my mother seems older than him because she's kind of religious."

"Like that nutjob fanatic mom in *Carrie*? I have that, have you read it? It's awesome."

"No, but I saw an ad for the movie on TV. She's not like that. She's just… I don't know. Old-fashioned."

"Bummer."

"Yeah."

Bummer. I liked that tidy summary of my relationship with my mother. It took something that made me feel freakish and confused and brought it into the light, transforming it into a typical teenagey complaint.

I didn't tell Casey she was sharing her cake with Sister Christian, or about how Pauline Knowland stole my bra during a shower after gym last September, so I'd spent the rest of the school day hunched over and red-faced.

I didn't tell her how hard it is in a small town, where you're shoved into a role in fifth grade and you can't escape it no matter what you do, how it squeezes the fight out of you, because everybody knows everybody and you aren't allowed to change.

And I didn't tell her that one of the things hidden in my bedroom was a homemade calendar taped to the inside back wall of my closet, where I crossed off the number of CDL High days I had to survive until graduation. 581.

Go Astros.

Instead I said, even though I wasn't that interested in horror novels, "Can I borrow *Carrie* sometime?"

"Sure." Casey jumped off the crumb-strewn bed and went through boxes, tossing books on the floor.

She had more books than I did, and I had a ton. I even had a first edition of *Little Women*. Casey had *Little Women*, too, I noticed, and I picked it up off the floor, about to ask if she liked it and if she'd ever read *Little Men* or *Rose in Bloom*, which could be preachy but had some entertaining parts.

Only when I looked closer I realized it wasn't *Little Women*. It was *The Little Woman*.

And judging by the cover, it was definitely not an homage to Louisa May Alcott. It had a lady sashaying down her hallway in a skimpy white nightgown, with a gun stuffed down her cleavage. Behind her, at the other end of the hall, you could just make out a shadowy male figure.

The perfect wife is about to get the perfect revenge, it said.

"We had this fantastic used bookstore down the street from our last place," Casey said, her head down in the moving box. "It's one thing I'll miss. That and foghorns. And pork buns."

"Found it," she said, lobbing a paperback of *Carrie* at me. "Keep it as long as you want. And take this, too. You might be into it, being adopted and all. I went through a phase where I totally imagined I was adopted because of that book. It seemed so romantic."

"It's not, believe me."

The cover of *Carrie*, with a pop-eyed teenage girl covered in streams of blood, creeped me out. I'd probably just skim it. The other one looked pretty good, though. *Lace,* it said in pink, on a black lacy background. *The book every mother kept from her daughter* at the bottom. Which sounded promising.

This daughter would definitely keep it from her mother. Maybe I could stuff it down one of my winter boots. It was too big to conceal inside my Kleenex box.

"You're lucky your mother lets you read whatever you want," I said.

"My mom's annoying, too. She can never stick to one hobby. She gets totally into something, then just when *I* get interested she's onto something else. It sucks."

It didn't sound sucky at all. It sounded kind of great. My mother hadn't developed a new hobby in decades. She was content with her baking and her needlepoint and her charitable bustling-around. Even my father was pretty stuck in his ways. He had his crosswords, and his never-ending house repairs, and his twice-a-week volunteer job at the Historical Society which consisted—as far as I could tell—of playing backgammon with Ollie Pedersen above the hardware store surrounded by old photos.

"Last month it was pressure valves," Casey said.

"Like, plumbing?"

"No. This philosophy on stress relief. She got this book by some lady named Alberta R. Topenchiek and it's all she talked about for weeks. Pressure Valves and Self-Monitoring of Wants versus Needs and Minor Stress Triggers versus Major Triggers."

I laughed.

"I almost threw the book down our garbage chute, I got so sick of talking about it. Anyway, Alberta R. Topenchiek says everyone has to have a pressure valve. The thing they do when nothing else makes them feel good. My mom's is her art, and mine's swimming. What's yours?"

"Kayaking," I said. I'd never thought of it that way before, but of course it was.

"Will you teach me? I've never done it."

I hesitated a second but I didn't have a chance against her smile. Her smile, her ridiculous candy-wrapper curtain, her directness.

And her total confidence that the only thing separating us was a few hundred feet of lake water.

"Sure."

I stayed at Casey's for three hours that first day, helping her organize her books and clothes, listening to the Top 40 radio countdown CD for 1982. I'd never seen someone sing along so completely unselfconsciously to Toto's "Africa" before. Usually people sort of mumbled it in the back of their throats, looking around as if they were worried they'd get caught.

When she wasn't singing I tried to stick to safe topics. *The principal is married to the history teacher. Hot lunch in our district is $3.60, or you can do the salad and fruit bar for $1.80.*

But Casey kept steering the conversation back to exactly where I didn't want it—me.

"So what are your friends like?" she said, folding a green sweater.

"I used to hang out with this girl Dee, but she moved to Tahoe last year."

This was a lie. Dee and I had been friends in third grade, and she'd moved away in fifth, right when I could have used her. Fifth grade was when Pauline Knowland decided I had entertainment value.

"Are you allowed to go on dates yet?"

"It hasn't come up," I admitted.

"Right. It's early."

"What about you? Have you had a boyfriend yet?"

Casey got a funny half smile, looking at a spot over my right shoulder. She spoke slowly, as if she was in a witness box, enunciating for the court reporter. "No, ma'am. I have not had a boyfriend yet."

With the cake polished off, she set a big pink-and-white Brach's Pick-a-Mix bag on the bed. Root beer barrels, lemon drops, toffee, and starlight mints. No butterscotch.

"Sustenance, because we're working so hard," she said.

By the time I kayaked home, promising to return at ten the next morning, Casey's closet was organized, her CDs were lined up alphabetically along one wall, and my back molars were little skating rinks of hard candy.

I ran my tongue across my teeth as I paddled, trying not to smile.

3

Alexandra the Great

I spent five hours with Casey the next day, and seven the next, and as the long summer days ran on it became easier to count the hours we were not together.

She proved to be a quick study on the kayak but I still sat in back, where I could take over if things got dicey. She liked to go fast. We'd be floating along, lazy and destinationless, and she'd shout, "Let's do warp speed!" and we'd fly, enjoying a wind-blown rush for a minute until we inevitably knocked paddles and collapsed into laughter.

I showed her my favorite spots on the lake. The flat, sunny rock at Meriwether Point, where I'd always picnicked alone, and shady little Jade Cove, where tiny fish tickled your ankles and there was a downed pine tree that made a good, bouncy diving board.

One day I took her to Clark Beach on the North shore. We ate cheese-and-sourdough sandwiches and drowsed in the sun, and it would have been another perfect day if I wasn't slightly on edge, worrying that Pauline Knowland and her pack of blow-dried minions would show up. I hadn't taken Casey anywhere so public before. But Pauline didn't come. She spent most of her summer afternoons at the mall or at Pinecrest Lake Beach, where there was more action. Action was in short supply around Coeur-de-Lune.

Sitting behind Casey in the kayak day after day, I got to know the pattern of freckles on her shoulders. She didn't brush her hair before we met by her dock each morning so the back rose up in a snarled mat, revealing the flipped-up size tag of her purple bathing suit.

Freckles on pink skin, a tangle of red hair, an upside-down Jantzen Swimwear size six label: these are the strongest visual memories of that summer before high school.

I had a journal my dad gave me when I was seven, a puffy pink thing with *A Girl's First Diary* on the cover in gold script. I hid it inside a hollowed-out copy of *Silas Marner* on my bottom bookshelf, and concealed the key in a mint tin in my third-best church purse.

I wasn't a dedicated diary writer. My entries were sloppy and I sometimes went weeks without turning the key in the little gold lock. But on June 13, seven days after I met Casey, I wrote:

A summer friend. Ariel. She's…disarming.
TGTBT
Disarming. (One of my PSAT words.) *TGTBT.* Too good to be true.

The acronym—such an obvious attempt to sound like other fourteen-year-olds—wasn't the most pathetic part. It's that I was afraid she'd vanish if I wrote her real name.

It's not that I didn't think she liked me. I knew she did. I made her laugh, not polite laughs but snorty diaphragm laughs. I didn't talk much about my life at school, but my family was safe material. I told her how my dad and I once secretly replaced the gritty homemade apricot fruit leather in my mother's charity care packages with Snickers bars. How he always saluted me if we met in the upstairs hallway, because of my vaguely military cargo shorts.

"You'd like my dad," I said.

We were swimming in Jade Cove, floating on our backs, Casey in her purple one-piece, me in my loose black T-shirt and underwear, once again pretending I'd forgotten to bring a suit. I'd carefully rolled up my shorts in a towel and set the bundle on a rock, far from the water.

Disarming. She had disarmed me. I rarely separated myself from the charm I kept in my pocket, but for her I did. I wasn't ready to tell her about it, though.

"Would he like me?" Casey said, eyes closed, arching her back to stay afloat so her stomach made a little purple island. The skin on her nose was bright pink, and the freckles there merged closer every day.

"Definitely."

"Hey. Why do you always wear them?"

"Hmm?"

"Your cargos. I've never seen you in anything else. Not that I mind."

"I just like them. The pockets are good for collecting things. Hey, I have oatmeal cookies in my backpack. Are you hungry?" I splashed over to the beach.

Two weeks into summer we still hadn't met each other's parents. We rendezvoused at Casey's dock every morning and stayed on the water all day.

I said my mother got on my nerves and Casey accepted this. She kept me out of her house, too, telling me her mom wanted to fix the place up before inviting me over.

"She's dying to meet you, though," she said. "She just wants to get the house done first. She was mad you saw it before it was finished."

"Does this mother of yours really exist?" I teased. I could tease her by then.

"She's in some kind of retro homemaking phase. Yesterday she drove all the way to Twaine Harte for an antique firewood holder. I just hope she puts up my bedroom curtains before she gets bored with antiquing and moves on to rock climbing or whatever."

Casey scattered crumbs like this about her mother all the time. I stored them up, greedy for more. I was as fascinated by her fond, indulgent tone of voice as I was by the composite picture they created of this person I hadn't met yet.

On June 26 I wrote in my diary:

Ariel's mother—Alexandra Shepherd
Only 36.
+ Once a card dealer in Reno.
+ Makes lots of $ off her art. Scandalous art?
+ Let her boyfriends sleep over til Casey asked her not to.
= Exact opposite of Ingrid Christie

One afternoon in late June, as I was showing Casey how to make a hard stop-turn in the kayak, I got an official nickname, too.

"Slow down, Pocahontas, I didn't quite get that," she said.

Pocahontas. The four syllables were a sweet drumbeat in my head for the rest of the day. Casey had sort of called me Pocahontas the first day we met. But this was different. I'd never been given a nickname by a friend.

When I left her dock a few hours later, she sat on the edge to see me off, legs dangling over the silvery-gray wood. I was late for dinner and was already paddling hard when she called out, feet now churning the water, "I almost forgot, come early tomorrow. My mom wants you for breakfast."

I showed off my stop-turn. "Really?"

"The house is done so she wants to meet you. Nine, okay?"

I hadn't planned to say it out loud. I was giddy from the day, the breakfast invite, and my diary name for Casey just slipped out at the last second. "Okay. Goodbye, Ariel."

But when I felt myself saying it I got shy, and her nickname came out so soft it got lost crossing the water.

"What?"

I gathered my courage and repeated it, louder this time. "I said, goodbye, Ariel."

She stilled her legs and tilted her head, considering. Then she grinned, kicking out a high, rainbowed arc. "I love that."

As I started to paddle away again, Casey pulled the Disney figurine off the nail by her legs and waved it.

"Twins," she yelled. Then she set it on her shoulder and made a goofball face.

I smiled all the way home.

But in my diary that night, I wrote:

65 days til school. Wish there were zeros at the end. Infinite zeros.
00000000000000000000

Before I slipped the diary back inside *Silas Marner,* I filled in the string of zeros, making each oval into a sad face.

It's not that I thought she'd instantly transform on September 2. Change into someone cruel, from a fourteen-year-old who could still make dumb jokes about Disney princesses into a sneering wannabe grown-up like some of the high school girls I'd observed. I knew she was better than that.

It's just that she didn't know what a *machine* school could be. I'd already been processed through the machine, because our town was so small sixth through twelfth were in the same building complex, the high school separated only by a covered walkway. My reputation as Sister Christian had already traveled down that walkway, I was sure of it.

And the machine had decided that I didn't deserve a friend.

I had this fantasy that Casey would say she wasn't going to CDL High after all, that her mother would have an overnight religious conversion and send her to the Catholic girls' school four towns over. It would solve everything, and it wasn't completely ridiculous. I knew all about her mom's impulsive nature. If I scattered some pamphlets about St. Bridget's and maybe some enticing religious icons on her futon, I could probably make Catholicism her next obsession.

But even if I could pull it off, judging by what Casey had told me, her mother would end her fling with the Lord long before first-day registration.

Casey was definitely bound for CDL High.

It was bad enough, worrying about the time limit on Casey's friendship. Then I met Alex.

The morning of the breakfast, I wore my hair loose, and though I wasn't willing to alter my Ziploc-inside-cargos arrangement on my bottom half, I went fancier on top, with a light blue peasant blouse. It was the one nice shirt I owned that was sufficiently baggy.

Halfway across the lake I could see them waiting for me on their dock. Both of them short, with bare legs. Both with sun glinting off their red hair.

But as I got closer I could spot the differences between them. Casey's hair was shoulder length and bone straight; her mother's fell in spirals past the waist of her cutoffs. Casey was sturdy and slightly bowlegged, giving the impression that she was firmly planted on the ground. Her mother, though no taller, was fine-boned. All jumpy vertical lines. Alexandra was like Casey, made with more care. And though she was thirty-six, she could have passed for a college girl.

She reminded me of one of the redheads in my European art book, a full-page print I'd tried (unsuccessfully) to copy. Not the woozy Klimt lover, who looked like she'd been folded to pack in a trunk. I liked this painting better: a modern Russian oil of a young auburn-haired dancer surrounded by chaotic brush-strokes, her eyes defiant, her arms so fluttery they seemed to disturb her painted background. That's what Alexandra was like.

"Need help?" Alexandra darted across the dock as I tied up. To Casey she asked, wringing her hands, "Does she need help?"

"She's fine, Mom. Laura's a pro."

I climbed up the ladder, self-conscious under her steady gaze. When I tried to shake her hand she pulled me in for a hug, speaking close to my ear. "Alexandra Shepherd, but call me Alex, of course."

My dad's version of a hug was one palm rapping me on the back like I was choking on a chicken bone, and my mother limited her displays of affection to awkward shoulder pats.

This was a full-body squeeze, and the force of it, coming from someone so little, unnerved me. When she finally let go she didn't really let go. She only leaned back, still so close I could count the freckles on her nose. She didn't have as many as Casey.

"Laura," she said, cupping my jaw in both warm hands.

"Mom."

"Oh, I'm just excited. Your first friend in the new town. I'm sorry, Laura."

"It's okay."

It wasn't exactly okay, though. I didn't know where to look. She still had both hands under my chin and her gray eyes were darting and circling, scanning my features.

"Careful, Laura, she wants you to sit for her. When she analyzes someone's face like that, she's making plans. And it sucks, believe me."

"You caught me." Alex dropped her hands and stepped back. "Laura, you're welcome here anytime."

Some people pronounced my name Low-ra, and some people said Laah-ra, and neither was correct. It was just Laura, standard pronunciation.

Alex said it like there were three syllables, not two, adding a breathy cascade within the vowel. Lau-aura. She said it like a declaration, like I couldn't possibly be anyone else, and like meeting me confirmed that I was just as wonderful as Casey had said.

"I'm starved and you're freaking out my friend." Casey was already running to the back door. She was barefoot, wearing her purple bathing suit, but she'd pulled on cutoffs for the occasion.

Alex didn't speak as we walked up the path together, and as she held open the screen door, she watched me closely again, her eyes monitoring my face for a response as I took in the fixed-up house.

She'd transformed it. Newly white walls brightened up the long room and set off the blue of the lake and the green of the pines coming through the small, high windows and screen door. There were the antiques I'd heard about—a circular wooden table and chairs near the tiny kitchen, a deep armchair on a braided oval rug next to the fireplace, and a low yellow day-bed had replaced the futon in one corner. But she hadn't sanded away the marks in the floor from the old bunk beds, I was relieved to see.

"Like it, Laura?" she said, fidgeting with the hem of her white eyelet tank top.

"It's perfect."

"You did a good job, Mom," Casey said from the kitchen table, a croissant hanging from her mouth. "Now can you two please stop being so freaking polite so we can eat?"

When Alex was in the kitchen slicing an almond pastry, Casey whispered across the small table, "I've never seen her so quiet. She must really want to paint you. Watch out."

"I don't mind."

★ ★ ★

Alex was more relaxed each time I came over. She stopped saying my name more than the standard amount, and began to match Casey's description. She did talk too much. She did launch from one hobby to another so fast it was hard to keep up.

And she did want to paint me. I chalked up her odd behavior on that first morning to the overwhelming impression I'd made as a potential subject, and I was flattered.

By midsummer we'd settled into a routine. Mornings I sat for sketches on the back porch, muscles aching, but happy to let Alex and Casey entertain me.

One hot day in late July Alex had me in a stiff-backed dining room chair with my hair in a tight bun. She said she was trying to capture something in my eyes. That I was "an old soul but tried to hide it," and she hadn't managed to draw this to her satisfaction.

"You have a… What is it, Case? What's in her eyes that's so hard for me to get right? That bit of sadness mixed with… I don't know what."

"That's a neck cramp mixed with the desperate need to pee. I know the feeling well." Casey was sprawled in the sun by my feet, a paperback of *Peyton Place* tented above her face.

She read a section aloud: a couple writhing around, monitoring the status of the man's erection, panting out a play-by-play of their lovemaking.

When Casey wasn't acting out *Peyton Place*, making me laugh until I broke form, Alex would lecture us on her latest bird. Her birding mania had abruptly replaced a brief heirloom tomato kick. She'd even invested in binoculars and a leather journal for recording her sightings. Casey and I knew as much about the yellow-headed blackbird as the local Audubon Society.

"Their scientific name is *Xanthocephalus*," Alex said from behind her easel. "And the Tahoe basin has lost hundreds in the last ten years, isn't that awful? Their call is so unusual. Like…a rusty gate opening over and over, and—"

"Oh, my God, Mom. *You're* a rusty gate opening over and over. Give it a rest."

Alex popped her head above her easel. She had her curls piled on top of her head, and a double pine needle had fallen onto it like a hair ornament. "Laura's interested. Aren't you, Laura?"

"Definitely."

"She's just being polite. Laura doesn't give a shit about the Xanadu birds anymore and neither do I."

"Xanthocephalus," I said, laughing.

"Kiss-up," Casey said.

"Dang it all, Case, you made me mess up." Alex had the same laugh as Casey, full-throated and coppery. "Naughty girl."

A few days later, *Peyton Place* and the yellow-headed blackbird were replaced by *My Sweet Audrina* and the dark-eyed junco bird. The material varied, but the two-woman show did not. Alex the flighty. Casey the sarcastic.

And me. I was the audience. Sometimes the egger-on or the mediator. They each tried to get me on their side, and I loved every second of this gentle tug-of-war.

After lunch Alex would wander upstairs to her studio— painting was the one constant in her day—and it became me and Casey again, kayaking and swimming and picnicking until dinner. They invited me for every meal, but I only stayed one out of five times, figuring that this amount would not push my mother over the edge.

I told my mother the Shepherds' car was used and they couldn't pry the anti-Christian fish off. She hmphed at me, not buying it but not forbidding me to see them, either.

By August I'd thrown myself into the Shepherd household completely. Without a flicker of loyalty to my own slow-moving, well-meaning, predictable parents.

I kayaked across the lake every chance I got. I spent the night almost every Saturday, ignoring my mother's hmphs, her narrowed eyes.

On Sunday, I rushed over again as soon as I ditched my church clothes. Paddling hard, like I was racing backward across the river Styx, from the land of the dead to the land of the living.

I wished school would never start.

4

The Machine

September 2

Casey and I did walk to school together the first morning, just like my mother had commanded back in June. We arranged to meet at the gazebo in the park at 7:45, and everything about it felt strange.

It was strange to see Casey on land. It was strange to see her in jeans. It was strange to see her with her hair brushed.

When I walked over I found her using a stick to pick a tile from the crumbling old mosaic inside the gazebo. "A little first-day-of-school gift for you," she said, handing me the small green square. "For good luck."

"Thanks." I dropped it in my pocket, next to my Ziploc.

We walked up the shoulder of East Shoreline Road to town, Casey kicking pinecones and chattering, asking about every backpacked kid we saw on the way, me dragging my feet and answering in monosyllables.

Her whispered questions started out genuine. "Are they a couple? Is that girl on the bike a freshman?"

When we were so close we could see the brick and white plaster of CDL High through the pines, she finally picked up on my death-row vibe and tried to make me laugh.

About a pasty guy in a skull T-shirt taking last-minute drags off his cigarette—"That's the school nurse, right?"

About a sour-looking teacher in the parking lot wearing an ankle-length black skirt and a curious, drapey gray cardigan—"Ooh, I like the cheerleading uniforms."

I could manage only a tight smile.

I'd dressed carefully, in a denim skirt and my blue peasant shirt. As we walked up the broad brick steps together, surrounded by keyed-up, tanned kids, I tucked my blouse in and tugged it out for the hundredth time.

"You look great," Casey said. "Don't be nervous."

"I'm not nervous."

"Yes, you are. You're petrified. *I'm* the new girl. *I'm* the one who's supposed to be nervous."

Then, too soon, we were in the auditorium with the entire school—240 students. A puny enrollment by California standards, but we could still barely hear each other. We had to get our locker assignments and ID pictures, and I was a *C* and Casey was an *S*, so our lines were on opposite sides of the room.

"Meet me outside the cafeteria at lunch?" she shouted.

I nodded. We only had two classes together. PE and study hall, both in the afternoon.

Casey started to walk toward the *R* through *Z* line. But then she turned back to me and whispered, leaning close, "Is it your boobs?"

"What?"

"Is that what they tease you about?"

"What do you…"

She kept her voice low as the wave of kids parted around us.

"You always hunch. You wear those baggy old-man T-shirts instead of a bathing suit. I know you hate school, you've been dreading it all summer, and you won't talk about it. So is that it? Or is there more?"

I managed to look down at my extra-blousy blouse and say, "They don't help."

She didn't laugh. She just squeezed my wrist and said, "I'll kick their asses if they mess with you. See you at lunch."

I nodded and let the other kids pour in between us, so relieved I could have cried.

And the morning went fine. My ID picture came out pretty. Not one person called me Sister Christian. Even Pauline, who was of course a frosh cheerleader, was in a big pond now, with diluted influence, and seemed to be more interested in trying to get attention from the upperclassmen than messing with me. We had English together but she ignored me for the whole fifty-five minutes.

I was not Carrie, the hopeless freak with the bible-banging mother. I'd never been close. And by third period I was a little mad that I'd let an idiot like Pauline get to me for so many years.

By fourth period I was almost relaxed.

Then I found out about the rally.

I was in fifth period Spanish, happily conjugating sports verbs (to kick, to run, to swim), when Mr. Allendros said, *"Tiempo para ir al gimnasio."*

Time to go to the gym.

It was still half an hour until the lunch bell, so I thought it was part of the lesson until the sophomores started getting up. The other freshmen looked as clueless as me, but we all stood and filed out the door.

"What's going on?" I said to the girl behind me in the packed hall.

"Pep rally," she said, her notebook knocking my elbow as she got jostled from behind. "Sorry."

So I was swept along to the *gimnasio*, feeling far from peppy.

I hunted in the bleachers for a flash of red hair but I couldn't find Casey, so I gave up and sat near the door in the first row, hoping I'd at least catch her on the way out. For something called a *rally*, it was pretty tedious. Announcements about elections, and football tickets, and a fund-raiser over at the skating rink/bowling alley in Red Pine.

And once again, I let myself relax.

Until ten minutes before the lunch bell, when the cheerleaders started pulling kids from the bleachers. There was to be some sort of audience participation to cap things off, and I wished desperately that I'd sat in the top row, far from their perky reach.

They could have targeted the leadership types, but no. They recruited poor Dan Novacek, a boy I'd known since kindergarten who rarely bathed, and Ellie Jacobs, who always wore a fishing cap, and a sweet, gray-bobbed teacher who'd been standing by the exit minding her own business.

Still, I thought I might be safe. The morning had gone okay. I shrank down and sat very still.

But Pauline found me. Pauline, with her new Rachel hairdo and her old taste for cruelty.

She gripped my elbow and I shook her off, smiling wildly, unfocused. But I was pushed, pulled, prodded by others who were relieved they hadn't been singled out. Until I was onstage.

Not a stage exactly. The gym floor. But it might as well have been the Roman Forum. There were eight of us that the cheerleaders were arranging in various poses. I grasped that we were to act out some sort of cute chain reaction.

I was the first link in the chain. Someone handed me a fake coin the size of a small pizza, made of foam and wrapped in tinfoil. On my left was the teacher, who had to stand with her elbows locked together and her forearms up in a *V*, making a kind of receptacle. I was to pivot from right to left and set the tinfoil coin in her arms. The teacher/coin slot seemed about as happy about this as I was.

After I gave her the coin she had to shout "Beep" and turn to her left. Dan Novacek, who just for kicks had an inflated inner tube around his waist, had to spin and pat the girl next to him on her head, and she had to toss a football up and catch it. And so on.

When the chain reaction was over the cheerleader at the end yelled, "Go," and the audience had to shout, "Astros."

I did my part correctly every time, which wasn't easy since I was trying to keep my elbows pinned close to my sides to minimize what the bra companies call "wobble and bounce." The teacher did okay, too, and so did Dan in his inner tube. But the girl down the line kept fumbling the football, and when the crowd half-heartedly yelled, "Astros" the third time, I heard an "Assholes" mixed in.

I wondered where Casey was. Up in the bleachers, pity mixed with revelation. Seeing me clearly for the first time, as a victim. And there was nothing to be done.

We were all rattled, and while the football-tossing girl got it together, two kids at the end of the human contraption kept messing up. So by the fifth time there were almost as many voices yelling, "Assholes" as "Astros."

It was not how I hoped the day would go.

But as I turned with the weightless coin one more time, praying it would be the last, someone snatched it from my hands.

There was a ripple of confused laughter from the bleachers.

I caught a flash of Irish setter red hair. Casey had stolen the quarter. Casey had mucked up the machine.

She was running around the gym and the crowd was loving it. As if she'd planned it for weeks, she ran to a cluster of basketball players and handed the quarter off to Mitch Weiland, a popular senior. The basketball team never got as much attention as the football team, so this was a stroke of brilliance. He

sprinted to the basketball net and inserted the quarter in a gorgeous dunk shot right as the bell rang.

"What was that?" I said, as Casey and I walked to the cafeteria.

She shrugged. "It was pissing me off. You looked so miser-
able, it just came to me."

"You're crazy." I smiled.

Later, after Pauline Knowland high-fived Casey on our way
to the lunch line, pretending she'd found her improv as hilarious
as everyone else, and four juniors asked to sit with us, I whispered, "Thank you."

"You'd do it for me. We're best friends, right?"

"Best friends."

5

Bartles & Jaymes

2016
Thursday evening

Casey and I sat on the dock and watched the sky until there
was only a delicate tracing of red around the mountains. One
by one, people flicked their lights on, ringing the dark lake in
dots of glowing yellow.

"I forgot how beautiful it is," I said.

"It's changed, though. Not as quiet as it used to be."

"I go to sleep to the sounds of the #1 California Muni bus,"
I said. "It makes these horrible groaning noises as it struggles
up the hill. I feel like one day they're going to ask me to come
out and help push."

"Did you drive in through town or did you take I-5 and
Southshore?"

"Southshore."

"So you didn't see how fancy we are now. We have two

espresso places and a Chef's Choice. You know, so you don't have to haul all the way to Tahoe City for your triple-shot latte and your ten million kinds of chèvre."

"And there's a fantastic bookstore, I hear."

"Who told you, your mother?"

"Yeah, she—"

"Right. Like she would use the word *fantastic* to describe any-thing remotely associated with me."

"She doesn't—"

"Stop. Don't even try. So. Speaking of goat cheese. I think it's time to move this wild party indoors. Unless you think we'll be too *crowded*."

Jett was still sleeping when I opened the car door. I clipped her leash on before she was alert enough to go nuts. "Wake up, sweet girl."

She shook herself, jingling her tags, and perked up the second she got out, excited by new smells. I let her pee and sniff her way down the driveway while Casey switched lights on behind us.

My phone rang and Sam's face flashed on my screen. Sam was the "goofy foot," the famous surfing lefty, from his café's name. The picture I'd programmed in, though, was Sam as I knew him, not the cocky young surf-punk from the past that I emblazoned on his T-shirts and magnets and mugs, but forty pounds heavier and forty years older. Big and weather-beaten, kind of like an aging Beach Boy. I liked that Sam best.

He knew I'd been considering visiting my hometown this weekend. He was the only person I'd told, and he'd urged me to go, to take a risk. His exact words were *You need more friends besides that hyper mutt and some old has-been fatty ex-surfer.*

"I shouldn't have come," I whispered into the phone. "It's beyond awful. Are you happy?"

"I think the question is 'are you happy?'" He spoke in his best Yoda imitation. Which was a pretty poor one. There was a fine line between Yoda and Fozzie Bear from the Muppets, and Sam always veered too Fozzie.

"Don't psychoanalyze me, Sam. I'm not up to it right now."

"Sorry, sorry. But keep me posted. And if you wimp out and come home early, you're fired. Anyone can slap some doodles on a T-shirt. You're totally replaceable."

"Supportive as always, Sam."

"Email me. I want to live vicariously."

"This is all about you, then."

"Naturally."

"Bye."

Jett was about as eager to go inside as I was but I tugged her leash. "Time to go in, JJ-girl."

Time to trade one unfamiliar landscape for another.

Casey had told the truth; she and Alex hadn't made many changes to The Shipwreck. Though there was evidence of a child—a fairy book, glittery purple sneakers on the floor, one of which I had to wrestle away from Jett as Casey walked over from the kitchen.

"Behave, Jett. Sorry."

"She's all right." Casey scratched her under her collar. "Jett, you said? As in Joan? Right, the spiky black hair."

I waited for Casey to give me just a little more. For her voice to warm a few degrees as she said, *Remember the poster you gave me? That CD you used to hide at my house?*

"She's a troublemaker like her namesake," I said.

"She's a sweetheart. I love Labs."

"Thanks. And how old is your little girl? Elle, you said? Not that I mean she's the same as a pet…" I needed to stop talking. Or at least rehearse every sentence in my head a minimum of three times before letting it exit my mouth.

Casey waited for me to stop. No "no worries," an expression it seemed the rest of the world used ten times a day. No "don't be silly."

"She just turned ten. She's been with us since she was five."

"Can I see her picture?"

Casey pointed to the photos hung on the stairwell. "You can see dozens, we're running out of room."

I walked up the stairs to examine the pictures while Casey crouched and scratched Jett's stomach. Jett was in textbook passive pose, on her back, paws limp. Casey had already won her over. At least she was making an effort with my pet.

I didn't have to hunt long for the little girl's face. She was all over the wall. A plump child with wavy brown hair and brown eyes, younger in the photos closer to the center, older in the ones crammed around the edges. There she was with a smiling Casey, fishing. There she was with her face red from a Popsicle. Carrying a backpack in front of my old elementary school.

"She's adorable," I called.

"Thanks."

Alex had started the wall the September after she and Casey moved in, first with a handful of framed photos clustered where they were easily visible from the middle step. The collection had grown outward, the spacing tightening over the years as real estate got scarce.

I knew so many of the images. Casey blowing out birthday candles at three and four and seven, her cheeks round, her eyes bright. Casey jumping off dive blocks at swim meets, her age only discernible by the length of her blurry legs. Casey and Alex on the trip to Mexico when Casey was fifteen, toasting with their margarita glasses in some awful spring-break club. Casey in the garden, pretending to mash herbs with Alex's mortar and pestle, her raised eyebrows showing just what she thought of Alex's pagan phase. Alex at her pottery wheel, squinting into the sun, her cheeks and forehead flecked with white clay. Alex as a toddler on the beach in San Francisco, the ruins of the Sutro Baths behind her. I looked at that one closely, trying to identify the old

Victorian up the hill that Sam had turned into his shop, years after the photo was taken. But I couldn't find it.

I'd once been on the wall, too. Prominently featured. By senior year I was in ten pictures. My favorite had been positioned eight steps up. Me and Casey in the kayak, raising our paddles over our heads and laughing, water pouring down in shining streams around us.

But that one was no longer there, and neither were any of the others. I'd been curated out of the gallery.

I walked down the stairs, smiling so Casey wouldn't know what I'd been thinking.

"My mom still has them."

"Has what?"

"The pictures of you. She keeps the one of us in the kayak in her studio."

I nodded. What was I supposed to say? *No worries?*

"So," Casey said, walking to the kitchen. "Wine? Rosé all right? And I wasn't kidding about the cheese. I didn't know what you'd like so I got it all. Hard, soft, everything in between."

"What, no cookie dough?" I followed Casey across the living room.

"Cookie dough?"

"You know, trio of cookie dough."

She turned to face me.

"Trio of cookie dough," I said. "Manicures. Crank calls?"

"What are you talking about?"

And I realized it even before my hand closed around the invitation in my pocket.

The invitation Casey hadn't sent.

I'd handled the hot-pink envelope so much over the past three weeks it had gotten soft. I passed it to Casey and she pulled the card out. After one glance she walked over to the rolltop desk in the corner, so fast I didn't have a chance to read her expression.

She handed me a piece of filmy blue stationery. "We've been had."

The handwriting's resemblance to mine was impressive.

"'Dear Casey, I've been thinking about our friendship a lot lately, and missing you. Would you mind if I came for a visit? I'll be in town on…'"

I didn't need to read any more.

"Your mom," I said.

"I'm going to strangle her."

"Do you want me to go?"

"Do you want to go?"

When Casey stomped to the refrigerator for the rosé she found it had been replaced by a six-pack of Bartles & Jaymes wine coolers with a fat manila envelope taped on top. *Girls,* it said on the outside, in Alex's unmistakable curly handwriting.

Alex had even remembered our flavor preference from senior year. Junior year our favorite had been Snow Creek Berry, but by the fall of 1998 we'd transitioned to Peach Bellini, and that's what she'd bought.

We sat on the sofa with our drinks, Alex's envelope between us. Casey studied her bottle's label, circling the round B&J logo with her index finger.

"Do you want to open it?" I said.

"You're the guest, you should have the honor."

"I need a minute."

"She turned in a pretty goddamned good performance of acting surprised when I showed her the letter," Casey said. She swigged her Peach Bellini, her grip on the bottle so tight her knuckles blanched. "I mean, Golden Globe–worthy."

"She took that acting class in Pinecrest," I said softly. When was it? Sophomore year? It didn't matter, but it was all I could handle at the moment, that one fact, so I concentrated hard until

I pulled it from my memory. Spring of sophomore year. Endless monologues from *Uncle Vanya* and *Streetcar.*

"Right. Then suddenly she said it would be better if she wasn't here, if the two of us had 'quality time' together. And today she blew town with Elle." Casey's cheeks had reddened. Her angry clown look, Alex had always called it.

I could leave.

But Casey hadn't kicked me out. She'd hot potato'd the question of what to do right back at me.

In the Stay column, at least Casey was sharing a piece of furniture with me.

In the Go column—she could not be farther away. The sofa had two big seat cushions, and while I sat in the middle of mine, Casey was so far away, wedged against the opposite arm, that she'd made her cushion lift up in the center of the sofa like she was raising a little padded drawbridge between us.

Another for the Go column—she was gripping her wine cooler so tight I could see the raised outline of the delicate center bone inside her wrist.

I sipped my sickly sweet peach drink.

Jett settled on the floor between us. Casey stretched her leg out so her heel could rub circles around Jett's fluffy midsection. I put the fact that she was petting my dog in the Stay column. "Let's at least open the letter."

"You do it, I'm too pissed." Casey took another swig of her drink and set it on the coffee table. She squeezed her left hand into a ball, then radiated her fingers out again like a magician in the "abracadabra" moment of the act. A de-stressing technique I used myself sometimes.

I set my bottle down a respectful distance from hers and tore open the envelope. Alex had taped a hundred-dollar bill to the top of a handwritten note. I carefully peeled off the cash and waved it.

"What's that for?" Casey said.

I scanned the letter. It was all so perfectly, ridiculously Alex I couldn't help smiling in spite of everything.

"What's funny?" Casey said.

"You're not going to like it."

"The hundred's a bribe? It's not even a decent one."

"It's not a bribe, listen," I said. "'Girls. I know you must be a little angry, and...'"

"Ha. Just a little."

"'...'and I don't blame you. Okay, maybe you're more than a little angry.'

"'But remember you're angry at me, not at each other. It was always that way, wasn't it? I was to blame then, too. I was the adult.'"

Casey snorted.

"'Correction. I was supposed to be the adult.' *Supposed to be* is underlined..." I tried to meet Casey's eyes but she wouldn't look at me. She was staring at her bottle.

"'So please see this for what it is: my attempt to make things right.'

"'Or see it as one last scavenger hunt. They were fun, weren't they? At least at first? I want this to be fun for you, too.'"

I waited for Casey's comment.

"Fun. God, I'm going to kill her... Sorry, sorry." Casey held up her free hand in apology. "Keep going."

"'I've made up a list.'" I fished out another piece of white paper, this one printed from a computer and folded in half. I held it up for Casey, who had inched closer. I didn't open it. I set it between us, facedown, so it bridged our couch cushions.

"'There are ten things. Five photos to take and five things to find, just like when you were in high school. I put a lot of thought into choosing the items. I couldn't find the right film for the old Polaroids so I got you a new instant camera at the Sharper Image...'"

"Unreal." Casey closed her eyes. "Doesn't she realize we can take pictures with our phones now? Not that we're going to be taking pictures anyway..."

"Wait, listen... 'I realize you can take pictures with your phones now...'" I pointed at Casey and gave her a chance to get her sarcasm in. We had a nice rhythm going.

"Because that makes this totally reasonable," she said.

"...'but I thought it'd be more fun this way. More like old times, you know? The camera is in the top left drawer of my dresser. A couple of these clues will take you out of town (hint, hint) so the money is for gas and incidentals.'"

"My mom did not write *incidentals*. What is she, a corporate accountant all of a sudden?"

"She did write *incidentals*." I tilted the letter so she could see.

"'I'll be monitoring your progress so no cheating. This will only work if you do it right.'

"'When you've finished all ten things on the list I'll trade you for something you've both wanted for a long time. Something I probably should have given you years ago.'

"'Please trust me one last time. I know that's a lot to ask. But you have to complete this game before I give you your prize. You'll understand Sunday, I promise.'"

"That's it?" Casey said.

"No. She signed it. 'Love, Alex.'"

I unfolded the paper and skimmed the first few clues. They were written in rhymes, but didn't seem too hard. Not by Alex's old standards. "Want to know what's on the list?"

"Let me guess. A syrup jug from the Creekside. The mayor's watering can. A picture by the drinking fountain at school."

"You've got the basic idea. A guided trip down memory lane. It's all summer stuff."

"Adorable."

"So what do you think the prize is? Something we've *both wanted for a long time*."

"Right now I want to throw a Sharper Image novelty Po-

laroid camera at her face. No, I want to *punch* her in the face."
Casey clenched and unclenched her fist again, as if imagining
the satisfaction she'd get from delivering the blow.

She grabbed the list, crumpled it up without reading it, and
tossed it, aiming for the wall opposite us. It barely cleared the
coffee table. Jett bounded over and returned it to her, wagging
her tail. "She even got your dog into the act."

I patted my knees. "Give it, Jetty."

I unfolded the damp paper on my lap. "She wrote the clues
in rhymes. Five-line rhymes."

"Those are called quintains. You missed the morbid poetry
phase she got into after 9/11."

"The clues seem pretty easy," I said. "Listen to this one:

"'Here you used to glide and spin
Young and swift and free
On hoofs of brown and orange you'd…'"

Casey interrupted. "The skating rink. Tough clue, Mom."

"I don't think she wants the clues to be hard. I don't think
that's the point this time."

Casey pressed her bright cheek against the side of her wine
cooler. "She was good, I'll give her that. Acting as surprised as
me when your letter showed up. Talking me into how great it'd
be if you came and I should at least give it a chance, how hard
it must have been for you to reach out after all this time…" She
broke off. "Sorry."

"It's okay." I picked up the sheet of blue stationery from the
coffee table. Until half an hour ago Casey had thought I'd sent
it. And I noticed something that I hadn't the first time. "My"
letter had a tracery of lines in it. Casey had crumpled it up, too.
Maybe Alex even had to fish the balled-up letter from the garbage. I couldn't blame Casey; I'd resisted, too. But it hurt.

"She outsmarted us," I said.

"Those handwriting samples we did junior year…" Casey said.

"Sophomore year."

"Was it? Anyway, I can't even deal with that part right now, the idea of her holing up in her studio, plotting this twisted fiesta when I thought she was painting. She was up there copying our handwriting while I was down here reading Lemony Snicket with Elle, totally oblivious."

"She thought we needed an activity," I said. "Like toddlers."

"This says it all." Casey picked up the manila envelope and punched the word *Girls*, denting the paper.

I nodded, though I knew Casey was getting worked up for reasons that had nothing to do with being treated like a child.

The scavenger hunts Alex masterminded when we were in high school weren't just party games to keep us entertained. Maybe they'd started off that way. But they'd become something else, and the final prize, for both of us, had been the end of our friendship. Alex couldn't make that right with an apology and ten bad poems.

We sipped our drinks. Casey petted Jett with her foot and I read Alex's list.

Most of the items were in town. Walking distance, even. The only item that would take some effort was the last one.

Not that we were doing it.

The grandfather clock struck eight and after the final, resounding bong it felt even quieter than before.

"So I get that she wants us to make up," I said. "But why now?"

Casey shook her head, focusing on a spot in the air above my head. She whispered something.

I tapped her knee, then, startled by the familiarity of the gesture, pulled my hand back. "Did you say no?"

Casey cleared her throat. "I said, 'I know.'" She shook her head as if to reset her thoughts. "I know why she's doing it now."

"Why?"

She smiled, but her eyes were glazed. Jett whimpered and snuffled into her lap.

"Because you have your little girl?" I said.

She shook her head.

"Then it's…because we're thirty-five? Or I am, and you will be in August. And thirty-five is, I don't know, the age you miraculously become older and wiser and able to get over the past according to your mom?"

"No."

"So tell me."

Casey's hand trembled as she set her drink down. She shook her head again. Then, so fast I hardly knew what was happening, she was gone. Out the front door. Barefoot, launching herself into the cold night.

I waited five minutes. Ten. Long enough to feel the cool air coming in through the open door. I reread Alex's list, trying to find clues between the clues. *Why now, Alex?* The answer tried to burrow into my thoughts, but I couldn't latch onto it.

Jett whimpered, her nose pointed at the front door.

"Should we go after her, Jetty?"

She thumped her tail, and then ran to the door, where I clipped on her leash. At the last second I returned for the clue list.

6

Messy

Even before I saw Casey's green sweatshirt in the light of the gazebo, I knew that's where she'd be.

We'd dreamed away so many hours under its rotting roof, every morning before school and after every party.

The bright gazebo looked like a stage in the shadowy park, which was otherwise lit only by one weak streetlamp. Casey sat cross-legged on the floor, leaning against the lower wall with her eyes closed. "Sorry about that," she said, not opening them.

"It's okay. Jett was worried, though."

Casey held out her hand and let Jett snuffle into it. "I'm sorry, Jett. Your mom's old friend is crazy."

"No. It's been a crazy day."

I looked around. In my time the small park by Casey's house had been scrubby and neglected, but now it was spruced up. The grass was groomed and there was a red play structure on one of those rubbery black surfaces that kept kids from breaking their arms when they plummeted off the monkey bars.

The gazebo had been fixed up, too, repaired and painted a glossy white.

The upper wall of the gazebo was plain white lattice, curving into a domed roof. But the lower wall had always been special, even when it was falling apart. I knelt so I could examine the mosaic running around the bottom. It was whole again, a fantastical lake scene for small children to enjoy, built at their eye level. Swimmers, fish, swaying underwater plants, and the imaginary friendly water creature everyone called Messy. Loch Ness had Nessie, Lake Tahoe had Tessie, and we had Messy.

I crawled along the floor, running my hand on the cold tiles. "They did a good job on this."

"What? Oh, shit, I forgot. Are you okay being here?"

"Sure. It's beautiful."

A brass plaque by the steps stated that the gazebo was built in 1945 in memory of Lieutenant Rupert Collier II, who had died in Normandy during World War II. A shinier plaque below said the gazebo had been "restored in 2012 thanks to a generous gift from the Coeur-de-Lune Historical Society in honor of William T. Christie."

My dad. I'd sent checks to the Historical Society on his birthday every year. I'd donated an extra-large sum on what would have been his eightieth, four years ago.

"They had an artist out of Truckee do it," Casey said. "She spent months matching colors. So many tiles were missing."

"I wonder why."

"Some hooligans had been prying them off."

"How terrible."

She smiled, wiping her shiny cheek with her sleeve.

"Did you give her the tiles?" I said.

"I sneaked over in the dark and left them in a shoebox."

"And she used them?"

"All fifty-seven."

Fifty-seven blue tiles. Casey had counted them, and remembered.

Fifty-seven nights, sitting here in the dark, picking off loose tiles, talking over whatever we'd done that evening. As innocent and free and unaware of time as the creatures swimming in the mosaic.

"I want to see it in daylight," I said.

"What?"

"I want to see the old tiles against the new, in daylight. So I can decide if this so-called artist matched them up right. My dad would've wanted me to make sure. Will you show me, tomorrow?"

"You mean it? You actually want to stay?"

I nodded. "I'm here. I'll take your mom's dare, for a while at least. I'm in if you are."

"But you always picked Truth and I always picked Dare," she said.

"I know. But say we did give it a try. What's the worst that could happen?"

"You know whatever my mom has planned for us at the end of this, this…whatever this is…is going to be nuts. She hasn't changed."

"I still want to try it."

"Why, though? It's not so you can see what they did with your donations."

I shrugged, touching the cold, thin line of new grout between the restored tiles. "Jett likes the fresh air. And I need to check on the house."

"Right." Casey took a deep breath. "I'll try it for now. *Whatevs*, as Elle says. On one condition."

"Okay."

"You can't ask me why I'm doing it."

"You asked me why. Not exactly fair."

"Your answer was bullshit."

I nodded, slowly. "Okay."

"We'll see how it goes."

"Anyway we're already doing it. Your mom's psychic. Listen to Clue 1:

"'This little lacy room was not
True shelter from a storm
But the perfect place to shade yourselves
On summer days so warm
Bring me one square of blue, it's the least you can do.'"

I tapped the mosaic. "We're supposed to pry a tile off and bring it to her."

"My mother's such a delinquent."

"Unlike you. Anyway I paid for it. We can borrow one tile."

"What was that line about 'monitoring our progress'? You think she's watching from the bushes with night-vision goggles?"

"Bought at the Sharper Image with the Polaroid."

We stared out at the dark.

"We know you're out there," Casey called.

No answer except from the frogs. Casey walked down the steps, rooted in the bushes, and came back with a stick. She knelt and dug at the grout, trying to dislodge a tile near the base. "This grout is way stronger than the old stuff. I'm not making a dent."

I commanded Jett to sit, and after a minute she settled enough so I could split the flimsy ring of her collar with my fingernail and pull off the rabies tag. I handed the thin silver medallion to Casey. "Try this."

While Casey scraped I scooted to the center of the gazebo where the light was brightest. I pulled the hundred-dollar bill from my pocket. "We could make her pay for dinner. She owes us that, at least."

"But what about our gas and incidentals? Dare we risk not having enough funds for the incidentals?"

"I'm starving."

"Me, too."

"What are the options these days? Josefina's Pizza or the Creekside?"

"They'll be madhouses. Tourists up for the weekend."

"The Greek place?"

"Became a Taco Empire four years ago, then closed for health violations. We could do the skating rink clue and eat at the snack bar. Kill two birds with one stone. Except."

"The food? I can handle fluorescent orange nachos for dinner. It actually sounds fantastic."

"No. The food's not bad these days. But…"

"But what?"

Casey stopped scraping and glanced over her shoulder. "He owns it now."

"Who?" I examined the hundred. It was a 2008. Someone had carefully outlined the triangle above the pyramid, the one holding the eye, with blue pen.

I studied the bill, reading Latin over and over (*Annuit cœptis, Novus ordo seclorum*), but I could tell by Casey's silence that I hadn't fooled her. I knew who He was. She knew I knew who He was. There was only one He in Coeur-de-Lune, for me.

And it wasn't the He worshipped in my mother's old church.

I looked up from the bill. "So he's been here this whole time?"

"He has a house in Red Pine."

"You've been there? To the rink?"

"Elle loves it. We have every birthday party there."

"She's a good skater, then?"

Casey turned back to work on the tile, speaking to the mosaic wall as she scraped. "Is that really the question you want to ask me right now?"

Hardly. I could think of a dozen that interested me more than little Elle's aptitude for gliding around on eight wheels—*Is he married? What does he look like? Does he have kids?*

Does he ever talk about me?

Casey answered only the question I'd spoken aloud. "She's a

good skater." She paused, but couldn't resist adding, "J.B. helped me teach her."

Jett whimpered. I'd wound her leash around my wrist so tight she couldn't move.

"Finally!" Casey stood and held out the small blue tile triumphantly. "A little chipped in one corner but it'll work."

As we walked back to Casey's house, she said, "You're sure you're up for the rink? You don't want to work up to it?"

"It's not a big deal."

"Got it."

"We're all grown-ups."

I drove us to the rink. If I'd been alone I would have done some serious primping in the rearview mirror first. Lip gloss, extra mascara. I would have taken my hair out of its twist and done a Level Three hair brushing, which required flipping my head upside down in pursuit of what my stylist called "volume at the crown."

More than any of that, I wished I could try out reactions in the rearview mirror. Practice molding my face into various bland masks. *Oh, hey, J.B.*, I'd say. Neutral, composed. Over it. A "no worries!" tone.

But I could only manage the lip gloss. I did it stealthily, transferring a dot to my finger, then my lips, while we were at a stoplight and Casey was calling Alex.

Casey put her phone on speaker. "Hey, it's Alex! Sorry I missed you. Don't take it personally."

"Mom. You total sneak. We got your list, and we're maybe going along with it. Maybe. But only so we can figure out how soon we need to check you into the asylum. So don't think you're not in trouble. Laura's furious. I'm furious. Call." A pause. "And don't forget Elle's multivitamins and calcium. One of the clear gummies and one of the opaque sugarcoated gummies a day. Goodbye, liar."

I'd always envied the effortless way Casey talked to her mom, like they were girlfriends. Even when they were fighting, there was an easiness between them.

Casey sighed. "Elle worships her, naturally. It's my mom who found her, at this place where she was volunteering."

"An orphanage?"

"Tutoring center. She was born drug affected. But now she's doing brilliantly. It's the next turnoff."

"I remember."

Casey swung open the door to the Silver Skate 'n Lanes, unleashing a familiar mix of throbbing bass and arcade beeps. The rink smelled the same, too. Sweaty rental skates, overly sweet first perfumes, fake-butter popcorn.

"You're sure about this?" she said.

"It's no big deal. He wouldn't recognize me anyway."

Here's where she was supposed to say, *Of course he would, you look exactly the same. You look fabulous.* But she was silent, walking ahead of me down the dark, carpeted hall to the counter. I lingered for a minute by the entrance, watching kids play with the gleaming metal marble run on the wall. It was all in perfect order.

The middle-aged cashier smiled at Casey. "You skating? No Elle?"

"We're just getting a snack, Deb."

"Session's over soon. No charge." She taped glow-in-the-dark bracelets around our wrists. "Disco night, God help us."

We pushed through the turnstile to the rink. "Disco Duck" was blasting. The smiles on the faces whipping by said, *Yes, we're doing this silly thing, but isn't it glorious?* The wind, the hundreds of tiny near misses, the satisfaction of a graceful turn, the soothing repetition of it. The rink was as effective as any monk's meditation labyrinth.

"Let's see that clue again," Casey said.

We read silently by disco light:

Here you used to glide and spin
Young and swift and free
On hoofs of brown and orange you'd win
A game, a heart, a key
Visit the ancient chest of tin, take a picture to bring to me

"Is it the same one?" I looked around for the silver treasure chest. Automatically, illogically, because he would be forty now, I searched for another gleam of silver: a metallic uniform T-shirt, and The Boy with black hair who wore it.

"Still over there by the DJ. The prizes haven't changed, either."

The chest held the prizes you could pick if you won the Dice Game or the Shoot the Duck contest or did the most impressive Hokey Pokey. Someone in silver would glide out and hand you your prize ticket with a picture of Digby the Duck holding a key. Digby the Pirate Duck: the rink's unloved mascot. Tickets were redeemed for something in the snack bar or for a cheap carnival treasure. Cockeyed stuffed animals, paddleball games whose tethers broke on the second whomp of the ball, plastic glitter bracelets.

Casey asked the DJ, a stocky man in a Jimmy Cliff T-shirt named Mel, if he would take a picture of us in front of the treasure chest. "Sure, Case, I'm on autopilot 'til the next block of requests," he said, stepping down from his elevated booth. "You want to wear the pirate hats? Want me to get the giant Digby? He's in the storeroom, but I can—"

"We'll pass," Casey said.

He opened the treasure chest and set us on either side, instructed us to put a hand on the lid. I'd stood in this exact spot with a group of girls at a birthday party once. Tina Kammerer's eighth. Second grade. Tina in the pirate hat holding Digby, her mom shooting the photo. I'd just learned to skate backward, and I was beaming. That was all it took to make me happy.

Our photographer yelled something but all I could hear was "I will survive. Now go! Walk out the door!"

"What?" Casey shouted.

"I said, say, 'Aaargggh!'"

I obediently mumbled, "Aar" behind my smile but Casey yelled, "Just take the damn picture, Mel. We're not *ten*."

He handed back the camera, the photo flapping out like a white tongue. "I was going to ask if you had requests, but not with that attitude."

We waited in line at the snack bar, monitoring the image as it developed in Casey's palm. It was overexposed, compromised by the flash bouncing off fake jewels in the treasure chest. Two women who might as well have been strangers, standing so carefully apart from each other, gingerly holding opposite corners of the treasure chest lid as if it contained uranium instead of ten-cent necklaces. My smile was tight and Casey was scowling.

If we were in the mood to write a caption in the wide white band at the bottom it would say this: *What the hell are we doing here?*

But I knew the white plastic would remain empty. That space was reserved for summing up happier shots.

"It's a good one of you," Casey said, examining the photo.

I prepared my automatic denials. *I'm ten pounds heavier, I can't wear my hair as long now, I have three lines on my forehead and a third of my left eyebrow simply vanished overnight…* "Oh, please, I…"

"Stop. Can we not do that, please? Can we just agree not to do that?"

"Do what?"

"That thing some women do, looking for reassurance. That whole repetitive, tiresome thing. You look fantastic, and I look fine, and we're thirty-five. Done."

"Fine. So you think Alex is here? In a Farrah Fawcett wig?"

"Wouldn't put it past her."

We carried our burgers and Cokes to tables with little swinging chairs attached. Everyone ate while either pushing off from the table base and letting their chair return, over and over, or pivoting side to side. Even the adults did it; they just did it less vigorously. It was impossible not to. Casey was a side-to-sider and I was a pusher-offer. These chairs had probably absorbed a million man-hours of nervous energy over the decades.

"Have you seen your mom yet?" I pushed off from the table and returned, glad to have something to do with my legs. I tried to pretend I was looking for Alex, a lock of her red hair peeking out from under a blond, feathered wig. But I was looking for someone else. Someone tall, with shiny black hair and brown eyes.

Casey took pity on me. "He's not here much. He owns a miniature golf course in Tahoe City and a couple other businesses."

I gulped too much Coke and an avalanche of ice dislodged and fell down my chin. "That's good," I said, wiping my face. "I mean, good for him. He wouldn't recognize me anyway."

"You said that already."

"I did?"

She waited a beat, fighting some impulse, and I wasn't sure if she won or lost the fight but she said, so quietly I barely heard her over the music and games, the *boom-clacks* from the bowling alley, "He'd recognize you."

We ate our burgers and watched the skaters, and in the long silence I wondered if Casey was thinking the same thing. That Alex had been right to give us activities. A schedule.

"They're cute, right?" Casey said. "God, so young."

"That one looks a little like your…" Daughter? Foster daughter? "Like Elle." I nodded at a laughing girl skating past with long honey-brown hair.

"That's her friend from school. Mia." Casey waved, but the little girl didn't notice. We watched her pack circle around. She was a bold and graceful skater, her hair flying behind her. She navigated the corners with a flick of her eyes and an imperceptible pivot of her skinny ankles.

The music stopped and a voice on the speakers announced

the Dice Game. People had to stand by numbers spaced around the rink while a teenage employee rolled a fuzzy die the size of a washing machine. Anyone not standing under the number it landed on had to leave the rink. Finally, three boys at number seven prevailed, and they high-fived each other as if they'd won the lottery. Modern kids, supposedly so spoiled and warped by their video games and iPhones. Here they were excited about their trip to the plastic treasure chest.

"Why are you smiling?" Casey said.

"Was I? I was thinking I'm glad this place is still here. Swinging chairs. Digby the Pirate Duck. I'm glad it hasn't changed."

"Me, too," she said.

"Me, too."

The voice above me was older now, but unmistakable. I hooked my feet around the table leg to stop my chair from swinging.

J.B.

Also called The Boy Behind the Counter, and Skating Rink Boy.

For me, he was only, ever, The Boy. The boy who was different from all the rest. And now he was standing behind me, inches from the back of my chair.

"We're a real time capsule," the voice continued.

I looked up. He was leaning down over me, his black hair falling forward around his face. The only thought I could register was that even upside down and half-covered by hair, his brown eyes were kinder than any I'd ever seen.

And the only words I could manage were "It's you."

7

The Boy Behind the Counter

June 1996
Summer before sophomore year

The last time I'd been to the Silver Skate 'n Lanes Pauline Knowland had shoved me.

It was in fifth grade, right when things started to go south for me at school.

"Watch out," Pauline had said, in a tone wholly without fear or apology, seconds before her palms smacked the small of my back and sent me flying. I'd tried to slow down by dragging my orange toe stopper, a piece of cylindrical rubber like a giant pencil eraser. Instead I'd fallen facedown in front of the snack bar.

I hadn't been back since.

Casey thought it was time for me to face my fears. The shabby skating rink/bowling alley in Red Pine had become cool again ever since Erin Simms threw a *Roller Boogie*–themed Sweet Sixteen. Now every girl in our class was talking about some college guy who worked there. He'd gone out back, behind the Dumpsters, with Debbie Finch. Debbie described this as if it were the most romantic thing in the world.

Alex was driving us to Red Pine so we could see what all the fuss was about. She clearly wanted to join us and dropped hints the whole way. "I've always been curious about bowling, do people really wear matching shirts like on TV?" Two miles down the road—"You two are so brave, I'd probably be a total klutz on skates."

Never been bowling, never been skating. I added these to my list of facts about Alex. Didn't know what a friendship bracelet was, never heard of the game Red Rover. These gaps in her childhood education didn't surprise me anymore. Her parents had been strict, she'd said. *Strict* was always the word she used to describe them when I asked. Then she'd change the subject.

Casey was in the back seat, not speaking. I turned to her and raised my eyebrows, pleading silently. *We have to invite her.*

She shook her head. Casey was punishing Alex for something. But to me, even their rare fights were something to envy; they were the fights I imagined sisters had.

"She's mad at me for turning a pair of her jeans into cutoffs," Alex said. "I'm getting the silent treatment. You can wear anything in my closet, baby. You, too, Laur."

I smiled, unsure what to say, and looked out the window.

"That's a pretty song, what's it called, Case?" Alex blasted the radio.

Another fact: Alex hadn't been allowed to listen to pop music when she was younger. Now she didn't enjoy it so much as study it like someone cramming for an exam. Casey told me this was why she'd devoured the Casey Kasem countdown CDs, worshipped the guy enough to name her child after him.

Casey not only knew the exact name of the slow, hypnotic song Alex liked, she owned it. "Fade Into You" by Mazzy Star.

We'd both bought the CD the weekend before. But she didn't name the tune. I smiled at Alex apologetically.

"I'll listen for the title after I drop you off." Alex grinned at me—*don't mind her*—but quickly turned her eyes back to the road.

Alex was a cautious, nervous driver, never going more than a few miles over the speed limit, her hands always gripping ten and two o'clock on the wheel. She'd only gotten her license a few years before. Her parents hadn't let her take driver's ed when she was in high school, Casey had said, so Alex hadn't gotten around to learning until recently.

When we pulled into the parking lot and Casey and I scrambled out, Alex called a little too cheerfully, "I want a full report."

I watched her leave by herself like all the other mommy chauffeurs. "She *so* wanted to skate with us," I said. "And that was kind of mean about the song. You're really that mad about some jeans?"

Casey shook her head. "She was flirting with this boy at the car wash who squeegeed our windshield. He was like sixteen."

"I get that it's annoying but she'd never—"

"Don't. Don't even defend her. I know it's not her fault. Her parents screwed her up royally. But she has to learn she's not in high school anymore." Casey swung open the door to the Silver Skate, releasing throbs of music.

I tugged at her jacket, suddenly nervous. "Case. Don't you want to hang out at your house instead? Cookie dough and *Grease 2*?"

"We can do that any night."

"If Pauline's here I'm going to kill you."

"Repeat this to yourself. 'I'm not that girl anymore,'" Casey said as we stepped into the dark, disco-lit world of the rink.

"What girl am I?"

"You're Laura Christie. Sophisticated Mystery Woman," Casey shouted over the music, pulling me into line.

"Say that three times fast."

The woman behind the register sealed circlets of glow-in-the-dark pink plastic around our wrists and we shoved through the turnstile.

"My tracking bracelet, so I can't escape," I said.

Casey laughed but stopped abruptly, clutching my arm. "Oh, no no no. It's too good. Look."

There he was. The famous Boy Behind the Counter, handing out skates. The rental counter was elevated, and by a trick of the overhead fluorescents, it seemed he was under a spotlight. His black hair caught the light as he glided between the counter and the shelves of skates behind it. Our small-town god. On wheels.

Morgan Schiffrin and some of her friends (girls we called the Hair Petters because they compulsively ran their hands down their long hair) were clustered near the rental counter, even though they already had their brown-and-orange skates. It was like an altar.

"He's obviously loving the attention," I whispered as we lined up. "That is the tightest T-shirt I've ever seen."

"Maybe he accidentally shrank it in the dryer."

"Please."

"Maybe he had a late growth spurt and can't afford to buy a bigger one."

"He's rich. Related to the owner, supposedly."

"No offense, Laur, but you're nobody to judge someone by the fit of their shirt."

"This is a medium." My new shirt was actually a M/L, but I pulled the hem away from my hip to show Casey how little excess fabric there was compared to my old XLs. "And these pants are slender. They even say so on the tag. *Slender cut*."

"Hey, wear a potato sack if you want. Go back to your cargos. I'll still love you."

I'd had to ditch my Ziploc-in-pocket routine for my new, more fitted wardrobe. It seemed that the small front pockets in all my new pants were just for show, and the Ziploc kept creeping up. So I'd rigged up a new system. I kept the Ziploc inside an old chamois drawstring bag of my dad's, where he'd stored his silver dollar collection until I had it mounted for his sixtieth birthday. I safety-pinned the drawstring of the bag inside the bottom right leg of my pants. The system had worked well for me all year. I couldn't touch my charm as often, but I felt it there against my leg, its gentle weight in the velvety fabric a comforting presence throughout the day.

The rental line was long, so I had time to get nervous again, watching the skaters whip around the rink. No sign of Pauline, thank God.

I tried to distract myself by observing The Boy. Twitching arm muscles, teeth shining as bright as his silver T-shirt, too-long black hair tucked behind his ears.

The girls in front of us found excuses to talk to him, coming back for skates with extra-long laces, asking him how to request a song, even though the song request clipboard was right where it always was on the wall behind the DJ booth. I heard Darla Semmler say she was a size five when she was at least a seven.

When it was finally Casey's turn she asked, in a breathy voice, "Can I have a newer pair, please? Something with ankle support? Because I have *extremely* delicate ankles."

"Ankle support. I'll see what I've got back there." He skated deep into the racks.

"Casey. You're horrible."

"I got carried away. It's all very *Cinderella*, isn't it?"

"Very."

To his credit, the orange-and-brown skates he slid over to Casey didn't look quite as beat-up as the others.

"What size can I get you?" he said, slapping the counter in front of me.

"Nine," I said, without looking up at him. *Take that, Prince Charming.*

He rolled my skates over the blue-carpeted counter, but when I grabbed them he wouldn't let go. "No special requests? Extra-long laces? Blue brakes instead of orange? Double-shot of anti-fungal foot spray?"

"These are fine." I pulled at the skates, annoyed that he was messing with me. Even more annoyed that my hands were trembling, and he'd think it was because of him.

"Hey," he said, under his breath, leaning down. "Hey you."

He gripped the skates until I looked up.

"Stick close to the sides and you'll be fine."

Just as I met his brown eyes, he turned to the girl next to me and slapped the counter. "Size?"

I joined Casey, who was lacing up on a circular bench covered with blue carpet. Everything at the Silver Skate 'n Lanes was covered in blue carpet. The floors, the benches, the counters, the walls, the ball racks in the bowling alley. They hadn't changed anything since the '70s.

"You've got the Hair Petters in a tizzy," Casey said.

I glanced over as I unlaced my Nikes. Morgan and her crew were clutching each other, pretending to fall, laughing like mad. And, yes, a couple of them were looking over at us. I'd engaged The Boy in conversation. Me, in a T-shirt as loose as his was tight. Me, with my unpetted hair yanked into a ponytail.

"This town," I said.

"Was he hitting on you?"

"He asked if I wanted antifungal foot spray."

"That's hot," Casey said, laughing. "No, seriously. Let them think he was all over you. You're prettier than those bots with their lime-green bra straps."

I did up my skates and we clomped onto the rink. "Do not abandon me."

"You've got this."

We took it slow. I was scared at first, as tentative as a kid, and headed for the sides at the least sign of trouble. But after four cautious laps, "Greased Lightning" came on, and Casey flashed her sideways grin, her red hair flying, and it was all so wonderfully silly I forgot I'd been afraid. I skated a little faster each time around. We did a mini crack-the-whip. And I didn't fall.

Two older girls offered us a ride home. Soon, Casey was sure, we'd get asked to one of the house parties. The keggers and ragers that were usually upper grade only.

We were on our way out, wobbly after skating for three hours. For a second, I thought that's why my legs felt funny.

Then I realized, sick, that the chamois bag was gone.

"Case, we have to go back."

"We'll miss our ride, they're already out the door..."

"It's gone." I patted my pants leg, rolled it up, and saw only one open safety pin and loose threads where the other had ripped off. All that skating, bending my knees as I took corners, the bottom of my pants rubbing against the top of my skates, had been too much for my latest system.

"What's gone?"

But as her eyes slid down my pants leg, she realized. I'd slept over at her house too often for her not to spy the chamois bag. She still didn't know what I kept inside it.

"I'll help you look."

We ran back down the long, tunnel-like hall. It was dark and my eyes were fixed on the glowing rink, where I hoped my charm had fallen. Halfway down the hall I smacked into something warm and solid.

"Whoa, you okay?"

The Boy. No longer a giant now that he'd descended from his platform. In his shoes he was only a few inches taller than me.

"Is there a lost and found? I've lost something, please, I..."

"This?" He pressed something into my hand, and at the caress of the velvety pouch and the familiar weight I was so relieved I could have hugged him. The bag was open; maybe he'd uncinched the drawstring a little and peeked inside. But it was still heavy. Still full.

"It was inside your skate," he said. "Must've dropped in when you were pulling it off."

"You have no idea… I was sure it was…" I finished, simply, "Thank you."

"No problem. What is it, a pet rock?" He laughed, but not in a mean way, and vanished down the dark hall.

I slipped the bag up my sleeve before Casey and I joined the other girls, who were now looking at me like I was someone to contend with. Casey got a big kick out of it, especially when Donna Kellerman said we should come to her older brother's party the next weekend. We should *totally* come. There would be a keg and Everclear, secured through a complex network that involved someone's twenty-two-year-old cousin.

But I didn't care about Donna Kellerman's brother's alcohol connections. I didn't care about our social coup. I cared only about the soft weight of the bag concealed in my sleeve.

8

Morning, 35th day of camp

She'd hidden the length of curving driftwood up her blouse sleeve, tucking and rolling the cuff tight so it wouldn't slip out. It was a new hiding place; for more than a week, she'd kept the driftwood concealed inside her pillowcase.

She hoped the other girls wouldn't notice that she was working one-handed, or that her left sleeve belled out like a pirate's. The wood felt both awkward and strangely comforting against her forearm, like the splint she'd worn when she fractured her wrist trying to do a back handspring at recess in sixth grade. Her mother had been so gentle with her that day, propping her arm on pillows when they got home, offering her raspberry Jell-O as if she had a stomachache, not a broken carpal bone. They'd watched hours of junk TV together. Mork & Mindy, The Love Boat.

It had been a long, tiring, expensive day at the doctor's, but after they were both so happy and relieved, curled on the couch together in their pilled flannel nightgowns. They stayed up for Fantasy Island. *One woman chose to go back in time to meet Jack the Ripper, then had to be rescued before becoming one of his victims.*

Why, her mother had said, laughing, her eyes streaming. Why would she pick that? When she could choose anything?

They have to keep it exciting, Mom. There has to be, you know. Drama.

Smarty-pants, her mom had said, swatting her gently on the bottom. A feather of a smack. Drama, my twelve-year-old daughter says.

When, exactly, had her mother started to get sad? So sad that she needed to abandon her here?

She blinked hard, shook off the thought.

She was on boring a.m. canteen duty, as she was three mornings a week, but she had a special mission today.

Every other morning, for the thirty-five days since her mom had parked her here, she'd thrown handfuls of forks and knives into their cylindrical plastic holders as hard as she could, enjoying the crashes, like a series of tiny car wrecks, the extra clatter when a utensil skidded across the long metal table. More than anything, she enjoyed the irritation that bloomed on the other girls' faces.

Not today. Today she filled containers with cutlery as if she was arranging roses. She smiled at the others as she gently set white plates into the steam table's spring-loaded wells.

The others smiled back, each anxious to prove she was the most charitable and forgiving. They smiled at each other, relieved, and hovered around her. One offered to reverse-French-braid her hair before Scripture study. Another asked to sit next to her in the van on Wednesday, when Miss Cooke drove them to their weekly scavenger hunt on the beach.

She'd overdone it. Soon everyone else would arrive. He would arrive. And it would be too late to deliver her gift.

The girls were finally heading back to the kitchen. Now or never.

Pretending to double-check the head table, she backed her way to the front corner of the canteen, where the band stowed its gear.

Quickly, she slid the slender arc of driftwood from her sleeve and set it across the lip of the music stand. She had written it in the center, in wobbly upper-case letters, so he would remember their talk behind the craft cabin:

CURDILUNE

The name of his little town beside the crescent-shaped lake. It had been eight days since he'd drawn Curdilune for her in the dirt, and he hadn't spoken to her again, though once she thought he'd smiled at her in afternoon prayer.

When the girls called to her, swinging the kitchen door open and beaming as if it was the gate to heaven—"You coming?"—she was innocently confirming that everyone at table twelve had a water glass. But her heart was pounding.

Her cheeks warmed as he entered the canteen, his black guitar case slung over his shoulder. She lingered by the kitchen door, watching.

He dragged a stool to the section of floor at the front of the room that served as a makeshift performance space. He set the microphone into place, flicked it on.

Then the music stand. He pulled it by the base while talking over his shoulder to Miss King, the earnest middle-aged volunteer soprano who made up the second half of the band.

Her offering fell off the music stand, whatever sound it made as it hit the floor lost in the clatter of two hundred campers talking, grabbing utensils and dropping them on trays, shoving chairs across hardwood.

She feared the fall had damaged it. The driftwood was less dense in the middle, perhaps where the once-living branch had been weakened by insects, or an animal, or time. After she had rescued it, the driftwood had dried so the tips were almost white, remaining slate-colored only in the center. From across the room it looked like a bone.

She flushed, as if it was part of her own body up there on display.

She'd give him one minute to notice it. She squeezed her dishrag and counted. One-Mississippi. Two-Mississippi.

He sat, a honey-colored curl falling across his forehead as he began tuning his guitar. She could just hear the sunny string of notes over the chatter, the settling-in at tables. When Miss Haskins walked to the mi-

crophone and tapped it they would hush instantly, but they were allowed a few minutes of conversation before Grace.

He always bit his upper lip when he tuned.

Five-Mississippi. Six-Mississippi. On seven-Mississippi he glanced down, reaching into his case.

Yes. There, inches from your right foot.

He shifted his guitar to his hip and picked it up. He examined the curving driftwood, looking puzzled until he turned it over and saw what she'd inscribed in pencil:

CURDILUNE

He smiled when he read the name of his hometown. He set the driftwood on his knees and searched the cafeteria, his eyes sweeping the rows of round tables, the campers edging down the buffet past the oatmeal and hash browns, the too-pale orange wedges. She squeezed her dishrag until cold water trickled down her wrist.

He found her. Smiling, he raised the driftwood as if toasting her—quickly, a gesture for only her to see—and in that second, to her, after the long, lonely summer, he might as well have hung the moon.

9

Raptor Rock

June 1996
Summer before sophomore year

"Are we there yet?" Casey panted.

"Almost."

Something hit my shoulder. "Ow. Stop throwing pinecones at me."

"It's too hot to hike."

"I promised your mom we'd bring her leaves from this tree at the top."

Alex had been into leaves for four days now. She had a book called *LeafCraft! The Joy of Working With Nature's First Fabric* by someone named Gemini Duquet. So far she'd made six coasters, eight place mats, and a hat. The coasters and place mats worked out but the hat was less successful. The brim kept splitting.

Alex had given me four place mats, one inscribed on the back:

For Laura, our sweet girl. Love, Alex.

I'd hidden them in my bottom desk drawer. They were too beautiful to get stained. Alex had matched up the color gradations in the brown leaves perfectly, so they looked like burnished wood. And I could only imagine how my mother would mock them.

She tolerated me hanging out at The Shipwreck as long as I kept my grades up and didn't neglect my piano practice, but the Coeur-de-Lune Church Women's Auxiliary (Ingrid Christie, President) wasn't exactly an Alex Shepherd fan club. Alex had an anticreationist fish on her bumper, she went to the grocery store in cutoffs, and there was no husband in the picture. That seemed to be enough information for them.

More than anything, I didn't want my mother to read the "our" part of Alex's note on the leaf place mat. I knew what she'd think. *Presumptuous.*

"There are perfectly nice leaves in the gazebo park," Casey called. "This is brutal."

"They're really special leaves."

Alex would appreciate the glossy, six-pointed leaves from the top of the hill. But they were just an excuse.

I was going to show Casey what was inside my pocket, and Raptor Rock felt like the perfect place. Private, quiet. A little dramatic.

I'd decided after the skating rink; a stranger had handled it and my world hadn't collapsed.

I walked quickly, anxious to get it done.

Casey, hot and cranky as a toddler, was dragging. "You have to entertain me since you forced me on this death march. Truth or Dare."

"Truth."

"Do you have a crush on him?"

"Who?"

This time the pinecone hit my back. "I have a pocket full of these so answer or I'm turning back."

"You have to clarify. Who is *him*? There are so many crush prospects in this town. It's hard to keep them straight."

"J.B."

"Who's Jamie? Ouch!"

"You know exactly who J.B. is. The guy at the rink everybody but you stares at."

I held out my water bottle. "You have to hydrate."

She gulped, wiped her mouth. "Don't think you can distract me."

"What kind of name is J.B. anyway?" I said. "Sounds like some businessman from the '50s. Or a dude ranch. And those T-shirts. I think they're getting smaller."

"This is not how you play Truth or Dare. Answer."

"He's not my type."

"You don't trust me. And I tell you everything."

Neither statement was true, but I let this slide. Casey told me almost everything. But she hadn't told me one of the most important things. Same as me, until today.

Casey hooked a finger into my back middle belt loop. "Be my towrope." Linked together, we huffed up the hill.

At the top, Casey pulled down a branch to inspect its leaves. "Are these the ones?" she panted.

"They're pretty, aren't they? Like stars."

They were thick and glossy, chartreuse green. Casey didn't strip the branch—I'd trained her well—but she collected some leaves from the ground and tucked them into her cutoffs. "She'd better appreciate this."

A few more steps and we were at the clearing and the big, flat piece of granite called Raptor Rock.

"No dinosaurs." Casey stared at the sky.

"Dinosaurs?"

"Raptor Rock. Those dinosaurs in *Jurassic Park*."

"You're thinking of velociraptors."

"Velocity. Fast dinosaurs, right?"

"Right. But raptors are a family of birds. Small eagles, hawks. I don't see any but maybe they're resting in the shade today."

"They're smarter than us."

We ate our peanut-butter-and-marshmallow sandwiches. I wasn't a fan but I'd made them for Casey since it was a special occasion. Then we lay side by side on the warm rock.

"Case, know what today is?"

"The hottest day in Coeur-de-Lune history?"

"It's exactly one year since we met."

"Is it? Of course. You in your kayak."

"Yep."

"And you brought us here to celebrate. I'm an idiot."

"If you were I wouldn't show you this." I sat up and reached into the front pocket of my shorts. They were cargos, but at least they were size eights. I'd bought weapons-grade safety pins from the fabric store—the big ones people put on kilts. My best system yet: three kilt pins secured the chamois bag perfectly.

Casey sat up. "Oh, my God, oh, my God. You're showing me, finally?"

"Yes."

"I've been so good, not asking. Haven't I?"

"Yes."

"I've thought of a zillion possibilities. Drugs. But I know you too well now, there's no way. Then I thought maybe crystals. My mom went through a major crystal phase. Then I decided it was something boring like a rabbit's foot."

"It's not crystals or a rabbit's foot." I took it out of the chamois bag, unsealed the Ziploc, and set my charm between us.

Casey scrunched her nose. "It's a rock."

It did look like a rock. Not even a pretty one. Small, less than four inches across. And roughly oval, speckled gray-on-white. Against the granite of Raptor Rock it almost disappeared.

Casey tried to be respectful. She scanned my face for clues and examined my precious thing again. "Um, it's beautiful?"

I smiled. "It's not a rock. See this?" I held the driftwood up and tilted it so the thin silver hinges glinted in the sun and she could see that it had been split in half lengthwise to form a case.

"What is it?"

I opened it. My talisman.

My music box.

I only let myself open it on very special occasions. I knew exactly how much to wind it so it would play one time. I was afraid one day I'd overwind it. Then I'd either have to entrust it to some horrible clumsy jewelry repair shop or live with its cold muteness forever.

I wound the small silver crank four and a half times.

The tune was simple. Eighteen cascading notes, like a stone skipping on water. I knew the notes by heart now, sometimes played them on the piano—only if I was alone in the house.

"It's beautiful."

"I think so."

"What song is it?"

"I don't know. I wish I did." I'd listened to the radio for hours, the classical stations, the jazz stations, hoping to hear it. But I never had.

"Where'd you get it?"

"It was my mom's. My real mom's."

"Oh, Laur. Of course."

"She left it with me before she ran away."

The chunk of driftwood had been hollowed out to hold the small tin mechanism, like the kind that might go inside a little girl's ballerina jewelry box. The hinges were only simple ones from a hardware store, and the music box unit glued inside was cheap—even I could tell that. But the case had been made with care. I wound the small tin key four and a half times and played it again.

When the last note faded away, and we could only hear the birds, Casey said, "Your parents gave it to you when they told you you were adopted?"

I shook my head. "They told me when I was five but my dad didn't give it to me 'til I was ten. Only my dad. She doesn't know I have it."

"Why would she keep it from you?"

"She doesn't want me obsessing over her. Because she was a druggie. She was into bad stuff and she OD'd."

"Laur." She touched my hand.

"Guess nobody saves the dirty needles or crack pipes or whatever for the family scrapbook. But at least they saved this."

"I don't understand your mom. Adopted mom, I mean."

"That makes two of us. She has her ways, as my dad says." He used these four words, and a certain look in his eyes— half defeat, half apology—whenever he tried to explain something inexplicable about my mother. Like why she'd keep this strange, wonderful thing, the one object I knew my real mom had handled, had valued, from me. Whenever I said that—*real mom*—he scolded me. *You have a real mom*, he'd say. *A real mom who loves you.*

"They fight about it," I said. "How much to tell me about her. I've heard them through the heating duct."

"What else do you know?"

"So the official story is she 'made bad choices' and 'passed away.' But I've heard my mother whisper things like 'dredging up the past' and 'drug-affected' and 'prostitution.'"

Casey's eyes widened in shock before she could help herself. "She was...?"

"It doesn't make her a bad person."

"I know."

"She made bad choices. I think they agreed on the wording— *bad choices*. I think my mother was hoping I'd have more problems so she could be a martyr. All I had was low birth weight, and she'd signed on for fetal alcohol syndrome, brain damage, whatever."

"You know that's not true."

"Anyway. After the official speech my dad said she loved me, because she must've stopped using when she was pregnant, but my mother didn't say a word. Not a word."

"You could talk to her."

I shook my head. "What's the point?" I opened the driftwood case again. Just to see the music box's workings shining in the sun.

"So anyway," I said. "The summer I was ten, when my mother was on a church retreat, my dad gave it to me. He said he and my mother 'were of different minds' about it. But he thought I was old enough, and he wanted me to know that everybody has beauty in them."

"I like that."

"So now you know as much as me."

"You have to find out what the song is," Casey said.

"I've gone to seven different antique dealers. And you know that syndicated radio show on KZSY Classical? *June Names That Tune?* Where people try to stump her, humming part of a song?"

"You know that's not exactly my station."

"How embarrassing is this? I used to call in. Every Sunday night at ten, I'd hide in the pantry with the phone and hit Redial. I finally got through when I was thirteen but when it was my time to go on the air I panicked and hung up."

Casey's eyes had gone so glisteny I couldn't look at them. I stared off at the view. "I had the portable radio on really low, and I heard June make this joke. Without missing a beat. She said, *That's an easy one. It's 'Static,' composer unknown, 1994.*"

"I can see why you wouldn't want to do it on the radio. Too public."

"I've tried record stores. Everyone says it sounds familiar, but they can't place it."

"Some dumb teenager in a record store wouldn't know. We'll go to a music professor. Or we'll… I don't know. We'll think of something."

This was why I loved Casey. This was why I'd needed to show her.

We.

I sealed the box inside its bags and slipped it in my pocket, fastening the giant safety pins.

Casey squeezed my hand and scooched off the rock. She stayed close, though. I could see her, gathering leaves, occasionally glancing over to check on me. She waited for me to wipe my face with my sleeve, and take a long drink of sun-warmed water from my bottle, and tell her when I was ready to go. We were quiet the whole way down.

The next Sunday morning, while Casey was sleeping, Alex and I sat on the dock and I showed Alex the music box, too.

"Thank you," she said, practically in tears as she examined the swirls and knots in the driftwood cover. "Thank you for showing me."

"I could have ended up like that," she said, when I told her about the drugs that killed my birth mom. "You fall in with one wrong friend, date one wrong boy."

"My mother thinks she was weak."

"She doesn't understand."

That night I wrote in my diary—

For a second I had a stupid idea. If only it were true.

10

Critical and Confusing

The Creekside Café
Last Saturday of August 1996

We sat at the good window table at the Creekside, waiting for our two short stacks of brown-sugar pancakes. We had an hour to kill before the next bus; Alex couldn't drive us to the rink tonight because she had a date.

We knew the men who picked Alex up only by their cars. The blue Pontiac, the black Porsche, the gray Camry, the white Lexus. Some cars only came once. Some came a bunch of nights in a row, then, just when it seemed Alex was about to declare the impossible—that she had a steady boyfriend—they disappeared from the rotation.

Tonight she was going out with some guy she'd met in a pagan store in Sacramento called Moonshadow. She'd come back with bags full of herbs and seeds, a mortar and pestle, a book

on "good witch" gardening, and a date with a guy in a beat-up
Nissan. We called him The Warlock.

We were playing Things That Don't Belong, the game you
played at the Creekside. It was just a regular diner, but had once
been a fish-and-chip joint, and the current owners had embraced
the nautical theme. The ceiling was strung in fishing net with
stuff artfully hung throughout—treasure chests, plastic starfish,
an octopus. Right above our heads was the lake monster everyone called Messy.

Along with a water-themed word search and a drawing of
Messy for coloring, the kids' menu had a section where you
wrote down the Things That Don't Belong once you spotted
them overhead. There were always ten nonaquatic things up in
the ceiling net, and they got rotated every month.

"Kazoo. Near the ladies' room," I said.

"Stuffed lion by the door." Casey craned her neck. "Pink
high heel."

Before we got all ten, Scary Sue dealt us our plates, banging
the syrup jar down between us without a smile. Casey poured
on a ton of syrup, until her pancakes were surrounded by a
gooey brown moat, but I was used to her sweet tooth by now
and didn't say anything.

When Scary Sue passed us a minute later, delivering biscuits
and gravy to the next table, Casey said to her yellow-uniformed
back, "When you have a sec could we have another syrup please?"

Scary Sue thumped another bottle down without looking at
Casey.

"Nice try," I said.

"I thought I'd at least get a smile out of her."

Casey was going to "break" Scary Sue, like the guards at
Buckingham Palace. She'd been trying for a year.

"She's pretty," I said.

Casey stopped chewing and covered her mouth with her hand.
"What does that mean?"

"It means she's pretty."

She swallowed, stared at me. I wished that instead of saying Scary Sue was pretty, I'd pointed out that Messy's tail was wrapped around a plastic ice-cream cone. It would be our fifth item.

"It means much more than that, and you know it."

I don't know why I said it. I hadn't planned to. Ever since I'd shown Casey the music box, I'd waited for her to tell me the secret she carried around with her every day. I guess I'd gotten impatient. I was anxious to show her how fine I was with it.

And the stupid thing was I already *knew* how totally self-centered this was, and how common. I'd read about it. All my pamphlets said—*don't push*. If Casey didn't want to talk about it now, if she wasn't *ready for or receptive to the conversation,* I wasn't supposed to force it. You were never supposed to force it.

I'd figured it out months before, after a hundred clues. Her expression one time when I asked her if she thought Daniel Day-Lewis was cute in *Last of the Mohicans*. Why she was the only girl in our class who wasn't nervous around the skating rink guy. Why she changed the subject if anyone asked who she liked.

I knew when we finally talked about it I'd say everything right and we'd become closer than ever, like with my music box.

She clattered her fork down and said, "I'm not that hungry." Pink spots blossomed on her cheeks, the spots Alex called her angry clown look. The last time I'd seen them was in the hall at school after Mr. Travertini, our geography teacher, asked her if Alex was dating anyone.

"Case. I only wanted you to know that…that I know, and of course I'm fine with it, and we can talk about it anytime you want." Seeing her tense jaw, her red cheeks, I blathered on, going way off-script. "I read about the Kinsey scale, and I'm probably a one, maybe even a one and a half, because I haven't liked a girl in real life but I think my first crush was on Julie Andrews. I mean. Mary Poppins." I finished limply.

"You know, I'm actually pissed," she said. "You're *fine with it*? You're *maybe even a one and a half*? Well. Lucky me."

"I'm messing this up."

"Yes."

"I'm sorry."

"You should be," she said. "Not everything is about you." She stared out the window, and I followed her gaze. An old man was shuffling from the bait shop to his truck, a white Styrofoam cooler in his arms. Casey waited until he folded himself into the seat and drove off before turning to me with a sigh. "How many times did I ask you what you keep in your pocket?"

"Never."

Scary Sue was slamming down plates of fried chicken two tables over so I lowered my voice before continuing. "I read this pamphlet from the library that said I was supposed to let you know I was available for an honest conversation. So this is me, Case. Being available. And being an idiot. I'm sorry. Forget I said anything."

I took a bite, but my pancake, delicious a second ago, was now flavorless.

For a few minutes Casey stared at the ceiling as if she was still playing the game. Concentrating hard, cataloging things that belonged and things that didn't.

Finally she sighed and looked at me. "You have a pamphlet?"

I nodded. "From PFLAG. That's Parents and—"

"I know what it is. What's the title of the pamphlet?" The pink circles in her cheeks had faded a little.

"It's called *Let's Talk: Supporting Gay Youth During a Critical and Confusing Time*. I have more but that's the best one."

"Sounds like a page-turner." One corner of her mouth curled up.

"It's okay."

"They actually had that at the library in CDL?"

I shook my head. "I took the bus to Reno and got it at the main branch. A couple of months ago."

"So tell me about this time. This 'critical and vulnerable' time."

"Critical and confusing."

"What else do you know about it?"

"That I should listen without judgment. Offer support. Not pretend I know how hard it is."

"How long have you known?"

"A while now."

"How?"

"Little things."

"Such as?"

"The way you look at Ms. Maplewood in trig when she wears that purple V-neck. When Courtney was bugging you at lunch about who you liked so you finally started listing football players just to get her off your back. Bob Shipoluly was the clincher."

The corner of her mouth twitched higher, so I ventured on. "Really, Case. Nobody's into Bob Shipoluly. He's like a WWF wrestler."

Scary Sue refilled our waters, not apologizing for the pond she made on the vinyl tablecloth. When she went into the kitchen she immediately started yelling at the cook.

"Most. Embarrassing. Crush. Ever," Casey whispered.

"Nah. She's got a certain quality. I get it."

Casey smiled. "You're a weirdo. But I still love you."

"Does your mom know?"

Casey shook her head. "She has no clue. Miss Free Spirit. I think it's because she's so boy-crazy herself, or maybe the way her parents were. So old-school. It just wouldn't occur to her."

"You know she'll be fine with it. I mean—accepting. She's not like..." Certain other mothers.

"I know."

"This town. Alex not realizing. It can't be easy. Can't you tell her?"

She waited a long time to answer, mopping up Scary Sue's water spill with her napkin. "For now I just want to go skating. Go fast and fall a couple times and eat junk food."

We would laugh about that day later. We called it Pancake Day. Our code name for Scary Sue was Syrup. But if we were alone, hiking up to Raptor Rock or kayaking, Casey would say, "Remember that day you ambushed me and forced me to admit I had a crush on Scary Sue? Worst way to get someone to come out, ever."

It *was* funny. But Casey had shown me a part of myself I didn't like. An ugly streak of insecurity. Selfishness pretending to be friendship. If I was completely "fine with it" would I have tried so hard to prove I was? I wasn't sure. I knew this, at least: I'd wanted to prove how close we were so I could sleep easier, reassured that the happiness Casey and Alex had brought into my life wasn't going away.

We went to the rink and skated fast, and the music was so loud we couldn't have talked if we wanted. It was Glo-in-the-Dark night, and the white printing on Casey's I Heart San Francisco T-shirt became phosphorescent under the special lights. The heart was red so it was invisible: I San Francisco. We even played the Dice Game. I got knocked out early but Casey was one of the last skaters standing. I saved her a seat at the snack bar and watched.

He was running the game, of course. The Boy. Someone else was calling the numbers over crackling speakers, but The Boy Behind the Counter had left his counter, skating around, making sure nobody cheated, helping the little kids.

At one point he was just on the other side of the low wall from me. My table was positioned between 5 and 6, and a little girl had parked herself there, at the invisible 5.5. "You have to skate to a number every time," he explained to her. His voice was gentle.

After three more rolls Casey won, and The Boy handed her the ticket she could exchange for a prize or free slice of pizza. She laughed at something he said as she dug through the treasure chest.

She glided up to our table waving a green stuffed giraffe on skates.

"Congrats," I said. "I got you a Coke."

"Thanks. And Jasper says thanks, too. This is Jasper." She set him on the table and drained her Coke.

We swiveled and swung in our chairs, watching the rink. When The Boy skated by in his tight silver uniform shirt I said, "Want to hear something gross?"

"Jasper does." She skated the stuffed animal across the table and pulled his ears up as if he was listening.

I watched The Boy on the rink dodge and weave. "He went behind the Dumpsters with Pauline Knowland last week. She said he took his shirt off. She was telling everybody."

"That is gross."

"Want to hear something grosser?" I said.

"You still like him."

I nodded.

We watched him skating. He was too tall. His shiny black hair, flying behind him as he skated, was too long, and his silver T-shirt, glowing in the dark, seemed tighter than ever.

She smiled and said, kindly, "He has *a certain quality.*"

11

Yes, No, Wow

2016
Thursday night

I swiveled to face J.B. so fast he stepped back and held his hands up, a "don't shoot" expression on his face.

"Sorry I scared you," he said, looking past me, at Casey.

Yes, there were lines on his forehead. Yes, the hair on his temples was brushed with silver. His stomach, once concave, was now ever-so-slightly convex.

But his eyes were still wide and kind, the hair that fell across his forehead was still black and shiny. *Pretty as doll's hair,* one of his elementary school teachers had called it in front of the whole class. He'd told me about this humiliation one day as I was curled up on his chest in bed, playing with his hair. Kids had teased him at recess after, for being a boy with pretty hair.

"How are you?" I said.

"Can't complain. Can't complain."

"Casey told me you bought this place?"

"Crazy, huh?"

"No. I'm glad someone's keeping it the same."

"Ah, but it's not the same. We have veggie burgers now. How was your food?" He checked my plastic serving basket. It was the closest he'd come to looking at me.

"It was great."

"Great. Great." He was answering everything in duplicate. His smile was too wide, his eyes wouldn't rest anywhere.

He was nervous, too. Confirming this made me feel a tiny bit less nervous myself.

"What else is different?" I said.

He knelt between my chair and Casey's so we could hear him better over the music. I had imagined the theme song from *Elvira Madigan*. Or maybe that wistful Italian string piece they played at the end of *A Little Romance*.

But because we don't get to choose these things, my reunion with J.B. played out to the tune of "Shake Your Booty."

"Let's see, we have compostable paper plates available for the birthday parties." He drummed the table with his fingers. "Digital music. Queer skate night. This one's a regular. Or she was before Elle."

"Don't blame her," Casey said. "It's because you insisted on all those atrocious fix ups."

"So ungrateful."

"Please," Casey said. "That last chick was into NASCAR. *NASCAR*, J.B."

"I thought you'd hit it off."

"You have the worst taste in women, ever."

They both laughed. I pretended to. We were going to power through this mess with laughter. We'd be world champion laughers.

Then all three of us realized the implications of Casey's com-

ment at once and stopped laughing. I stared at the ketchup bottle, my smile frozen.

J.B. tried to undo her goof, speaking fast. "We have another
one in three weeks, so come, okay? No setups. I promise."

Now all three of us were staring at the center of the table,
the condiments becoming some sort of safe zone for our eyes.
"Disco Inferno" was on.

Burn, baby, burn.

I could take the most direct route to the exit—hurdle over the
blue-carpeted half wall in front of us and run straight across the
crowded rink. I'd shove aside toddlers, the gang of tough-looking
older women zooming past in matching black satin jackets that
said Hell on Wheelz, whoever. But I was an adult now so I only
smiled harder.

Then Casey did what she always did. She couldn't just let the
moment pass. She had to try to neutralize it by calling it out.
"Sorry. That was awk, as Elle and her friends say."

"What does *ock* mean?" J.B. said. He was, as they say, *strenu-
ously avoiding* looking at me. I'd never really understood the expression until that moment. It was actually a perfect description.
Because such avoidance takes exertion. I was worn-out from it,
and I was only an observer.

"Awk," I said. "As in awkward."

He turned his head toward me at last. I smiled and shrugged
a little, meaning it was okay. It wasn't his fault. It wasn't anybody's fault.

Casey watched us. Missing nothing. "No more setups, okay?
Your setups are…what's the word?"

"Awk?" I said.

They laughed, relieved I'd attempted a joke, lame as it was.

"You stay home every Friday and Saturday night," J.B. said
to her.

"Suits me fine."

They went on like this, teasing, lobbing inside jokes across the Formica table. And while I knew they were only doing it to take the pressure of conversation off me, I could tell that their friendship was genuine. So Casey and J.B. had gone on without me, getting closer each year. It was astonishing. In my mind, they'd stopped having any contact after I left. What did I think, that the whole town had been frozen like Pompeii for the last seventeen years?

That age-old internal complaint, insistent and tiresome. *Me, me—it's all about me!* I worked my napkin in my hands, pulling it as tight as my smile.

Finally, Casey said, "Did you know about this little scheme of my mom's?"

"Scheme?" J.B. said.

"Tricking Laura into coming? The scavenger hunt she set up?"

"Scavenger hunt, huh? Are you doing it?" His expression way too innocent.

"So you did know," Casey said. "We're not sure yet. We're only trying it out." Casey pulled the Polaroid from her pocket and handed it to him.

He examined the picture for a long time and I wondered what he was thinking, studying this overexposed image of me and Casey posing on either side of his plastic treasure chest. He handed it back to her. "So what's she got you doing besides coming here?"

Props. Thank God for props. I pulled the list of items from my purse. "We've done two out of ten."

J.B. leaned over my shoulder, close enough that I felt his breath on my neck. "Poems, no less."

I remembered, too late, the line in the roller rink clue about winning a heart. *On hoofs of brown and orange you'd win / A game, a heart, a key...*

"You should finish it," he said abruptly.

"Why?" said Casey.

"You just should. Trust me."

Why should I trust you, J.B.?

And yet I wanted to. After everything, I wanted to.

"Spill it," Casey said.

"No. But I'll contribute this." He picked up a purple plastic birthday goody bag from the floor and set it on the table. "Use it for your loot."

Casey slipped the Polaroid into the bag. I reached into my pocket for the blue tile and dropped it in.

"You should finish." J.B. looked at me again and walked away.

"Well," I said.

I studied the goody bag, which hadn't changed since I was in grade school. It had a picture of Digby the Pirate Duck doing a skating trick where you drop down with one leg extended in front of you and hold your ankle as you roll along, like you're aiming a hunting gun. The trick was called Shoot the Duck. Kind of twisted for a kid's birthday goody bag. A duck doing Shoot the Duck. And the design was cluttered, the purple background clashed with the yellow Digby and made it hard to see his pirate hat.

A *No*, definitely, on the *Yes, No, Wow* spectrum I learned about in art school. (If a design worked, it was a *Yes*. If it didn't, it was a *No*. And then there were *Wows*—rare, brilliant, elusive. What we all aimed for but almost never reached.)

Maybe J.B. had inherited a lifetime supply of the goody bags when he bought the place. He had better taste than that, or at least he used to.

I smiled at Casey. "That went fine, don't you think? We were very civilized."

"He's not married."

"I'm surprised. He's a good guy."

"He was living with someone, five, six years ago. But nothing's lasted."

"That's too bad."

"Is it?"

"What about you? Anyone serious?"

"I lived with someone in Tahoe. In my late twenties, but she moved to Boston ages ago. J.B.'s not dating anyone right now."

"So what d'you think? Should we keep going?"

"He's definitely in on it."

"Definitely."

We looked across the rink, but he'd disappeared behind the sea of gliding skaters. "Night Fever" was playing, rainbow lights strobing in time to the Bee Gees' plaintive falsettos. A portly man did an impressive Shoot the Duck spin in the center, under the disco ball.

"I'll keep going if you will," I said.

Casey swiveled to face me, her eyes narrowed. "Is he why you want to stick around?"

I waited a long time to answer. Seeing him had been intense. *Yes, No, Wow* all at once. But J.B. was only one reason I wanted to stay. There were others, some so small I'd feel foolish offering them out loud—the smell of the skating rink, the satisfaction of rocking back and forth in my chair, the way the light hit the lake.

But most of all Casey, looking at me, not letting me get away with anything.

I didn't want to go home yet. "I'd like to know what your mom's up to. Aren't you curious?"

"It could be a disaster."

"You're right."

"It could be a *disaster of epic proportions*."

"Could be."

"Oh, hell. What's the next clue?"

Clue 3

Well-planned clutter overhead
To distract the hungry young

You searched long after others stopped
Noticing what had been hung
One child of the sea dives from the nest; free her from
the rest

"The Creekside." Casey pushed back from the table triumphantly. "The junk on the ceiling for the Things That Don't
Belong game."

"*Child of the sea*. They still have those mermaid toys?"

12

Things That Don't Belong

The Creekside's waiter was male, and friendly. When we ordered only two hot teas to go he scolded Casey. "You should have your visitor try our brown-sugar pancakes." He pointed at me. "You'd love 'em, specialty of the house!"

Punk. I'd eaten hundreds of brown-sugar pancakes at the Creekside before he was even born.

"Just the tea, Griff," Casey said.

After he'd walked away I said, "So no more Scary Sue?"

"Long gone. Moved to Arizona."

"I'm sorry."

A hint of a smile. "I was not, I repeat, *not* pining away for Scary Sue all these years."

"Got it."

"You spot one of those mermaids?" Casey said, yawning, scanning the ceiling. "I'm pretty wiped."

I pointed above the ladies' room door, where a mermaid plush toy's fin poked out through the net.

I crossed the small restaurant and glanced around dramatically, as if I was about to commit a Class C felony, while Casey observed from the entry, her yawn turning into a smile. Reassured that nobody was watching, I stood on my tiptoes and plucked Clue 3's fin from the netting. The mermaid slipped out easily, as if she'd been waiting there seventeen years for me to rescue her.

We stood on Casey's porch. Her tired face was sepia-colored in the glow from the single, old-fashioned lamp over her head. She took her keys from her pocket, studied them. "Well," she said, the word almost lost under the high, insistent vibration of the cicadas.

"Well." I pulled the mermaid plush toy from my waistband and held her up to the light so her cloth fin sparkled. "Three down."

Casey took the purple goody bag from her pocket and handed it to me. I dropped the mermaid in.

"We're good at this," she said.

"We've done it before."

She jangled her keys. "This is pretty strange, huh?"

"Yes."

I wanted to ask her if she felt like I did, if the years when we'd been friends still seemed more important than anything that had happened since.

But I feared she didn't feel the same. Maybe for Casey, this was merely *strange*. A weekend of forced déjà vu that would go as quickly as it came. An awkward, tricky, emotionally exhausting weekend, sure. But no more.

Casey unlocked her door and Jett burst out. She pushed her nose at Casey's hand, reminding her of her scratching ability.

"She likes you," I said. "She went for you before she hit the bushes."

"I'm honored." Casey dug her fingers into the precise spots behind Jett's ears that made her eyes go blank with pleasure.

The door was wide-open, the lights shining in The Shipwreck's living room. My place would be dark, and cold, and uninviting.

"We have Clue 4 tomorrow." I rattled the goody bag.

"Raptor Rock, isn't it? A hike."

"We should start before it gets too hot. What time should I pick you up?"

"Stay here tonight."

"Don't be silly, you don't have to…"

"It's almost midnight, you're tired, the dog's tired. You probably don't even have food in your fridge. If we're going to do this thing we should do it right and start early. So…stay here. And don't call me silly."

I lay on my back in Casey's old bed, exhausted but wide-awake. Jett was snoring at my feet. Her soft, familiar rattle usually worked better than any white-noise machine.

But when I closed my eyes too many images crowded in. Casey sitting on the dock, her blanket on her shoulders like a tiny superhero, and J.B.'s kind brown eyes avoiding mine. The willowy sea monster on the mosaic, and the treasure chest spilling over with cheap loot.

I wondered if Casey was asleep. I wondered if J.B. was, or if he was tossing and turning, remembering.

The hands on Elle's purple glow-in-the-dark clock progressed to 12:30, then 12:45, as I counted sheep. I tried counting by threes from one hundred, backward. Then I gave up and dedicated myself to important thoughts like—why do they only say Toss and Turn? Why not Flip and Flail? For those nights of aggressive non-sleep.

At 1:05, I stopped trying since I never slept through the 2:00 a.m. to 4:00 a.m. stretch anyway. Other people napped from two to four in the afternoon; I was awake between two and four at night. My reverse siesta.

I sat up and Jett twitched in her sleep because she'd been using my leg as a pillow. I turned my phone on and found a text from Sam. He was another night owl. He woke up at dawn to surf and took a long afternoon nap, so he was always free to pester me late at night:

How goes the Big Reunion in the Big Woods, Laura Ingalls? Send photo of devirginizer stat. Need chuckle. Picturing your gentleman in combination spangled Olympic skating costume/woodsman outfit.

P.S. Don't eff this up. It took guts for your friend to reach out after so long. Life is short and all that jazz. S.

The "devirginizer," as Sam put it, was J.B.

How I regretted it, the one night Sam and I had gotten drunk in North Beach to celebrate his shirts going national. Seeing a brunette at the next table who'd reminded him of his first girl-friend, he'd reminisced about his first time, and, halfway into the second bottle of estate Sangiovese, I'd finally told him about mine.

Only the bare facts: an older boy, an empty skating rink, a dark room, a pile of ski coats.

I'd kept the important parts to myself. The sweetness of it, the buoyancy of that pile of down and nylon under my bare skin, the way we'd laughed together, after. And his name. I hadn't told Sam any of that.

I typed back:

Can't sleep. Reunion constantly veering between disaster and mid-dling success. Not sure where we'll land. Found out it's not my friend who reached out after all. Long story. It was someone else, but we're going along with it. For now.

You know perfectly well a certain PRIVATE incident shared in mo-ment of weakness was at roller rink, not ice-skating rink. Request for photo too ridic. to honor. Denied.

L

He responded four minutes later:

Intrigued by invitation conspiracy. Wasn't me, I swear.

P.S. Middling success is all we of middling age can hope for sometimes. Embrace this fact, offered free of charge. P.P.S. Like roller
skating is less embarrassing. I still picture your dude in spandex and
rhinestones. And I say: Excellent. Let bygones be bygones and rip
that spandex off. S.

I typed Mansplainer and shut my phone down.

San Francisco felt far away, but Sam was there. I'd made a life
away from this town. Small and self-contained though it was.

I stretched my toes to Jett's warmth, going over the list of
Alex's scavenger hunt clues in my mind, wondering how she
had settled on these ten.

But that only made me more restless. Each item so carefully
chosen. Alex's sharp little shovels for unearthing the past.

I forced myself to count the star stickers on Elle's ceiling instead.

13

It was a clear day, not a wisp of fog.

Her teammates ran ahead to hunt for strands of kelp, a white shell, a soda can.

The clue sheets that their middle-aged chaperone, Miss Cooke, passed out in the van always had the same easy, obvious items. The rules were always the same, too. They could not leave the sand. They could not talk to strangers, though there were never strangers. Maybe on weekends, but not when they visited this ragged stretch of beach—only on Wednesdays, for one precious hour.

And her mom had sold Three Pines to her as a beach camp. Look, sweetie, she'd said, showing her the brochure. Beach outings. Crafts, music, nature walks.

Was her mom allotted more than sixty minutes of beach time a week, over at the adult camp?

Did she know that the three pines in the clearing were supposed to be miraculous replicas of the three crosses on Mount Golgotha? Golgotha, such an ugly word; it sounded like choking.

Did she, too, sit on a hard chair all day as strangers railed about chastity, sober apparel, obedience? As they echoed verses that should have made them furious, smiling and nodding along, eyes closed in bliss?

For the man is NOT of the woman, but the woman of the man!

Someone yanked her shirttail. "Bad night?" It was her cabinmate, Sandy, a girl who carried a gold-and-black Good News bible with her everywhere.

"What do you—"

"I heard you crying."

"I wasn't—"

"Also you usually get your shoes wet right away. You pretend it's an accident but it's on purpose."

"Why would someone do that?"

Sandy considered, biting her lip. "To feel the ocean, to feel normal. But your shoes are dry today. The beach hour is the one semidecent part of camp, and you're not showing gratitude."

She glanced over Sandy's shoulder. Miss Cooke wasn't looking at them. She was at the picnic blanket up the beach, smiling beatifically. Miss Cooke never lost that broad, unnerving smile, even when she had to undo a girl's stitches for the third time in embroidery lessons.

Miss Cooke was organizing their snacks for after the scavenger hunt. They always got one Ants-on-a-Log and two vanilla Hydrox cookies apiece. Then it was back in the van. The winning team got to choose which songs to sing on the ride back; that was the prize.

It was pathetically wholesome.

But Sandy was right. The scavenger hunts were the only time she felt close to normal.

"That's a sin, you know, being ungrateful." Sandy stared at her, monitoring her reaction.

It was the first time she'd heard actual sarcasm all summer. She'd almost forgotten what it sounded like.

"So pray for me."

"Take this instead. Stay awake tonight, and keep your shoes handy." Sandy pressed something into her hand and ran ahead to help her team hunt for a sand dollar.

She uncurled a scrap of paper. It was a pencil drawing of a crescent moon. Her crescent moon, the Curdilune one, with knots and swirls and shading to suggest the texture of driftwood.

There was a thick, curved line near the bottom of the crescent, to represent a smile, and a small circle at the top for an eye.

She smiled back at it.

14

Velocity

2016
Friday morning

When I woke I had the oddest feeling. I closed my eyes again so I could hold on to it.

I knew I was an adult, that Casey's old bedroom was now her daughter's. But in that cloudy minute between dreaming and waking, all of my senses remembered what it felt like to wake up at The Shipwreck on a Sunday in high school.

At home I had always risen to the sound of a creaking oven door, the air already heavy with my mother's checked-off tasks. But I was usually the first to get up in the Shepherd house.

Casey would be snoring lightly next to me, her arms flung over her head. I'd crawl out from under her soft yellow comforter slowly so I wouldn't disturb her. I'd set my feet on the cold hardwood floors. My church dress would be hanging on the closet door, waiting, but my eyes would skim over it; my other life didn't start until 8:45.

Alex would still be asleep, crashed on the daybed in her studio. I'd take my sketchbook and pencil from my bag, tiptoe downstairs. Then I'd have an hour outside to draw, wrapped in the scratchy red wool blanket against the morning chill. I always got my best ideas on those Sunday mornings on Casey's dock. I sketched fast, without second-guessing.

After an hour or so Alex would join me. It would be just the two of us for a while.

The third phase of Sunday mornings at The Shipwreck: Casey would open the screen door, say "Why are you two so awake?" and we'd laugh at her bleary eyes and red hair sticking up.

Then there was another precious half hour or so, just the three of us, before I had to scramble home in time for church. That was the deal I'd made with my mother.

I opened my eyes, staring at the top of the tidy vanity, where Elle's hairbrush and ponytail holders and ChapStick were neatly laid out. She had a small white metal earring tree. This, too, was tidy: the pairs of studs and tiny danglers matched up and carefully secured to the perforated leaves of the little tree.

It has been seventeen years. Casey has a daughter you've never met. And you are only an uninvited weekend guest.

I shushed Jett as we walked past Casey's door.

Outside it was crisp and windless, the lake glassy. I breathed in the clean smell of pine resin, the smoky complement of wood fires. I turned my phone on, wrapped Jett's leash around my wrist twice. My city dog was thrilled with her new surroundings— the biggest park she'd ever visited. It felt like she'd tug me straight into the water.

I had an email from Sam: a picture of a black Lab on a surf-

board. A "meme." Sam loved to crowd my inbox with memes
and emojis. (He called them "mojos" though he knew the right
name perfectly well.) "Every wave is a fresh chance to be a bad-
ass," this one said.

When we came inside Casey was awake and dressed, her hair
neatly brushed. "Did you sleep okay?" She scooped out coffee,
in hostess mode.

"Perfect. It's so quiet here, it's fabulous. Thanks." I unclipped
Jett's leash. Casey had set a bowl of water on the kitchen floor
and Jett bounded for it. I crossed the living room, pretending
to appreciate the tree view out one of the small windows so I'd
have something to do.

"The bed's not too soft?" Casey said. "I've been meaning to
get a new one."

"It was perfect."

"Good."

She was so polite. Too polite. Not like on the porch when
she'd ordered me to stay. As if she'd spent the night regretting
letting her defenses down, and plotting a reversal.

We'd taken two steps forward and one step back. Or maybe
that was overly optimistic. Maybe it was one step forward and
two steps back, and Sunday we'd part with the veneer of good
manners painted onto everything.

Was it better that way? Less honest, but safer? Maybe that's
how it had to go when you got older. You couldn't bear the
truth—we're not friends anymore. But you could be polite.

On Sunday we'd say, "We did it. See you in another seventeen years." Or never.

"Cinnamon-swirl bread for your toast, or walnut whole grain
or sourdough?" Casey said, breaking into my thoughts. "I didn't
know what you'd like so I got everything."

"The walnut, but please let me help." I moved toward the
counter.

"Stop. Sit."

I obeyed, settling in a kitchen chair.

Casey bustled around, prepared a tray with fruit, juice, toast, butter. She warmed the milk for my coffee in a tiny saucer. When we'd been in high school Casey had eaten straight from the Cap'n Crunch box, holding it out to me teasingly because she knew I didn't like it.

"Any word from your mom?"

"Called her again but of course she didn't pick up. The chicken."

"You told her we're doing her list?"

"Yes. I said we're expecting a big prize on Sunday. Preferably in cash." She set the tray on the round kitchen table. "How many clues do you think we can knock off today?"

I pulled the list from my purse. "The hike will take a few hours. Until two at least."

"Are we sure this is right? I can see us dripping with sweat up at Raptor Rock, then realizing we misinterpreted the poem."

Us. I wondered if Casey'd let the word slip unintentionally. It was so much like something she'd have said as a teenager.

We read silently:

An airy, aerie place
Where you gathered stars for me
A climb to reach them, but there you two were free
Above, the birds, below, the stone
You never went alone

"It's definitely Raptor Rock," I said. "The stars are those pointy leaves she liked."

"Guess she wants us to get some exercise."

"We'll bring water. Take it slow. And I guess… Should I leave my stuff here 'til we get back? I'll get over to my house this afternoon."

"Whatever you want."

★ ★ ★

Jett came with us, tugging on her leash, delighted by the new smells around every corner. In high school I practically had to tow Casey uphill. Now she seemed determined to push herself.

"It seems like you do this trail every weekend," I said.

"Haven't in seventeen years. Since you left."

"Oh." Dangerous territory, this. What to talk about? Work. Work was safe. "How did you decide to buy the bookstore?"

"Phil Pinkerton needed to sell during the pit of the recession. 2007. Nobody wanted it. Remember Phil?"

"Of course. Mr. Pinkerton got most of your allowance. We used to read dirty paperbacks in the back room."

Here's where she could grin.

Or not.

"Yeah, so I had a little money. My mom said I could take the rest of my college money… You know I dropped out halfway through freshman year, right?"

I made a sound that was supposed to be a yes, but trying too hard to convey my lack of judgment (how cool of you, who needs college, I didn't need to finish my BFA to do my job). I went overboard and it sounded like Yayyees.

Casey looked at me strangely. "So since I dropped out she said I could do whatever with the rest of the money she'd set aside. And I bought the bookstore. Turned out to be a good investment—the real estate part."

"That's great. How's the bookstore part doing?" I said. "If you don't mind my asking."

"Netted two thousand dollars last quarter. That was good, for post-Christmas."

I nodded, unsure if I should offer a "that's wonderful" look or a sympathetic one.

"That's great?" I said.

It didn't sound great. I'd broken $120,000 the year before, largely thanks to Goofy Foot.

Casey smiled. "Eight thousand a year? We're not exactly living like lords. But my mom's generous, we have free housing. It's working out."

I nodded.

"Now, your business is going well, obviously."

"I like working for myself."

"How was *S-C-A-D*?" She sounded out the four letters of Savannah College of Art & Design, which nobody did. Everyone said *scad*.

I concentrated on the path, strewn with dry leaves. One foot in front of the other. We were getting into treacherous ground.

"I was lonely at first. The South felt...foreign. Like another country. But the program was good for me. I got through it."

I held my breath, waiting for her to respond. I'd planned to go to CalArts. Casey'd been accepted at UCLA. She'd turned down her dorm assignment. We were going to live together. We'd put a deposit down on a ratty studio near Lake Balboa, splitting the distance between our schools. We were going to laugh at La La Land together. Me and Casey and J.B. The three of us against the starlets and the surfers.

And then, at the last minute, leaving her with nobody, I'd taken off for Georgia. Like the division of property in a divorce. *You get the Pacific Ocean, Casey. I'll take the Atlantic.*

She had every right to yell. Pelt me with pinecones, rocks.

"I saw that movie," she said. "That one set in Savannah."

"Midnight in the Garden of Good and Evil."

"I rented it the day it came out, because I knew you were there. I wanted to see what it was like."

I reached to her. "Did you? Case."

But she marched past me and didn't stop until we'd ascended the hill.

We got to Raptor Rock in less than ninety minutes. A record. We'd gone many times after the first visit, when I'd shown Casey my music box, but even at seventeen we'd never propelled our-selves up as fast as this.

I'd tried talking for a while. Halfway up the hill I said, "Re-member that first time, how you pretended you thought rap-tors were dinosaurs?"

"Oh, yeah."

After another hundred feet—"We're walking fast. Giving the velociraptors a run for their money."

"Hmm."

Casey was all business at the summit. Though sweaty and clearly worn-out, she didn't let herself rest on the rock with me and stood closer to the edge, looking out at the view. As Jett lapped from her portable water dish, from the corner of my eye I watched Casey pick up a leaf and stuff it into her pocket with-out examining it.

There would be no confidences shared on the rock today. We'd ventured too close to the heart of things.

"Is your mom still making her leaf crafts?" I called. "Remem-ber that book? That awful hat?"

"Kind of."

"Remember the place mats she gave me? It was one of her better phases, don't you think?"

"Guess so."

Yell at me. Shove me. Look at me.

She didn't say another word as we walked back down the hill.

15

Stepping Stones

Friday, late afternoon

I hid in Elle's bedroom, spying on Casey from behind her daughter's purple curtains.

She'd been sitting on the dock, her back to the house, for hours. She hadn't said anything about tackling the rest of the list. She hadn't spoken to me at all.

At two I'd taken Jett for a walk by the water, hoping Casey would thaw, at least speak to me.

Every sense on high alert, Jett sniffed her way up the rocky shoreline just north of The Shipwreck, along the western curve of the lake. At one point she spotted a duck and barked furiously, then froze, some ancient instinct from her bird-dog lineage transforming her into a furry black arrow from nose to tail.

I turned to face Casey and smiled, hoping she would notice, call out. We were only twenty feet from the dock, so she had to have heard Jett barking.

But she remained stone-faced, staring out at the water.

It was too much, what Alex had tried to do. She thought she could lay out memories for us, simple as the chain of stepping stones in the deep part of Meriwether Stream. Like all we had to do was hop from object to object to get over the past. As if a flimsy Polaroid, a small tile could hold us.

Whatever her reasons for reaching out now, it had been too long and some things couldn't be repaired. It was time to go home.

I was packed, my clothes rolled into neat cylinders in my suit-case, when my phone vibrated.

New message from
goofyfoot@goofyfootsf.com to
lchristie@lchristiedesign.com

I wasn't in the mood for one of Sam's digital pep talks.
But the subject line said—

Urgent!!! Concern Re: Design Modification on Youth S. Slv. Tees

So I clicked on it.

Gotcha.
How goes it? Impressed you haven't chickened out. Don't chicken out, LC.

Then there was a chicken drumstick, a skull and crossbones, and what I thought was a smiling chocolate kiss but on closer examination turned out to be poo.

Below that was a link to his twitter, @goofyfootSF. Sam spent hours on Twitter, posting surfing photos and inspirational memes that he hoped would go viral and rack up followers. It made his day when he got retweets, or when a C-list celebrity responded. He called it "starfuckery," as if he didn't care, but clearly reveled in it.

I clicked the link. His latest creation wasn't bad. An old photo of him bailing out on a huge, crystalline wave, taken at the second he'd jumped off his board and gone airborne.

Below it said, "If you never wipe out you never get better."— Sam "Goofy Foot" Gilman. 1981, Waimea Bay.

Well played, Sam.

But I was going. Casey didn't want me there; she was perched at the end of the dock, her chin on her knees, still as a gargoyle.

I checked under the bed to make sure I hadn't dropped anything, zipped up my suitcase, and felt inside my purse for my car keys. My hands brushed against something smooth and flat. A photo. I'd found it in a box of keepsakes in my closet and tucked it into my purse Thursday afternoon in a moment of optimism.

I sank onto the bed, lost in the old picture, for a long time. Waiting for it to lose its power. But the longer I stared at the overexposed image, the more my chest ached. Its smiling subjects had no idea how complicated life could become.

I would try talking to Casey once more. If only to say goodbye.

It was getting dark when I sat next to Casey on the dock. Twenty-four hours into our weekend, and we were right back where we'd started. No, worse. She was chillier than she'd been when I'd arrived.

Casey was folding the clue sheet into a paper airplane on her thigh. She held it up, scrutinized the neat creases, and adjusted the nose, then lifted it and aimed at the center of the lake.

When she pulled her arm back to launch it I clutched her wrist. "Case, don't."

She turned, eyes flashing, pulling her arm but unable to free it from my grip. "Why do you still go along with every stupid scheme she cooks up? You still worship her that much?"

I let go, surprised by how tightly I'd gripped her. How frag-ile Casey's wrist bones felt in my hand. And how desperate I'd been to stop the list from sailing into the water.

She watched me, her eyes daring me to stop her as she re-coiled her arm again. "Buh-bye, Scavenger Hunt. Buh-bye, Terrible Poetry."

Buh-bye, tatters of what had once been friendship. She was right. It was too late for us anyway. "Throw it, Casey."

Her eyes softened and she dropped the list on my lap. "Oh, hell. You throw it."

I touched its edges, sleek as the real gliders people flew off the bluffs near Sam's shop. Sam and I watched the gliders sometimes. I always said it looked like fun, pure freedom. Sam said I was a brave chick, that he'd never fly in anything lighter than he was.

I set the clue sheet on the dock, securing it under Casey's sandal, and pulled the old Polaroid from my back pocket. "So I carried this all through college. All four years."

She accepted the photo but didn't look at it. "Tell me you didn't wear cargo shorts all through college. The South is for-mal, I hear."

"I had these linen drawstring skirts with zippered pockets. Very artistic. Very weather-appropriate."

"Good to know."

"The other thing I wanted to tell you is this. My college roommate was this girl named Elaine Carter. She was from New York and she was into ceramics. That's pretty much all I ever learned about her. She tried to be friends at the beginning but... Anyway. She was so nice. She'd ask me to go to parties with her but I'd hide in the studio all night. Ask me to wake her up so we could sit together at breakfast. But I'd sneak out while she was still sleeping."

"Poor Elaine."

"Yes. Poor Elaine. And another thing I wanted you to know about, besides the Polaroid, and poor Elaine, is I bought a Greyhound ticket Thanksgiving break of freshman year. I was going to come see you. Forty-four hours on the bus each way. I made it all the way to the depot."

Casey kept her eyes fixed on a couple of kayakers across the lake.

"I just wanted you to know," I said. "In case it makes a difference."

"Anything else you wanted to share?"

"Yes. I still want to finish your mom's list. If you're up for it. I understand if you're not, but I'd very much like to finish. We were doing okay until the hike."

She studied the picture. "God. We're so young."

"Sixteen. You can tell my age in our high school pictures by the thickness of my eye shadow." Like figuring out a tree's age by the rings in the trunk.

"Summer after sophomore year. Those awful keggers. We thought we were so cool at first, getting invited to senior parties. God. Look at us."

I leaned a little closer to study the girls in the picture.

Alex had taken it. We were in Casey's bedroom, ready to go out. Casey was in a tank top and jeans, her hair in a sloppy bob. I'd just exchanged my cargo pants and shorts for a happy discovery—cargo miniskirts. My hair was carefully styled, cascading down my shoulders, and my heavy eye makeup didn't belong with my innocent smile.

I had another photo like it at home, taken a second later. That one was more posed and clear. But I preferred this one. We'd turned to each other and laughed, goofing off right as Alex had pressed the button, so my right arm and Casey's left were blurs, as if one.

"We look happy," I said.

"We were happy." She handed the picture back.

We were quiet for a few minutes, then she said, "I guess we owe it to those girls to finish off the list. I guess I can do that."

"Good." I'd had almost the exact same thought, examining the picture up in Elle's room. *Those girls wouldn't have given up so easily.* "Number five isn't far. Jade Cove."

Casey gazed to our right, toward the distant clump of trees on the east shore of the lake that hid our old swimming spot. "The picture'll be dark, but I doubt my mom'll disqualify us for that."

"Or we could blow off the list until tomorrow. We have plenty of time. I want to see your bookstore."

She smiled. "Tour of the failing businesses of Coeur-de-Lune?"

"No, actually I've wanted to see it for years. Ever since my mom told me you bought it."

"Sure. I'll take you. Do you…" She hesitated, then went on. "You want to drop your suitcase off at your place first?"

We both glanced across the water at my empty house.

"No. I want to stay here for the rest of the weekend. If you'll still have me."

Casey set her head on her knees and looked up at me, the corner of her mouth raised in the faintest hint of a smile. "I guess I can handle it."

One step forward.

16

Dreaming Shepherd Books

I liked Casey's bookstore right away. It felt like her: unpretentious and lovely.

There was a big stencil in the window, with the store's logo. An elegant line drawing of a shepherdess napping on a rock, her book tented over her eyes, a single sheep jumping over her. A *Wow*. I wondered if Alex had designed it.

At the front of the store was a window seat catching the sun, overstuffed armchairs in the corners, and of course a wall of used paperbacks.

The teenager at the counter guiltily hid his ACT prep book and hopped off his stool. "Didn't think you were coming in today."

"Tim, this is Laura." So I'd earned an introduction at last. I'd have preferred "Laura, my old friend," or "Laura, she grew up here." But I'd take it. "You can go. I'll close up."

She looked around the empty store. "We do actually get customers once in a while. It's just that it's ten minutes 'til closing."

"Of course. Did your mom design your shepherdess?"

"Yep."

"I love it."

"You don't think it implies our books put people to sleep?"

"No."

Casey watched silently as I walked through the small, over-stuffed rooms, running my hands along shelves. She had a table of local history books; my dad would have approved. A whole LGBTQ wall, clearly marked, right up front; our town had changed with the times.

In a back corner by a window there was a giant hollow papier-mâché tree with a generously sized cutout in the trunk. A mound of overstuffed pillows waited on the floor inside, winking out invitingly, but mostly obscured by a curtain of candy wrappers strung across the opening in the tree. Not just butterscotch this time. Sheer pink, pistachio, translucent red. It was magical, shot through with sunlight. I climbed in through the crinkly cellophane strips and smiled from behind it. "Casey."

She leaned down to peek inside at me. "The kids seem to like it."

In her back office she made me coffee. She held up a stack of envelopes and grimaced. "The HVAC bills are brutal. This place has zero insulation."

I sipped my coffee. "But look what you created, all by yourself."

"I know I should probably sell, take the gain on the building and run, but...I love it too much. I love being part of the town." She clenched and unclenched her left hand.

"Is your hand okay?"

She looked down and shook it. "Yeah, touch of carpal tunnel. Overdid it on the ten key. The one part of owning the store I don't love, data entry. Anyway, I do like being my own boss."

"Me, too. Some of my clients require major hand-holding, though."

"Like that Sam guy who keeps texting? Your boyfriend?"

"He's most definitely not my boyfriend."

"Got it."

"He's seventy, only a friend. I hang out at his café sometimes. He's funny, you'd like him, though he can be an unfiltered know-it-all."

She started to say something but sipped her coffee instead.

"What?"

"Nothing."

"Tell me."

"I was going to say he sounded like the father-figure type."

I paused, tried to laugh this off. "Sam's way too obnoxious for that."

"I'm sorry, it was a dumb thing to say. Your dad's not replaceable."

"It's okay."

It was unsettling, that she could size up my life so quickly, so well. Sam's sense of humor was the opposite of my dad's. Inappropriate to the point of infuriating. But there was something to Casey's assessment. My closest adult relationship was platonic, with an irreverent, much older man.

Casey grabbed a canvas Dreaming Shepherd tote bag from a box, dropped in a bunch of bookmarks, and handed it to me. "Shopping spree, on the house. I recommend the Highly Flammable section. But take whatever you want."

"That's so generous, are you s—"

She closed her eyes and pushed her hand toward me like a traffic conductor. *Stop.*

"Thank you. But you pick them out. Surprise me."

As Casey filled the bag there was a rap on the door. Though it was obviously after-hours, the assault on the glass continued, surprisingly loud given that the customer seemed about eighty. When Casey opened the door a sweet voice trembled out, "Oh, dear, are you closed?"

I should have guessed who it was from the passive-aggression.

One glance at too-pale face powder, white hair teased into a cotton helmet, a yellow handbag, and I knew: Barb Macon, my mother's ancient church friend.

I ducked inside the papier-mâché tree.

Casey rang up her purchase, not complaining about the intrusion. And, mercifully, not calling for me so Barb and I could chitchat about old times.

"I heard you had a visitor. Ingrid Christie's girl?"

I held my breath, afraid exhaling would set the wrapper curtain a-wafting.

"She's at the house."

When Barb left Casey laughed. "You can come out now."

I crawled out of the tree trunk. "She's nosy as ever. I didn't even tell my mother I was coming."

"She must've heard around town."

"What did she buy? Religious poetry? The complete works of Rick Warren?"

"She special-orders large-print romance novels. She has a special passion for Scottish lairds."

Raunchy old busybody.

I rummaged through the tote bag as we walked to Casey's house from the grocery. She'd given me e.e. cummings poetry, Candice Bergen's autobiography, *The Bluest Eye*, and *Valley of the Dolls*.

The last one I pulled out was an oversized paperback with a pink stain on the spine.

The Girl's Total Guide to Beauty.

"No way." I smiled at the familiar cover. A woman's face divided into four quadrants, a different "look" in each section. One eye was rainbowed in blue and yellow shadow under fluffy bangs, one sported false eyelashes under gelled hair. One side of her lips was baby pink, the other scarlet. "I can't believe you kept it."

"Elle found it in a box of your stuff from the vanity. A few months ago. My mom had held on to all of it—your old makeup, an embarrassing collection of scrunchies, and of course, *The Girl's Total Guide.*"

"God." I flipped pages. "I *studied* this. I thought I looked so mature. Remember when I tried to do highlights and burned my scalp? My hair was coming out by the roots for weeks." I examined the price sticker. "You priced it at a dollar and still no takers?" I laughed. "Smart girls."

Casey peered into her canvas bag, rearranging groceries. "Oh. I only had it out for a few days. Some teenager tried to buy it but…" She shrugged. "I gave her a free copy of this other makeup book instead. Aren't you starving? I'm starving."

17

Vanity

"So which rager am I getting ready for?" I said to Casey's reflection.

Casey was lying on her back, a paperback of *Queenie* tented over her head. I was doing my makeup at her antique vanity, the one Alex bought at an estate sale in Twaine Harte. I'd never seen her use it; Casey's beauty routine consisted of scraping a comb through wet hair as she pounded down the stairs two at a time.

"Hmm?" She was absorbed in the book but bouncing her legs along to Sheryl Crow. Her green giraffe, Jasper, by her feet, was bouncing to the beat, too.

"Which party are we going to—Matt Pomeroy's or Deva Vance's?"

"What difference does it make? All the parties in this town are the same."

"True."

I had *The Girl's Total Guide to Beauty* open to the section on eyeshadow. Subsection: The Four-Shade Method. I leaned close to check my work in the mirror. My four shades were Smoky Taupe, Amethyst, Midnight Pearl, and Buff. The book said if you only blended well enough you could make any colors work together.

I loved Casey's dressing table. But the fine grain of the wood was hidden under papers and books and the dirty mosaic tiles Casey pried out of the gazebo in the park nearly every Saturday night. She had twenty tiles now and tossed them onto the vanity carelessly before we'd climb into bed. I arranged them in a neat grid whenever I came over, but when I returned they'd be disturbed again. I'd redo my work while Casey laughed at my compulsion. (*You're borderline OCD*, she'd say. *Could you even fall asleep here without doing your tile rows?* The truth: probably not.)

"Matt Pomeroy's in love with you." Casey licked her finger and turned the page.

"Please."

"Matt Pomeroy's throwing this whole party for you. It's all very *Great Gatsby*."

"Matt Pomeroy's never spoken to me."

"He said you have the prettiest eyes he's ever seen. He clearly wanted me to pass this info on to you."

"He's never looked at my eyes. He's never looked above my neck. Boys think if they say they like your eyes it makes them sound deep." I beaded mascara onto my lashes, stretching my mouth wide. "And that you'll have sex. You're lucky you don't have to deal with them."

"Girls can be shallow, too."

"That's true." I leaned close to the mirror to study the line where my Amethyst eyeshadow turned into Midnight Pearl. Something seemed a little off. Maybe I just hadn't blended enough.

Casey stopped bouncing and stared at me upside down in the mirror. "So why are you putting all that goop on if nobody looks at your eyes?"

"Because it's fun. Because I like it."

"No, it's because your mother doesn't allow it. And it gives you a twisted little thrill that she doesn't know you're running around like…like Joanie over there." She pointed her book at her Joan Jett *Bad Reputation* poster. Joanie had slashes of hot pink on her cheeks and her eyes were lost inside raccoony black ovals.

"My makeup is way more subtle than Joanie's. No offense, Joanie," I said to the poster.

"If your mother saw you looking like that she'd never let you spend the night here again," Casey said.

"I'm careful."

"What do you do when you have a date and the guy picks you up at your place?" Casey set her book on her chest and met my eyes in the mirror again, genuinely curious.

I was allowed to sleep over at Casey's on Saturdays if I got back in time for church the next morning. I was allowed to go on one date a week—in town—as long as the "young man" introduced himself, I kept my grades up, and got home by nine.

I smiled at Casey's upside-down reflection. "I keep makeup in my purse and put it on in the rearview mirror. They like to watch."

"Yuck."

"And I keep makeup-remover pads in my purse. I wipe myself clean on the porch. At two minutes 'til curfew I look like a choir girl again."

"What if your mom finds your makeup stash? She's no dummy." Casey rolled onto her stomach, saving her place in *Queenie* with her thumb.

"I take extra precautions." I smiled mischievously and pulled a gray film canister from the lining of my purse, shaking it. "The makeup-remover pads are in here." I fished out what looked like a magic marker, but was actually a white mascara tube I'd disguised with a purple Crayola sticker and marker cap. I'd slid a pen cap over a short eyeliner. "Everything's camouflaged."

Casey sighed and picked up Jasper, flopping onto her back and tossing him up and down. "You get a charge out of the whole thing, admit it. That gunk on your face, your whole disturbingly elaborate system. It's your way of sticking it to your mother behind her back."

"Maybe." I returned my makeup-in-disguise to my purse lining, set the other tubes and compacts and my hairbrush in the vanity's top-right drawer. My drawer.

Casey went back to her book and I stared at my painted reflection, listening to the radio. I wondered who this Billy character in the song was, the one Sheryl Crow got a good beer buzz with early in the morning. Did Billy look at Sheryl above her neck? He sounded like he might.

"Hey, Case?"

"Listen to this... This person in *Queenie* keeps a special pillow next to her bed for holding her underwear during sex. A *scented* pillow. Is this something people do?"

"How would I know? Case?"

"Hmm?"

"Do you think I look slutty?"

"Don't say that word in front of Jasper. That's an ugly word and Jasper is innocent."

"But tell me."

Casey set her book on her chest and stared at the ceiling. "I think you're enjoying the attention."

"Is there something wrong with that?"

"'Course not. Who got you to throw out your extra-large shirts and stand up straight?"

"Maybe you created a monster." I studied my carefully shadowed eyes and glossed lips.

"It's not you. It's this town. There's a reason all the girls flirt with some older guy in a silver shirt and roller skates. There's nobody else to obsess about."

"You have you-know-who at the café. Syrup."

"You know what I mean. Ruler-girl obsessions."

Ruler was our code word for straight. For gay, we said *Cheerful*, and Scary Sue was always *Syrup*. Just in case someone overheard.

Few people at school knew Casey liked girls. She'd decided to keep it quiet for a while, maybe even until after graduation. We were going to live in San Francisco together, after college, where it would be easier for her. No more code words.

But the fact that Alex hadn't clued in baffled me. It had become some sort of test, and every week that went by she was failing miserably.

I'd promised not to say anything, but I worried that if Alex didn't figure it out soon, one day I'd come over and find that Casey had replaced her candy-wrapper door with a real one.

"This Ruler girl isn't obsessed with him. Not anymore."

"Obsessed with who?" Alex whooshed in through the crinkly curtain.

"Nobody, Mom."

"This college boy who works at the skating rink," I said. "Who thinks just because he wears his T-shirts too tight and his hair too long and goes to UCLA everyone is automatically supposed to swoon."

"Sounds fascinating." Alex had on a silky white blouse and black skirt, with her hair up in a skillful twist, a single red spiral escaping down her temple. She held up two necklaces. "Quick, he's going to be here any sec. Green or blue?"

"They're both fabulous," Casey said without looking. "Stunning. To die for."

"Laura will help me."

I touched the long chains of semiprecious stones swinging in her hands. "The green, because the stones go all the way around. It'd be nice with your hair. I like it up like that."

"You should wear yours up sometime. Show off that long neck." Alex pulled the necklace on, dropping the other carelessly on the dressing table. She stood behind me and piled my hair on top of my head, evaluating the effect in the mirror.

"You two are out of control," Casey said. "Now I know why that thing is called a *vanity*."

"Who's your date?" I said. "The guy from your tennis class?"

"He's waaaay over," Casey said before Alex had a chance to answer. "Lasted exactly as long as the tennis phase. She dumped him for someone she met at the beach. Then it was some glass artist from Truckee. Then last Sunday some forest ranger picked her up."

"Completely unfair," Alex said. She smiled at me in the mirror. "*I* picked *him* up."

"That's who you're going out with tonight?" I said.

"Dinner and dancing at the Catamaran. Tahoe."

I sighed. "That sounds so much more romantic than Deva Vance's sweaty kegger."

"You two'll get there," she said, leaning over me to rub her teeth, checking for lipstick smudges in the mirror. "I feel it in my bones. Someday very soon one of you'll kiss a boy and your knees will turn to jelly."

I winced at the "boy," working hard not to glance at Casey's reflection.

"There are no knee-jelly kissers at CDL High," I said. "Believe me."

"Well, try to enjoy these years. When I was in high school I would've given anything to go to a keg party."

"Was your mom as horrible as mine?"

She fiddled with her collar and when she finally spoke she didn't really answer at all. She only tugged my hair and said, "Your mother's not so bad. Give her a chance."

I wondered if Alex would be so generous on the topic of Ingrid Christie if she heard the conversations through the heating duct.

"That mother," my mother had said only that morning, her whisper carrying up the old metal duct as well as any shout.

"So she's a free spirit, Ingrid."

"Is that what they're calling it these days? Free spirit?" *Spirit* came out in a hiss.

"She's happy, Ingrid. Truly happy. She has a real friend. Don't kill this for her. She's a good girl."

And my father, who trusted me, had won. He didn't realize that my new preference for the correct T-shirt size was the least of the changes in me. I kept the bargains I'd made—introduced them to my dates, maintained my B-plus average. I was never a second late for church.

But the unspoken agreement? The important one? I'd broken that many times. I'd attended sermons parched and headachy from Everclear. I'd let more than one "young man" delve his fingers inside my underwear at 8:50. Only that, so far. But I knew the truth.

I was not a good girl.

"Gorgeous girl." Alex held my hair in two ponytails and pulled them out to the sides, Pippi Longstocking–style.

"You two have quite the mutual admiration society going," Casey said, small and distant in the mirror.

Alex jumped on the bed and kissed the top of Casey's head. She tickled her until she dropped her book to the floor and curled into a defensive ball, shrieking and gasping, and Jasper bounced off the corner of the bed.

"Say *uncle*," Alex said. "Say *uncle* or I'll go for your underarms. I'm your mother, I know your weak spots."

"Uncle!"

As soon as Alex pulled her hands away Casey said, "Is your park ranger going to be wearing the whole outfit, Mom? The Smokey the Bear hat and everything."

We burst out laughing, and Alex spread her arms, wiggling her fingers in a tickle threat, one hand aimed at me in my chair and one toward Casey on the bed. But she only picked up Jasper and tossed him to Casey as she got up. "Naughty children. And to think I was going to take you to the Creekside for pancakes tomorrow before Laura has to go to church." Alex kissed the top of our heads and pushed her way through the cellophane curtain.

"We're sorry we laughed," Casey called.

"Please take us to pancakes," I yelled.

I dropped my voice so only Casey would hear. "We have a craving for maple *syrup*."

Jasper bounced off my head.

"We'll see, naughty children," Alex called.

We listened to her light thumps on the staircase. A few minutes later there was the crunch of a car in the gravel driveway. A masculine chuckle, Alex's low murmur. Different from the voice she used with us.

"And *we're* the naughty children," Casey said.

I picked Jasper up from the floor and inspected his ear. It was starting to come off, dangling by loose green stitches. Casey was already annoyed, so I felt a surge of guilt as I asked, "Why were your grandparents so strict? Not letting her go to parties, not even letting her learn to drive? I mean, at least my mom is letting me get my permit."

"You know we don't talk to them. They were awful to her."

"Yeah, but. Do you know why they were so awful?"

"I think they were super religious. She told me once if she talked back—or even used a tone her dad didn't like—he used his belt on her. Real backward, scary stuff. It's hard for her to talk about."

"That's horrible."

"You can add it to your list of fascinating facts about my mother. For your files."

She said this in the same light tone she always used to tease

me and Alex about our closeness. But as I watched her carefully in the mirror, I realized she wasn't turning pages anymore.

"Hey. Case."

I tried to catch her eyes, but she pretended she was deeply absorbed in *Queenie*. "Did you know this book is based on Merle
Oberon, that actress from the thirties?"

"Case."

"I'm going to get her biography."

"Hey. Lady."

She finally looked up, meeting my gaze in the mirror.

"Stop with these jokes that aren't really jokes. Macaroon?"

Our code word. Our reset button. *Macaroon* meant *I'm sorry*,
but more than that. It meant we had to take a deep breath before
things got ugly. *Macaroon* meant—remember what's important.
Let's not fight. Be sweet. Life is short.

We'd come up with it during a party back in October, when
I'd wanted to stay and Casey wanted to go. Our only real fight.
That was back when the parties, and the boys at the parties who
wanted to go off alone with me, were a novelty.

I swiveled my chair so I could face the real Casey instead of
her speckled reflection. "Double Macaroon. For Jasper's sake?
He doesn't like when we fight." I held him up and swayed him
to the radio.

She smiled. "Macaroon."

18

Sorry

Deva Vance's rager: infinite red Solo cups, beer pong on the Vances' walnut dining room table, Pauline Knowland telling everyone in the kitchen she'd worn a ponytail holder around her wrist so she could pull her hair back later when she threw up.

Pauline and I had an unspoken agreement. We simply pretended the other didn't exist. But I couldn't help rolling my eyes at Casey when Pauline snapped the brown elastic around her wrist, calling it her "puke bracelet." It was only nine, but it appeared she'd need the bracelet soon.

"Just when you think she can't get any classier," Casey whispered. She went to the dining room to set up a variation on beer pong she'd invented. (It involved arranging cups of beer in circles with stacks of dollar bills in the center. She called it Solar Pong.)

Casey played Solar Pong while I watched, sipping a drink that looked like everyone else's Everclear and Sprite but was really only Sprite. I'd taken a break from drinking after I'd overdone it at a party in April. I'd thrown up all night in The Shipwreck's tiny bathroom and Alex and Casey had brought me cold cloths in alternating shifts. I'd almost missed church the next day.

Around ten a boy named Everett told me I had beautiful eyes and I was so bored I let him kiss me at the dark end of the hallway. His tongue swept all over, even venturing between my upper lip and gums. As Everett swabbed out my mouth like a dental hygienist, his cold hand on the back of my neck, my knees had never felt more stable.

Casey came over while Everett was refilling my red Solo.

"Five minutes?" I said.

"Can you hold out a little longer? I'm about to win. Who's your new friend?"

"Someone's cousin who goes to UC Santa Cruz. Majoring in linguistics." I leaned close. "Slimiest. Kisser. Ever."

"He should be good with his tongue. Majoring in linguistics and all."

"I just remembered the mascot at Santa Cruz is the banana slug," I said and laughed. Everett, waiting in line politely by the kitchen counter, thought I was smiling at him and grinned.

"You're terrible. Look at him over there, all happy. He doesn't know he's a slimy kisser. He really likes you."

"I don't know what's wrong with me."

"Well, at least you're not hustling Robbie Gilman for ten bucks." She laughed. "He keeps bragging that he plays his best after his second bong. And he can barely grip the paddle at this point."

"Let's do something different next Saturday. Take the bus to San Francisco like we always say we're going to. Anything but this."

"Amen."

"Casey Kasem!" The kids around the dining room table were summoning her for the semifinals.

"Gotta finish up."

"Then we leave?"

"Then we leave."

Soon we'd be at the gazebo. Soon I'd be looking through the lattice at the stars while Casey got her weekly tile. We'd make fun of the party, and make fun of ourselves, too—of how much we'd wanted to crack this inner circle, and how empty we'd found it once we got in.

When Everett wasn't watching I bolted down the hall, opening the first door I saw. The laundry room. I shut the door, sank onto the linoleum, and leaned against the dryer. It was off, but still ticking and warm through my thin T-shirt (new, stylish, size small).

I opened the dryer door, curious. Who'd done laundry so late? Maybe Deva's older sister; Deva paid her twenty bucks per party not to narc her out when their parents were away. I touched the jumble of fabric. So warm, so soft. Who'd know if I borrowed from the pile for half an hour?

I pulled on a large man's sweatshirt, tucking my hair in and pulling the hood up. I'd wait it out in my warm sweatshirt, in the soft glow of the rainbow trout night-light, inhaling the purifying and familiar scent of Rain-Fresh Cheer.

But the second I leaned against the dryer and closed my eyes someone jiggled the doorknob. I held it tight as they politely asked if the bathroom, or what they thought was the bathroom, was occupied. "I'm gonna piss myself, dude. Hurry up."

I held my breath, gripping the doorknob. Whoever it was thumped off, but he'd ruined my little sanctuary. I opened the room's other door, which I'd assumed led to the garage.

No: a narrow staircase down to a wood-paneled basement rec room. Someone had attempted a tiki theme. A hula girl lamp in the corner, giving off a weak orange light, a mound of floral quilts on the sofa, a straw skirt on the coffee table holding dusty issues of *People* and board games.

I settled cross-legged on the floor by the couch, spreading game boxes on the carpet. I played with the Trouble automatic dice roller, punching the clear dome until I got snake eyes. (It took twenty-three punches.) I tried Battleship but the batteries were dead so it wouldn't do any torpedo sounds. I made black-and-red patterns in the Connect Four rack. Horizontal stripes, diagonal stripes. A sad face.

I played Hungry Hungry Hippos against myself, which took a great deal of dexterity.

I hadn't had this much fun at a party in months.

"You're cheating."

"Owahhohmygod." I whacked the Hippos arena so hard white marbles bounced off, disappearing into the green shag carpet.

"Shit. Sorry. Are you having a heart attack?"

I looked over my shoulder. Him. The Boy Behind the Counter. Horizontal, sleepy-eyed. He was lying on the couch, buried under quilts from his chin down.

I rested my head on my knees. "I'll live."

"I cover my face when I sleep. It freaks my mom out."

"How can you breathe like that?"

"Exactly what my mom says." He slid down to the carpet next to me, stretching and shaking off blankets. Instead of his tight silver T-shirt he wore a loose blue one. "You look so familiar. You're a Trojan?"

I glanced at the gold USC on my chest. *No, I'm only in high school. We talked at the rink, remember? You found something of mine…*

I said none of that, and though my hood had slipped down I made no attempt to free my hair from the sweatshirt, swoosh it around to jog his memory. Later, I would analyze this decision to lie, and realize that either I wanted to punish him for making out with Pauline Knowland, I was hurt he didn't recognize me, or both. And I liked the idea of being a college girl. It felt like normal rules didn't apply here, in this funny place you could only discover by going through the laundry room, like finding Narnia through the wardrobe.

"Yeah," I lied.

"Maybe I've seen you down there. I'm at UCLA. Grad school next year."

I nodded as if this was news.

His cheek had a thin pink sleep line stamped into it. I fought the urge to touch it. Instead I hunted for marbles in the carpet.

He crawled around, helping. "You *were* cheating, though."

"How could I when I was playing against myself?" I lobbed a marble into the box.

"You were favoring the green hippo. Pink didn't have a chance. Found one!" He held out his palm.

"That's a popcorn kernel."

"Oh. Guess my eyes haven't adjusted." He took the lid off the Sorry! box, the only one I hadn't gotten to. "Wanna play? You can even be green since it's your favorite."

For a few minutes we played silently, rolling and tapping and sliding.

"So why aren't you...?" J.B. pointed his red plastic piece at the ceiling, at the epicenter of the party sounds. (Sheryl Crow again. I couldn't escape her that summer.)

"I was having so much fun I couldn't handle it."

"Right." He tapped my Connect Four frowny face.

"I guess I'm busted." I smiled.

"I get it. I only came because my mom forced me. She says I work too much."

"And you're humoring her but catching up on your sleep."

"Exactly. So did you go to CDL High?"

"Yeah." Not, technically, a lie. I *did* go. And I'd go for two more years. "Soooorrry." I bumped his red piece with my green, sending it skidding across the board.

"Unnecessary roughness. This isn't air hockey." He picked up his piece, squeezing it tight. "Hey."

His voice had gone soft; I looked up. He leaned an inch closer, his eyes scanning mine. "Did anyone ever tell you..."

Don't say I have beautiful eyes. Don't say it.

"Did anyone ever tell you your eyes are sort of sad?"

"Yes, actually."

"I'm supposed to be the one with sad eyes," he said.

"They don't look sad to me." I leaned over the game board to study his brown eyes, balancing with my fingertips on his knees. I was bold, here in Narnia.

"It's this stupid stereotype. I'm part Ohlone." He held still, maintaining his joking-around smile. But he hitched his breath and spoke in a rush. "What's your name?"

"Laura."

"That's extremely pretty." He tucked a stray lock of hair back into the neck of my sweatshirt. His index finger remained near the corner of my jaw, making slow, tiny circles beneath my earlobe. And now I was the one who had to concentrate on breathing.

"What's yours?" I whispered.

He answered into my neck, where he'd replaced his fingertip with his lips. I couldn't hear him, but of course the question was another lie; I knew his name.

J.B.'s hand moved to my hip, inches from my pocket. I usually maneuvered away when hands ventured too close to that pocket. But right now I didn't mind his hand there. I didn't care about my lies, or how many girls he might have taken behind the rink. I closed my eyes, rested my hands on his shoulders. The softest fabric, still warm from his nap.

"Fade Into You" was on upstairs. Unmistakable after all the times Casey and Alex and I had played it on repeat. Such a strange song, languid and sad.

This could be my knee-wobbling kiss. I'd finally found it, and I wasn't even standing.

But the kids overhead must have sensed what was about to happen under their feet. Light on the stairs, a nasal laugh. We pulled away.

"Dude, check it out." More obnoxious laughter.

I knew that laugh. It started off snorty and ended in a cackle. It belonged to Rob Pedersen, Ollie's son. Rob was a few years older and used to work, or pretend to work, at the hardware store.

"Hey, listen," I whispered.

"You *know* her dad keeps the good beer down here."

"Hey," I whispered. "I have to tell you—"

J.B. clasped my hand, whispering hurriedly. "Can I get your number? I'm here all summer, I'm working a ton but—"

"Robbing the cradle, J.B.?" Rob snorted.

J.B. looked toward the two boys, illuminated by the open minifridge.

"Watch out for those high school girls," Rob added, twisting open a beer.

"High school?" J.B. turned to me. Still smiling, still giving me a chance.

"Uh-oh, sorry to break it to you, J.B. She's cute, though." Rob or his friend. I couldn't tell, they were both snorting so hard. But it didn't matter. J.B. was already pulling his body far from mine.

"Laura, don't worry, I'll tell your dad you played board games all night." Rob, then. He acted like a completely different person in front of his father.

But then, so did I.

"Shut up, assholes. What grade are you in?" J.B. said, not taking his eyes off me. "What grade?" I could tell that it hardly mattered. Now his eyes were sad.

Rob and his friend were cracking up at our little shag-carpet drama. They thought it was hysterical. I wished J.B. thought it was a little funny, too.

But he said coldly to the boys, "Take your beer and get out."

They obeyed, clomping up the stairs with beers in their back pockets. I hoped they'd forget about the bottles. Sit down hard and need a hundred stitches in each of their butt cheeks.

J.B. still had the rosy line on his face, though it was fainter now. His hair was still messed up. I wished, more than any-thing, that I hadn't lied.

I spoke quietly. "I'll be a junior next year. At CDL."

"So you're what? Seventeen?"

"Sixteen."

"Perfect. And you lied because?"

"You assumed... I borrowed the sweatshirt."

"So it's the sweatshirt's fault."

"You didn't care how old Pauline Knowland was," I said quietly.

"What was that?"

"I said, you didn't care how old Pauline Knowland was. At the rink. And the other girls."

"What are you talking about? Polly who?"

"You went behind the Dumpsters with this girl in my class. Pauline. She said. And your silver shirts. Everyone says you wear them so tight to...you know."

"Nope. You'll have to elaborate."

"To show off. Get high school girls to make out with you or..." I trailed off, realizing how lame this sounded. Freaking Pauline. Ruining my life even now.

But I was the idiot, for believing the rumors.

"Well. If Pauline says." He pushed the plastic lever on my Connect Four rack hard, so my sad-face design clacked down the grid and the red and black chips whooshed onto the carpet. "So the talk around town is I'm only working there to hit on girls?"

"I guess."

"Anything else?"

"That you're rich. Related to the owner, so the only reason you work there is... It's stupid. Forget it."

He stood. "So I don't know who this Pauline chick is. But I'm at the rink to make money. When I'm not spraying out skates or handing out those crappy prizes I'm on cleanup in the snack bar, EZ-Offing sludge so there won't be a grease fire from the next day's corn dogs.

"With all that glamour I don't have time to go outside. With anyone. It's one of three jobs I have lined up for the summer. I also work at your buddy's store when I can, doing odd jobs and deliveries. And when I'm not doing that, I'm tutoring."

I couldn't look at him. He wasn't yelling. He got quieter as he went on, which felt worse.

"And that shirt you and your friends think is so hilarious? The owner of the rink is this scumbag named Andy. No relation, thank God. He's too cheap to buy new uniforms, so I took the biggest one in the bin. My mom tried to help me stretch it. She got it wet and tried to expand it out on the line with clothespins behind her place in Green Creek."

Green Creek was the trailer park.

The images hit. Trailer. Clothesline. Mom. I'd never felt so foolish.

"But you believe what you want."

By the time I was able to choke out "I'm sorry," he was already on the stairs.

"You're quiet." Casey sat cross-legged at the lower wall of the gazebo, attacking the mosaic with a stick. She kept a good one under the stairs specifically for tile removal.

I lay on my back, staring at the quarter moon through the lattice. The lamp in the gazebo had been busted forever, but the moonlight was usually enough for Casey to get her tile. We went no matter how cold and tired we were, or how sad and defeated we felt. Like tonight.

"I said, you're quiet," Casey repeated. "That translates to 'what's wrong' in passive-aggressive."

"I met someone tonight."

"Banana slug?"

"No. The Boy. J.B., from the rink. Tight T-shirt."

"No!"

"Yes."

"You kissed him?"

"We played Sorry!"

"Naturally. And is he all that everyone says? Did he take off his shirt?"

"He's not like that. It's all lies. The girls in this town are a bunch of liars. Especially Pauline Knowland."

"Shocker."

"Why would she make that up? So much detail, going behind the Dumpsters, taking his shirt off?"

"I have an idea. But don't worry, I do *not* have a thing for Puke-bracelet. I won't test out my theory."

"You think? Pauline?" But it would explain a lot.

"I do think. If she wasn't such a horrible human being I'd consider it. She's got incredible shoulders."

"You and your shoulder obsession."

"Back to your guy. You really like him."

"It doesn't matter. It was a disaster of epic proportions. He hates me."

"Impossible."

I closed my eyes and listened to the *scritch-scratch* of Casey defacing the mosaic. Finally, she said, "Ah—got you."

Casey held the tile up to the moonlight as we walked home down East Shoreline. "That was a stubborn one."

"You're a vandal."

"Which makes you my accessory." She handed me the tile. "Here. It can be your something blue for your wedding with J.B."

"I don't think I'm going to be needing it. Keep it for your collection." I tried to hand it back but she clenched her fist.

"You never know. He may come around. Put it in your pocket with your...you know."

I slipped the tile into my jeans pocket. It made a neat clink against the music box.

★ ★ ★

Casey fell asleep almost immediately but I couldn't. I tossed and turned next to her warm back, trying not to disturb her, trying to find comfort in the section of my pillow that was slightly firmer than the others, because of the music box hidden under it.

I replayed the basement scene in my head, hoping to recapture the feeling. The sequence of feelings. I cataloged them: contentment, lust, frustration. Embarrassment. Regret. All in the space of an hour, when I usually felt nothing the entire night of a party.

I touched the tender spot under my jaw where his fingers had circled.

My face got hot, remembering. But it wasn't the same.

19

41st day of camp
Two hours after lights-out

Every time she remembered setting the driftwood on the music stand,
her cheeks warmed. Camp was making her into someone else. Some-
one bold, reckless.

She lay in the dark, waiting for Sandy to signal to her.

By now she knew her cabinmates' nighttime symphony well: their
moist, regular breathing, their snores and sleeping-bag swishes, and the
trickles of their occasional shy trips to the bathroom, where they peed re-
spectfully, without turning on the light.

She'd been lying awake for hours in her upper bunk, pinching her wrist
when she felt drowsy. Her tennis shoes waited by her feet, hidden under
her gray Monterey Bay Aquarium sweatshirt with the sea lion on it.

She and her mom had visited Monterey every June since she was five.
They always went the day after school got out.

Her mother was a school nurse in a rough section of Daly City. Nine
months of the year she tended to black eyes, kids who called her "bitch"
and "cunt." She'd always said the students didn't mean it, that they

were hurting. The job's tough days were worth it because she was helping young people who needed her, and because she got summers off. Summers they could spend together.

They'd started the aquarium tradition the June after her dad left for good. They got up while it was still dark and drove down the coast in her mom's wheezing old white Pontiac, singing along to Pop100 radio, both of them giddy about the weeks of freedom ahead, time ribboned out in front of them as long as the highway.

They always stayed at the aquarium until closing, lingering in the blue light of the tanks, mesmerized by the silent, floating creatures in the kelp forest. There was a large, bright orange fish called a garibaldi that they liked best. It stood out against the olive drab of the kelp, the skulking, homely eels. Last summer she'd bought her mother a key chain from the gift shop with her allowance money: a plastic garibaldi.

You can look at it when you're having a bad day at work next year, she'd said, and her mom had hugged her.

On the drive home from the aquarium they always stopped at the same chowder shack in Pescadero, and her mother would laugh because she'd devour three packets of oyster crackers before their orders came.

This June they hadn't gone on their pilgrimage to the aquarium. Something had happened at her mother's job in May; something she wouldn't talk about. A meeting with a parent that went bad.

That's what her mother's friend Lolly had said the afternoon this all started.

Lolly had whispered, Don't worry, she's fine.

She'd seen her mother's head on the kitchen table before Lolly shut the door.

Those murmurs behind the kitchen door, the whistle of the teakettle. Her mother's strange, humorless laugh rising up: Like tea will undo it, Lolly.

Lolly's soothing tone.

The untouched cups of tea in the sink after.

Her mother needed more than elephant seals and the garibaldi to make her happy this summer. She needed more than her.

So her mother chose to spend their precious free weeks apart, living with strangers at the adult camp. And here she was stuck with girls who could recite all of First Corinthians by heart.

Lolly had told them Three Pines was idyllic, a bargain. Fun for the kids, peaceful for the parents, who got four weeks of "personal retreat time" thrown into the deal.

Do this for me, her mother had said. Lolly says the adult camp's just down the road. We can see each other all the time.

But she hadn't seen her mother once.

In daytime, when something made her think of home, she got an ache in her throat. To make it go away, she concentrated on the parts of camp that were the most absurd, the bits that would be funny later: the way the girl next to her in morning service scrunched her eyes shut while she sang "Open My Eyes, O Lord." The fiasco of a cross lanyard she'd made in crafts: how the strips of white plastic poked out every which way, and how Miss Cooke only smiled and said, We have extra materials if you'd like to perfect this, dear. She saved up these stories to tell her mom on pickup day.

At night, in the dark, lying on her top bunk while the others slept, she welcomed the pain in her throat. She summoned it. Thinking of certain things made it come, right away: her mother's old laugh, from before the tea day. The denim beanbag chair in her bedroom, under the window. The garibaldi-fish key chain, a small packet of oyster crackers, her mother's tan, fringed leather purse. Any of these images would do the trick. Alone, in the stuffy air of her sleeping bag, she let the tight feeling in her throat soften into tears.

It was after eleven when she heard rustling across the cabin, soft footsteps. Sandy stood next to the door, a flashlight in one hand, sneakers dangling by the laces from the other, their reflective stripes shining in the moonlight.

She climbed down her bunk ladder, reached for her shoes and sweatshirt, and tiptoed past the stacks of sleeping girls.

Silently, they crept out of the cabin, padding down the front steps in their socks, slipping into their shoes only when they were safely on a blanket of pine needles.

"He's meeting us in his truck," Sandy whispered. "On the logging road."

*She hesitated. Summer was almost over and it seemed foolish to ven-
ture into the woods with this strange, unpredictable girl when she was so
close to escape. There could be bears. The flashlight batteries could die
and they could get lost.*

*"Come on, it's not far." Sandy tugged her by the elbow, her voice
soft and reassuring.*

"Want to tell me where we're going?"

*"The promised land. Glory, hallelujah." Sandy did not have her
gold bible with her tonight. The gold bible was a prop, a decoy; that became clear after they passed the hillside clearing with the three pine trees
that marked the north edge of camp. Sandy tucked the flashlight into
the waistband of her khakis and raised her arms above her head like the
show-offy girls at camp, the ones who reached to the sky when they were
especially overcome by the Lord, as if they were bench-pressing heaven.*

*She curled eight fingers down, pivoted her wrists, and, turning, pointed
the two center digits in the general direction of Camp Three Pines.*

*The girls followed the trail to the logging road, where a red pickup idled,
the passenger door open.*

*She hesitated but Sandy squeezed her elbow. "Don't worry. I've
been there before."*

Sandy climbed into the middle seat and after a second she followed.

"You made it," the musician said, smiling.

*She stared ahead, her cheeks warming. Her hand hesitated on the
door pull, her right foot stayed planted on the dirt road.*

"You okay missing your beauty sleep?" he said.

*It was an old-fashioned expression. He looked older without his guitar,
under the harsh light of the truck. She'd guessed he was in his twenties
but now thought thirties was more like it.*

*The driftwood moon lay on the dashboard, wedged against the wind-
shield by a crumpled take-out bag.*

She had sent him a message, and he had answered.

20

More than Fun

Late July 1997
Summer before junior year

The three of us lay on the dock on the red-plaid picnic blanket. For half an hour I'd heard only the lake's gentle lapping and the occasional whistle of Casey spitting watermelon seeds off the dock.

I'd owned my purple two-piece for less than a week, and the sun on my bare stomach felt deliciously forbidden. My mother had meetings at church or I wouldn't have risked it.

Alex was so quiet I thought she was asleep. But when she thumped the dock with her hand and said, "Let's talk about your party," I realized she'd been quietly obsessing again. Casey's birthday was all she'd talked about for weeks.

"I don't care as long as I get strawberry cake," Casey said, then spat more seeds.

"How about a *Little Mermaid* theme," I said. "Casey wears a tail and shell bra."

This got a laugh out of only Casey. Alex was serious about throwing Casey the perfect sixteenth birthday, a party that would shake Coeur-de-Lune up. Too bad Coeur-de-Lune didn't know it needed shaking up.

"Be serious," Alex said.

"Can't the three of us just go to the Creekside like last year?" Casey said.

"You know what I would have given for a big party when I was your—"

"Mom. The six words. You promised."

"Six words?" I opened my eyes.

Casey sat cross-legged in front of the watermelon bowl, digging for a good wedge. "*What I would have given for.* She agreed to stop saying it. We know all about your poor, deprived, sheltered childhood, Mom." Maybe realizing how unkind this sounded, she softened it by reaching across the bowl and snapping the back of Alex's blue bikini top. "But look at you now."

Alex didn't answer for a long time. She didn't bat at Casey's hand and say, "You naughty child," laughing, like she usually would.

I watched Casey, watching Alex, lying so still on her stomach, on her third of the picnic blanket. And I knew Casey was quietly surrendering to the idea of an over-the-top party.

"Okay." Casey sighed. "Big party it is."

Alex sat up, smiling. "Yeah?"

"Yeah. Sure, Mom. Go nuts."

"Okay, so think." Alex stared out at the lake as if it could offer ideas. "What's the most fun you two've had recently?"

"Watching *Grease 2* and making peanut-butter-cup cookie dough last night was pretty fun," Casey said.

"We could have it at the skating rink," Alex said. "You two used to go all the time."

"Mom? Remember? Laura's boy works there so she doesn't want to go anymore."

"He's not my boy."

"Right. Sorry, honey. Though I still think you should try to talk to him. How could he resist our Laura?" She tickled my knee.

"He can," I said. "Next idea?"

"A swimming party?" Alex said. "We could decorate the dock."

"That'd be fun," Casey said.

"But it has to be more than *fun*," Alex said. "It has to be extra special."

"We can buy the good dip," Casey said.

Alex didn't acknowledge her snark. "Let's analyze these town parties. The ones you always say are so sucky. Why do you go? How can we make yours *not* sucky?" She said *sucky* without irony, in her anthropology mode. Casey and I had accused her of secretly researching a book on teenage living in America. "Laura? Help me out."

"We go because…because the parties are the center of things," I said.

"But what do you do there that's fun? Talk with your other girlfriends? Make out with boys?"

Casey shot me a look that said, *I told you so—can you believe it?* It reminded me not to come to her aid with any pamphlety hints. The look was resigned and a little sad, too.

Because Alex still didn't know. She didn't have a clue. It bothered me, that Alex's eyes were so restless she couldn't see her own daughter. But Casey said it was just the way Alex was raised, with strict, religious parents and an expectation of straightness. *Just the way she was raised.* The same phrase my dad used to pardon my own mother.

"Laura, help me. What's the best time you've had at a party this summer?"

When a certain older boy touched a one-centimeter-square section of my jaw. "I had fun playing board games," I said.

"Games," Alex murmured. "That's it, you brilliant, brilliant girl." She got up and ran down the dock to the house.

Casey and I watched her, then turned to face each other. I wondered if my smile was as fond and indulgent as Casey's.

"It could be fun," I said. "Pictionary. Charades..."

Casey groaned. "Please let it not be charades."

The day of Casey's party started off drizzly. A rare summer storm. Alex fretted, worried that people wouldn't come, or that the rain would put a damper on the game.

She'd planned a scavenger hunt. She must have spent ten hours a day writing in a yellow Mead notebook. Obsessing over rules, what to put on the list.

"What'll we do about the food?" she said, rearranging the furniture yet again. We'd pushed most of it against the walls because The Shipwreck's living room was tiny.

"We'll hold an umbrella over Laura's head while she barbecues. Stop stressing," Casey said, not looking up from *Princess Daisy*. I'd given her a huge bag of used books as a birthday gift. I'd gone to her favorite bookstore in Sacramento, and even found two of these lesbian paperbacks from the 1950s that cost sixteen dollars each. We'd pored over them that morning, fascinated, but now they were hidden under Casey's bed.

"Why did it have to rain today?" Alex picked at her cuticles.

"There are only twelve kids coming, Alex. We'll make it work."

"Mom. Chill."

Alex walked down the dock to survey the clouds again.

"Remind me why I agreed to do this?" Casey said.

"Because she's your mom and you love her."

"Oh. That."

I peeked in the fridge. Casey had made Alex promise to keep it simple. Hamburgers and chips and carrots and celery sticks. And Alex had obeyed. But there had to be four dozen hamburger patties in the fridge, carefully draped in cellophane. The peeled carrots were little fancy ones, green tassels still attached. And the celery sticks had been cut so precisely it looked like Alex had used a ruler.

"We'll be living on hamburgers for a month," I said.

At 4:35 it stopped drizzling, and at 5:15 Alex took her worries indoors. She filled bowls with chips. There were so many bowls that they kind of made the room look smaller, but I wasn't about to say this to Alex.

At 6:02 Alex said, "Where are they?"

"Mom. It's okay."

It occurred to me that she'd never thrown a party before. My own mother oversaw parties—or what passed for parties, at church—all the time. Bible study coffee klatches and spaghetti suppers for one hundred and Palm Sunday brunches in the church's ugly yellow banquet room, with three coffee urns glugging and ten women on the committee obeying orders. My mother managed these events with the cool confidence of a general.

At 6:04 we heard the first voices in the driveway.

At 6:14, when Taylor Rockingham said she'd thought Alex was Casey's sister, Alex couldn't hide her pleasure. And she started to relax. Small as it was, the house was a good icebreaker.

"This really used to be just for kids?" someone said.

Casey and I showed off the marks from the bunk beds, the hidey-holes under the upstairs floorboards where we'd found comic books and arrowheads.

We told the kids who didn't know Coeur-de-Lune's legends how the Collier boys and their cousins used to run free all summer, the town their playground. We told everyone how they had slept there with a babysitter, like going away to camp. We pointed out the wooden beams in Casey's bedroom where boys had carved their initials: *R.C. D.C. F.C. T.C.*

So many *C*s.

"A bunch of them died young, though," I said, a bit dramatically.

Casey echoed my solemn tone. "Nobody knows why."

This wasn't exactly true; some were said to have moved east, or maybe it was south, and the wars and heart attacks and illness that had felled the others were perfectly reasonable, dull explanations, as my father had told us.

But reasonable and dull couldn't compete with fantastic and ghoulish.

Mark Supringer poked his head in from the hall through Casey's candy-wrapper curtain, draping everything below his neck in the rustling strands like a colorful mummy. Mark was on the swim team—green-tipped blond hair, an inverted triangle of an upper body. "The Collier curse," he hissed.

He pushed through the lengths of plastic and leaned close to me, his lips humming near my earlobe. "Scary stuff."

When I pulled away, he continued in his regular drawl as if he'd been addressing the whole group all along. "Maybe it's the house that's cursed. Or, like, maybe you should check for lead paint."

My father would have chided us for exaggerating about the Colliers. *The Collier curse is about as real as the lake monster*, he had said more than once.

"Case? Come down, it's almost time." Alex's wavery voice called up the stairs. It was almost seven; Alex had planned everything to the minute.

Alex passed out the scavenger hunt lists shyly that first time. She had none of the impresario about her—that would come later. And the list wasn't written in clues—that would come later, too. Alex hadn't let us help and as I read the list I worried, just for one disloyal second, that maybe the items were too easy, too childish: a restaurant sugar packet, a coupon for something frozen, a *Thomas the Tank Engine* item, a cowboy hat.

"You have two hours," Alex said. "Back by nine or you're disqualified."

"What's the prize?" Mark called.

"You'll find out later," Alex said.

Casey seemed unconcerned, but I thought how awful it would be for Alex, if at nine o'clock nobody bothered to come back.

But everyone huddled, concentrating harder than they ever did in class.

Casey and Will Benton and I got five things. We ran back ten minutes before the deadline, sure we'd won. Sure, I guess, that nobody else would have taken the game seriously.

But not only was the house full, another team had gotten eight items. Alex checked the hauls carefully, beaming, listening to her sweaty young guests laughing and recounting their successes and failures. She handed out the prizes—twenty-dollar gift certificates to Tower Records in Tahoe City—and was rewarded with Mark Supringer's official stamp of approval. *Cool.* Alex had done everything right.

Alex pulled Casey's cake from the fridge and we sang, and Casey's eyes shone, and she clutched Alex's hand in a thank-you after she set the fiery rectangle in front of her.

Before Casey made her wish, she smiled at me.

Kids didn't linger after. Not that first time. A game and a cake, then time to leave. Like in kindergarten, back when the game was musical chairs or pin the tail on the donkey.

I knew, of course, that people like Mark were off to other parties. Less innocent ones.

But Alex had tapped into something the town needed. Something *more than fun*.

Everyone asked if we were having another scavenger hunt the next weekend. They kept calling.

Alex pretended to resist at first. "They're just being polite." But she couldn't hide her pleasure, and it didn't take much urging to get her to agree.

Fourteen kids came to the second one. I remember we lost again. I remember searching desperately in someone's pantry for

a container of real vanilla extract. They only had artificial. My
mother had real, but I hadn't wanted to ask her.

The next weekend fifteen kids showed up.

By the middle of August there were so many kids The Shipwreck's living room felt close and stuffy until everyone burst
out into the night at the start of the game.

And Alex's clues had started to show signs of genius.

Sometimes the items were linked, so you had to plan ahead.
One night near the end of August we had to get a kids' menu
crayon from the Creekside before we could do a grave rubbing
in the cemetery. Scary Sue handed a red crayon over to Casey silently and Casey and Monica Eblingshire and I ran to the church.

It was a warm night, the warmest of summer so far, and we
were all a little loopy at that point. Summer was coming to an
end and we'd been tearing around town for nearly two hours,
trying to hold on to the last days of freedom. It was almost time
to run back to Casey's house.

As the headstones came into view, the three of us stopped
running. I peeled the wrapper off the red crayon as we walked
through the stone archway.

"Well, this is creepy," Casey whispered. "Thanks, Mom."

"Totally. Laura, why aren't you freaked out?"

"My dad takes me here all the time." I held the clue list against
the closest headstone and started rubbing, wishing I had masking
tape and an oil pastel and a bigger piece of paper to do it properly.

Letters began to emerge in white on a background of red:

COLLIER
RUPERT T. COLLIER II
1892–1944
Loving husband and father

I whispered as I worked. "Case, look."

"Sorry to disturb you, Rupert," she whispered.

"I don't think he minds," I said softly. "He was a fun father, letting his sons and nephews sleep in a separate cabin all summer."

"Maybe he couldn't deal with the racket," Monica said. "Parents were like that back then. Drinking their martinis away from the kids."

We sprinted home. We had the fake tattoos, the baseball, the crayon, the grave rubbing, the pool noodle. Monica had stuffed it down the back of her jeans, and it bobbed as she ran, like a pink tail.

As we passed the back of the hardware store I glanced up. I knew my dad was up there, playing backgammon with Ollie in the cluttered storage room that served as the Historical Society's headquarters. The society would be drinking coffee and eating my mother's blueberry cake, reading old newspaper articles aloud between games.

My dad always said the town's settlers were self-important because when they shoved out the Native Americans they changed the Washoe name for the area, Tibye-Talyawi, or Black Moon, to Coeur-de-Lune, Heart of the Moon—as if the lake had no soul until white people began to live out their little dramas within its arc. But he liked nothing more than studying these lives.

If I hadn't glanced up at the window I would have run right past him.

Him. Standing by a pickup truck on the concrete loading bay that led to the back of the store.

No chance of him mistaking me for a mature college girl this time. I was running like a crazy person, a unicorn tattoo on my cheek. His mouth opened as I passed.

So what if he thought I looked like an idiot. I sped up, running so fast I had to keep my hand down my pocket to make sure my music box wouldn't pop out. I was experimenting with a new system—Velcro tabs—but it hadn't been tested in extreme conditions before.

"Hey, High School!" he called.

I slowed down. Only a little.

"Hey, High School. Where's the fire?"

I jogged back to J.B., letting Casey's and Monica's laughter recede ahead of me.

"Scavenger hunt," I panted, hands on my knees.

"You're always playing games when I see you. You winning?"

"Maybe."

"What do you have to get?"

"Oh, a bunch of stuff. A crayon from the restaurant. A grave rubbing. Pool toy. Fishing bob."

"We have tackle. I can lend you the bob, Ollie wouldn't mind. I was just returning the truck so I have to go in and hand over the keys anyway."

"We got it already. Thanks, though."

"Nice tattoo."

I touched my cheek, smiled. "So you're talking to me. Does this mean you're not mad anymore?"

"Not sure yet. My mom said it sounded like I was kind of a jerk to you."

So at some point since the party in June he'd talked to her about me. Interesting. "I like your mom."

Another team was running down East Shoreline, hooting and belting, "We are the champions!" Beth Cohen wore a child's pink life jacket.

"I should catch up," I said, not moving.

He tucked a lock of black hair behind his ear. "So," he said.

"So."

We both glanced up at the sound of scraping wood. Ollie was opening the window, trying to see what the ruckus was. Any second and my dad would be at his side.

Far up the road, Casey's voice floated to me. "Come on, Laur!"

"Gotta go," I said. "I can't let my team down."

"Hope you win."

I was already grinning when he called after me, "Hey, High School. No cheating!"

21

Honor System

Last Saturday of August 1997
Summer before junior year

Next weekend was Labor Day and everyone would be gone, so tonight's hunt would be the last one until June. Casey convinced Alex it was better this way. Less chance of Saturday nights at The Shipwreck becoming like all the other parties. We told everyone, "It's a summer thing," and they looked so disappointed Alex beamed.

To mark the last game Brett Nealey brought a twenty-four pack of Bud, covering it with a coat until he got inside. "For after," he said. "And nobody's driving. It's only for after."

There was a moment's hesitation. People had figured out that the normal parental rules didn't apply at The Shipwreck. They'd sneaked beers in their coats but until now they'd kept their stash hidden from Alex.

This was new ground. A test. Casey and I exchanged a long look.

We often met each other's eyes when Alex was being particularly Alex, like parents did when they caught their child
doing something out of line but weren't sure how much disci-
pline to mete out.

That night Casey's eyes stayed fixed on mine longer than
usual. In a few seconds she must have calculated, weighed the
risks of letting this happen against what it would cost Alex if
she told Brett he couldn't keep his beer. Casey didn't care what
they thought about her. It was only about Alex.

So she didn't protest. Nobody did.

"Only for after," Alex said.

My dad thought the hunts were wonderful. Every Sunday dinner, he asked me what had been on the list the night before,
why we went for some items and not others, who'd won. He
said he had ideas for Alex. That she should feel free to consult
him or Ollie.

My sweet father. He wanted to make Alex's Saturday nights
into a history lesson.

"Instead of any old grave rubbing she could have you get one
of an early settler's headstone," he said on the last Sunday of August, pointing with the pepper mill. "Someone from the town
founding. And there's that plaque marking the site of the skir-
mish with the Me-Wuk in 1747, you know, out at North Beach?
Or how about a pinecone from the Sideways Tree?"

I swallowed a bite of pot roast. "But how could we prove it
was from the Sideways Tree?"

The Sideways Tree on the thinly populated west side of the
lake was a fir that went horizontal three feet up, where it had
swerved to avoid the other trees that used to grow nearby. Years
before, my dad and Ollie had propped it up with a wooden brace
to keep it alive. (As far as I could tell, this was the sole accom-
plishment of the Coeur-de-Lune Historical Society.) When I

was little I asked my dad why the tree's pinecones looked the same as other pinecones. He always got a big kick out of it.

"Smarty-pants. It would have to be on an honor system," he said. "The whole game is built on trust, right? She doesn't have you stealing, does she?" He winked, as if this idea was absurd.

"No," I answered quickly. Too quickly, because I could tell by the ever-so-slight narrowing of my mother's eyes that she'd noticed. So. There'd been talk among her church biddies about the sinfulness factor of the scavenger hunts.

Casey made everyone promise to put back anything we "borrowed." And it's not like Alex had us taking anything valuable— last week there'd been restaurant saltshakers, a handful of pink powdered soap from the gas station bathroom. But she was lax about oversight, and Casey and I had given up trying to control who joined the games.

"I think it's marvelous, don't you, Ingrid? So creative."

"Jeannette Archer said a pack of girls woke her up last Saturday. Screaming like the devil. She found a beer can in the alley the next morning."

"Everyone knows Kyle Archer has to sneak his beer in the alley after fishing. She should be grateful to Alexandra Shepherd, giving the kids something to do on a Saturday night so they don't get into trouble. What's the harm? It's good, clean fun."

He winked at me. My dear, clueless dad. I shoved aside a mental image of Alex making room in the refrigerator for Brett Nealey's beer. *Only for after.* But for some kids the "after" had become the main draw of Alex's Saturday night games.

"…and carrying on the legacy of that summerhouse, too. Those Collier cousins used to tear all over town in the forties and fifties, playing pirates, cowboys and Indians."

"You're supposed to say Native Americans, Dad." I prayed he and Ollie had never said anything like that in front of J.B.

I hadn't seen him again, but whenever my dad mentioned

"that nice college boy who works at Pedersen's," and how he was a better worker than Ollie's own son, my cheeks fired up.

"Right. Cowboys and Native Americans. Anyway, there's a great old photo of the Collier boys on the dock with fireworks. I'll show you."

"I bet Alex...Casey's mother would love to see it, too."

"Ingrid, did you ever join their games?"

My mother pursed her lips and stirred the gravy.

In my diary that night I drew two houses. One made of thick, straight lines like bars, another that was a whispered suggestion of a house, the lines curved, the roof open. A girl in the middle, eyes closed, hands touching the side of each. It was impossible to tell if she was pushing them away or pulling them closer.

22

June Names That Tune

Sunday before Labor Day
Two days before junior year

I woke with my heart pounding. The noise was terrible. Like someone had unspooled a roll of aluminum foil to perform a gymnastics ribbon routine on Casey's bedroom floor.

It was only Casey opening her white Levelor blinds, letting an uncivilized amount of morning sun in. "Wakey-wakey, rise and shine."

I hated that nasty metallic sound: *rap-rap-rap-rap-rap.*

I pulled a pillow over my face. "Why are you so perky? You sound like a deranged camp counselor."

Casey hopped onto the bed, shaking it. She yanked the pillow away. "And you look like a dead raccoon." She laughed. "I'm sorry, I love you, but you should see your eyes."

"Removing my makeup was not high on my list of priorities last night. Why am I facing the wrong way?"

"You were like that when I came in. I had to inhale your feet all night."

"Mean." I rolled onto my side and curled up at the foot of the bed so I could face her. She'd stayed up even later than me, to finish watching *Xanadu* on cable. She *never* woke up before me. Yet she was miraculously alert.

"What gives?" I said.

"We're going to make our last Sunday before school count."

"Good. Let's go back to sleep."

"No way. You have church." Casey nodded at the navy dress and white cardigan I'd hung on her closet door.

"Maybe I'll skip."

"You always say that."

"Sometime I will."

"Not today. If you skip, she'll blame the evil, pagan Shepherd women and your sleepover deal will be off. And you'll ruin my plans."

"What plans?"

"You're going to clean up, and put on your church dress, and get home super early and make nice with your mom. Extra nice. This isn't bake sale week, right?"

"No. I helped her last week."

"You're going to ask her really sweetly if you can go back-to-school shopping in Tahoe with some girls from school. Tell her you're having pizza after but you'll be back by eight. And this is important. Tell her *Tish Mayhew* might be in the group."

"Tish Mayhew? She hates us. She said the scavenger hunts should be against the law because someone borrowed her mom's stupid plastic elephant watering can and forgot to return it. No way am I spending the day with…"

"Chill. We're *not* spending the day with Tish Mayhew."

"Then what?"

"Your mom approves of the Mayhews because they go to your church."

"Not my church. My mother's church."

"Right. But Tish is basically your mom's wet dream of a best friend for you."

"She wouldn't put it exactly that way, but sure. So what're we really doing?"

"After church meet me in the parking lot behind the drugstore so we can catch the 10:39 bus to San Francisco."

"Are we finally going to that club? You know, the…*Cheerful* club?"

"That's not it. Not this time. It's a surprise. Go shower." She pushed me off the bed.

As I stared at myself in the vanity mirror, realizing Casey hadn't exaggerated much when she compared me to a dead raccoon, she said, "And, Laur?"

"Hmm?"

"Don't forget to bring your you-know-what. It's important."

Even when the bus rumbled out of Coeur-de-Lune she wouldn't say where we were going. It obviously had something to do with my music box, though. When I wore my navy linen dress it went inside a wide pocket on my right hip. (I used six safety pins to secure the pouch.)

Casey's outfit didn't offer clues. She was dressed as she always was in the summer, in cutoffs and a T-shirt and black Chucks with no socks. She hadn't even freshened the grubby *Little Mermaid* Band-Aid on her right palm, the one covering the blister she got gripping the paddle too tight during our three-hour kayak Friday.

"So, tell me," I said, as the bus lumbered onto the freeway.

"When we're closer. God, it feels good to get out of town. I can't wait 'til we move away."

"I'll miss the lake," I said.

"You'll have a vacation place on the lake. We'll have apartments in San Francisco."

"In the same building."

"Naturally. And I'll stay with you every weekend in the summer while you get your kayaking fix."

"What color do you want for your guest room?"

"Blue."

We decorated our fantasy homes. My lake house would be rustic, but bigger than my family's. The city apartments would be sleek and modern. Walking distance to clubs and restaurants and a zillion bookstores with used paperbacks, and a bunch of sophisticated friends. These friends were shapeless, faceless, a blurry backdrop to our adult fabulousness. But we knew they'd be different from the people in town.

I dozed and Casey read a book called *Love Bites*. Something about slutty vampires.

When we could see the triangle of the Transamerica building Casey finally said, "I got us ten minutes with June."

It took a second to register.

I grasped her elbow. "*The* June? June Le Forestier? *June Names That Tune?* No!"

"*Oui.*" She checked her watch. "We've got to be there by three. That's her break."

"You talked to her?"

Casey shook her head. "I got the station's intern on the phone. I said I had a family heirloom music box but couldn't identify the tune. I pretended you'd called the program like a thousand times but never gotten through. And she said she'd help."

"You're incredible." I touched the outside of my pocket automatically. Even through three layers—plastic, chamois, linen—I could feel the hard case.

"There's a catch. June doesn't know we're coming."

Radio KZSY was on Mission Street. An old brick building wedged between a burrito restaurant and a stucco apartment. The

intern, a girl getting her PhD in musicology at Berkeley, ush-
ered us into a break room reeking of burnt microwave popcorn.

When she left Casey said, "Look, Laur. In case this doesn't
work. If she won't see us, or doesn't know the song…"

"She *always* knows the song."

"But. Just in case. We'll keep trying. So don't be too crushed,
okay?"

"She'll know it."

I'd listened to *June Names That Tune* every Sunday night for
six years. I'd heard her voice in the dark so many times I knew
its bronzy richness, its hills and valleys, as well as Alex knew
Casey Kasem's.

June had a couple of signature lines. One was "deep into the
vault."

I'm going deep into the vault this time, she'd say, and sometimes
she pretended she was pushing aside old cobwebby synapses
and dendrites to get to the memory. And just when it seemed
someone was finally going to stump her she'd come out with
the answer. Composer, date, everything. And it would be obvious she'd known all along.

Her other big line was "the cold and brutal judgment of time."
She used that to describe works that were, in her opinion, un-
derappreciated. *Shostakovich's "Symphony 15,"* she'd say. *A lovely
thing. Shame that one has gone out of fashion. Lost to the cold and
brutal judgment of time.*

When her heels clacked in the hall I straightened into my best
church posture to greet her. Hers would be impeccable, regal. I
pictured her in a black dress suit, with short black hair and red
lipstick. Elegant as the words that poured out of her so beautifully on the radio.

June Le Forestier stomped in with an annoyed expression and
a commuter mug the size of a beer stein that said Composers
Do It In Double Time. She wore plastic clogs, not heels, and

stalked over to the coffee machine in the corner without glancing in our direction.

The uncharitable thought came immediately: *Mrs. Piggle-Wiggle.* The heroine in a series of books I'd been addicted to when I was little. Soft and bulging, great shelf-like bosom, gray hair in a center-part bun.

"One minute," she said. "I'm shit-tired."

A foulmouthed, lobotomized Mrs. Piggle-Wiggle.

"What's this again? Family heirloom?" she eventually asked.

I froze, trying to reconcile this barking creature with the patrician June Le Forestier I'd worshipped in the dark.

"Show her," Casey said.

I fumbled with the safety pins in my pocket, cutting my thumb. I finally managed to pull the music box out, remove it from its protective bags, and set it on the table. I glanced at Casey, uncertain, but she nodded so I opened the lid.

As the music played June gulped coffee, her back to us. When the last note rang out, haunting and sweet, she didn't speak. She flipped the lid of the coffee maker and lifted the plastic cup from the top, then banged it against the trash can to release the soggy filter and grounds.

Casey turned to me, pity in her eyes.

"Let's go, Laur." *I'm so sorry*, she mouthed.

So. No song name after all. The tears threatened, a watery film blurring the room. My thumb pulsed and there was a glistening red oval of blood under the nail bed where I'd scraped myself on the safety pin. I wiped my hand on my dress but the blood welled up again, and I felt a familiar rushing in my head.

I looked away from the blood, reaching for the box with my left hand so I wouldn't stain it. I examined the whorls in the driftwood I had come to know so well, distinctive as a fingerprint.

It was just an object my mom happened to have, a trinket. She probably never knew what song it was any more than I did. My attempt to give it more meaning seemed childish now.

June was scooping grounds into a fresh filter when she spoke
again. "Got a pen?"

Casey scrabbled in her backpack and pulled out a pen and
Love Bites.

"*'L'Amour est Bleu.'* 'Love is Blue.' Composed by André Popp
in 1967. Popularized by Vicky Leandros."

Casey scribbled on the inside flap of *Love Bites*, scrambling
to catch up. "Can you spell her last name?"

"*L-e-a-n*—" June swigged her coffee "—*d-r-o-s*."

"*Love is Blue.*" I couldn't speak.

Casey filled the silence for me. "Thank you so much. This
means a lot to us."

June, glugging coffee, gave a careless wave.

As she passed on her way out she noticed the music box and
paused. "Unusual case. Stone? Marble?"

"Driftwood."

"Unusual," she repeated. "Pretty tune, too. Never hear it
anymore."

I nodded. She was almost out the door when I blurted out,
in an effort to make up for forgetting to thank her, "I guess it's
been 'lost to the cold and brutal judgment of time.'"

She seemed surprised for a second, then looked me in the eyes
and snorted her appreciation. "One sec."

While she was gone Casey tore a strip of brown paper towel
from the dispenser over the sink and wrapped my thumb. "You
got blood on your church dress."

"I don't care. It doesn't matter."

"Press this tight. You *hate* blood, remember? Those cow hearts
in bio?"

"I don't care," I said again. "It doesn't matter."

"That woman actually talks on the radio for a living?" she
whispered. "She's not exactly a fountain of conversation."

I didn't care. It didn't matter. I loved June Le Forestier again.

Loved her with more childlike fervor than I'd ever loved Mrs. Piggle-Wiggle.

June came back with an album. The cover was pure sixties, a nude woman with a monarch butterfly painted on her face, a vine climbing her midriff. "Take it. We've got it on CD."

"You're sure, thanks, this means so—"

June waved her hand and disappeared.

Casey slept against my shoulder on the bus ride home. I stared out at the sunset, holding the record carefully in my lap.

"Love is Blue." June had given me the instrumental version but I could look up the lyrics. I could buy the sheet music and play it on the piano. Not just the eighteen-note fragment of melody I'd memorized.

The whole thing.

But only when I was alone, so my dad wouldn't worry that I was getting obsessed, just like my mother had predicted.

She'd liked the tune. She'd liked it enough to pass it on to me, even when life got the best of her. And I finally knew its name. "Love is Blue." A sad message from her, maybe. Or maybe the only version of the song she'd heard was the music box's tinny excerpt. But I knew its name, and for now, that was enough.

Casey stirred and leaned close to study the album. "Groovy cover."

"Groovy is more seventies, isn't it? This is… What'd they say in the sixties?"

"Trippy? Where are you going to hide it?"

"Your place."

"Shocker. How's the cut?"

"You look." I unpeeled the paper towel.

"It's not bad."

Her *Little Mermaid* Band-Aid dangled from her palm. The blister was still raw.

"We should've stopped for bandages," I said. "And tetanus shots."

"We're a mess." Casey inspected her blister. She pressed my thumb against her palm, matching up our tiny wounds. "Blood sisters," she said, laughing.

23

Band-Aids

2016
Friday night

"Damn!" The knife clattered to the floor and the onion Casey'd been dicing rolled off the chopping board. She sucked on her finger.

"Is it bad?"

She shook her head. "It's nothing. But guess you can tell I'm not exactly a gourmet cook. I was trying to show off."

"I'll get something." I ran to her bathroom and rummaged in the medicine cabinet, returning with a *Cars* antibiotic Band-Aid and a box of gauze pads.

"Let me do it," she said.

"I'm not squeamish anymore." I forced her to uncurl her hand and show the half-inch line of red on the tip of her index finger, under a flap of skin. I would have been fine except for the skin flap. As I was blotting it with gauze I felt the old, in-

furiating rushing in my ears and had to sit on my bar stool with
my head down.

"You okay?" Casey laughed, snatched the Band-Aid from the
counter, and wrapped her finger.

I handed over the wet wad of gauze without looking at it.
"God, I hate being a 1950s cliché. A woman woozy at the sight
of blood." I smiled. "Guess I was showing off, too. Trying to
prove I'd grown out of it."

Casey returned to chopping the onion. "Now, that—" she
paused, pointed the knife at me "—would be utterly disappoint-
ing and boring." She turned to check the pot of pasta water.

Another small step forward.

She slid the pile of glistening, pale yellow onion off the chopping board and into the pan of olive oil. It sizzled and spat, a
drop landing on my arm. Casey had the pan on too high. But
I wasn't about to tell her. I was celebrating inside. Sally Field in
that old Oscars speech. *You like me, you really like me!*

"That smells so good," I said. "Please let me help." I hopped
off my bar stool.

"No, you're the guest. Sit."

And just like that, another giant step back. I was still a Guest
with a capital G. I climbed back onto my stool and sipped my
red wine.

Casey stirred the onions. Their edges were browning too fast.
"You can entertain me, though. Read me something."

Forward progress again. Or was she only humoring me? I
couldn't keep up, her mood changed so often.

I dug through the bag of books she'd given me. This wasn't an
e.e. cummings moment. I needed something campy and juicy,
to make her remember how we used to be. *Valley of the Dolls*
seemed to be the ticket. I flipped through for a scene Casey and
I had mocked many times: the one where a grown woman re-
assures her mother that she's doing her bust exercises.

I worked hard, reading the lines aloud in my most earnest

voice, as if the bust exercises were life-and-death. Sally Field had never reached so deep.

I worked too hard, of course. Because though Casey smiled throughout my reading, bustling around the kitchen stirring tomato sauce and draining pasta, she didn't reward me with the helpless snorts and tears of laughter I was after.

And she wouldn't let me carry a single dish from the kitchen to the table. "No. Just sit, *sit*."

"This is delicious."

"Thanks."

We chewed, sipped, smiled politely at each other.

"More wine?"

"I'd love some."

Chew, sip, smile. "More bread?"

"No, thank you. It's good, though. So good."

"Good."

Bad. So bad. We were stuck. We'd done better over our junk-food dinner at the roller rink, with something else to look at so we didn't have to strain for conversation.

We should have put on music. I'd have preferred "Shake Your Booty" to this tense silence.

Finally Jett took pity on us. She set her front paws on Casey's lap and sniffed at her plate to see if there was anything to her liking.

"Jett, off! She never does that. I'm so sorry."

"Guess she knows I'm a softy." Casey rubbed at her head. "Elle wants a dog."

"Are you getting one?"

"I think so. The three of us keep going to the shelter but we can't agree on who to pick. They all look so desperate to be adopted, you know? They have that look, like love me, love me, please be my mommy... Shit."

"It's fine."

"Shit, shit, shit. I'm sorry. You'd think I'd have more tact, with Elle and all. But tact was never my thing."

"It's okay. I got over it a long time ago."

She drained her wine, leaned back in her chair, and looked up at the ceiling fan. "It's a goddamn minefield. A black hole. We try to stick to safe topics but keep getting sucked back in. It's a disaster."

"I think it's kind of funny."

She faced me again, shook her head.

I smiled, nodded. "Casey. It's funny. Admit it."

"No."

"It's not as painful as when I compared Elle to Jett. Or when you told my first boyfriend he had bad taste in women right in front of me. I think that was probably the low point."

"Stop." But she started laughing. At first just hints of a giggle behind her napkin. But after a minute she was snorting, wiping at her eyes. "I'm sorry. It's not funny. It's not funny at all."

We sat on the couch together with our shoes off and a box of sea-salt toffee between us.

"Music?" Casey said, chewing and scrolling through her iPhone. "Would you like Elle's G-Rated Hip-Hop Dance Mix, or the *Soothing Sounds of the Harp* album I play at the store when I'm doing the books, or... Oh, brother."

"What is it?"

"Just a text from my mom."

"Everything okay?"

"They're fine, she just never fails to freak me out." She handed the phone to me and started digging in the bottom of the container for toffee bits that had fallen off. "The woman needs to open a psychic shop in the back room of the bookstore."

At first I didn't get it. Alex had sent a picture of Elle biting into a drippy triple-stack ice-cream cone in front of a shop I recognized from its white siding and green shutters—the Cinnamon Bear in South Lake Tahoe. Below the picture she'd texted:

Sweetheart. Hope it's going well. We're having a ball. I'm even making her floss, don't worry! XXOOXX Mom. P.S., there's cookie dough in the freezer for your dessert, in the back. And I made a new song playlist for you two. All your favorites.

"Wow."

"Right?" Casey crunched another piece of toffee. "Wish I'd known about the cookie dough before we bought this. This is too salty for me. I'm over the salty everything trend." She went to the kitchen and dug around in the freezer.

Above the message about the playlist was an older text from Casey to Alex: Call me back!!!! Then an angry-face emoji. Casey and Sam would hit it off.

And one above that, from Alex to Casey. Without thinking, I scrolled up an inch so I could read the whole thing: Give Laura a hug for me. I just know in my bones it's going well.

The hug, of course, had not been delivered.

I realized with a start that I was snooping and set the phone down on the sofa as Casey walked back with two spoons and a big glass bowl half-covered in tinfoil. "Looks like chocolate chip, peanut butter, and something with M&M's in it. Hard as a rock, though." She set the cookie dough on the coffee table.

"Elle's so cute," I said.

"Thanks."

"That *is* freaky about the music. Think she has nanny cams and hidden microphones?"

"I wouldn't put it past her." Casey scrolled and tapped, looking for the playlist. "Here it is. Casey and Laura Mix, June 2016."

"Let me guess. 'You've Got a Friend.'"

"'The Way We Were.'"

"'Memories.' Mixed with Casey Kasem musical countdowns?"

Casey smiled. "It's just music from high school. Nineties music. Twenty-four songs, good Lord, when did she do all this?"

She pressed a button and a small wireless speaker on the bookshelf sent a low Bluetooth tone before playing the first song.

Mazzy Star, "Fade Into You."

"This is *so* my mom," Casey said, laughing. "I do love this one, though, don't you? So pretty." She started digging at the cookie dough, managing to scoop out a shard.

"Yes." I closed my eyes and listened, trying to hold on to the light mood we'd had only moments before, laughing at the table.

"You okay?" Casey said.

"Sure." I opened my eyes, smiled. "Just tired."

"No. It's something else."

I hesitated. "It's the song. It was playing the first time I was alone with J.B. At that party."

"Oh. Shit."

"It just surprised me."

"Bad DJ'ing, Mom. You screwed that one up."

"She didn't know."

Casey forwarded to the next song. Chumbawamba. "Tubthumping." A tune that sounded like drunk soccer fans shouting in a bar. No painful memories attached to that one.

"Better?"

"Better. Thanks."

Typical Alex. Trying to be helpful but getting things a little wrong.

I tossed and turned, flipped and flailed. Too many memories. One minute they wrapped around me gently, warm and welcome and comforting as a blanket. The next they were acid.

24

Liquid Hiding Place

Saturday morning

Casey slept late so by the time we got started for Jade Cove it was eleven.

She wrapped Jett's leash around her right wrist, and I slung the camera around my neck, following her along the narrow, sandy trail winding through the trees.

For twenty minutes we walked through a dense cluster of pines without speaking. The only sounds were the rhythm of our footsteps on the trail, Jett's contented panting and jangling tags, the chirrups and twitters high in the trees. The feeling came before I made the connection. A view of Casey's back, birds, the clean smell of the lake. So familiar.

It was like when we'd kayaked together. Casey in the front, always. Long stretches of silence.

The path curved close to shore, where the trees thinned out, and the lake was so bright I tripped on a tree root, skidding and clutching a branch to right myself.

"You okay?" Casey called over her shoulder.

"I was admiring the lake instead of looking at my feet."

She glanced to her left only a second, not slowing her stride. "It's a dinky old thing, but I guess it's kind of pretty in the right light." Her voice had all the grudging fondness of a local.

Was I no longer a local? Because I couldn't pretend the midday sun hitting the lake was anything less than searingly beautiful.

I'd written a report about the lake in third grade. Everyone else in Miss Burkitt's class had used plain blue marker for their drawings, but I'd experimented with crayons, layering the wax, rubbing until I achieved the shade I wanted. Iridescent blue-black, like a fly's wing.

I'd loved the lake, known its sounds and colors, the names of water bugs and trees, the location of every shady swimming hole. It had been my only friend, before Casey.

A curve in the path, and there it was. The name romanticized it. Jade Cove was only a shady, C-shaped notch of pebbly beach under a clump of trees. The water wasn't really green as the name implied. It was the same deep, murky blue as the rest of the lake. But we'd liked it because it was cool even on the hottest days.

The downed pine tree we'd used as a diving board was gone, and Casey tied Jett's leash around a new sign: No Fishing No Swimming.

"When did this happen?" I said.

"The owner of the Jet Ski rental place made a fuss, said it was a public safety issue."

"So ban the Jet Skis."

"Exactly. I take Elle fishing here anyway. And there's a new petition to prohibit motorized stuff on the lake again."

"I'll sign. I'm a property owner."

"Write in a comment quoting my mom, how it's the gem of the East."

"Jewel of the East," I corrected.

"You're sure?" She drew Alex's list from her sleeve and read dramatically, "'One picture lost forever now/Taken in the jewel of the East.'"

"My bad," she said. She continued in a rapid kindergarten singsong:

"'Four boys were naughty there
But I was the only beast.
Long before our silly race this was your liquid hiding place.'

"The apology tour continues." Casey stuffed the clue sheet back in her pocket. "God, I was so pissed that night those boys went skinny-dipping, remember?"

Silly. Naughty. Were those accurate descriptions, Alex?

I smiled, but my smile was too wide or too tight, and didn't fool her.

"You okay?" Casey said.

"I'm just tired."

Casey nodded, and let this excuse pass. She shed her clothes, revealing a blue bikini, and ran in. Her shoulder blades seemed more prominent than they used to be, but she'd always been thin. Maybe I was remembering wrong. Or envious. Where the lines of Casey's body had sharpened with age, mine had blurred.

"How cold is it?" I said, kicking off my shorts.

"It's positively spa-like."

She submerged again, shot back up, and started swimming, falling effortlessly into her perfect crawl. Then she trod water and turned toward me. "What are you waiting for? Too much of a city girl to jump in?"

"You're going to laugh at my suit."

"Does it have a skirt?"

"Almost that bad." It was a simple black one-piece suit with a magic waist-whittling panel. I draped my pants and blouse over the no-swimming sign, hating myself for being self-conscious, and checked one last time for a pack of tourists buzzing by on Jet Skis. I held the camera above my head as I waded in. "Jesus, it's ice water. Let's get this over with."

Casey floated next to me and I extended my arms awkwardly, guessing at the camera height that would best capture our faces, fumbling for the button with my left index finger. Polaroids were not made for selfies.

"Remember that night she first brought out the cameras?" Casey said, laughing. She was exuberant from the cold water. Always happiest when she was swimming.

The water felt good on my skin, too. Bracing and familiar. But I couldn't match her mood.

"Remember how shocked we were?" she went on. "She's actually mellowed out, at least, I thought she had until she pulled this stunt, but—"

I pressed the button before she could finish. She turned to look at me, surprised.

The photo was the worst yet. Casey's profile was blurry. I was shivering, my smile fake.

"Halfway done," Casey said on the walk back.

"Hmm."

"What's wrong? Are you sad about how much the cove has changed?" She paused to dip her head forward, squeezing out her dripping hair.

"Yes. And…" How much to tell her? Alex had written part of her apology only for me. Casey didn't seem to know. "I was thinking about the cameras," I said. "I guess it hit me. How elaborate it all got."

"*Elaborate*. That's one word for it."

25

Gamemaster

July 1998
Saturday night
Summer before senior year

"C'mon, Alex. Tell us what's inside." Julia Masich reached for the white bag on the kitchen counter.

Alex swatted her away. "Not 'til everyone's here."

Finally she unveiled five brand-new Polaroid cameras with straps. One for each team. Casey and I exchanged a quick look. I wondered how much they'd cost her. But money never seemed to be a problem for Alex. I didn't understand Alex's work, a fusion of natural materials—sand, pinecones, stones—with garish slashes of acrylic in primary colors. To my untrained eye it looked pretty bad. But somewhere in America, people appreciated sand art.

"Something new this week," Alex said. "Half the things aren't things, they're places or stuff to do. You'll take pictures for proof." Alex, so flighty and fluttery most of the time, was in control on Saturday nights. "You know the rules. Back by ten."

She passed out the clues. Since the last week of June they'd been written in couplets. As everyone huddled with their teams Casey whispered, "She must've spent five hundred bucks on those cameras. This is officially getting out of control."

The first summer I'd been entranced, so proud of how we'd managed to upend CDL High's social scene. I'd recorded details in my diary. Team members. What they'd found and how they'd scored, who'd played it too safe, who'd rushed inside a minute past deadline. I'd glue-sticked in the clue sheets.

It was different now. Sometimes I remembered to grab a list from the floor at the end of the night. But just as often, I forgot.

I was still in awe of what Alex had created. Kids were even coming from other schools. The number of players continued to grow—as did the length of the after-party, and the number of beers in the refrigerator. (*Only for after*, Alex said. *Only for after* and *only beer* and *no hard drugs* and *absolutely no driving*. Though the week before a guy on my team had brought a flask of vodka, swigged it between clues. She also said, *If your parents find out they'll kill me*.)

So maybe I wasn't as enthralled as I'd been in the early days. But there were still moments of pure exhilaration for me, running around in the dark. It felt like we'd wrested something away from the Collier boys—their swagger, the way they strode around Coeur-de-Lune like young gods.

Casey was over the scavenger hunts, and had been for a long time.

For Casey Saturday nights, once *more than fun*, had become *more than annoying*. She worried about what would happen if someone snitched about the after-parties, or worse, if some stupid kid got alcohol poisoning on Alex's watch. Coeur-de-Lune society wasn't particularly fond of Alex to begin with.

Casey objected to the scavenger hunts for other, more personal reasons, but these were harder for her to articulate. She said Alex had lost it, that she was determined to ingratiate herself with a bunch of high school students because she didn't know how to relate to adults. It was creepy, she said. Unhealthy. For a long time, I resisted Casey's dark view, believing it was tainted by more than a little jealousy.

But when Alex started pulling those brand-new Polaroid R-2000s from the bag, I had to admit Casey was right. The scavenger hunts meant something to Alex I couldn't quite understand, and it worried me, too.

"Come *on*, hurry *up*," Allison Naitland yelled back as we walked—walked, it was unheard of—the last half mile to the house. Allison was approaching her first scavenger hunt with the same intensity that had propelled her to the regional Constitution Team championship in May.

Casey flipped her off behind her back. "I'm so done with this."

"I have an idea," I said. "If you want a break from the hunts."

"Explain."

"My mother's church retreat is coming up in August, remember?"

"Oh, yeah. I love retreat week. I actually get to set foot in your house."

"So we'll say it doesn't make sense to have the hunt that night because you're sleeping at my place."

"She'd probably organize the game without me. Definitely the party."

"Casey. She wouldn't. Anyway, I'll invite her for dinner that Saturday."

"Okay. But when your mom finds out my mom was in your house she'll make the priest come over with a cross and holy water to disinfect it."

"That's Catholics," I said, laughing. "Anyway, I think maybe

we should just talk to Alex, don't you? There's got to be a way
to explain without hurting her."

Casey half closed her eyes, shook her head: *Not worth it.*

I knew she was right. I couldn't think of a kind way to tell
Alex that the Saturday nights she planned so carefully had become less than fun for Casey. There was a fragility to Alex that
neither of us quite knew how to navigate.

We were the last team back. When we walked in Kip Soscia's
all-boys team was boasting about how they'd made it home before everyone else, with nine items, even though they'd wasted
time skinny-dipping at Jade Cove.

Great, Casey mouthed, and I smiled in sympathy.

Alex was verifying everyone's booty in the kitchen behind
me, laying items and photos out on The Shipwreck's narrow
counter. I caught her voice over the din. "You boys."

Only a teasing murmur and a low laugh, but something in
the tone made me look back to where Alex stood, the nucleus
within a cell of smiling, bare-chested, wet-haired boys. Alex
handed Kip Soscia a Polaroid, shaking her head at him. Play-
fully scolding. He grinned and stuffed the white square down
his jeans pocket. Alex had only asked each team to bring back
a picture of themselves on the sand. But I guessed Kip and his
friends had taken a more pornographic approach—and Alex had
laughed it off when presented with the evidence.

I glanced across the room at Casey, relieved she hadn't noticed.

When the party moved outside, Casey stayed in, curled on
the sofa with her eyes closed. A protest of sorts, or another test.
One Alex was failing; any time Alex's laughter rose up above
the others' Casey stiffened.

I wandered to the fireplace mantel, sweeping up the purple
nubbins from the vase of dried lavender Alex kept there. "You
okay?"

"Dandy."

I'd thought we were alone in the house but there was a sputter of male laughter from the staircase. I couldn't see who it was; they were hidden below the angled pine half wall that ran up the stairs.

Casey muttered, "Isn't it time for their mommies to pick them up?"

"I'll ask them to go outside."

It was Kip and Mark Engles. Two of the big winners from the skinny-dipping team. They were hunched on the third step, a small collection of Polaroids laid out between them like trading cards. I hovered over their bent heads, and they were so occupied, studying and sorting, they didn't notice me. Their hair, damp from the lake, emitted a puppyish smell.

The first photo I saw was of three boys knee-deep in dark water, mooning the camera. Their butts looked sort of sad and undernourished in the harsh flash.

It could have been much worse. It wasn't frontal, at least. But one boy had his legs apart slightly more than his friends did. I leaned closer, holding my breath, and noticed there was a ruddy curve below the shadowy cleft of his buttocks that made the picture less innocent.

There was a photo of Alex, too, in her pink peasant blouse. Her heart-shaped, laughing face was turning away from the camera, and she'd extended one arm in graceful protest. It was taken in the kitchen before the game, because Alex had her hair in the low ponytail she'd worn earlier in the night.

Kip picked up the skinny-dipping photo and hovered it facedown over the Alex one, lowering and raising it, crying in grotesque falsetto, "Uh, uh. Fuck yeah. More."

"You wish." I let the lavender buds in my hand fall to the steps so I could scoop up the pictures. "Is this all of them?" I spoke quietly, peeking over the staircase wall. Casey was still curled on the couch, thank God.

The boys, drunk and shocked to realize I'd been looming over them, nodded.

"Swear to God?" I said. "I'll find out if you're lying. And…" And what? I'd tell my parents? Their parents, who'd shut down the parties?

"I'll tell Alex," I whispered. "And I'll make sure you're never allowed back here."

"Swear," Mark said. "This is all of them."

"Go," I said.

They stood unsteadily, still stunned, leaving me holding the contraband like a school principal. Mark opened the front door, contrite. I enjoyed a heady moment of victory at their obedience.

I wasn't just the principal. I was the party's 120-pound bouncer. Alex's savior. Casey's protector.

But Kip looked back, checking that Casey was still on the couch. He smiled, leaned close. "Anytime *you* want to skip the game…"

"What?" I said.

Mark punched Kip in the arm, yanked him out the door. "Nothing. He's had three beers."

"What's going on?" Casey called.

Quickly, I sifted through the small stack. Two more skinny-dipping photos, neither as bad as the first one I'd seen.

Another of Alex in her pink blouse in the kitchen, laughing and feinting at the camera with her slender arm.

And one picture that made me sink down onto the bottom step.

Of course. That odd, snickering emphasis on the *you* in Kip's offer.

Anytime *you* want to skip the game.

"What was that about?" Casey called, walking over.

I was concealed by the low staircase wall and had just enough time to stuff the photo down my back shorts pocket, to rearrange my features into a mask of normalcy, before Casey appeared at the base of the stairs.

"What are those?" she said, nodding at the stack of pictures on the step.

"Just idiots. Idiots naked. They took pictures of the skinny-dipping." I handed her the Polaroids.

All except the one in my back pocket, in which Alex was up against the big fir behind the house, kissing Stewart Copley.

His skinny body pressed close, his hands tangled in her red hair. Awkward, nervous Stewart Copley in his olive green canvas jacket. He was a year younger than me. He'd been in my precalc class. His jaw was always raw and rashy from clumsy shaving.

He could have caught Alex off guard. Kip or whoever had taken the picture, returning early from the hunt, might have gotten lucky, pressing the red button seconds before Alex pushed Stewart away.

She could have been joking around.

But it didn't look like it, and I wasn't about to show Casey. She was furious enough about the images in her hand. "Goddamn it," she said, pushing past me and taking the stairs two at a time.

When I entered her bedroom she was already hard at work with the scissors. She cut the pictures in pieces, tore off each segment's top layer, and rubbed at the sticky middle. Until the only traces left of the bare-assed boys in Jade Cove, and laughing Alex in her pink blouse, were the black smudges on her fingers and the pile of curly plastic shreds in her trash basket.

She threw the scissors at the wall, creating a deep pockmark. A spider against the white paint.

"Those boys watch her like she's a dirty joke," she said. "You know she doesn't have one female friend her age in this town? Not one."

I could feel the photograph of Alex and Stewart Copley through the thin cotton of my shorts. "She didn't ask them to do it. She wasn't swimming with them."

No. She was back here, doing God knows what with another boy.

Stewart had stayed behind with Alex, opting out of the scavenger hunt. By invitation?

I thought over recent Saturdays, trying to remember if there was always a boy who ran to home base early, or didn't play at all. But maybe Kip was just being filthy. Jealous, because he wished it had been him pressing Alex against the tree.

"She wasn't with them," Casey said. "But she's letting things go too far."

I sat on the floor next to her, touched her knee. "We can talk to her."

"Like that'll help."

"And you got rid of the pictures. Without them it's just rumors."

"Rumors are enough in this town."

"Would you rather have a mother like mine? Bake sales and bible study?"

"Stop defending her!"

"I'm not, I'm only saying you shouldn't worry so—"

"You can't *see* her, Laur! You never will."

But I could see her. I saw her, and perhaps felt a small, vicarious thrill at her daring, at becoming the custodian of her secrets.

When Casey finally fell asleep I tiptoed down the hall to Alex's studio. The light was on, and Alex was looking over some flat lake stones she'd gathered. They were spread out on one of her sawhorse tables, in columns sorted by color, darkest to lightest.

She turned with a warm smile. "Can't sleep, sweetie?"

I shut the door behind me gently and joined her by the table. "What are you going to do with these?"

"No idea," she said, laughing, tapping a stone the dirty gray of a rain cloud.

"I'm sure it'll be great," I said. "So I...I need to tell you something."

"Are you okay? Is it Casey?"

I shook my head. "She's fine. We both are. It's... Were you joking around with Stewart Copley tonight? The thin boy in the green jacket. Did he try to kiss you or something?"

She had the grace to flush, to close her eyes.

"It's okay, I won't tell anybody, but a couple of the other boys…took a picture. I got it back. Want to see it?"

She shook her head, eyes still closed. "I'm mortified." Her lids fluttered open. "It was a stupid, stupid thing to do. He surprised me."

"I thought it was something like that."

"I stopped him before it went too far. Of course I stopped him. It's just that he's so shy. So sweet."

"I know."

"I knew it was a mistake the second it was over. And it *was* just a second, honey. We'd been talking while we waited. He wasn't in the mood for the game, he said. He's having a hard time at home and…" She rubbed her temples. "Oh, God, tell me Casey doesn't know."

"No. I didn't tell her. She was already so mad about that team going skinny-dipping. The town might not understand…and… Anyway, you should talk to her tomorrow."

She nodded. "I'd never—"

"I know. Just…maybe…" I couldn't meet her eyes. She was so wan and sad in the unflattering light of her studio lamp, I almost didn't say the next part. I didn't want to be like the church people I loathed, the ones who judged her.

But there was Casey, sleeping in the next room, trusting me even though I'd lied to her about the picture. I had to make my lie okay.

I said it fast. "Just be more careful."

"Of course."

"We don't have to talk about it anymore." I turned away.

She gathered a handful of my T-shirt in one hand, pulled me toward her. "No. We do, Laur. Let me say this."

"You don't have to—"

"I do. Listen. You know how Casey makes her jokes, saying

I have Peter Pan syndrome. How I'm trying to redo my teenage years. Because of my...how I was raised?"

I nodded.

"I'm not saying it's a good excuse." Her eyes were wide, contrite. She clutched the fabric of my T-shirt with both hands,
leaning forward on her stool like she was praying. "I guess what
I'm saying is I'll do better from now on."

I smiled. "Good."

"Now go get some sleep." She tapped my nose.

I was near the door, my back to her, when she spoke again.

"Laura. The picture?"

"I'll get rid of it."

"My sweet girl. Thanks for understanding."

I didn't want to embarrass her further, so I didn't bring it up again.

And I had my own theory about why Alex had fallen into the
kiss with Stewart. It wasn't just because she had uptight parents
and couldn't go to parties when she was a teenager, no matter
what she said.

That could be part of it. But Alex was also a little lost, a little
scared right now. Casey was growing up and would be gone in
a year; before Alex passed out the lists tonight Casey'd spent half
an hour talking to a girl whose sister went to UCLA. Grilling
her about housing and majors and the best places to live. Alex
had overheard and joined in, forced a smile. She had to be sad
about it.

So Alex was clutching at whatever was closest. Even skinny
Stewart Copley.

The next morning after I finished cleaning up from the church
bake sale, I cut up the picture in the dark Sunday School room,
using stubby purple child's scissors. I sliced the Polaroid into
pieces smaller than my pinky nail so that Alex's transgression
was reduced, on each sliver, to a color: the pink of her blouse,
the green of Stewart's jacket.

I took perverse satisfaction in disposing of the scraps. I tossed a few down the white feminine-hygiene canister in a ladies' room stall, a couple in the leather waste bin of the library, two in the kitchen garbage, one in the big granite trash can behind the sanctuary, near the pansy-lined path to the cemetery. My mother had raised the six hundred dollars for that trash can.

Alex knew she'd screwed up. And summer would be over before we knew it.

26

42nd day of camp
12:30 a.m.

The musician's house was a few towns away from camp, on the other side of the mountain. She recognized the gas station they passed when they pulled off the main road.

It was the same Arco Quik-Stop she'd run into for Cokes and Fritos, the afternoon back in June when she and her mom had driven here from San Francisco.

Might be our last chance for decent junk food, her mom had joked, and they'd giggled, imagining the deprivations of camp: powdered eggs and Tang. Like astronauts, she had continued, laughing, making it sound like an adventure. Not realizing that camp really was another planet, a terrible one. She couldn't have known.

Her mother had driven them here because she was fried from what had happened in that parent meeting that went bad. That's what she'd said.

I'm fried.

Do this for me.

I never ask you for anything, hon.

Summer was almost over and in another week, she and her mom would pass this same gas station on their way home. Laugh again, about what a fiasco their little experiment in retreating had been.

And everything would go back to normal.

It was well after one in the morning by the time they arrived. There was someone snoring in the hammock on the porch, another body passed out in the front hall.

"Friends," he explained in a considerate whisper, leading them through the dark house to the kitchen. "I'm a softy; everyone crashes here when they move to California."

Something about the musician made her want to lie. Or maybe it wasn't him; maybe it was camp. The months of forced good behavior bursting into rebellion, making her into a person she didn't recognize.

She'd lied and said she was seventeen.

When he'd asked what her favorite drink was, as the truck rattled down the hill, she'd lied and said it was rum and Coke.

When rum and Coke was the only drink she knew, and she was no more seventeen than he was a real Christian. He'd been a last-minute replacement at Three Pines. He'd said the regular guitarist had backed out to can salmon in Alaska. His sweet singing in chapel and at meals, his smiles at Miss Veach and Miss Cooke and the rest. It was all an act.

They sat on the kitchen floor, the radio on low. The guitar player held out her rum and Coke in a chipped mug. When she reached for it he didn't let go right away.

"Seventeen, huh?" He smiled, not buying it. "Well. Guess you're entitled."

She took a too-big swallow, sputtering at the unexpected burn. Embarrassed, wiping her watering eyes, she said the first thing that came to mind. "How old are you, Sandy?"

"Sandy?" He laughed. "Who's Sandy?"

"I only go by that around church people," her cabinmate said. "My real name's Alexandra."

"*Sandy,*" he said. "*I like it.*" He stood and fiddled with the radio on the kitchen counter. "*Sandy isn't allowed to listen to the radio at home.*"

Sandy/Alexandra sipped her drink, closed her eyes.

"*What about you?*" he said. "*Your folks as religious as hers? Or do they let you play devil music?*"

"*Yes. I mean, no. They're not religious. And yes, I can play anything I want.*"

He turned the dial until crackles gave way to organ chords, a low, robotic drone she recognized instantly.

"*Name that tune,*" he said, settling on the pale yellow linoleum between them, leaning against the oven. "*Ah. Too old for you two, I'm sure.*"

Alexandra shook her head. "Not a clue."

"*The Doors,*" she said. "'*Riders on the Storm.*'"

"*Gold star,*" he said, grinning. Impressed.

Her mom's ex, Tim, had played The Doors over and over when they'd painted her room last summer. Tim was a good guy. He'd laughed when she'd complained that the songs all sounded like a haunted house.

Her mom had laughed, too, had reached down from the ladder to daub yellow paint on her nose. The color was Banana Cream Pie; they'd chosen it together.

She sipped her drink, and each time a new song came on she got another gold star. She was relieved that this was all they seemed to expect of her.

After her fifth gold star the song "Daniel" came on, by Elton John, and he didn't quiz them. He closed his eyes and sang along, picking chords out on the leg of his jeans. He looked younger with his eyes closed. He sang in a jokey way, exaggerating the emotion in the long vowels, but he was unable to mask the sweet timbre of his voice, and she remembered why she'd watched him all summer, why he'd sent a warm tickle down her spine when he'd first spoken to her, out of all the girls, behind the craft cabin.

When the next song started he didn't sing along. He opened his eyes and took a long swig of rum. "That's freaky. This song is about some-one named Daniel, too."

Except it wasn't. "Only the Good Die Young" was about a girl named Virginia; everybody knew that. She and her friends had ana-lyzed it. Virginia the virgin.

"Swear you didn't call the request line to mess with me, Al?" She couldn't tell by his expression if he was serious or not.

"It's just a dumb coincidence, Daniel," Alexandra said.

He reached up and swirled the dial aimlessly, landing on a fuzzy country station. "Don't mind me," he said. "That song just gets to me."

They were speaking in code. She glanced from him to Alexandra, waiting for one of them to explain, to give a name to the new frequency in the room.

"Oh, Al," he said. "I got you that gum you wanted. On my dresser."

"Thanks." Alexandra stood up.

She was alone with him now. Daniel, like the song—she could hardly forget his name now. Daniel, who closed his eyes to Elton John but couldn't bear Billy Joel.

"Is this your first time at Camp Jesus?" He said it in Spanish, mock-ing. Hay-zoos.

She nodded.

"You're having a tough time." Not a question. "Are you from San Francisco like her?"

"Yeah."

"Miss it?"

"I miss my mom."

"Of course you do," he said, his eyes softening. "You poor kid. I've got some Ghirardelli chocolate around here. Might make you less home-sick. What, you think I'm teasing?"

"Yes."

"Not at all. This woman threw it in my case when I was playing the cable car turnaround. You wouldn't believe what people throw in. Doughnuts, beef jerky. Apples with a bite out. I got a potato once."

"Really?"

"Yeah. A big old raw potato long as my hand." He grinned. "I took it home and baked it. Right here." He knocked on the oven door. "I baked that thing at 400 degrees for an hour, got sour cream, some bacon, some chives... You have a nice laugh. Darn. Called attention to it. Made you stop. Anyway. They mean well. They think I'm homeless."

"You own this house?"

"Sure do. So now you're wondering why I play on the street."

"I wasn't—"

"It's all right. I'm not sure I know myself."

It was after four by the time they left. They drove through dark streets, passing the gas station, cutting over the hill on the logging road.

When the truck coasted to a stop and she slid toward the door he touched her wrist lightly. Just touched it, but she froze as if he had cuffed her.

"Hey. I forgot to thank you in person." He reached across her for the driftwood. "This is something special. Something worth holding on to." He tossed it up a few inches, caught it, then brushed it tenderly. He looked up and smiled. "No, really," he said more softly, no more teasing edge in his voice. "It was kind of you. You're a sweet girl."

When she got out he called, "Careful, now! Stay on the trail!"

They spoke quietly on the walk down the hill, staying close within the flashlight's wobbling oval of light. It was cold, and the crackling sounds outside the oval made them walk quickly.

"He was in a weird mood," Alexandra said. "He gets like that sometimes. He's okay, though. He bought me a cupcake for my thirteenth."

"This summer?"

"No...my birthday's in May. I see him in the city sometimes. When I can get away."

"What was that Billy Joel stuff about?"

"Billy Joel?"

"'Only the Good Die Young.'"

"Oh. His older brothers both died young. And his favorite cousin or something. Sad, huh?"

"That is sad."

"So your parents," said Alexandra. "You get along with them?"

"Yeah."

"But you said they're not religious."

She shook her head.

"Then why'd they stick you here?" She pointed the flashlight down the trail toward camp. The dim glow of the overnight cabin lanterns was still visible against the gray light.

"My mom needed a rest. Three Pines is what she could afford. Her friend told us about it."

"Are your folks doing the adult retreat this month?"

"Yeah. Since July."

"They must be rich, to take off work so long."

"My mom's a teacher. She gets all summer."

She didn't volunteer that it was only her and her mom. Her father sent her birthday cards and Christmas presents, but it had been ten years since she'd seen him so she could only remember that he'd had a silky brown beard, that he'd let her play with his pile of change on the front table.

They crept across pine needles past the craft lodge toward the circle of cabins. It was getting light; it had to be after five. They'd cut it close, but still had half an hour before the early risers would stir.

She wanted to ask Alexandra about the name thing. Why had she decided to be Sandy at church? "Hey, Alexandra," she whispered.

"What?" Alexandra whispered back.

"You girls are up early."

They turned. It was Miss Cooke, their beach chaperone. She was on the trail from the parking lot. Smiling and looking snappy in a yellow turtleneck under a stiff plaid coat, her brown hair scraped into a bun. She carried a wide pan draped in foil.

Alexandra met Miss Cooke's broad smile with her own. "We hiked up to see the sunrise. From the clearing. It was incredible." A lie so effortless, so Eddie Haskell brazen, it seemed she must have rehearsed it. "Do you need help with that? Smells good."

Miss Cooke raised one thin eyebrow.

She thought they were busted.

But after a second Miss Cooke's disapproving expression gave way to that unnerving smile. She gestured with the pan, flipping a corner of foil up to indicate they should help themselves. "For the deacons. But take a couple. I won't tell."

27

Women's Retreat

Late August, 1998
Summer before senior year

My mother would be gone for a whole week.

I looked forward to her church retreat at Three Pines as much as any kid ever anticipated Christmas. For months I'd been counting down the days until the gifts arrived. These were the gifts: time alone with my dad, seven days free of my mother's looks and clucks and hmphs, a household schedule that would go beautifully loosey-goosey the second her friend Barbara Macon's sagging brown Buick carried her out of our driveway.

There had been a frightening moment, the afternoon she left, when she asked me to come. I was at the table helping my dad finish the *Times* puzzle. She was carrying a stack of freshly ironed Land's End button-downs to my parents' bedroom, where her suitcase, toiletries, and pants were laid out on the bed. She paused halfway across the living room rug, as if the idea had just occurred to her. "You could come along, Laura, you're old enough now. There's still space. Barbara would love it. You know how fond she is of you."

Not *I'd* love it. Barbara.

It must have cost her a lot to ask me.

Since I'd met Casey I'd trimmed my commitments at church to the bare minimum. I still sat between my parents during 9:30 service every Sunday, holding the red-and-gold hymnbook, turning to the page numbers that someone posted on the oak board in front of the sanctuary. (Though I knew most of the page numbers by heart: "Softly and Tenderly" on seventeen, "How Great Thou Art" on fifty-six).

I still helped with bake sales in the narthex every other week, selling Blue Moon cakes and peach streusel pie and waxed paper bundles of divinity to raise money for things like oak hymn boards. But I'd quit choir. I hadn't helped at vacation bible camp in four years.

I was supposed to feel a special connection with Mrs. Macon because she'd helped arrange for my private adoption. She'd heard I was "available" through a charity for mothers with drug-affected infants where she volunteered. All my mother's church friends knew about it, and Barbara always said modestly that it was nothing, that she'd only made a phone call, knowing my parents were looking to adopt.

But she loved it when they called her "the stork." The whole thing made me want to slap her across her ancient, powdered, pious face.

This was a final appeal. My mother knew it. I knew it.

"I told Mrs. Cooper I'd babysit Kit this week."

"Well. See she pays you what you're owed." She shuffled into the bedroom.

"Next summer, maybe," I called.

My dad and I worked the crossword. We got 11-across (Aesop) and 18-down (centennial) before he spoke.

He said quietly, "That true, the babysitting?"

"Hmm?"

"Funny thing is, I heard Mrs. Cooper telling Ollie the Coopers were off to Yosemite Monday. She was in the store buying a tarp."

"Oh."

"Shouldn't lie, Laura. I think better of you."

"I know," I whispered. "I'm sorry. It's just, a whole week with her church people. I couldn't stand it. And it's the only time you and I ever get to hang out, just us, and…"

"Still. Shouldn't lie."

"I know."

Silently, he worked the puzzle. 8-across, 11-down, 19-down, 19-across. He filled in four more answers without speaking. I thought I'd ruined our week.

But as he wrote in 22-across (quotidian) he winked. "Ah well, mothers and daughters. You'll be best friends one of these days, I'm told. People change, if you let them."

"She won't."

"You both will. You'll go on all kinds of trips together."

"Maybe, Daddy."

"Just you wait," he said. "All kinds of trips."

I kissed my mother on her cheek when she left. "Well," she said. "See that your father takes his blood pressure pills."

"I will."

She patted my back clumsily. "Casseroles in the fridge."

I smiled at Barb Macon, who was powdering her nose in the driver's seat. She wore a white blouse and yellow polyester slacks. White hair, black old-lady wraparound sunglasses, pointy little nose; she even looked like a stork.

After she'd tucked her compact into her yellow handbag she said sweetly, "Shame you're too busy to come, dear." She might as well have said, *I help find you a good home and this is how you repay me?*

My dad struggled down the gravel driveway with my mother's heavy blue suitcase. I didn't hear what he said as he helped her into the passenger seat, but he leaned close, and I guessed his goodbye included the word *love*.

After the stork's Buick disappeared from sight we went inside to check out the casseroles. They were stacked up as always, towers of red Tupperwares so high they blocked the refrigerator light.

"She went to a lot of trouble," I said, pulling a few out and setting them on the counter.

"Very wholesome assortment. Very healthy." He took the lid off a container labeled "Porcupine Meatballs—350 for 30 mins." "How about these tonight?"

My mother was an excellent baker. Her stew was tasty, too. But porcupine meatballs were horrible little spheres of ground beef studded with rice that never cooked through.

"Yum," I said. "I'm hungry now. I'll preheat the oven if you get out the timer."

My dad pulled out the red KitchenAid timer, actually turned it. We leaned over the counter and stared at it, listening to it tick.

We got better at this game of chicken every year. So a whole minute went by before my dad cracked. His eyes crinkled up. "Pepperoni or sausage?"

"Pepperoni."

"I'll call Josefina's."

After our early dinner—pizza on the dock with paper towels as plates; my mother would have gone catatonic—he handed me a piece of folded-up graph paper. "This year's project, if you're up for it."

I opened it. My dad had sketched the back of the house with

his mechanical pencil. For years, he'd been saying he wanted to fix up the deck.

"We'll push it out a bit there—" he ran his fingertip along dotted lines "—and here. Shore it up, broaden the steps."

"It'll be perfect, Daddy."

"It's a big project." He folded the graph paper and slipped it into his back pocket.

"Casey'll be back from her swim meet Wednesday, she'll help."

"Ollie recommended that young man who used to deliver for the hardware store. He's home from school for a couple of weeks and trying to earn some extra cash. He's bringing the cedar in his truck tomorrow."

Merry Christmas to me.

28

Whistle While You Work

Monday
High of 87

"Up already?" my dad said over his paper. "I thought you teen-agers all slept 'til noon."

I wasn't sure I'd slept at all. I'd been dressed since five. My hair had been in and out of a ponytail twice already. I'd put on lipstick, rubbed it off with a tissue, put it on again, then rubbed two-thirds of it off so I'd still look like a girl who was going to spend the day expanding a deck with her father.

All summer, I'd hoped to see J.B. I'd even dropped into the hardware store in June, when I knew UCLA was out for sum-mer break. But he wasn't working there, or at the rink. And I was crushed when Casey found out a few weeks later that he had an internship in LA.

At seven I was changing into my third pair of shorts when

I heard the crunch of the gravel driveway. I spied J.B. through my window blinds.

There he was. Right below my window. I could see the red top of his baseball cap and a few inches of black hair tucked behind his ears.

My dad bent to show J.B. a rotting board. J.B. knelt next to him respectfully and laughed at something he said. I wanted to make my entrance when they were far apart so I could greet J.B. privately. I didn't want him to think I'd planned this.

I waited at the window and watched until J.B. took the wheelbarrow around the house. Hoping to catch him on the side path, I finally went outside, but before I could make it around the corner he was already on his way back, the wheelbarrow loaded with boards.

"Laura, meet J.B.," my dad said.

J.B.'s grin widened with every step closer. When he set the wheelbarrow down in front of me he said, "You."

"We've met." I tossed my hair over my shoulder. "Around town." I slipped my dad's old leather work gloves on and immediately started pulling boards from the wheelbarrow. No professional had ever unloaded a wood order so fast.

My dad glanced from me to the wheelbarrow to J.B., then examined his handmade blueprint, his neatly written list of supplies. When he planned even the smallest project, he accounted for all possible factors. Mishaps, delivery delays, rain. It was the ex-contractor in him.

This was a variable he hadn't penciled out on graph paper, whatever spark existed between me and J.B. But he hid his surprise well. "Good. Let's see what we can get done this morning. Going to be hot as blazes."

By eleven it was eighty-three degrees and we had half the framing done. When my dad was inside filling our big thermos dispenser with water and we were grabbing more boards, J.B. said in a low, confidential tone, "How's USC?"

"You're hilarious. How's UCLA?"

"Money's tight, I worry about my mom when I'm gone, but I'll push through."

"Worry?"

"She had lymphoma. She's okay now."

"I'm so sorry."

A pause, a nod. "I like your dad. You two do stuff like this a lot?"

"When my mother's at her church retreat we always pick a special project. When I was young we'd make little things—a bird feeder, shelves for my room. Guess it's our summer ritual. He used to be a contractor."

"Unusual," he said, "Someone as old as you still getting along with a parent like that, wanting to spend time with them. Thought I was the only one."

"So now I'm too old?"

He took off his baseball cap, using it to wipe his forehead. He smiled and stared straight ahead. "I didn't say too old."

Then my dad was back bearing the big lemon yellow water dispenser with the push button. "Drink up, troops," he said.

We fell into an easy rhythm. The three of us were serious, quiet workers, and it was too hot to talk much anyway. By noon it was so hot my shirt was pasted down my back and under my arms, but I didn't mind. I didn't mind that I was wearing bulky kneepads and oversized work gloves. My gear made me feel braver.

Anytime my dad went inside to the bathroom, or to fill up the water dispenser, or into the shed to find a tool, J.B. and I stole a few words.

When my dad walked down the beach to evaluate the deck from far away, J.B. handed me one of my gloves. "Lose this?" he said. "Saw it fall out of your pocket over there."

"Thanks. You're always finding things I've lost."

"What?"

"The skating rink, two years ago? You found something. Something important to me."

He still looked puzzled.

"I was younger. I wore my hair differently." I bunched my hair up behind my head until he smiled, recognition dawning on his face.

"Oh, yeah!" he said. "I can't believe I didn't realize that was you."

"It was dark in the rink."

"Still." He shook his head. "What was it you lost? A little stone in a coin purse?"

"No. More important than that. A sort of…lucky charm."

My dad was back.

"How does it look from down the lake, Daddy?"

"Not too shabby. Don't think we'll be a blight on the landscape."

At two, as I was kneeling, placing boards, and J.B. was lying on his side on the ground to measure the grade where the new steps would go, my dad ran inside to answer the phone.

"What does J.B. stand for?"

"Guess."

"John Boy."

"Nope."

"James Bond."

"Wrong."

"Umm… Jelly Belly?"

He sputtered out an astonished laugh. "Actually, kind of."

I laughed, glancing at his stomach. It was flat, practically concave, under his sweat-soaked shirt. He smiled, but I saw from his eyes that he was serious.

"Sorry. I thought you were kidding."

"I'll tell you about it sometime."

Tuesday
High of 89

We finished the framing early and broke for lunch. When my dad was inside ordering pizza I said, "It's supposed to be even hotter tomorrow. Hope you're not sorry you took the job."

"I'm definitely not sorry."

(A beautiful word, *definitely*. I savored it and all it implied.)

"You have air-conditioning?" He nodded at the house.

"Yeah, but we hardly ever use it. If my room's too hot to sleep I go swimming. My wet hair's usually enough to cool me off."

"You swim last night?"

"Yeah."

"Which one's yours?" He looked up at the two possible windows.

I pointed.

He stared up at my bedroom window, then got busy picking up scraps below the table saw.

My dad came through the sliding glass door, whistling "Bolero."

"Josefina's says one hour."

That night when my dad was watching a tape of *60 Minutes*, Casey called from a pay phone in Davis, where her swim team was competing. It wasn't an official meet, but they'd finished strong this year and their coach wanted them to stay sharp. Casey was one of the best on the team.

"Hallelujah," she said. "Finally, something interesting happens in this town."

"He hasn't even asked me out."

"Minor detail."

"Tell me about your trip. Any progress with butterfly girl?" Casey had a long-standing crush on some raven-haired pre-pre-Olympian from another school who was 1. gorgeous and 2. smoking everyone in the 200 meter fly.

"She's definitely straight. Or thinks she is. This giant boy-friend in a baseball cap came to cheer her on. I'm heartbroken."

"Idiot girl. I'm sorry."

"Well. At least one of us has a love life. I can't wait to check it out in person."

"Don't look at us too much, you'll make me nervous."

"I won't."

"But don't *not* look at us."

She laughed. "I'll look a totally normal amount of times. Even if you rip off that tight shirt and lay him down on a pile of sawdust."

"Case."

"Kidding."

Wednesday
High of 92

Casey swam over at nine. She emerged from the lake like a sel-kie, in cutoffs and a tank top, and my dad laughed as she trot-ted over, barefoot and dripping. She and my dad had hit it off immediately, though he rarely saw her outside school functions and church retreat week.

"You'll need shoes, Red," he said. "Otherwise we'll be driv-ing you to Emergency with a nail through your foot."

"Whoops."

"I'll lend you sneakers, Case. J.B., this is Casey."

She waved. "Hey."

"Nice entrance," he said.

"Red's the local mermaid, she lives in the lake." My dad looked up from his graph paper blueprint to wink at her.

"Actually I live over there." She pointed across the water.

"I delivered something to that house once, for Pedersen's," J.B. said. "Sawhorses. I met your mom."

"Sure, she's still got them in her studio."

"Cool old place."

"Thanks."

Casey was good to her word. Our work site got more lively with her around, but she didn't stare. She threw herself into the project.

Near the end of the day J.B. was placing the last few boards on the steps and I was securing them with the nail gun. Casey was by the back door, sanding the old section of the deck, producing a steady music of whines and hums with the electric sander. My dad was mixing an old can of wood protectant, the sound exactly the same as when my mother beat cake batter with her wooden spoon.

He held the stick up to the sunlight, checking the varnish color. "Better bring two gallons tomorrow," he said to J.B. "In the Light Amber. Thought I had an unopened can in the shed, but guess my mind's not as sharp as I thought it was. Guess I'm no longer the sharpest tool in the shed."

"Daddy," I groaned, but J.B. and Casey laughed.

"I'm going to have one more look."

His lanky denim form disappeared into the shed but we could hear him whistling.

"Is your mom's sense of humor like his?" J.B. said.

This produced a curious sound from me. A choked-off, dry laugh that no one would mistake for real amusement.

"What?"

"She's nothing like him." I braced the nail gun at a forty-five-degree angle, fingers curled back, the way I'd learned when I was twelve. *Whoosh-bam.* Such a satisfying, complete sound.

J.B. changed the subject, speaking in between the nail gun's reports. "So you've been kayaking a lot this summer?" *Whoosh-bam. Whoosh-bam.* "You're into that, right?"

I turned to him in surprise. He must have seen me on the water or asked around about me. Maybe both.

Casey moved as far from us as she could, pulling her orange extension cord taut and turning the sander up to High.

"I don't get on the lake as much as I should," he admitted. "Here, this one's good to go."

Whoosh-bam, whoosh-bam. "I could take you out sometime," I said.

"Definitely. I'd like that."

He stayed for dinner. The four of us sat on the dock and devoured the best of the Tupperware provisions. Cold fettuccine with ham and-peas, cold chicken croquettes, cold salmon cakes. The secret to my mother's heavy, old-fashioned food was eating it straight from the fridge after a full day of manual labor. Sitting next to a certain older boy with a wood shaving in his hair, an inch above his left ear, didn't hurt, either.

"Good day's work," my dad said when the Tupperwares were empty and the sun was an orange glow behind the mountains. He stood and rubbed his shoulders. "Well, I'm turning in, kids. See you bright and early tomorrow. We need all hands on deck."

Good-natured groans all around this time.

"Daddy. How long have you been waiting to say that?"

"Couple days." He winked and raised his hand in a salute as he walked down the dock.

"I love your dad," Casey said once he was inside. She stood up, flapping her sweaty tank top away from her stomach, then stretching as if she were every bit as achy as my sixty-six-year-old father. "I'd better go, too. If I wait too long my muscles are going to get so stiff I won't be able to swim home." She kicked off my blue Keds and dove in before I knew what was happening. When she bobbed up ten yards away, she called, "It feels fantastic, you two should cool off."

J.B. and I watched her cross the lake, efficient and graceful. Not looking one bit tired.

"It's a trippy little house," J.B. said, squinting at The Shipwreck. "Marbles and stuff hidden under floorboards, old initials carved everywhere. Ollie was worried somebody'd bulldoze it."

"You know about the Collier boys?"

"Sure. The famous Collier boys. There's an old newspaper photo of them, it's pretty cool. Ollie taped it to the register at the hardware store."

"The black-and-white one? My dad found that. He had a copy blown up for Casey and her mom, but it's a surprise so don't say anything."

"I don't think I'd have made a good Collier boy. Sounds like they were real hell-raisers. I spent my childhood watching *Star Trek* and taking the toaster apart."

"That's rebellious. In an indoor way."

He laughed. "Not if you put it back together every time."

"It's sad, though. A lot of those Colliers died young."

"Don't tell me you believe in that curse stuff?"

"No."

"They're probably retired in Florida. Bored and happy."

"That's what my dad thinks. This town does like to make up stories."

We were quiet for a long time, looking at the water. The heat was no longer brutal, but my shirt was still pasted to my back.

"So," he said. "You swim as well as her?"

"Not nearly. But I'd go in for a little."

"I can wait for you to get your suit."

"It's okay." I unlaced my tennis shoes and went down the ladder. I pushed off and floated on my back, tipping my chin up to soak my hair.

He hesitated, started to tug his shirt up, then left it on and jumped off the edge of the dock.

He emerged sputtering, his hair slicked back. "How are you not freezing?"

"I'm used to it. This is pretty warm, actually. It's *ice water* in June."

"You're lucky, living right on the water," he said, his voice strained from treading water.

"I know."

In one of Casey's books we'd have stripped down to nothing by now. We'd be clinging to each other, bare chests slick and heaving.

But it was exciting enough for me, hearing his splashes nearby in the almost-dark. It was plenty.

"So tell me what this Jelly Belly stuff is about," I said.

Water poured off his back as he climbed up the ladder and settled on the top step. He wrung out the hem of his T-shirt and ran his hands through his wet hair, staring across the lake intently.

"I was a heavy kid," he said. "When I started fifth grade, this was back in San Mateo, not here, I weighed 170 pounds and I was only five-two." He paused and glanced down at me. "Here's where you say, 'No way.'"

"Keep going." I swam up to him in a lazy sidestroke.

"I was unhappy. My parents had separated. I used to polish off a box of Little Debbie cakes on the way to school. In sixth grade we went on a field trip to the Jelly Belly candy factory, and there you go. Instant nickname."

I held on to the sides of the ladder, looking up at him.

He shrugged. "My initials really are J.B., so this kid Trad Whitaker thought he was being ultraclever."

"Trad? Not Tad? Trad?"

"Trad. I lost the weight after we came here. You're getting out?"

He moved off the ladder so I could climb up. We sat next to each other, our legs dangling off the dock. Casey or Alex had flipped the porch light on at their house. Soon my dad would flick ours on, too, and he'd realize that J.B.'s truck hadn't rumbled away. It was almost time for him to leave.

"I hate Trad Whitaker," I said. "What do your initials really stand for?"

His hand curled against my cheek in a pretend megaphone.

I froze, clasped my knees with my hands, as his lips hummed against my earlobe. "Julian Baker."

Did his mouth linger near my ear a second longer than necessary? It was so close to that tender, hidden spot under the corner of my jaw, the one his lips had discovered back in Deva Vance's basement. (In one of Casey's books I would shiver, and turn to him, and we would slide into a perfect kiss and I'd hear bottle rockets that would wake the Collier boys from the dead.)

But our porch light flicked on.

He pulled back and cleared his throat, speaking normally again. "Julian Archuleta-Nuñoz Flynn Baker."

Very little sleep that night. My fingers were too busy moving back and forth between my earlobe and jaw, and other places, and my mind was too busy imagining him, also awake, also imagining, over in Green Creek.

29

The Moon and Stars

Friday
High of 93

We'd pushed ourselves Thursday, despite the heat, and were now ahead of schedule. By two Casey and I were sprawled in the shade with our eyes closed, waiting for the first coat of sealant to dry, and J.B. and my dad were in the garage, working on a secret project with the leftover cedar.

"I like him," she said. "And he clearly likes you."

"He goes back to school Sunday morning."

I felt something ticklish on my nose and cheeks and opened my eyes.

Casey was sprinkling pine needles on my face. "Admit you're excited. Admit it."

I wiped a pine needle off my lip and tossed it at her, trying to hide my smile. "I admit it."

She lay on her side, her head resting on her arm. "This has been nice. Working outside."

"I know. I wish…"

"You wish your mom wasn't coming back so soon."

"I'm a rotten child."

"So am I. It's been good to have a break from my mom, too."

"You're fighting?"

"No. She's just off lately. You know how she got into that Wicca stuff last summer?"

"The stinky herbs, sure. Thought she got bored with it."

"Well, it's back. Now, it's like *extreme* witchery. Blood Magick, it's called. Magic with a *K*. She actually wanted to take my blood to do a 'binding spell' on me. To keep me safe at meets, keep the team bus from crashing."

"No way."

"Way. She laughed it off when I wouldn't do it, but I know she really wanted to. She has this blood-gathering pewter thingy, special-ordered from that store in Sacramento. Remember that place? Moonstruck?"

"Moonshadow."

"Moonshadow. So you put this silver thing over a syringe…"

"Ugh."

"Right. You and blood. Anyway, it's pretty out there even for her, right?"

"It's Alex. She told me she was worried about the bus."

"I guess. Anyway, I'm taking her to this spa in Reno Sunday. Thought it might get her to relax. You'll come?"

"You're a good daughter. I know how into facial masks and pedicures you are."

"Different kind of spa. Come. Watch her for me. Let me know what you think."

Saturday
High of 95
Project status: complete

After we finished Alex walked over for dinner. She was trying to act the adult, shaking hands with my father, who she'd met at school events. But Alex trying to be an adult was unsettling. If Casey hadn't said anything I would have assumed she was only keyed-up because she was around company, but there was something else. She did seem off, jittery.

When I introduced her to J.B. she said, fluttering her hands, "He looks familiar. Why does he look so familiar?"

"We met when I delivered your sawhorses for Pedersen's," he said.

"The sawhorses, of course. I still use them." She whirled to face the deck. "And this looks amazing. I'm impressed." She paced around, admiring.

"Have a seat in the shade, Alexandra," my dad said. "You, too, Red. I have a little something for you two. Nothing much." He pulled a flat brown package from under the table and set it on the picnic table.

"You got us a present?" Alex said. "You shouldn't have."

"Laur, know what it is?" Casey said.

"I do. You'll love it."

"Just tear into it, Mom."

Alex picked at the masking tape carefully, keeping the stiff brown paper intact as it slowly revealed the framed black-and-white photo.

Casey leaned close. "This. Is. Awesome."

"July 4, 1945." My dad pointed at the caption. "See the flags and bottle rockets? Sorry it's so grainy. Gal at the photo place did her best."

"It's the kids who used to sleep in your house, Alex," I said. "See the dock?"

She nodded.

Casey breathed out, "So cool. I'm surprised they didn't burn the dock down. Mom, look at this tiny barefoot guy with the pirate flag. He's my favorite. I wish we had a flag like that for the dock."

"I know some of these boys didn't meet a happy end, but thought you might like it just the same," my dad said.

"That's *why* I like it," Casey said. "They don't know they have the Collier curse."

"Small-town gossip," my dad said. "Plenty of boys around here died in the wars."

It really was a wonderful photo. The kids were in front, showing off their arsenal of homemade fireworks, and the adults were standing behind them, so the photographer had only captured their lower halves. The grown-ups existed merely as a backdrop of skirts, wide pants, a couple of martini glasses cradled in fingers. The boys' arms were blurry from movement, legs planted wide apart. Expressions daring the camera. Even the littlest one seemed bold—a boy no more than two, his honey-colored curls shining in the sun.

It seemed they might stride out of the photo and tell us a thing or two about how to have fun on their lake.

I'd been so sure Alex would go crazy over it, I got a little annoyed with her then. She still hadn't said a word. My dad had paid a lot of money to have it blown up and framed. He'd driven all the way to Tahoe City.

"Gal thought the frame would go with anything," he said, worried. "But let me know if you want to change it out."

Finally, Alex remembered her manners. "No, I love it. Thank you." She wiped her eyes, a swift upward flick of her pinky fingers.

Dinner was take-out chicken and potato salad and corn on the cob. A feast; I'd bought too much. The photo of the Colliers leaned against the trunk of the big pine by the picnic table, facing us as we ate.

"Join us, boys, there's plenty," my dad called, and everybody laughed.

Alex laughed a beat behind everyone else.

I continued to watch her closely, as I'd promised. But she was polite during dinner. Calmer. She asked J.B. about his summer jobs, how he liked grad school.

"Casey's going to UCLA, too," she said.

"Stop, Mom. I probably won't get in."

"You will," she said. "And Laura will have her pick of art schools in LA, you'll see."

Casey and I had a master plan. If I got into CalArts and she got into UCLA we'd live together.

Later Alex pulled me behind the shed and squeezed me, whispering something about the perfect first boyfriend, her eyes filling again.

"He's hardly a boyfriend," I whispered, wiping chocolate ice cream from her chin.

"Oh, he will be," she said.

"Are you okay? Casey's worried."

"I told her I'm fine. Tell her I'm fine."

"It'd be normal to freak out about her leaving for college next year, with her gone at the swim meet."

"I'm just getting used to you growing up. My sweet girls."

"We'll drive home all the time."

"Of course you will. So stop worrying. I'm fine."

"Promise?"

"Promise. Come on. Your boy's over there eating ice cream all by himself."

At eight my dad called out, "Another tiny surprise."

We followed him to the shed to see the secret project.

Two secret projects. Twin benches made from the leftover cedar. One for our house and one for Casey's. Casey's had a mermaid silhouette and waves cut into the back and mine had a half-moon and stars.

"For your hard work," he said. "Didn't want that good cedar to go to waste."

"Daddy," I said, hugging him. "You made these in two days?"

"Oh, they're nothing. Simple things. This young man's a fast worker."

"Thanks, J.B. I love them."

"I know where mine's going," Casey said. "In the shade by the garden gate. It'll be my reading bench. I'll sit there every chance I get, until I'm an old lady."

"I can bring it over tonight," J.B. said.

We were all admiring the benches, circling around. So I didn't notice right away. I turned only because I caught the expression on Casey's face.

Alex stood apart from the four of us. "They're just so beautiful," she said, her face distorted from crying.

"What was that?" J.B. said.

We were alone in his truck, rattling through the dark back to my house. Casey was spending the night and had oh-so-casually decided to keep my dad company while we dropped off Alex and the bench and photograph. Alex had carelessly shoved the photo of the Collier boys on the mantel next to her vase of dried lavender, so some of the kids were hidden by purple branches. But I'd repositioned it, carefully rearranging the stalks of lavender until the grinning, cocky boys could see the entire room without obstruction.

"Alex is always pretty high-strung. Up and down. She's freaking out about Casey going to college."

"Tough one. My mom hides it but I know she gets lonely. So you're looking at art schools in LA, huh?"

"That's the plan."

He grinned as he drove the short distance back to my house.

"Another question," he said, when we were idling in my driveway. "Will you be around over Thanksgiving break?"

"Definitely."

"Good."

"Well, good luck with school." I opened the car door.

"You, too. Good luck with senior year."

Before I could think about it, I leaned across the cab of the truck and kissed him. It was a fast, imperfect kiss; he was startled and I aimed too low, scraping my lower lip on stubble. I started to pull away, embarrassed, but he cupped his hand around the back of my head and said, "Hey."

"Hey."

"Can you do that again?"

I kissed him again, slower this time, a hand on his bare knee, my mouth open the slightest bit. His hand moved from my hair down to my neck, closing around the strap of my tank top and slipping it down, resting on my bare shoulder.

When I finally pulled away, and said, "I should get in," he laced his fingers in mine and said, his voice low, marveling, "I've wanted to do that for two years."

30

Doctor Mona's Hot Springs and Holistic Spa

Sunday

Casey, Alex, and I lay on our backs. Getting pummeled.

Casey had done a Netscape Navigator search to find Doctor Mona's Hot Springs and Holistic Spa in Reno. Eighteen dollars got you a relaxing deep-tissue massage, a detoxifying mud bath, a refreshing shower, and a soak in a mineral hot tub. We hadn't seen the fine print until we were in our robes signing liability forms on clipboards: *Staff may include trainees.*

"We don't have to go in, you guys," Casey said when we pulled up, taking in the green, barracks-like building. "This looks a little sketch."

"You planned our whole day, honey, of course we're going in," Alex said. "This is probably where the locals go. We don't need all that touristy wildflower and wind-chime stuff."

Now Alex, on my right, was letting out strange little whelps and gasps, trying to conceal them with conversation. "Oh, whoa, guess I was a little tense there." A minute later—"Eeohmy, you're strong for such a petite person."

I turned my head to watch. Alex, suppressing laughter, mouthed, *Help.*

I turned to face Casey. "Sorry," she whispered, giggling.

Even though my masseuse was pulling my arm so aggressively I worried she might dislocate my shoulder, I looked up at the mildewed ceiling tiles and smiled. It was so good to see them laughing again.

Alex tried to reassure Casey in the mineral bath. We sat on the edge in our scratchy white robes, soaking our feet next to a silent older lady.

"I feel so relaxed," Alex said. She sipped from her cone-shaped cup of lemon water.

"Mom. It's been a horror show. That mud bath nearly gave me third-degree burns."

"My neck actually feels *amazing*," Alex said. "I don't stretch when I paint. Honestly. My body hasn't felt this good in months."

"You shouldn't drink that water, Mom. Those lemons look like they've been there for a decade."

Casey was right about the brown lemon slices bobbing in the dispenser. I hadn't said anything, but I'd passed on a drink even though my tongue was sticking to the roof of my mouth from thirst.

Alex took a big, showy sip and clasped Casey's hand. "Let's come here every summer. Laura, don't you want to come back next summer?"

"Sure," I said, in such an artificially high tone that Casey laughed, and even Alex had to smile.

"Laura, you should see your skin, you're glowing!" Alex said. But the floodgates were open. She was giggling. Our tubmate gave us a sour look and decamped for the locker room.

Alex, trying to suppress her laughter, threw her cup at Casey.

"I know why Laura's glowing," Casey said, laughing, peel-ing the cone-shaped white paper cup into a strip and bouncing it like a spring.

"Don't start. He's probably already met someone else in LA."

"I saw the way he looked at you," Alex said. "He's sweet. And cute."

I tensed the same way I had on the massage table, anticipat-ing my masseuse-in-training's hands. We'd been having a per-fect day. Alex hadn't teared up once. I didn't want anything to spoil it. But Alex went on.

"...I wish Casey'd find somebody. Some nice boy like your J.B."

"I've gotta pee," Casey said, dropping her torn paper cup and scrambling out.

"Is she mad?" Alex asked, her eyes on the locker room en-trance. "Guess she doesn't want me teasing her like that, about dating. I should know better."

"Alex."

"What?"

"Nothing."

"Tell me. It's because I was teasing her about boys, right? I was being a typical mom?"

I picked up Casey's paper cup strip and studied the shiny wax coating on the inside.

When Casey returned she still wouldn't meet Alex's eyes. "I think that massage did something to my bladder. I've never had to pee so much. Ready to go?"

"Casey," Alex said. "I'll stop teasing you about boys. I didn't mean to be annoying."

"It doesn't matter, Mom."

"It does. Of course you should date on your own time. What's the rush?" She knotted her robe tighter and picked up her towel.

Tell her, I mouthed behind Alex's back. I moved to leave, standing up and cinching my own robe.

"No. Don't go, Laur. Mom?"

She was actually going to do it. Finally. Now. In front of me. Wearing a Doctor Mona–issue robe and towel turban, an arc of detoxifying mud in her right eyebrow. "Hey, Mom."

"Sure, we can go. Although I'm a little disappointed we didn't get to meet the actual Doctor Mona. Do you think she—"

"Mom, I don't like guys I like girls I've known since forever so there you go." Casey inhaled.

Alex looked from Casey to me. Back to Casey.

"Are you going to say anything?" Casey said.

I held myself as still as I could, hoping one of Doctor Mona's other patrons wouldn't choose this moment to troop in, disrobe, and plunge into the mineral bath.

"You're…?"

"Gay. Yes."

"Why didn't you tell me?"

"You never asked."

We were silent for a minute. Finally, Alex spoke. "I'm the worst parent in the world."

"No, you're not."

"Did you think I'd mind or act weird or…"

"No."

"Laura, you knew?"

I nodded, hoping Casey wouldn't volunteer that I'd figured it out on my own.

"It's okay, Mom. I'm not mad anymore. Laur sees me with kids at school all day. It's different."

Alex hugged her. Their robes were so big that for a second they seemed like a single creature made of white terry cloth.

Quietly, I padded away to the locker room.

We ate dinner at the Lucky Duck Casino. An all-you-can-eat $5.99 buffet, complete with a guy in a tall white hat sawing away at a roast.

"I don't know about this meat." Casey laughed, poking a hunk of wobbly pink beef with her fork. No matter what she'd said before, I knew it hadn't been okay, Alex not knowing. Because I'd never seen her so happy. "It looks kind of weird."

"It's prime rib," I said. "No, wait. The menu says *primo* rib."

We watched as Casey got up for more shrimp and waited in the buffet line behind a man with a walker. He had to scoot his plate down, push the walker, dish out his food, then repeat the process. But she was patient.

"I can't believe I didn't realize," Alex said quietly. "I'm furious with myself. Look at my sweet girl."

"Look how happy she is."

"I thought I was helping her, when those boys started hanging around on Saturday nights. I thought she'd love it. Because *I* would have loved it if my parents had… I'm screwing everything up."

"Alex. Do you have any idea how my mother would've reacted if I'd told her what Casey just told you? She'd kick me out of the house. I'd be living with you."

"You'd be welcome to." She smiled, wiped her eyes. "But you don't know that. You're much too hard on her. And too easy on me." She paused before going on, her forehead scrunched, and I knew what she was going to ask. "Laura. Have you and Casey ever…"

"Never," I said, laughing. "There's never been anything remotely like that between us. We've joked about it, how it would feel completely wrong. We're just friends."

"I was only wondering."

Casey was now dishing out green beans for walker man.

"Are the kids being jerks about it?" Alex said, her eyes crinkled in worry.

Were they? Casey didn't go around scattering rainbows, but she'd decided after a lot of thought not to hide who she was, either.

One Friday in January Kirk Elfinger had muttered "dyke" as he walked past our cafeteria table. At first I'd been mute and useless, frozen in shock, my turkey sandwich halfway to my mouth.

Casey had thrown her Coke at Kirk's feet, told him to fuck himself.

Only when soda was fizzing on Kirk's high-tops had I stood, hands shaking, and said the first thing I could think of, my voice thin and strained, "Elf weiner!"

We laughed about the Kirk Elfinger incident now—mostly about my absurd, impulsive insult.

I could tell Alex about the Kirk Elfinger day, but then she would feel even worse. And it wasn't my story to share. "Most of them are okay," I said. "Unless Casey's hiding things from me."

"Like she did with me." Alex shook her head in disbelief. "She couldn't be herself with me. I've made so many mistakes, wasted so much time."

"What are you talking about? You two have all the time in the world."

She faced me with an expression I didn't understand at the time, but would never forget. It was a kind look, full of pity. Because I truly believed what I'd said. I was seventeen.

31

Early morning, 42nd day of camp
The night after meeting Daniel

She lay in her top bunk licking icing and pasty cinnamon filling from her fingers. Not even trying to salvage half an hour of sleep before the lights snapped on. She'd be exhausted by lunchtime.

She guessed that across the room, Alexandra had already slipped into unconsciousness, relaxing into sleep after their overnight field trip as effortlessly as she told her lies.

Alexandra. She hadn't gotten the chance to ask her why she'd invented Sandy.

But she thought she knew.

Another name meant it wasn't really Alexandra who'd been dumped at a camp with no visiting day. It wasn't Alexandra who had to endure Miss Veach reading Revelation for an hour, pounding the podium, her voice hoarse with rage: Those who practice magic arts, the idolaters and liars, the sexually deviant—they will be consigned to the lake of burning sulfur! Who had to raise her hand at the stage-whispered finale, instead of laughing at how ridiculous it all sounded: Can you smell that sulfur?

Yes, she could understand it.

But Alexandra would go back to a home like Three Pines. The rules and the shame pressing her down, keeping her small. No boys, no radio. Acting a part, sneaking over to the cable car turnaround to see the strange, older Daniel, flipping off her life in the dark.

Not her. One more week, and she and her mom would be home. Together. Her mom would apologize for signing her up for this weird place, and laugh at how boring her adult retreat had been. They'd trade stories, make up for lost time. Blast their stereo so loud their upstairs neighbor, Mrs. Crawley, would stomp on the floor, and her mom would turn it down a little but give the ceiling the finger right in front of her.

They'd keep playing music until it erased every minute of this summer.

One week later
Last day of camp

She was the first one in the parking lot on pickup day.

When the white Pontiac pulled in she didn't give her mom a chance to park. She knocked on the trunk until it popped, threw her sleeping bag and duffel in, slammed the lid, and heaved herself into the passenger seat.

"Honey I have to sign you out, and don't you want me to meet your new friends, I—"

"Just drive, Mom. Let's just get the hell out of here." She laughed, giddy. Goodbye, Three Pines. It's been real.

Her mother's fingers tightened on the wheel. She didn't laugh. "Don't speak like that, Katherine."

And she knew everything had changed.

32

Another Tiny Surprise

2016
Saturday, 3:00 p.m.

Items 6 and 7 shared a clue:

> Twins, these are
> A pretty pair
> Welcoming one or two to sit
> One like the water and one like the air
> Time has weathered them but there's much they share

We sat in the sun on Casey's mermaid bench, just inside the garden gate.

"She's not going to put Yeats out of business, is she?" Casey asked, her knees up inside the oversized Dreaming Shepherd T-shirt she'd thrown over her bathing suit after Jade Cove. "And did she have to imply *we're* weathered?"

"The garden looks pretty," I said. The old fence was nearly hidden in greenery now, the rusty gate spray-painted white. The puny starter flowers that Alex had planted the year she and Casey moved in were now higher than our heads. Raised wood beds held vegetables, fairy furniture tucked among the stalks. "Where's Alex's witchy section?"

Casey smiled. "She lost interest. Now we have swiss chard instead of colt's foot. Snap peas instead of valerian. Though the growing season sucks at this elevation."

I ran my hand along the arched back of Casey's bench. She'd taken care of it over the years, stored it inside for the winter, protected the wood. It was cracking a little, and grayer now, but still beautiful.

Casey pulled her legs out of her T-shirt tent and we took a selfie. She shook the picture to help it develop, hopping off the bench and nodding her head toward the lake. "Now yours."

I didn't move. I was back in high school, that last unspoiled summer. I touched the rough old wood of Casey's bench, ran my hand inside the mermaid and wave cutouts. My dad had carved it himself, with the router.

The wind had played with a tuft of his white hair as he unveiled the benches, one for me, one for Casey. He'd twitched his eye at Casey in a wink. I'd been so happy that my two favorite people in the world liked each other so much.

Years after I left home for good, I'd regretted leaving my bench behind. But by then I was afraid to see it. I was sure it would be a wreck, the wood warped, the slats broken. Abandoned.

Casey turned, took one look at my face, and sat down again. "You okay?"

"I'm fine. Sorry."

"Don't be. It's too much."

"When I read seven on the list I was *fine*. I knew I was going over there today. I was planning to check in on the place." I grabbed my shirttail and wiped my nose on periwinkle silk.

"Let's save your bench for later. We'll skip to number eight."

"I can handle it." I brushed at the tear that had escaped below my sunglasses. "I'll wash my face and we'll go." I stood.

She shook her head. "Seven's on hold. Let's do eight first. I haven't been to Reno in years."

Casey said she was tired and wanted to rest up for the drive to Reno, though I guessed she knew I wanted to be alone.

While she slept I swam near the dock, not minding the cold this time. I bathed my eyes in lake water as I swam far out, daring Jet Skiers to cross my path, but I didn't see any. Only a single yellow kayak in the distance, crossing the north point of the lake.

I watched its progress with a pang. My old kayak had been stolen years before, when somebody broke into the shed. I was informed via a curt email: Kayak and inner tubes stolen. I'd written a fat check for new ones and a top-of-the-line digital lock for the shed. But maybe the kind of people who rented our house these days preferred Jet Skis.

After I lazed on the warm dock, throwing tennis balls for Jett, Elle's brilliant orange-and-purple beach towel wrapped around my lower half. Jett eventually got tired and stretched out next to me in the sun, but every five minutes she stood and shimmied to dry herself, spraying me with water and making every hair on her body stand on end. I sprawled on my back with my eyes shut, talking in the goofy, love-drenched voice I used when we were alone. "You crazy girl, Jetty, now I'm soaked."

"Great dog."

And every hair on my body stood on end. I scrambled to sit up, my legs jackknifed awkwardly under me, as J.B. walked to my end of the dock.

"Sorry," he said, staring down at the wood near my feet, clearly wondering if he should sit, or kneel, or offer to pull me up. He settled for taking off his sunglasses and stuffing them carelessly in his back shorts pocket. "I'm always creeping up on you. It's not intentional, I swear."

"It's fine."

"Where's Casey?" He scanned the lake, squinting against the shining water, hand still fidgeting in his back pocket.

"Napping. We're driving to Reno later. Clue 8."

"Seven down? Impressive." He crouched to scratch Jett's ears.

"We're skipping around a little," I said. "You can report that to Alex."

"What makes you think I'm spying for her?"

"Please." I met his eyes.

He feigned innocence at first, his forehead crinkled as if the accusation was absurd, but he gave in fast, sighing. "Okay. Okay, I told her I'd check on you. So I can say it's going well?"

"No major explosions."

"But…" He stopped himself, biting his upper lip, stretching out the tiny ski slope of flesh above it. I'd learned in a portrait class that this part of the body, the gentle groove between the nose and the center of the upper lip, was called a *philtrum*. (J.B. had a particularly sensitive philtrum, as I recalled, especially when he was freshly shaven. Nice to touch with the pad of a finger, nice to brush with lips or tongue…)

He shook his head. "Never mind."

"What? Say it."

"Maybe explosions are better than running away."

I stared at Jett's silver license medallion shining in the sun. I would not cry in front of him.

When I didn't answer he said, "Sorry. Jesus. Don't know where that came from."

I took a long, controlled breath to try to steady my voice. "Yes, you do. You're mad I left."

He looked off to the center of the lake, where there was a slight chop, frosting the waves in white.

"So," I said. "Casey says you're some kind of family recreation mogul?"

He waved this off. "Dumb luck. My first job out of school was with this robotics start-up that went public. I made some money to invest. I wanted to be near my mom, she's had some bone trouble, from the chemo."

"Is she—"

"She's better now. Thanks. Anyway, they were going to demolish the rink so I got it cheap. The economy took off, people decided this was a happening vacation spot." He hitched his chin, indicating the lake. "One thing led to another."

"Do you like the work?"

"Occasionally." He fished a business card from his pocket and offered it to me.

I studied it politely. *Baker Recreational Properties.* "Do you still tinker?"

"On weekends. You still draw?"

"On weekends."

"You have your own business, too, right?" he said.

I remembered this about J.B., how he asked questions, how he didn't interrupt. I hadn't realized how rare it was until I was an adult. Most men I'd gone on dates with used questions only as a kind of conversational tennis backboard, to return the topic to themselves.

"I'm in graphic design, mainly local companies."

"I'd like to see your stuff," he said. "Will you show me sometime? Pull pictures up online?"

"Sure."

He nodded gravely, all business. *Let's have our admins set that up.* Then a small, self-deprecating smile broke the taut planes of his face and he ran both hands through his hair. "I'm full of shit. I've seen your work on your website."

I nodded, trying not to show how much this pleased me. Not Googling J.B. was one of the most impressive achievements in my thirty-five years on the planet. A superhuman act of willpower.

"You're good," he said. "Your head shot's good, too. Though you look better in person."

"Please, I don't…" *That thing some women do.* I adjusted the child's towel I was using as a sarong, securing the waist so there was no chance it would slip. I forced myself to stop, look him in the eyes. "Thanks. You look good, too."

He raised his eyebrows and grinned, patted under his untucked blue button-down. I caught a flash of brown stomach and glanced away. "A little jelly creeping back in there," he said.

"That's Trad Whitaker talking."

"You remember his name."

I concentrated on extricating a soggy leaf from Jett's paw.

"So you've been all right?" he said. "Happy?"

"I like my work, and I have this wild girl here, and a nice place in the city. I bought it seven years ago."

"Friends?"

"A few."

"But no family."

"I see my mother once a week."

"You know what I mean. Marriage, kids, all that."

"No. No marriage, no kids, no all that."

Casey would come out soon. Or he'd leave. "J.B., tell me. Please. Why did Alex do this now? Casey knows, but she won't tell me."

He glanced over his shoulder at the house, started to speak then stopped.

"What?" I said.

"I can't say."

"But you know."

He hesitated. "Try to talk to Casey." He gave Jett a soft pat on her head and stood. "Don't gamble away your business in Reno."

He walked back down the dock toward Casey's house. When he stepped onto the lawn he turned. "It's a good thing, you coming back."

33

Biggest Little City in the World

Saturday evening

Clue 8

Hands and dirt and water for sale
Physician, beautician…fake?
Days that don't turn out as planned
Are the days our hearts awake
Take a cone from the stack to prove you went back ☺

The for-sale sign was huge. "18,000 square feet, Broder &
Wakefield Commercial Realtors."

"Well, damn," Casey said. "I wanted some brown lemon water."

"Poor Doctor Mona."

We had dinner in Reno, settling on a place called International
Odyssey. The menu was the helpful type, with pictures of the

food. "Substitution's allowed!!!" The walls were painted in a wild mélange of scenes from different countries: a bullfight next to a pagoda, a man in a striped shirt holding a baguette in his underarm next to a camel.

"What do you think, as an artist?" Casey said. "Personally I think it rules."

"I'm not really an artist."

"As a design professional, then."

"I agree. It rules." I held up a napkin with a "Flags of the World" design. "This can substitute for the cup from the spa." I dropped it into the goody bag. "Substitutions allowed!" I said in a perky commercial voice.

"Cheers." Casey raised her plastic cup of red wine.

"Cheers."

"So, how many of these countries have you visited?" I said.

"A few."

"France?"

"Yep. With my mom, 2004."

"Italy?"

"Same trip."

"Thailand?"

"2008."

"I'm impressed."

"Also, Kenya, Namibia, Australia, New Zealand, the Cook Islands. Arctic Circle."

"Alex went with you on all of those?"

"Some were with a girlfriend. Ex-girlfriend."

"That must've been serious. What's her name?"

"Delia. She's in Sacramento, we still hang out. We're still friends, blah blah blah. And, oh, yeah, my mom and I took Elle to Machu Picchu last year."

Here I was, thinking I was the one who'd gotten away and Casey'd been stranded on the tiny almost-island of Coeur-de-Lune.

"I'm jealous," I said. "You've been everywhere. I can't imagine spending even one night in a hotel room with my mother."

"So you two. It hasn't gotten better?"

Our food arrived. Chicken teriyaki for me, fettuccine for Casey. I shrugged, poking at the syrupy meat and gray-green broccoli. "We'll never have what you and Alex have. I've accepted it. She didn't have an easy time of it, growing up."

"Neither did my mom, but she and I make it work. Most days."

"That's true."

Casey set her fork down. "But what do you mean, she didn't have an easy time?"

"Kids played tricks on her."

"Such as?"

I hesitated. "The worst thing I know of has to do with your house. It's a sad story, are you sure you want to hear it?"

"If you feel like telling me." Casey wiped her mouth with her napkin, leaning forward.

My mother had shared the memory a few years back when she was recovering from hip surgery at UCSF. A story she'd never told anyone, not even my dad.

About a summer day when she was young, when she thought the boys across the lake were going to let her play with them at last. There were eight of them, brothers and cousins. But it seemed like there were dozens; like they ruled the town. One afternoon thirteen-year-old Ingrid was invited over and made to sit on a bottom bunk, with blankets hanging from the top so it was like a cave.

A test, to join their club. She had to reach out and touch things, guess what they were. Something prickly: a pinecone. Something delicate: moss.

One thing was soft, warm. She caressed it, trying to be brave so she could join their club. Then she heard one of them say what it was, snickering. She knew the word from school. She started crying and they showed it to her, laughing: only a peeled hard-boiled egg.

You have a dirty mind, Ingrid, they called as she ran. *Stupid girl,* the youngest boy yelled, echoing the others.

A boy no more than five, my mother had whispered in her hospital bed, shaking her head.

"Little bastards," Casey said. "And everyone in town worshipped them. The idea of them."

"I wish she'd told me before. But still. Me and my mother, we never would've been best friends."

"She shared that story. That must mean something."

"She was on opioids at the time."

"Oh." Casey laughed.

"Anyway. We were talking about travel. I've only seen England and Mexico and Canada. I'd like to travel more." I wanted to say, *Maybe we could go on a trip together sometime?* But I stopped myself. We hadn't talked about what would happen after Sunday. I was oversharing after my glass and a half of wine. *Soggy heart.* I'd read that on some blog. The not-so-technical name for when you get tipsy and accidentally tell the truth.

A waitress led a pack of seniors to the table next to us. I scooted my chair to make room for a woman in a lemon yellow pantsuit to push her walker.

"Excuse me, dears," she said. She wanted to park the walker against the wall and Casey was in the way. But Casey was lost in thought, staring vacantly at the woman.

"Excuse me," the woman repeated sweetly.

Casey came back to earth, belatedly scooching her chair and draining her wineglass. "Ready to go?"

On our way to the car we passed a bar called Wally's. I calculated. One more drink in Casey's tiny body and she wouldn't be able to drive for hours. "I can't drive your car, Case. I never learned stick."

"We'll go for coffee after." She tugged me inside.

The bar offered something called Wally's Wall O' Daqs.

Twenty feet of daiquiri machines lined up behind the bar like the Slurpee dispensers in 7-Eleven. All colors of the rainbow. Melon Madness and Peach Pleasure and Blue Lagoon and Call-a-Cab.

Call a cab was what we'd have to do if Casey kept this up. Her mood had changed so suddenly, from light to serious and back again. But then mine had, too, all weekend. One minute I felt giddy as a teenager and the next, thinking of the time that had passed, how much we'd lost, it hurt so much I couldn't breathe. If Casey was in a Wall O' Daqs mood she was entitled.

She ordered Banana Bliss and I ordered Peach Pleasure and we toasted. I ran through possibilities in my head. Something serious, something sincere. *To friendship. To Ariel and Pocahontas. To being older and wiser.*

"To…Doctor Mona," she said.

9:00 p.m.

Casey ordered Wally's twenty-dollar signature drink, The Yardstick. A narrow, three-foot-long plastic cup like a giant test tube with a built-in straw. You could get a dozen daq flavors in there.

I wanted to have a private word with the bartender, ask him to secretly virginize it, but couldn't catch his eye.

10:00 p.m.
The Klondike Kate Casino

Casey was parked in front of a slot machine called Mythic Mermaid, sipping a free 7&7.

"Ten more minutes, Case. Then coffee."

"I just got the Splish-Splash bonus."

"What's that?"

"No idea but I think it's good."

A woman came by selling ninety-nine-cent white gloves to

protect against slot machine blisters. Casey bought one for each of us and settled in.

Maybe we could crash in a hotel.

10:30 p.m.

Casey decided Mythic Mermaid wasn't good luck after all. "Too obvious," she said.

We switched to the machines called Cougar-licious. Symbols spun around: the hourglass shape of an older blonde woman—the cougar, presumably. Gold car keys, cougar paws, credit cards, a boy with slick black hair like a young Kyle MacLachlan. I tried to make the game last. I'd already blown forty dollars. But Casey looked like a pro, pulling the arm incessantly with her white-gloved hand.

"There's a button, Case."

"It's better luck to do it this way. I deserve some good luck, don't I?"

"Of course you do."

She lifted her left hand and exercised it, splaying her fingers and clenching her fist, but maintaining her steady action with the right hand.

"Is your carpal tunnel really bad? Maybe we should take a break."

"Carpal tunnel's such a weird name. It sounds like carpool tunnel." She laughed. "They should call it accidental loss of strength. I have accidental strength of loss in my left hand. I mean loss of strength. Luckily it's not my slot-machine hand." When she stopped laughing she tilted her head, studying me. "Can I try something?"

"I don't know. You're being a little weird."

She reached behind my head with her ungloved hand, tugging at the pins securing my hair in its updo.

"Ouch, what are you—"

"I've been wanting to do that since Thursday. And take off that priss cape, too."

"Priss cape?"

She yanked at the sweater draped over my shoulders.

I tied my sweater around my waist and smoothed my hair, smiling at Casey's efforts to loosen up my style. I was contemplating feeding my last twenty dollars into the machine when bells started dinging on Casey's. I leaned over her shoulder: a horizontal line of four cougar paws and a red bra. A $282 payout.

Then we were both jumping. Jumping and laughing as the little siren on top blared and *ding ding ding* and quarters poured out so fast we couldn't keep up.

While Casey spent some of her winnings in a twenty-four-hour gift shop I called J.B. from within a rack of crinkly stretch dresses. I punched the numbers from his business card, fingers clumsy after two cocktails.

"Hello?" His voice was thick with sleep.

"It's Laura," I whispered. "Sorry, were you sleeping?"

"Not at all." Throat clearing, mattress bounces, the unmistakable swish of someone propping pillows behind his back. "Why are you whispering?"

"We're in Reno and I can't drive Casey's car because it's a stick, and she's pretty drunk. I hate to ask but—"

"I'll get there as fast as I can. Where are you?"

Midnight

When J.B. walked into the Klondike Kate Casino he found us wearing single white gloves, Michael Jackson–style, and giant new T-shirts over our clothes. Casey's said, What Happens in Area 51 Stays in Area 51 and mine said, I Was Addicted to the Hokey Pokey Then I Turned Myself Around.

We guided Casey out to his truck, settling her onto the bench seat in the back and clipping her seat belt. She conked out almost immediately, curled across the seats.

"Is she okay?" I whispered. "I've never seen her drink like that."

"She just needed to blow off some steam."

J.B. carried Casey to her bed and I tucked her in.

"I owe you," I said, walking him to his truck.

"Pay me back by wearing that shirt to the rink sometime. We'll put a spotlight on you and you can do a solo Hokey Pokey."

"I don't owe you that much."

"Well."

"Well. Good night." It felt so normal. So simple. J.B., me, porch light, moonlight, the gentle wind off the lake sighing through the pine branches, making them shiver. Making me shiver.

He kissed me on the cheek, tugged my T-shirt sleeve like a pal. "Well," he repeated.

I started to return his cheek kiss. But one of us moved at the last second—maybe we both did—and our lips met.

Then he was picking me up, and I don't know how we covered the distance, or who managed to open the door, but instantly we were inside the cab of his truck, and someone found the fancy motorized gadget that reclined the seat. We stopped kissing only long enough so he could remove my Hokey Pokey T-shirt, both of us laughing to find another layer under it.

"You. You," he said, his lips humming against my neck, his hands running up and down my sides.

There was a second when surprise dawned on his face, that this might be enough for me, me on top of him pressing close, tiny movements and just the right angles, the perfect pressure through the sweetly frustrating obstruction of our clothes. I held my breath, not laughing now. I closed my eyes, it was so perfect, and at the last second, when the warm rush was inevitable, I had one clear, unbidden thought that tipped me over the edge: *See what you missed.*

★ ★ ★

"Well," he said, one hand playing with my hair, one still clamped on my hip. "That was… You really…"

"Hmm."

"Multiple layers of clothing, confined space. Quite a feat. I'm proud of us."

"There's a word for it," I said, pushing myself up on his chest. "Two words."

"What are they? I'm not familiar with them." He widened his eyes, all innocence.

"Of course you are."

"Nope."

"Dry hu—"

"Don't." He laughed, clapping a hand over my mouth.

Playful, on a cloud, still thinking this was the beginning of something.

"Don't say the ugly words," he said. "The name does not do it justice. I'm a big fan of what we just did."

I looked into his eyes, as gentle as they had been in high school, after we first slept together, and I slid off that cloud. This wasn't high school.

I pushed his hand away from my mouth. "The name's accurate. And I should get in." I disentangled our limbs, scrambled off of him to the passenger seat.

"Why are you… I know you're…"

"You know I'm what? I'm exhausted."

"I know you're scared."

"I'm not. This was fun but it's been a long day."

"Fun."

"Yes. Fun."

He sighed, staring out the windshield at the dark hulk of the house. "Come to my place. I have an actual bed, and a shower, and a big kitchen." He faced me, touched my knee. "I'll make us breakfast. French toast, omelets. The works."

"Not now."

"I hope that means not yet."

"I'd better get in."

We stood on the porch, watching a moth batting at the lamp over the front door.

"Careful, little girl," I said, as the wispy creature floated close to the glowing yellow bulb over and over, making it buzz and tick. "You'll get zapped."

"She's fine. You've been in the city too long."

"I'd better check on Casey and try to get some sleep. We have to drive to the city tomorrow."

"I could drive you. You two could nap in the truck."

"No. Thanks, though."

He leaned close. "It's all right," he whispered.

He kissed me on the cheek, tenderly, near the corner of my mouth. Another centimeter to the left and we'd be at it again as if nothing else mattered, pretending it was 1999, drawn back into the cab of his truck by some rip in the space-time continuum.

I pulled away. He brushed my hand with his fingertips, but I wouldn't look at him.

This was a cheap moment in a truck. This doesn't mean anything. This doesn't hurt at all.

34

Rainbow of Glass

Sunday morning

The chirps of a text woke me at nine thirty:

Hey you

Three dots boogied on my screen, then disappeared as J.B. composed another message, deleted it. Finally, he settled on:

When do you need me to drive you to the city?

First I typed, It was a mistake. Please forget it happened. I deleted that, deciding to ignore what we'd done in the truck: Casey sleeping. Don't worry about it.

Him: I'll see you in a little bit. No expectations, promise.

Three dots again.

Then: I lied. I'd love to take you on a real date once you recover from your weekend. Just consider it, L.

I closed my eyes.

If only it was as simple as it'd felt in J.B.'s truck. In daylight it was clear; what happened had been a onetime thing—the result of a lethal cocktail of selective déjà vu and lust.

It—J.B., me—was impossible.

You still there?

It angered me that he'd pretend otherwise.

Casey slept until nine thirty. She padded down the dock in sunglasses, draining a tall glass of water, still in her rumpled Reno ensemble.

"How goes the battle?" I said.

"Remind me never to do that again."

"You won $282."

"And you let me blow it on this?" She yanked the hem of her Area 51 shirt. "Do I remember correctly? My car's parked at some random restaurant in Reno?"

"I have the address," I said and then paused. "So J.B. offered to drive us to the city for Clue 10. But I'll take us, I'd rather—"

"He called me and I told him absolutely. Though I'm sure it'll be a total *chore* for him to sit in a small confined space with you."

"Casey, please don't." My voice came out sharper than I intended. I sighed. "It's nice of him to drive us. It's been good to catch up."

"Think you could date him?"

"No."

"You're still crazy about each other," she said. "That hasn't changed."

"It's complicated."

"Got it." Casey's tone was final, accepting that it was the end of the discussion. But she bit her lip and tilted her head, so I'd know she didn't accept my vague excuse. "So what's the clue before the San Francisco one? You said it's in town?"

"Rainbow of glass."

"My head's pounding too much to figure out my mom's cutesy verses."

I knew Clue 9 by heart now:

A rainbow of glass and a song
Double creatures trapped in a hall
Here you stayed caged so long
Then, suddenly, climbed over the wall
In your photo you'll capture it all

"Rainbow of glass is the stained-glass window," I explained. "Creatures trapped in the hall is the Noah's ark mural outside the Sunday school room. She must've remembered from that Christmas service."

"Your church."

"Not my church."

We walked toward town along East Shoreline. When we passed my old street Casey paused. "We're right here, do you feel like—"

I shook my head. "Later."

Tactfully, Casey didn't say another word about Clue 7, my bench.

I pulled the clue sheet from my back pocket. Friday it had been white as the fresh powder up at Sugar Bowl. Now it was a raggedy, stained thing. It had been crumpled up, dampened, torn in one corner. Pierced by dog teeth, folded and refolded. "I guess we can take a picture outside the church if late service is still going."

"It'll be over. There's only one now."

"You know the schedule?"

"I took Elle once."

"You're kidding."

"She'd been begging for months. 'What do they do there? The stained glass is so pretty.'"

"But you're an atheist, aren't you?"

"I didn't want her to be one of those teenagers who joins a cult because they were deprived of religion as children."

"So how'd it go?"

"She was bored out of her mind. Hasn't asked since. But I kind of liked it. I loved the music."

"That's how they get you."

She didn't say anything.

"Sorry. I sound bitter."

"A tad."

The steeply pitched white roof came into view. So elegant, so proud. I could see why Elle would want to peek inside. There were still worshippers chatting in the parking lot, scrubbed and dressed-up and happy. Purified after their hour in the pews.

I was painfully aware of Casey's rumpled T-shirt and cut-offs, my exposed shoulders in my black racerback dress. It was a packable "travel" dress that rolled down to nothing in my suitcase. Minimalist and classy—but now I felt nude. Sinfully cardiganless.

"Good morning." A young blond minister on the steps shook our hands, smiling, not giving our outfits a second glance. "Welcome."

"Mind if we look around?" Casey said.

"Not at all."

Casey tapped a rainbow sticker on the propped-open door. "That's how they get you," she whispered.

We wandered into the sanctuary. Sunlight filtered through the stained-glass window, painting the aisle in yellow and blue and red. Casey positioned herself inside the light, so she was tat-

tooed in shifting diamonds of color. "Better than disco night at
the rink," she said, laughing.

I brushed past her quickly and sank into a pew, out of reach
of the stained-glass colors.

She sat next to me, craning her neck to look up at the old
wood rafters. "Another way they get you?" She squeezed my
hand, and I welcomed the soft, reassuring pressure, recognizing
it as an apology for teasing me. I had not thought this building
could still affect me.

"It smells the same," I said. "Exactly the same. Perfume. Candles. Paste from Sunday school." We were in the tenth row from
the pulpit. Farther back than where I'd sat with my family for
sermons, but the same distance from the front I'd favored in
college lectures. (Close enough to see the projector, far enough
away to duck out early if I wanted.)

Women's Studies 201. Sophomore year. Dr. Alice Palmer. A
slender, graying professor who wore chunky-knit scarves in all
Savannah's heats and humidities: *Modern religion is an institution
created by men to police women's sexuality. Discuss.*

Oh, the hands that had shot up that day. Not mine, though.
I'd kept my own hands, twisting and fidgeting, in my lap, too
overcome by the bell-like simplicity of the professor's statement,
too angry at how long the world had waited to articulate it to
me clearly, to speak. By the end of the fifty-minute class my
palms were wet.

"You want to take this one?" Casey offered the camera.

"You do it."

She took a quick shot of our faces.

I flipped through a hymnbook as she shook the picture. The
books were new. Black, with modern illustrations. Easier to read
than the old red, gilt-edged ones, but not as pretty. "How'd it
turn out?"

"I look hungover and you look pissed." She handed me the
picture.

I smiled because she was right. We had the makings of one painfully honest photo album.

Casey started working her left hand again, making it into a starfish, then a fist, over and over.

And I knew. I let myself know.

I touched her thumb. "What is this?" I said softly. "And don't tell me it's carpal tunnel."

"No. It's not carpal tunnel."

"Parkinson's."

She shook her head, examining her hand as if it didn't belong to her. "ALS. Amyotrophic lateral sclerosis. What they used to call Lou Gehrig's."

"Accidental loss of strength," I whispered.

She looked up. "What?"

"You said that last night."

"Did I? That's not bad. I should have Elle call it that. Amyotrophic lateral sclerosis is hard for her to pronounce."

A man in my mother's building had ALS. Walkers, wheelchairs, the gradual loss of every muscle, even though the mind was fine. It was the cruelest disease.

"Laur, don't cry. Not yet. Later, we'll cry."

All I could see was Casey swimming like a mermaid, skating like a little kid. I'd just gotten her back.

"When did you…" I could barely mutter the words.

"Four months ago."

"And what's your…"

"You can say it. *How long do you have?*"

"There's research now, money. That ice-bucket thing. And Stephen Hawking, he's had it for ages, right? Maybe…"

She laughed. Actually laughed. "Everyone says that about the ice buckets and Stephen Hawking. But there's no cure yet. And Hawking's an outlier. Nobody understands how he keeps going."

"Still, that means there's hope, there must be—"

"It's moving slowly for me. I might have five or six years. Depends on what I'm willing to live with. I might have 'til Elle's twenty-one, if I'm lucky."

"How is she? You said she knows."

"She knows the basics. It's the worst part. She'll have my mom. But…"

"I'll help. I'll…" But who was I? Someone who'd walked out on her friendship nearly two decades before. Who'd never even met her little girl.

"You being back is pretty nice," she said softly. "Sitting here. I'll take that for now."

When I trusted myself to look at her I found her eyes swimming and had to look down. I concentrated on her small sunburnt hand in mine.

35

She had another name now. Just like Alexandra became Sandy, clutching her gold bible like a shield so they couldn't take all of her, Katherine became Kate. That's what she wrote on her name tags.

Her mother had made new friends at her church retreat. Lolly was out. Lolly wasn't really saved, her mother had said. She thought she was but she wasn't, like most people, even most people at the church.

The two of them joined a new church, one formed by her mother's retreat friends. True believers. Her mother said she'd never seen so clearly before.

For months Katherine reasoned, pleaded, cried, shook her mother's shoulders in a useless attempt to rattle the blankness from her eyes.

Then Katherine retreated to some small fortress within herself.

Now it was Kate who prayed for eight hours on Saturday and ten hours on Sunday, who didn't complain as she shivered in the industrial building in Daly City that Reverend Brockwood had leased to hold his swelling congregation.

The warehouse had once been used to pack chowder and still held a lingering cologne of dead fish. Katherine would have giggled and poked her mother, crinkled her nose when Reverend Brockwood preached about Fishers of Men. And Katherine's mother, wherever she had gone, would have giggled, too, whispered, Let's get the hell out of here. But this meek, obedient woman was not Katherine's mother.

It was Kate who surrendered her old clothes, even her favorite embroidered cutoffs and the sheer, vanilla-colored blouse they'd bought at the mall only last March, the blouse her mom once said made her look like a medieval princess. Kate who accepted her new costume of long skirt and high-necked shirt.

March seemed like so long ago now. Their lives before seemed made-up, a dream. Had her mother been unhappy with their old life, but hidden it all along? She must have been, to want to replace it with this life just because she was fried.

Her word. Her excuse for going to Three Pines, spending summer apart. She was fried from her job, her life, and had needed a change. A rest. That's how they'd been trapped in this new life.

Fried. A silly-sounding expression until you thought about it.

Now, it scared her. Her mother's old personality had been burned up. Like it wasn't beautiful.

Her wild, somewhat whooping laughter, and her ideas about how to parent, like the time they'd both called in sick and gone to the Redwoods instead of school and work. Mental health days, her mother called these outings.

The way her mother had always tickled her. Even the way she'd sobbed quietly under her covers after her last boyfriend had split, served Campbell's tomato soup for five dinners in a row, her red-rimmed eyes caked with too much orangey-pink Erase concealer, but still not concealed. She would have preferred even the sad days, like the tea day, to this blankness. The terrifying evenness of her voice.

Her mother hadn't been fried before like she'd said: They had fried her over the summer, while Katherine was just down the road. They had cooked her circuits. Rewired her.

But Katherine wouldn't let herself be fried like her mother; she had Kate to protect her.

Kate let them dunk her in a plastic wading pool while they sang and cried and raised their palms to the metal roof. And Kate stopped herself from running, screaming, through the phalanx of worshippers in their metal folding chairs after she emerged, dripping and sputtering, and saw her mother's blue eyes streaming with joy, her face as wet as her own.

Kate kept Katherine alive.

And Alexandra kept her sane.

Alexandra rolled her eyes from across the room whenever fat Reverend Brockwood beat his podium. If they managed to sit together, Alexandra found secret ways to entertain her. She passed her notes, rolled like tiny cigarettes, that said Scavenger Hunt! She listed things to find in the vast room: polka-dot scarf, man with three-plus folds in his neck, bird's nest in rafters.

Once she tilted her bible so Katherine could see the faint pencil sketch drawn in a corner of the glossary page. Two girls in braids, half-hidden under an umbrella. The meaning was clear; Reverend Brockwood was a spitter, and the more fired-up he got, the more vigorously he railed about lust and wickedness, the hypocrisy of other faiths, the more the saliva flew from his tiny mouth, anointing the lucky worshippers sitting front-row center.

These small gestures made her new life bearable.

So one Sunday morning, when Alexandra and Katherine met in the far-right ladies' room stall for a few stolen moments before they had to become Sandy and Kate again, Katherine asked only one question when Alexandra pulled a piece of foil from her turtleneck.

It was smaller than a stamp, with two fuchsia disks affixed to it like candy buttons.

"What are they?"

"They make everything wonderful. They make everything…soft."

Alexandra peeled them off and touched her tongue to one, swallowed. She held her palm under Katherine's chin.

Katherine mimicked her friend, accepting the tiny pill with her tongue. Their own secret communion.

And just as Alexandra had promised, twenty minutes into afternoon service, the warehouse's right angles blurred and melted, her metal folding chair became velvet, and even the bloated, waxy face of Reverend Brockwood changed to warm liquid color. He spoke of lambs, and she saw lambs trotting down the aisles, reached out, and petted their billowy wool. He recited from the book of Hosea: "And the old king will float away like driftwood on the surface of water." And she floated.

Wonderful.

Winter

The candy buttons got her through January.

In February Alexandra said she was running away. Her parents had told her—had told the Sandy version of her, the only one they knew, who could be trusted with such news—that the elders of the church had voted to sell off the Three Pines property.

The church was officially splitting. No more arguing between the older members and the new ones. Alexandra's parents and some other families were following Reverend Brockwood to a piece of land he owned in Idaho. Seventy acres. Privacy. No other faiths nosing around, questioning their rules.

The church in Idaho would have its own school, just for them. There was a boy they had their eye on for her; they would have their own house.

It would be wonderful.

Alexandra had fifty-eight dollars, ones and fives she'd pilfered from her mother's purse.

And she had a plan: a ride, a place to crash. Just until she saved more money, waitressing, maybe. Then she was going to move on to Los Angeles or New York. She was going to act, or paint, or sing. She was going to do everything.

"You're staying with him, aren't you?"

"Come with me. He likes you."

Katherine shook her head. "She wouldn't make us go. She wouldn't quit her job."

"She's changed. They change."

"She wouldn't."

Alexandra has to run away, she thought, but if the church splits up and the craziest of them move, my life will go back to normal.

Later that night, after she found the packed bags in her mother's closet, after she saw the check for unused vacation days endorsed to Reverend Brockwood, after she confronted her and she said, "Yes. Yes, of course we're going with them," and Katherine pleaded, begged for things to go back to how they were, and her mother smiled that empty, empty smile and said of course she didn't want things to go back to the way they were, Katherine called Alexandra.

"When do we leave?"

36

Sacred Institutions

Late June 1999
Summer before college

"You gave me too much, dear." Mrs. Sheehan pressed a nickel
into my palm.

Before I could apologize for making wrong change she was out
the propped-open front doors, nibbling her square of blueberry-
lemon cake. Blue Moon Cake, my mother's neat penmanship
spelled out on the sign taped to the table edge. Everyone said
how clever she was, inventing this cake, how the shiny crescent
moons of blueberry pie filling in each piece of lemon sponge
were so perfect, how she should open a bakery. The way people
raved, you'd have thought she'd cured malaria.

I'd sold four cakes and a dozen slices, plus assorted brownies, blondies, and muffins, during the usual sugar frenzy after
Reverend Talbert's send-off from Ephesians: "Know the love

of Christ that surpasses knowledge, that you may be filled with all the fullness of God!"

Filled with the fullness of God. And baked goods.

Now it was only me, a few stragglers, and Mrs. Pettit, manning her own card table—for choir sign-ups, I assumed—across the room. Any minute the deacon would unprop the front doors and I'd be free.

J.B. was home from LA for the weekend so he and Casey and I were driving to a beach we liked in Pinecrest. They were picking me up at 11:30 in his truck.

J.B. Now officially, gloriously, my boyfriend.

We'd exchanged emails all fall and spent Thanksgiving break talking and kissing in his truck cab, listening to the radio, fogging up the windows.

At Christmas I agonized over his gift and decided to sketch him instead of buying something. A small black pen-and-ink, only three by four inches, as if trying to capture his soul would seem less intimate in miniature. As if its size would make it a casual present.

Though I spent more time on those twelve square inches of Bristol board than I had on anything I'd ever drawn. I mimicked the intense gothic style of the woodcut illustrations in my 1943 edition of *Jane Eyre*. J.B. staring across the lake, remembering the cruel boy who'd taunted him. His hair wet, his eyes soft, lost in another world.

We sat outside my house in his truck for our gift exchange. The Pogues belting out "Fairytale of New York" on KALT-FM. He handed me a heavy rectangular package wrapped in flocked red-and-green paper and I gave him his almost weightless little present swathed in gold tissue.

His gift for me was a gorgeous color hardcover about the painter Lee Krasner.

"It's perfect," I said, carefully turning the pages. "I love her."

He held my line drawing up to the truck's overhead light for a long time before speaking, then nodded. "It's me," he said simply.

After that we emailed daily and talked on the phone three times a week.

I made him tell me about the four other girls he'd been with. Names, ages, the where, the how often. I told him about my unremarkable dates in town, my explorations before the good-nights.

I confessed what I hadn't told anyone except Alex—that I wanted to draw. I told everyone else I wanted to be a graphic designer. Practical. Safe. He told me about his favorite buildings in LA, that he'd wanted to major in architecture but had switched to straight engineering for the sure money. For his mom.

The messages zipping up and down California between JulianB@netzero.com and kayakgirl96@aol.com got longer, warmer, until he sent one sweetly official, brief missive in January:

Subject: technical?
are you my girlfriend? used word today, describing you to nosy fellow TA
terminology accurate?
ps hope it is

During the academic year he had to work on campus most weekends, tutoring and in the engineering lab. But he stole away one Saturday in February. Driving six hours to meet my bus in Sacramento, where we found a quiet café. Hitting the road again three hours later in the opposite direction, a quad espresso in the cupholder.

By spring I was so jelly-kneed in love I could barely concentrate on my classes, but I'd gotten into CalArts. Casey'd been accepted at UCLA, where J.B. had one year left of grad school.

We'd all be in LA soon. Me, J.B., Casey.

I was happy, anticipating my freedom, so close now, and the afternoon ahead in Pinecrest, the swimming and sunbathing and lazy kissing on damp towels, fingers laced together. Casey would call, "Get a room, you two," and throw a towel over us or splash us in her good-natured way, pretending to be shocked. I was in such a good mood I accidentally smiled at Mrs. Pettit.

She pinched her face up. "Wonderful sermon."

"Wonderful."

As if I knew. I'd been too busy reliving scenes from the night before, entangled with J.B. on Casey's bed while the sounds of the postgame party drifted upstairs. We hadn't slept together yet, though I wanted to.

Fragments of Reverend Talbert's message had intruded into my daydreams, creating an unholy but undeniably sexy hodge-podge: J.B.'s hand exploring the curve of my waist *(...and he spoke to the Apostle Paul...)*, the way I'd tunneled my hands under his shirt, turning his voice ragged *(...fishers of men, he said, and it was so...)*. That's how I entertained myself in church these days, crossing my legs tight in the sunny pew. Then feeling guilty.

"Where's your mother, dear?" Mrs. Pettit asked.

"She has her committee meeting in the library."

"And which committee is that, now? It's so hard to keep up."

"The one remodeling the bride's dressing room?"

"Now, won't that be charming. When our Emily was married it was in a pitiful state. Torn carpet, rusty faucet. I don't know what we'd do without your mother."

"Yes."

"Will you give her one of these for me, dear?" Mrs. Pettit walked over with a slim red pamphlet. The tightness of her smile made it clear she hadn't forgiven me for dropping out of choir sophomore year. Neither had my mother.

I'd assumed Mrs. Pettit was drumming up support for youth choir, or adult choir, or canticle singers or bell ringers. She was in charge of pretty much any group making noise in special robes.

But when I glanced at the pamphlet I realized this was something else. Something new.

I left the unsold goodies, the money box, the powder blue napkins with the trotting lambs on them, strewn across the table. I left without saying goodbye.

When Casey was swimming and J.B. was curled on my towel, his head in my lap, I showed him the pamphlet.

"Oh, man." He sat up.

The pamphlet quoted a senator from Mississippi who compared homosexuality to a condition like alcohol abuse or kleptomania. *A pathology in need of treatment*, it said.

Mrs. Pettit's pinchy smile took on a sinister meaning; I wondered if she knew about Casey. Dina Pettit, her daughter, went to the parties on the sly, so even though she knew Casey was gay she probably wouldn't have said anything. But Coeur-de-Lune was small.

"You going to show her?" J.B. said.

"No."

"Is your mother part of it?"

"I don't think so." I folded the pamphlet and rolled it inside my dress, wrapping the fabric tight, tucking it into my beach bag. "But either way I'm done. I should have stopped going to church years ago. You should've seen the way they treated Alex one Christmas."

"Alex never struck me as the religious type."

"She surprised me at a carol service I was playing piano in. Sophomore year. She was all dressed up, but…" I shook my head, remembering the long, sliding glances, the insincerity in the greetings that cold December night. *So good to see you here finally!*

"They said stuff?"

"It was the way they looked at her."

"Why? The scavenger hunts?"

"All of it. The parties. The cutoffs, the boyfriends, her age. That's all they see. And if they know about Casey? They're probably thrilled. Proof they were right all along, not to be friendly to Alex. Also…never mind."

"Also what?"

I'd never told him about Alex kissing Stewart Copley the summer before.

"What?" J.B. repeated.

"Nothing. You need lotion. You're burning." His skin wasn't burning at all; he didn't burn. I touched my favorite part of his shoulder, where various muscles joined under smooth skin.

He kissed the shoulder where my bathing suit strap was supposed to be, and for a few disloyal seconds I wished we were alone, or that Casey had brought a date.

Then I looked out at the shining water. She wasn't at full speed, but even her laziest backstroke was a beautiful thing to watch, liquid and controlled. I wanted to run into the water and scoop her out like those parents in *Jaws*. She didn't know what was going on under the surface of our placid little town.

"What'll you tell your mom about…" J.B. pointed at my bag.

"That I'm eighteen and I'm done pretending."

My mother stood in the entry, inhaling and exhaling in a deep, showy way. *See what you do to my respiration, wicked child?* "You've been out with that boy all day?"

That boy. She said it like she said *those Collier boys* or *that mother*, meaning Alex. No adjective necessary.

"You know his name."

My dad crept in as she took another "Lord help me" breath.

"The state you left the bake sale table in. Marjorie Pettit said—"

"Did she tell you about her little cause?" I took the pamphlet from my bag and held it out to her, then at the last second offered it to my dad instead.

He read it and sighed. Handed it to my mother.

She barely glanced at it before handing it back to him. "Marjorie Pettit's a fool. Always has been."

"That's it?" I said. "*She's a fool?* She probably knows about Casey. And I know you know, too, the way those old bitches gossip."

"Laura." My father's voice was sharp, but he didn't look up from the pamphlet. I hadn't told him about Casey, but I wondered if he'd guessed.

"Witches, then," I said, softening my language for my father's sake. Not for her.

"It's that Shepherd woman," my mother said. "That house. That's why she's acting like this."

"Alex has never done anything to you. And The Shipwreck is just four walls and a roof. Just because you were too uptight to play with the kids who used to live there—"

"Laura!" my father said.

I took my own deep, showy breath, and when I finally said the words, I sounded like an actor enjoying her monologue too much. An ugly part of me was glad about Marjorie Pettit's pamphlet. Because now I could say it at last:

"I'm never going back to that church."

First week of July

The week after I finally told my mother I wasn't going to church anymore, I waited for my punishment. None came. I was even allowed to take the bus to Tahoe with Casey for fireworks.

I guessed that my father had intervened, told my mother I was almost a grown-up. It's what he'd said to me twice since my birthday, bashfully: "Eighteen. Hard to believe."

J.B. came home almost every weekend now, and on Saturday night I went over to Casey's as usual, and as usual J.B. and I spent most of our time on her bed half-clothed, stopping just short of sex.

I said, "I'm sure. I'm eighteen."

"Soon," he said.

While he was down the hall splashing water on his face, I drew the shade up halfway and spied on the remnants of the party from Casey's window. There were still kids in the lamp-lit garden drinking beer. Alex sat on the bench, a small bowl in her lap. It was the one she'd bought during the high point of her witchy gardening phase, stone with a matching pestle. On a towel next to her were small objects I couldn't make out.

Ginny Ambrose and Dina Pettit sat at Alex's feet, laughing and dabbing their arms with paper towels. At first I thought perhaps they'd simply spilled beer, but I realized, from the way Casey stood slightly apart from the others, unsmiling, that this wasn't the case.

"What's going on out there?" J.B. settled behind me on the bed.

"I'm pretty sure it's Alex's version of a Wiccan blood ritual," I said. "Seems to be a crowd-pleaser."

"You're kidding." He stared over my shoulder at the scene.

"Casey's annoyed. I should go help."

"You're not her mother, Laur."

I pressed my forehead against the cool glass. "You mean Casey's or Alex's?"

"I meant Alex."

A boy picked up the mortar and pestle and began drumming. *Click-thrum. Click-thrum.* The set cost fifty dollars from the Moonshadow occult shop in Sacramento; I'd seen the price sticker the afternoon Alex bought it.

"Want to hear something embarrassing?" I said. "Promise not to tell."

"Promise."

I made my confession to the window. "I used to imagine Alex was my mother."

I waited for him to answer, or laugh, but he didn't.

I turned to face him. I couldn't read his expression. It was kind, inviting me to continue my explanation, but was there pity mixed in?

"Alex was so *interested* in me and…I had it all worked out. We don't look anything alike, but our feet are almost identical. Narrow, and we both have super-small pinky toenails, did you ever notice? Freakishly small, like basically dots?"

I extended a leg, settling my foot in his lap so we could study my toes.

He tapped my pinky toenail. "I've never noticed Alex's toes. But I like yours."

"You know they're weird." My pinky toenails really were odd. They were like flattened seed pearls inserted into my flesh. The one time I had a professional pedicure, before homecoming sophomore year, the lady at the salon had bluntly asked if I wanted to "overdraw" them. She'd painted varnish straight onto my skin, a trompe l'oeil effect that made it look like I had a respectable-sized nail. I'd told Alex about this salon visit and she'd whipped off her socks to show me how her toenails were almost as tiny.

That means we both have Greek ancestry, she'd said. She'd read a book on this. Casey had held her foot up and it was nothing like ours; her toenails were standard discs and her toes swerved into each other like puzzle pieces.

I withdrew my leg, settling cross-legged on the sagging mattress.

"So, the feet thing," I said, staring out the window again. "I thought maybe my parents hadn't told me my real birthday. Because otherwise it wouldn't be possible. Casey's is more than two months later. Dumb, huh? Like that kids' book with the bird. *Are You My Mother?*"

"It's not dumb. I'm sure every adopted kid does that."

We watched Alex quietly through the window, leaning close to catch puffs of breeze from off the lake, welcome after our sweaty tangling on the bed.

"You wouldn't still want it to be true, would you?" he said, scratching the window screen to indicate the scene outside. "About Alex?"

I looked down at her, holding court with teenagers, oblivious to Casey's fury. Or, worse, not so oblivious, but unable to resist the attention. She was selfish, foolish, infuriating. But brimming with life.

I shook my head no. But I knew the answer was yes.

J.B. left at midnight and I curled up in Casey's bed to wait for her.

When she collapsed next to me, she sighed.

"That bad?" I said.

"If you'd been down there she would've poked a needle in you, too. Your church people are going to burn her at the stake."

"Tell."

"Love spells for some lifeguards Ginny and Dina worship. The crowd ate it up."

"No. God, Alex." I laughed, but stopped abruptly when I saw Casey's expression. She was right, of course. Certain parents would go ballistic if they found out Alex had tapped their daughters' tender arms like sugar maples.

"Don't take the Lord's name in vain. What would your congregation think?" Her voice was bitter.

"Stop with the church stuff," I said to Casey. "I'm not going back."

"You're pretty girl-who-cried-wolf on the subject."

"I know, but I mean it this time. And I know I said I'd keep an eye on Alex and I haven't done that, either. But I'll help you with her next weekend."

"You don't have to babysit her on your Saturdays with J.B."

"He won't have sex with me anyway. It's totally frustrating."

"Poor Laura." She smiled.

I was so relieved to see her smile. "Help me. Should I take him to a hotel?"

"With a heart-shaped bed."

"They have those in Reno," I said.

"You could ask my mom to do one of her spells."

"How would we get his blood?"

"You could bite his tongue while you're kissing and secretly save the blood and spit it into the magic stone bowl."

"He might notice."

"It's not a perfect plan."

For the first time in the hundreds of Saturdays I'd slept over, Casey didn't set her alarm.

"You're sure?" she said, her hand hovering over her plastic Eiffel Tower clock.

I said the same thing I'd told J.B. "I'm sure. I'm eighteen."

When I came home the next morning I expected to find the house empty.

But my dad was out back, sanding the teak side tables from the den. They nested together in a way that had fascinated me when I was little. My mother said they were a royal pain because they showed every drop of water.

"You're here," I said.

"That I am." He didn't look up, maintaining a steady scritch-scratch with his sandpaper. Finally, he blew at the fine powder and said, "I always thought Minister Talbert was a decent character. Bit of a windbag, but not one to allow an ugly business like that under his roof. Can't abide it."

"Thanks, Daddy. Was she really mad?"

"It'll blow over." He nodded across the water at The Ship-wreck. "Casey's a good kid. Nobody's business, the other stuff. Anyone giving her a hard time?"

"Nothing too bad."

He smoothed a small section of wood, blew again, and inspected it. "Give your old man a hand. See if you can find the teak oil. Blue can, top shelf."

I watched him from inside the shed as he bent over the lowest table in the set, his jeans loose on his skinny form, his stooped posture making him look frail. He had such a quick mind that I forgot sometimes, he was nearly sixty-seven.

My father never went back to church after that. I don't know what my mother told people. I imagine it hurt her deeply, him siding with me that last summer. We never discussed it again, and although I listened at the heat vent for weeks, I never heard my parents fight about it.

Quiet as it was, the schism in our little family, it turned out, was deep and irreparable.

37

Counting Down

July 1999

Casey was worried about Alex. She'd started dating this guy
Casey didn't like. Older. Gary something. We even got to meet
him and he was dull. (*Dull. Dull, dull,* I wrote in my diary). He
lived all the way down in Palo Alto and drove up to Coeur-de-
Lune every chance he got.

"It's because you're leaving," I said to Casey about the Gary
guy. I didn't mention that Alex was drinking while we were out
on the scavenger hunts. I'd seen her slide a wine bottle behind
the knife block one Saturday night when our team returned.
"She wants someone to hold on to."

"You mean it's because *we're* leaving," Casey said. "You, me.
Her excuse to have a fan club at CDL High. That's what Saturdays have become. Alex Shepherd fan club meetings."

By midsummer Alex had become distant and distracted, unpredictable even for her, her graveyard of abandoned projects more

sprawling than ever. Her scavenger hunt lists were all over the place—either repetitive, dashed off the night of the game, or written in overly obscure rhymes.

She started smothering Casey, kissing her, squeezing her. But she continued the parties Casey hated, and continued to date the dull, humorless man from Palo Alto. And she kept drinking. I could tell by her pink cheeks, the wildness of her laughter in the garden after the scavenger hunts.

Alex was shattered about us leaving, no matter how much she tried to deny it. She kept talking up the amazing things that awaited us—a big city, the college classes she always wished she'd taken.

I'm so excited for you girls, she'd say, often. Too often.

Casey and I sat near Alex on Saturday nights, limiting her drinks. When J.B. came, he helped.

But at eleven Casey would urge J.B. and me to go inside. We'd hold hands as we left, pretending to be casual so nobody would tease us. We'd walk upstairs slowly, examining the photo wall.

At the top there was a picture of Alex as a toddler on the beach in San Francisco. There weren't many pictures from when Alex was little, because she didn't talk to her family anymore. But I liked this one of her in a skirted swimsuit, her bobbed red hair shining in the sun. She was tiny, standing in the sand against a low rock wall.

I'd noticed J.B. studying it more than once.

"Alex looks cute in that one, doesn't she?" I said one night, when he was lingering by the pictures even longer than usual.

"Yeah, but that's not why I like it. See the wall of this building behind her? Or what used to be a building—it burned down a long time ago. I went there for a project when I was an undergrad. It's the Sutro Baths, out by the Cliff House. They used one hundred thousand panes of glass." He drew in the foggy sky with his finger, showing me where the roof had once been. "At high tide, the salt water would flow right in from the ocean. Pretty innovative for the time. Shame it burned down."

He started to follow me upstairs, then looked back at the picture. "How old do you think she is here?"

"I think she said one or two. She couldn't be much older. Look at those chubby cheeks."

"Yeah. Cute." He stared at the picture until I reached down for his hand, tugging him up the last few steps.

I could have helped Casey stop the Saturday nights at The Shipwreck. But they were everything to me. They were my excuse to see J.B.

Behind Casey's gold candy-wrapper door, J.B. and I spent a hundred hours kissing, exploring, peeling off more and more clothing but keeping it close by, listening for footsteps.

One night he pulled my drenched underwear to the side and ran his tongue up and down my very center, until I cried out and dug my hands in his hair.

The next week I took him in my hand, my mouth. *Soon.* We both said it now. We knew the rest would happen *soon.*

In late July, we sat on Casey's bed, the light from the garden lamp below bathing us in gold, and I finally showed him my music box. He hadn't seen it since years before, at the rink, and that time he'd thought it was a stone because he hadn't removed it from the bag.

I opened the lid and played the song, and he didn't say a word until it was done.

J.B. ran his index finger over the swirling grain of the driftwood case for a long time. "Handmade," he observed. "Ever see another like it?"

"Never." I told him how Casey had helped me find out the song title. Softly, I sang the sappy lyrics I'd memorized. I'd never done this before, not even with Alex or Casey. The song was wistful, listing the colors of loss, doubt, regret. Someone's heart had turned green, or jealous. And that made life gray.

"Sad," he said.

"I thought there could be a message in there for me. Maybe she was even a painter. You know, the colors?"

"Maybe."

"I play it on the piano when I have the house to myself."

He brushed his lips on my temple. "Play it for me sometime."

August

"Soon we can spend the whole night together," I said. We lay on Casey's bed on our backs, feet up on the wall, fingers entwined.

"Soon," he said. "Thirty-seven days."

We would all be in LA by September 13.

"I love that you're counting. I thought I was the only one. I've been counting down in my diary."

"I didn't know you kept a diary."

"I'm pretty hot and cold with it. Now I usually start off the entries by apologizing for not writing."

"What do you say about me?"

"That's private. But you come out okay."

Entries in *A Girl's First Diary*

Aug. 8

36 days until LA: Casey and I found an apartment 17 miles from CalArts and 18 from UCLA. (Oh, yeah, and drumroll, only 21 from J.B.'s new rental, ahem-ahem.)

Carpet unfortunately rust-colored and shaggy but everything else v. nice. We can buy two single beds and couch from people living there now (also students) for $250 and probably will. Complex is The Pacific Breeze but we are nowhere near ocean of course. We have eensy-weensy balcony over pkng. lot.

Put down $750 deposit. C & I both screamed in car on drive home, so excited. C asked if I wanted J.B. to live with us (very shy, for her) and I said of course not. Not ready for that.

C & I hope she'll meet fabulous g.f. in LA. I asked C to describe her ideal, perfect g.f. She says I'm too hung up on perfect. Maybe. But if J.B. not perfect, haven't seen evidence yet.

Major plans to check out her "scene" there & I'll come along for moral support. Clubs, coffee shops, etc.

(C still doesn't know about Mrs. P's stupid red leaflets. She started stuffing them in mailboxes. Last Sat. we got one and I ran over to The Shipwreck to hide theirs before C saw. Told Alex. We agreed not to tell C.)

CDL looked so tiny when we came back from LA. We felt sorry for it.

Aug. 10

34 days until LA: Daddy ordered pirate's flag from a catalog for Alex. Exactly like the one in the picture. Another of his perfect gifts.

Will miss him so much. He's promised to check in on Alex next year.

Aug. 12

32 days until LA: Shipwreck as usual. J.B. and I came close. I think if we'd had a condiment with us it might have happened. (Condiment is what C calls them to tease me.) Alex gave me some. She's taking me to Sacramento next week to get on pill. But need to be on for month to be extra safe, she says, over and over, like I didn't learn in Health. She asks a lot of questions about me and J.B., making sure I'm okay.

Know it'll happen soon. In a real bedroom, with real door, when we can spend the whole night together. Not in Reno. Tacky... One of those cozy cabins in Pinecrest? Candles, fireplace, everything perfect.

He said, "I love you but I want you to be sure."

I said, "I love you. I'm sure."

I really do. I really am.

★ ★ ★

Aug. 15

29 days until LA: C and A and I went shopping in Sacramento for setting-up-house things for apartment.

Had saved $170 in babysitting funds. M & D paying tuition and share of deposit and rent but didn't want to ask for extra. I was running out & who came and stuffed ten crisp $20 bills in my hand? Mrs. Ingrid Christie. Truce w. my mother?

So surprised almost forgot to thank her. I hadn't asked her to come shopping with us, felt tiny bit guilty (but only tiny bit).

When I said thanks, she said, "Your father and I discussed it," awkward patting of arm. Nice of her.

Bought carload of stuff for apartment with C & A. Our own coffee maker, our own purply-blue-gray bath towels (oh-so-sophisticated), our own silver soap dish. Even got fancy soaps like starfish & mermaids & sand dollars, but for show/guests only.

Alex kept squeezing us. Saying she was so proud of her grown-up girls. We had her pick out her own towel and pillow for when she sleeps over. I caught her crying in the comforter section.

I think she'll be okay once we're gone and everybody adjusts.

I wrote the twenty-seven-days-until-LA entry in three-inch-high letters: *Perfect. Perfect. Perfect.*

38

Lost and Found

August 16, 1999
28 days until LA

The rink and bowling alley were closed until one on Mondays,
but J.B. was home for a long weekend, earning some extra cash.
The owner had promised to give him a hundred dollars if he
could fix the marble run by the entrance. It was a metal thing,
an intricate series of chutes and windmills and pulleys, that had
been broken longer than I could remember.

I watched him through the glass door. He was kneeling, parts
and tools spread on a towel. I liked his face, so serious, so intent on his task.

When I finally knocked, he grinned and ran over to let me
in. "How long've you been spying on me?"

"Not long. Can you take a break?"

"Definitely." He kissed me, a strangely chaste, hands-free kiss.

We usually couldn't control our hands—they roamed, dug, pet-ted. "I'm greasy." He held up his smudged palms.

"I don't mind." I examined the marble run. "Any luck with that?"

"Getting close." He sent a heavy silver sphere down a slide at the top and we watched it traverse its little course. It made its way through the contraption, gliding along ramps and into tun-nels, merrily swinging on a miniature trapeze, getting scooped up by a long metal stick like a metronome with a cunning bas-ket on top.

"Whee," I said softly, following its ride in the basket. Then, abruptly, the silver ball stopped, tripped up by a ridge in front of a sloping tunnel. "Aw, poor little guy. How frustrating to make it so close."

"I'll get him to the finish. Need to make this ledge lower, here. What's in the bag?"

"Our lunch. Ham-and-butter sandwiches. And brownies. I thought you'd want a break from nachos and mummified hot dogs."

"How long can you stay?"

"I have a babysitting job at two. Are we really alone?"

"See any other cars?"

"Nope."

We walked down the long, carpeted hallway. The two of us had never been alone in the rink before. Even at the end of the nighttime skate sessions there was always someone there besides J.B. People cleaning up in the snack bar, or Andy, the owner, looking stressed through the glass door to his office.

J.B. headed for the snack bar but I tugged him toward the dark rink. "I have a better idea." I pulled the picnic blanket from my backpack and kicked my Nikes off.

"What are you in the mood for?" he called from the DJ booth.

"Bach. 'Goldberg Variations.' But I doubt the rink has that."

I'd been trying to master part of it on piano for a year but had put in woefully little practice time since J.B. and I got together.

"Sorry, no Bach. But let's see how close I can get."

I recognized drowsy steel guitar, the opening chords of "Walkin' After Midnight." Patsy Cline. The beginning of a four-song Patsy medley the rink played on '50s night. The glitter ball began to spin, layering the rink in shifting white lights.

"How'd I do?" He slid over in his socks.

"Perfect. This song always makes me wish I knew how to waltz."

He pulled me to my feet. "But we can slide."

So we slid to Patsy. We dragged and pushed each other, did a sock-foot crack-the-whip, competed in a distance contest. We slid until our stomachs were growling.

After we ate we lay on our backs, looking up at the spinning fake stars and listening to "You Belong to Me." I picked out the notes on the rink with my hand. "Remind me to get this sheet music sometime."

"Did you reserve that music room at school for next year?"

"Mmm-hmm. Ten hours a week free if you're a music minor."

"Good." He leaned onto his side.

I swept a lock of hair from his eyes.

He kissed my bare shoulder. "Salty."

"Andy should charge for this." I closed my eyes. "Rent the place out for…"

"What?" He murmured into the hollow between my shoulder and neck.

I dug my fingers into his hair. "Rent it for…" His mouth slid higher. "For private dates…"

"I'd rather save it for us," he said, his mouth traveling up my neck, jaw, chin. Taking my lower lip between his. I forgot where we were until we rolled off the blanket and I felt the cold surface of the rink under my back. We rolled back onto the blanket, onto the little island we'd made.

I gripped his hand, he pressed back. And I knew.

It was daytime. We were both sweaty, in grubby work clothes. No candles, no fireplace. I had to leave in an hour for babysitting. "Now," I said.

"Here, though? Exotic, but maybe not the most comfortable. And if someone comes in early…"

"Andy's office?" I said.

"It's locked."

"I know where." I pulled him by the wrist across the rink, onto the carpet. To the storage room behind the arcade, the one holding the big box of lost-and-found clothes. Coats and sweaters and scarves left behind, never claimed. "I always wondered what happened with lost-and-found stuff nobody came back for."

"This might be a first."

We made ourselves a big, buoyant nest of forgotten clothes, draped the picnic blanket over it. With the door shut, there was only a faint glow on the floor from the rink lights. But we could still hear Patsy's lonely contralto singing "I Fall to Pieces."

I was too on edge to let go completely in our narrow, dark hiding place. He tried to hold off, to help, but though his fingers were well acquainted with what I needed now, it was a lost cause right then. I whispered, "It's okay," and he sank into me one last time, spoke into my neck: "Vyou. Itso. Itso." *I love you. It's so. It's so.* He shuddered and cried out.

After, I curled up on his chest. Sticky, marveling, proud.

"You didn't come," he said. "I wanted you to so bad."

"I was thinking too much." I brushed his wet hair off his forehead.

"Did it hurt a lot?"

"A little," I admitted, my hand drifting down to where it had stung, mostly at the beginning.

"I'll make it up to you."

"It wasn't as bad as they tell you." I sat up, my hands on his shoulders, my thighs around his abdomen. He circled his hands around my waist and closed his eyes, and we playacted for a second, moving our hips. "I wish I didn't have to go," I said.

"You have no idea how much I wish that... God, you're. It's." He leaned up. "Can you get away after babysitting?"

I leaned forward so he could take my nipple in his mouth, pulled back. Leaned forward again. "Maybe my babysitting job will get miraculously—keep doing that—extended."

"And maybe." His voice hummed into my breast. "Maybe I'll—is this nice?—call in sick."

"Yes. It's nice. Keep. Don't."

His mouth was now fully occupied, and I was intent on my small, rocking movements. Though some separate, vigilant part of me was on alert for sounds outside our lost and found, and wishing we had all afternoon, I was able to stop thinking. Just long enough.

We checked into a cabin in Pinecrest at four. Hard workers, for seven hours we devoted ourselves to contrasts, comparisons, combinations. We resisted sleep even though we were both exhausted.

When we drove home it was after eleven. It was a chilly, breezy night, but we left the windows down. J.B. and I clasped hands, hanging on even when he shifted gears.

I leaned against the window. Smiling, letting the wind dry my still-sweaty hair.

J.B. parked a block from my house so my parents wouldn't hear his engine. "I love you," he said, lacing his fingers with mine through the truck's window.

"I love you, too."

39

Again

Casey and I walked slowly from the church back to her house.
For five blocks we didn't say a word.

We let the town fill the silence with its Sunday noises of buzzing lawn mowers, kids shouting, Jet Skis on the lake.

This time, as we passed my old street, Casey didn't ask if I
wanted to take the picture of the bench my dad and J.B. had
made me. But she touched my shoulder. The tiniest, swiftest
brush of her hand, to say she remembered our happy week working outside, the summer before senior year.

She thought she knew everything I'd lost in this town.

All the reasons I'd run away.

When we reached the park across from her house, Casey
stopped, watching a little dark-haired boy and his ponytailed
mother, or nanny, pumping their legs in the swings. They swung

in opposite time, high-fiving when they passed each other. Each time they clapped hands, the boy shouted, "Again!"

"So that's why Alex wanted us to get together now," I said. "Because you're sick."

Casey turned to face me. "You're not supposed to say sick. My counselor says I'm 'showing early, manageable symptoms.'"

Casey had always been a natural mimic; I could envision the counselor, some prim no-nonsense nurse in a white uniform, an irritatingly all-knowing expression in her eyes, a sheaf of pamphlets in her hand. But I couldn't laugh at her imitation. Not yet.

Casey's sick. I screamed it, in my head.

And I almost hadn't come.

But maybe Alex had known I would, or cast a spell on me from afar to make sure.

A good witch, after all these years.

40

February

Daniel picked them up in his truck at Lands End Beach. Four hours traveling north, curled up against the window in the passenger seat, fighting the urge at every stop to scream that it was a mistake, she wanted to go home.

She leaned against the glass and closed her eyes, seeing things she needed to forget. The orange garibaldi-fish key chain, the rectangle of morning sun on the faded red living room sofa they'd found secondhand. The denim beanbag chair under her bedroom window, her mom's fringed saddle purse.

The messy blue counter in their small, shared bathroom, its grout stained orangey-pink from loose chunks of Apricot Velvet blusher. They'd shared this blush. Until her mother discarded anything that didn't conform to the church's idea of modest womanhood and they had to leave their faces bare.

Her mother's cheeks were soft, slightly plump. Like her own.

Katherine opened her eyes and rolled the window down, as if the cold ocean air could pull every unwanted picture from her mind. Scatter them on the wind, send them out to sea.

She had no home. The closest thing to home was Alexandra, sitting there between her and Daniel, her unbraided red hair swirling in wild ropes.

When they pulled up to Daniel's white clapboard house he said, "The place is pretty full right now. Friends I've met on gigs, friends from college."

The word college was reassuring. Katherine counted twelve other houseguests the first day but it was hard to keep track. They crashed on the sofa, the floor, even the kitchen floor. Sometimes they slept in the hammock strung on the wraparound porch.

He gave her and Alexandra the second-best room, upstairs, next to his, with a door that locked, an actual bed. Daniel said they could use the small bathroom that connected their room with his. Nobody else could.

He said they could stay as long as they wanted.

The first week, the back of her throat was hot and tight, threatening tears at the slightest memory of home. But she didn't let herself cry in her bed as she had at camp. Instead she bit the inside of her cheek, hard. A pain she could control.

She didn't want food, even the warm honey-walnut bread Alexandra brought upstairs one morning, wrapped in a paper towel. "It's good," she said. "Derek baked it."

She took a bite so Alexandra would leave her alone.

"Come outside. Trina's showing me how to make those dangly earrings. She says I can help her sell them at the farmer's market next weekend."

Alexandra had thrown herself into the household. She knew all the names already. Derek the Baker. Trina the Jewelry-maker. Like they were living in a nursery rhyme.

"I'll come down later. I'm tired."

She woke to the sound of guitar, Daniel's low voice singing Beatles songs. "Blackbird."

"Let it Be."

"Julia."

The lyrics, though soft, carried through the closed doors of their shared bathroom.

He played scales, strings of notes from low to high, like a question. Then he strummed "Johnny's So Long at the Fair." Low and sweet, swapping in his own words:

"O dear, what can the matter be
O dear, what can the matter be
Katherine's so long at the door.
I'm worried about her, she seems oh, so lonely..."

She tiptoed to the bathroom, opened the door inch by inch so it wouldn't squeak. The door on the other side, the one to his room, was ever-so-slightly ajar. She rested one hand on the sink to still herself, held her breath.

"She's a quiet one, Katherine / Does she feel like talking?"

She opened his door.

He stopped singing and laughed, picking out a meandering string of notes. "You doing all right?"

She nodded. "You're a good singer."

He waved this off, setting the guitar on the bed. "I'm a mimic. Wish I was more than that."

He'd fastened the driftwood crescent to his brass headboard with wire wrapped around the center. At first she thought the curving driftwood ornament was supposed to look like miniature bull's horns, like the ones people strapped to the grills of their trucks.

Then she got it. A ninety-degree tilt to the left and the crescent moon became something else entirely.

"Like what I've done with your present?" he said.

"Yes. It's clever."

"Don't tell me you guessed why I wired it on that way. With the points up."

"For good luck," she said. "You never hang a horseshoe upside down."

"Exactly." He nodded in delight, reaching up to make a minute adjustment to the driftwood so it sat level. "You're the one who's clever. You found it for me. My good-luck charm."

Katherine wandered over to the window. Alexandra and some of the others were out back, sitting at the picnic table under the big tree. They were smoking, laughing, making their odds and ends to sell.

"So you're not into our little jewelry and candle workshop?" he said. "Don't worry, it's not a requirement."

"It's not that. I like the things they make. I'm just…"

"Homesick," he said.

"I guess."

"I have something perfect for that."

"Chocolate?"

"Nicer than chocolate." He pulled a piece of foil from his pocket. "But only if you want it. Again, not a requirement."

41

A Pirate

Late August 1999

Perfect. Perfect. Perfect. I wrote in my diary on August 17, the morning after my first time with J.B.

Maybe this was tempting fate. The number three has a dark power, according to one of Alex's books. Maybe, if I hadn't written the word, or had written it only once, that last summer would have simply rolled on, one perfect day after another.

J.B. and I sneaking off together every chance we got, shaky with desire.

Casey and I visiting favorite spots on the lake to wish them goodbye. *See you at Thanksgiving, Jade Cove. See you at Thanksgiving, Raptor Rock.* We tried to act solemn during these farewells, but usually overdid it and ended up laughing.

LA was so close we could taste it.

★ ★ ★

The last scavenger hunt was August 21. A cool night for August. We'd zigzagged across town until we were breathless, and our team won.

"The last winners," Alex had said, handing over twenty-dollar gift cards for the Creekside. And we'd been relieved that we didn't have to tell her this was the end. We'd worried, privately, that she'd somehow try to keep the hunts going next summer when we were home from college.

Alex seemed better. More in control. Focused. We thought she'd accepted us leaving. And though someone had brought a case of beer and a case of Zima and a case of wine coolers, Alex didn't take one sip that night. I watched her.

She sat on the bench in the garden next to me with Casey on her lap. Casey smiled at me, cradled in Alex's arms.

"Just look at that," Casey said, pointing up at the half circle of the moon, brilliant against the black dome of the sky. Such a clear night, so many luminous pinpricks around it.

I drank two wine coolers, watching the stars, waiting for the crunch of J.B.'s truck wheels on the drive even though he wouldn't be there for another hour. I was wearing my oldest cargo shorts, the zippered pocket soft and worn-out from my music box, and J.B.'s blue long-sleeved UCLA T-shirt, huge and cozy, smelling of him. Now that the night had gotten chilly, I was grateful for the long sleeves. I'd almost worn my peach short-sleeved T-shirt instead, but it had a blueberry-lemonade stain on the front. If only I had taken the time to scrub it out.

If only I'd worn a short-sleeved shirt, and if only Marjorie Pettit hadn't been quite so pickled in her particular vinegar of fear, and if only Alex had been into some other hobby that summer. Or, if what happened had to happen, if only it had happened two months earlier. One month, even. So I'd have had time to make it right.

If only.

I closed my eyes, happy, loosely following the conversation

in the garden, the unmistakable sighs and whispers of a couple making out on the back steps. The girl giggled, the back door creaked, and they stumbled inside together, laughing. I couldn't tell who it was, but they were probably heading up to Casey's bedroom, which would have annoyed me on any other night. Everyone knew J.B. and I got Casey's room.

Jessie something, a loud sophomore who'd never come to a Shipwreck party before, read aloud from a book she'd found on the potting table. I knew the book well, a fat volume called *The Ancient Garden Witch*, serene gray-haired woman on the cover. Casey and I teased Alex about it.

"'Blood spells are the most personal of spells. They can never be anonymous.' You've really done this, Alex? With actual blood?"

"Sure."

Ginny Ambrose was bursting with pride. "I let her do it on me once. Swear to God."

"Yeah, right," Jessie said. "They're kidding, right, Casey?"

"They're not," Casey said. "She's been after me for a year, but I've managed to fend her off. Watch out or she'll go vampire on you, too."

I was happy to hear the fondness in Casey's voice. When I opened my eyes she was pretending to bite Alex's wrist while Alex twisted away, laughing.

Jessie begged Alex to get out her gear. "C'mon, Alex. You did it for Ginny."

"And Dina," Ginny said.

Dina Pettit wasn't there, but everyone confirmed that she had, indeed, opened a vein for a lifeguard.

Poor Dina was stuck at home. Probably folding nastygrams for Mrs. Pettit to pass out at church the next morning.

Jessie went on. Her boyfriend, smoking pot on the path by the dock, was being *a tool*. She needed Alex's help, she said, begging, making everyone laugh. Other voices joined her, with other requests. "I need more help than Jessie, Alex. Just give us a tiny demonstration."

Alex looked at Casey.

Casey looked at me.

I smiled, sent her a fraction of a shrug across the bench. Alex was just being Alex. Let her have this one last night.

Finally, Casey said, "It's fine, Mom. Do your thing."

Alex's eyes slid from Casey to me. "How about a protective binding, to keep you two safe next year at school?" She couldn't hide the excitement in her voice.

"No way, Mom. You know how she is about blood. I'll let you take mine finally, or you can do Jessie's love spell for her, whatever, but leave Laur alone. Don't do it, Laur."

The little hushed crowd of Alex worshippers watched us. I liked it. I liked everyone knowing how important I was to Alex. They were as in awe of her as I'd been the summer I'd first met her. "It's that important to you?" I said.

Alex nodded.

"Don't do it," Casey said. "Mom. She had to put her head between her knees when we dissected the cow's heart in bio. Just do me so you can show off your gadgets, and put in a lock of Laur's hair or whatever."

"I won't faint." I sat up, twisting the sleeve of J.B.'s shirt.

Alex dashed up the back porch steps. "Good girl," she called. "It'll be over in a flash."

"You don't have to," Casey said, nudging my knee with the tip of her sandal.

"It's fine. I want to."

Alex came back with a shoebox and sat between us on the bench. She inserted a clean syringe into a small pewter holder with a dragon design wrapped around it. There were many appreciative *oohs* over this dragon. "The lady at the store recommended it when I bought the book," Alex said. "Purely for show, but she's cute, isn't she?" She uncapped a bottle of rubbing alcohol.

"That's kind of modern, isn't it?" Jessie said, leaning so close over the back of the bench that I could smell the beer on her breath.

"It's an old and beautiful practice, but that doesn't mean I have to give anybody an infection," Alex said.

Casey went first, doing everything she could to mess with Alex's air of ritualistic solemnity. She extended her left arm like a ballerina beginning a port de bras. "Do your worst, Glinda. I'm *so* telling a therapist about this someday."

A few seconds later—"It would be much simpler if we just got pepper spray."

"Shush. I'm buying you pepper spray, too." Alex wiped Casey's arm above the elbow. I didn't look again until the tiny operation was over and she was capping the vial of ruby liquid, wrapping it carefully in tissue to protect it from breaking, and setting it in the shoebox. Casey, pressing a piece of clean gauze to her arm, rolled her eyes at me.

"And you bury it in the garden now or what?" Jessie said, her voice reverent.

"Later. Have to look at some charts, consult the stars, you know." Alex got the laugh she expected.

Then it was my turn.

By then I was no longer in the devil-may-care, end-of-summer mood I'd been in just minutes before. Hoping I wouldn't have to put my head between my legs like Casey'd warned, I tried bunching up the sleeve of J.B.'s shirt, but there was too much fabric. I looked over my shoulder to check that the boys were still pretty far away, congregating around the path and dock. The boy and girl up in Casey's room wouldn't be looking out the window anytime soon; I could tell by the fact that they'd switched KJAZ on low, by the lapses between their soft, intimate laughter.

It was only girls in the garden tonight, and I wanted to get the bloodletting over with, so I pulled off J.B.'s shirt.

Some girl started to tease me about my lacy aqua bra. "I'll bet J.B. looooves that one, Laura—"

"Shut up. Do it fast, Mom." Casey's voice was sharp.

I didn't look. Alex rubbed my left arm with alcohol and I shivered at the cold.

Then—a sting, a warm pulling. It didn't take long. It was so fast, so small. A tiny poke, something that would barely qualify as pain.

"Almost done, don't move," Alex said, her voice soothing.

Casey cradled my head in her lap and caressed my hair. "Mom, you owe us big-time. It's almost over, Laur. You're doing great. Don't look yet…"

I was looking up at the moon, so I didn't see him at first. I only heard the whine of the gate.

Thinking it was one of the boys from the dock, I scrambled up from Casey's lap, my arm over my chest, distantly registering a thin, slicing pain as the needle in Alex's hand twisted in deep, then slipped out.

He froze for a moment, just inside the gate. He'd unfurled the black pirate flag. Maybe he'd been planning to wave it, to enter making a joke. *Ahoy.*

I touched my punctured skin and felt warm wetness, but I didn't feel queasy. Only tired.

And everything slowed down. The voices in the garden, the sounds of Casey and Alex fussing over me, receded to a distant hum. The romantic jazz turned on low, the laughter from Casey's room, were soft and indistinct, miles above me. Part of the sky.

Everything but my dad's eyes seemed slow and far away, smeared into the background paint.

Then he was at my side and it all speeded up, sharpened into sickening clarity.

He picked up the syringe, full of my dark red blood, sniffed it, then dropped it to the ground again. He stepped on it, his foot turning, ankle swiveling with a violence I'd never witnessed in him. He didn't stop until the syringe snapped, emitting a distinct, plasticky crack.

"Oh, shoot, sweetie," Alex said, fumbling on the ground for pieces of the syringe. "Mr. Christie. It's not what you think. We were taking the tiniest bit of blood for a game. A silly game…" She knelt by me, clumsily pushing a gauze pad against my arm with one hand, but I let it fall.

Casey picked it up and held it in place. "Here, Laur." She draped J.B.'s shirt over my chest. I stared down where the syringe had broken. The glinting fragments, the dark spot in the earth that now held my blood.

Alex's old and beautiful practice looked ugly to him. My father had thought she was putting something inside me, something terrible like what had killed my mom.

He walked to the gate, and for a second I thought he was leaving. But he was picking up the flag he'd dropped. He crossed the garden, set it on the white wrought iron table. "This isn't the one from the picture. Ordered it from a catalog."

The girl laughed from Casey's window, her boy murmured, and one of them turned up the music.

My father glanced up and then quickly away. As if he could see through the wall at whatever passion was unfolding in Casey's bedroom.

His eyes slowly traversed the silent girls, the empty bottles. He stared blankly past the bench at the dock, toward the distant sound of someone cracking open a can of beer, deep male hoots, splashes.

What's the harm?

Good clean fun.

Giving the kids something to do on a Saturday night so they don't get into trouble.

"Group from the church coming by soon," he said, not looking at Alex. Or me. He stared up at the moon, bright even against its field of stars. "There's been talk. You'll want to call it a night, Alexandra."

My voice sounded raspy, foreign. "Daddy. Alex was only showing us this funny witchcraft thing, it's not what you…"

But he was already pushing through the rusty garden gate.

42

Spring

At first it felt like a family.

They had their roles, their routines. Chores and inside jokes.

Daniel was the parent, resolving squabbles, letting them borrow his truck, peeling money off a thick roll for food or gas. Though he was their unquestioned leader, presiding over the house because it belonged to him and he was the oldest by nearly ten years, he had a streak of boyish recklessness.

When yellow jackets took up residence on the back porch, it was Daniel who made everyone stand on the lawn as he evicted them. Fearless, he scraped the gluey nest from the beam with a broomstick and carried the buzzing, dust-colored lump high as a flag to the driveway, where he threw a match on it. He got stung five times but said of the welts rising on his temple and hand only this: "Guess I'm not allergic."

He only went out at night. All day he talked on the phone or played his guitar. Few people were allowed in his bedroom.

Others stayed inside all day, too, or disappeared for hours. But even on the coldest days Katherine joined the group out back in the untended garden, at the picnic table under the aspen tree. It was mostly the younger kids there. They talked, the air was sweet, the radio played.

It felt like freedom.

She learned to make things to sell at the farmer's market. Discarded kitchen chairs were thrown into the truck, the seat pieces trimmed and polished until they were smooth as stones, engraved with sayings like Life's a Beach. A piece of wood that countless strange bodies had worn down, and now it would adorn a fancy vacation house.

Twigs and a bag of garish feathers from Goodwill became dreamcatchers, three dollars each. Bath bars plucked from the housekeeping cart behind a Motel 6 up the highway were wrapped in strings of blue and green wool pulled from a moth-eaten sweater. Felted soap: three bars for a dollar.

They all knew how to make something beautiful out of something ugly.

She understood that there was another economy in the house that didn't involve her. Housemates who never worked at the picnic table. Strange cars that drove up, drove off.

There were two types of customers at the farmer's market. Some were well dressed, carrying baskets or canvas bags to hold their heirloom squash and pies and local handiwork.

Others didn't have baskets and didn't make eye contact. They strolled casually from the blanket to the truck with Daniel or the tall, blond boy named Finn. They left in a hurry, their purchases hidden.

In April, whispering in bed, Alexandra admitted to Katherine that she sold for him, too, evenings. At the skate park behind the high school.

She'd sold for him in San Francisco all fall. "Nothing terrible," she said. The pills called Skittles, or Eve, or Malcolm. The ones kids used at the under-eighteen clubs.

"They're not even illegal for adults," Alexandra said.

Now Katherine knew; those wonderful candy buttons Alexandra produced from her turtleneck in the church restroom—they'd come from Daniel.

One afternoon she ran upstairs for a sweatshirt and heard Daniel and Finn and a man who didn't live in the house, arguing.

"Don't trust those guys...that last batch was No-Doz cut with Raid...probably fucking Easter Egg dye."

She crept into the bathroom and peered through the half-inch opening of the door, holding her breath.

"I'll give them a try," Daniel said. "Unless someone else wants to be guinea pig for a change?"

The other two were silent.

"What a surprise. More for me."

"Don't, dude. Test it on one of your little groupies."

Daniel scraped a gobbet off a piece of foil and popped it in his mouth.

"Man, you have a death wish."

Daniel grabbed his throat, bugged his eyes out. Then laughed, crumpling the foil and throwing it at Finn. "It'd take more than this to kill me."

He rolled up his jeans, showing off the three long, pink scars on the side of his left leg. Shiny parallel lines gouged into the hair, as if a precise animal had raked its claw down his calf. "See this fucker?" Daniel said. "My mutant mark. Only one in the world." Daniel seemed proud of this scar, but Katherine had to be careful not to stare at it when he wore shorts.

She shut the door between her room and the bathroom quietly, so they wouldn't know she'd eavesdropped. He didn't act tough or speak like this with her. He was gentle, telling her she was his favorite.

He didn't expect her to sell. He confided in her. He told her they were the same, how he was homesick, too. He missed Coeur-de-Lune, the town where he'd grown up, but couldn't bear to visit it, even though it was just over the mountain.

He missed his two brothers, who had died young. They'd both gotten sick but he'd been spared. One night he said he knew it should have been him who died.

One afternoon he showed her what he kept in a boot at the back of his closet: a child's thermos with a cowboy on it, a lasso forming the word Gunsmoke in the blue sky. He'd had it since he was a kid, he said, though he'd lost the matching lunch box. The thermos concealed a thick

roll of cash. He said she was special, that she could ask him for any-
thing she needed.

Everyone knew she was his favorite. He treated her gently, protec-
tively. He saved the pills stamped with stars just for her. They were the
best ones. When she took them, every fear, every longing for the past
dissolved into the giddy certainty that she was exactly where she was
supposed to be.

He played music for her through the bathroom doors.

He'd sent Alexandra to rescue her; she could never forget that.

43

Eighteen

August 21, 1999
The night of the last scavenger hunt

It was my mother who'd tipped my father off about the church people coming that night.

Marjorie Pettit had asked her to confront Alex but she'd refused to come along, said something to my father about people with nothing better to do with their evenings.

At the time I thought it was malicious. My mother's brilliant plan to shame me, to out me as a liar and a fraud.

But it's possible she was simply being decent. She couldn't have known that he would go. Certainly not what his going would set in motion.

My father walked over when she was sleeping. I think he brought the pirate's flag as an excuse, planning to slip in the warning to Alex about Marjorie Pettit casually, so as not to embarrass her.

Casual. The decisions that flay us often begin this way.

★ ★ ★

I called Casey from the pantry while my parents slept.

"How bad is it?" she answered.

"Bad. I tried to explain but he only said, 'You're eighteen. Sorry I intruded.' His voice was so *cold*."

"He's just embarrassed. It'll be okay, Laur."

"Did the posse of church people come?"

"Is two people a posse? It was only Marjorie Pettit and some other lady. By the time they came we'd cleaned up and it was only me and my mom. They said something about a noise complaint and stomped off. It would've been a nightmare if your dad hadn't warned us."

But it was a nightmare.

"Laur. You still there?"

"Yeah."

"I meant, a nightmare for all of us. Not just you… My mom's dying to talk to you, here…"

"I can't talk to her right now."

A pause, then Casey's underwater-sounding murmur. She'd put her hand over the phone to tell Alex I didn't want to talk to her. A wail of protest: Alex's. Loud enough to break through Casey's hand barricade. *Just let me talk to her.*

"J.B. then," Casey said.

More murmurs, knocking sounds—the handset being dropped on a table?

And then J.B.'s low, slightly raspy "Hey." His voice sounded so warm and concerned that I felt better immediately. We could fix it.

"Hey."

"You think if I talk to him it'll help?"

"Maybe. He won't even look at me. He's always defended Alex and now…"

"I know. Alex is crying, she really wants to talk to you…"

"I can't right now."

"Are you sure, she's—"

"Tell her I'll smooth things over."

★ ★ ★

I hoped when I walked into the sunny kitchen the next morning things would feel better.

But my dad didn't look at me. He concentrated on his crossword.

"I'm sorry, Daddy. What you saw. Alex was just playing around."

"You're eighteen," he said, studying his puzzle.

I was eighteen, but I'd kept my secrets well. He was sixty-seven, and it had looked ugly to him—me in my bra with boys nearby, a needle piercing my flesh, a trail of blood on my arm, couples in the bedrooms, beer bottles, the sweet cloud of pot on the path. We'd made a fool of him.

Still, I knew I could fix it. He just needed time.

Casey said Alex was writing him a letter. She wanted to get it perfect. Casey read it over the phone, "'You trusted me with your daughter, and I'll do whatever it takes to regain that trust. I know what you saw looked awful. There's no excuse. I'm responsible; I was the adult...'"

But my dad never read those words.

Five days after the party he had a heart attack in the hardware store, playing backgammon with Ollie. By the time I got to the hospital he was "stable but serious," and they told me he was very lucky. Only a moderate "event," a warning sign. Doctors were talking about stents and balloons and catheters. He was sleepy, but when I came into his room he reached for my hand.

"There's my little one," he said, smiling. He showed me the glowing red monitor attached to his index finger. *"E.T.,"* he said, lifting his hand and winking, then drifting off to sleep. We'd seen *E.T.* together at the theater in Red Pine when I was little.

They told me he was fine, to go home.

The next morning when I came downstairs my mother was already at the kitchen table gripping her mug of coffee with two hands. She'd set out another mug for me; that's how I knew.

I stared at the sun on his empty chair.

"He went very peacefully."

44

Skipping Stones

Five days later

Everyone came to my father's service, which was short, and which he would have liked. I stayed near my mother's side, grateful for her steely reserve. She wore a thick black wool dress and I studied the embossing on the skirt, like overlapping clovers, while people spoke about my dad's goodness.

"Bill Christie loved digging into the history of this town," Ollie said. "And now he's part of it. And if he had a choice he wouldn't want me talking about him. He'd want me to remind you that this building was completed in 1853 and restored in 1962, and you should all appreciate the joists in the corner over there."

Relieved laughter.

Food after, at our house. Our kitchen counter paved in casserole dishes. J.B. with his hair tucked down his collar. Casey and Alex in long blue dresses I'd never seen.

Alex trying to talk to me, the worry on her face so raw I had to look away. Me finding excuses to avoid her.

The whole town was there. Pauline Knowland hugged me, genuine tears in her eyes, and I thought about what my dad said. *People change, if you let them.*

Casey slept at my house that night for the first time. My mother didn't object. We lay in the dark for hours, talking. I couldn't sleep, but around one I pretended to so Casey would sleep for real.

When her breathing slowed, I carefully crawled out from under my comforter, leaving my music box under my pillow, and tiptoed downstairs in my thin nightgown. I pulled my dad's biscuit-colored Fair Isle sweater off the peg by the back door and wandered outside to my kayak. The moon was nearly full, an almost perfect circle, but on the water it was a great, shivering diamond, and I thought: *if only I could paddle out to the very center of that diamond. Lie down in the middle of it in my dad's good-smelling, thick sweater and close my eyes. Then, maybe, I could sleep.* I pulled the sweater on, hopped into my kayak, and paddled hard.

But when I saw the garden lamp on at The Shipwreck I changed course, my arms making the decision before my brain.

I wanted to see Alex. I wanted to tell her it wasn't her fault, that I was sorry I'd avoided her all day.

No one had forced me to surrender my body to her. I could have helped Casey get control of the parties long before. And I'd liked it, sneaking upstairs with J.B., being at the center of things, keeping Alex's secrets along with my own.

That part wasn't Alex's fault.

Alex would hug me, say my name in her special way, make me tea from some foul-smelling garden herbs. Tell me it would get better, that my father would have come around. Of course he would have.

I tied up on the Shepherds' dock and walked across cold sand, grass scattered with sharp pine needles.

There were voices in the garden. Alex's and someone else's, a man's.

It hurt, realizing she'd gone on a date after my father's service. The anger rushed back, a dry heat filling my chest, my tired head.

I turned, headed back toward the water. Then froze. Because the male voice was now rising up loud enough to recognize.

"We should tell her, Alex. Not now. Not right after her dad. But soon."

"No."

"I could tell her, if you can't."

I crept back, holding my breath. They were sitting together on the garden bench, their backs to me. Alex had her hand on his elbow.

"We can't tell her," Alex said. "Can't you see? She'll tell Casey."

"It's not right, Alex. Lying."

"Would you want to know, if you were her?"

If he responded, I couldn't hear it.

"See, we can't tell her," Alex said. "I have to protect Casey."

"What a hopeless fucking mess," he said. "Sometimes I wish I'd never delivered to your studio that summer."

"No one made you come back this summer," Alex said sharply.

For a minute there was only my shallow breathing and the whisper of a breeze ruffling through the pines.

"I know." He sighed. "I should have just forgotten about it." He choked out a bitter laugh I'd never heard. "You know she used to pretend you were her mother? She almost convinced herself it was true? You mean that much to her. She trusts you that much."

"Sweet girl."

Slowly, Alex rubbed his shoulder. Slowly, she moved closer

to him on the bench. Sank against his chest, crying. "I know it's wrong," she said. "I didn't mean for it to turn out this way."

J.B.'s hands stayed stiffly at his sides for a moment. Then he reached up and touched her hair. "We'll figure it out," he said.

There was a second, even after I heard this surreal exchange, even before I saw Alex in the warm nook where I'd rested my own head so many times, when I still believed it wasn't possible.

But I was already looking at my memories differently, shading and highlighting, just a few lines and erasures here and there, as if I was sketching with my worn-down graphite pencil.

The way Alex had teared up the day I introduced J.B. The way he stared at her photos by the stairs.

The way she'd looked in the Polaroid, kissing poor, shy Stewart against a tree. *Of course I stopped him.* But in the picture she'd been closing her eyes.

You can't see her, Laur!

When had it started? The summer they moved in, right before Alex and Casey became my life? J.B., driving for Pedersen's, innocently delivering paint, garden mulch. Delivering those sawhorses for Alex's studio. Lugging them upstairs... *Thank you, no problem.* And then.

And then the two of them. Not just before J.B. and I were together.

I should have just forgotten about it.

No one made you come back this summer.

This summer. Trysting secretly, planning their lies. Pitying me, biding their time.

I allowed another wave of grief to join the others that had been trying to drown me for days, and it was done.

When I saw her for the last time, Alex was sitting in perfect stillness as J.B. consoled her.

I paddled home quietly and slipped under the comforter next to Casey. She was still dreaming, unaware that everything had changed.

★ ★ ★

Years later I would wonder: If I had heard this conversation any other time, when I wasn't feeling so ashamed, so raw about my last week with my father, would things have been different? Would I have burst through the rusty garden gate, demanded explanations? Details? Told Casey to get my revenge?

Would I have listened to that weak voice in my head whispering *something's not right here*?

But I felt certain I'd made it happen. Pushed the two of them together somehow. I'd done it with my greed, my secrets. The terrible power of my longing for something different.

I sent Casey away at dawn, telling her I needed to be alone. I didn't leave my house or answer the phone for five days.

When I finally called Casey back one morning she said, "Hey, lady," with such love and relief in her voice I had to get it out fast before I changed my mind.

I'd decided. I would never tell Casey; I owed her this. It was all ruined anyway.

"I'm not going to CalArts, Case. I'm so sorry. You can have my half of the deposit."

"I get that. But you can't stick around Coeur-de-Lune being sad. Move into our place anyway. Go to the beach all day. Start next quarter when you're ready. Or—"

"I'm not sticking around Coeur-de-Lune. I'm going to SCAD instead. Savannah College of Art and Design, remember? It's a good program. I start September 18 but I'm flying out early."

"You turned them down. You've never been there."

"I told them about my dad and they're letting me accept after the deadline."

"You're not thinking straight. Freaking *Georgia*? J.B. said you won't talk to him or see him either and—"

"I'm so sorry, Case. I've got to go."

"Laur, please—"

Click.

I sent J.B. one email.

Things have moved way too fast. I need a break. A fresh start. Time to grieve. I hope you will respect that. I'm going to school in Savannah instead of LA.
Take care,
Laura

I hit Send then blocked him. JulianB@netzero.com could no longer send anything to kayakgirl96@aol.com. I hid under my covers, cowardly as someone starting the timer on a bomb.

He created a new account, sent me an email that I read in spite of myself:

Please. Don't. I love you.

But JBaker@readymail.net got blocked, too, and after that he stopped.

He called fourteen times that day. Nine the next, seven the next. The refrigerator door was papered in phone messages. My mother took down every one faithfully. I eavesdropped, tiptoeing down the hall so I could hear her murmuring to J.B. on the study phone. "Yes, I've given her all the messages." Her voice was surprisingly soft. "Yes, I will tell her. She's resting." Another time—"Thank you…No, you're not intruding…That's very kind." And I wondered what he'd said to warm her at last, now that it didn't matter.

I avoided Casey. When she came over I told my mother I didn't want to see her, that I had to rest.

Casey wrote me a letter. "I love you, L. Please don't shut me out. Please."

Alex wrote, too. "I'm so sorry about what you're going through, sweetie, and about the garden. Your dad loved you and was so proud of you, always. Nothing could have changed that. I want to help you. We all want to help you…"

But of course Alex's words were as false as everything else about her, and there was nothing anyone could say to make it right, to take us back to how it was. How I'd thought it was.

If I stayed in Casey's life, I'd surely spit out the truth someday. And I didn't want her to know. Alex was right about that. Casey couldn't know. If I told her she'd never forgive Alex, and she'd lose her family, too.

I could save her from that. I could do that for her, at least.

I visited Casey one last time before I left.

I went on a Wednesday night, when Alex would be at her Reiki class. I walked over. I wanted to make sure Alex's car was gone. Anyway, I hadn't felt much like kayaking lately.

Casey was sitting at the end of the dock, kicking her legs in the water, staring over at my house. When she heard me she turned, happiness and relief spreading across her face. "How are you doing, I've—"

"Can you give this to J.B.?" I sat next to her and handed her his blue shirt. I'd soaked it in ammonia, but the sleeve still had the ghost of a bloodstain where it had rubbed against my arm as I ran home.

"Sure, but—"

"And this is for you." I pulled the music box from my pocket, held it out.

"No."

"You keep it. Keep it safe."

She clenched her fists. "Laur. It'll get better. We'll help you, all of us."

"My dad was my family. This isn't my family. Please, take it." I dropped the music box in her lap and stood.

"Laur. Don't."

"I have to pack. My flight's first thing."

"Laura." Casey stood up. She shook my shoulder with one hand, gripping the music box with the other, her voice rising when I wouldn't meet her eyes. "Don't."

I whirled away from her, hoping to make it down the dock before the tears came.

"So you're leaving? Just like that? Talk to me! You're mad at her, but I get punished?"

Halfway down the dock now. Not much farther to escape her voice.

"Right. Perfect. Prude little church girl's embarrassed in front of Daddy, and the world has to end. She has to do penance for her sins. No, Laura. We all have to."

I stopped walking, and she went on, screaming now.

"Nobody forced you to join her stupid...*performance*. If you hadn't *followed* her so fucking blindly, if you hadn't wanted her to be your *mommy* so fucking bad..."

I wiped my face, turned toward her. "Good to know what you really think of me. Have fun at school, Casey."

"Laura, wait!" Her voice was strained, frantic.

But mine was strangely calm now. Calm, and certain, and cold. "I have to go. Goodbye, Casey."

Her arm flew out.

The gesture was not planned, or even conscious. I knew it. Even then. She threw it because she didn't know what else to do. Like slapping someone when they're a danger to themselves. That's all. Even then, I knew she didn't mean to throw it.

I watched it soar over the sunset mirror of the lake. There was a strange beauty in it, like Casey was skipping stones. The moment stretched out so slowly it was almost as if we could stop it, if we wanted to.

But I didn't want to. It would make it easier for me to give Casey up.

She watched my most precious thing hit the water. An animal cry escaped from her throat, and she jumped, but I knew it was too late. The metal inside would take it down. Before Casey had one arm over her head in a half stroke, a silver hinge glinted in the sun and disappeared.

Casey was resurfacing, sputtering lake water, when I turned and ran. I heard her scramble onto the dock, her feet pounding behind me.

"Laura," she cried as I passed the garden gate, the break in her voice almost enough to pull me back.

Almost, but not enough.

45

Extreme

Casey and I sat on her bench in the garden, taking inventory. One by one, I pulled items from the goody bag and set them between us on the wooden slats. Four rows of two. A tile, a stuffed mermaid. A leaf, a napkin. Four pictures.

"Look at your perfect grid," Casey said. "Just like the ones you used to make on my vanity."

"Always trying to make sense of the disorder," I said, smiling.

"And does it make sense, when you arrange it like that?"

"I wish." I shuffled the items around, messing up the grid.

"Can I ask you something?" Casey said.

"Of course."

"Are you happy? Have you been happy?" She faced me, her eyes serious, searching.

I clutched the simple armrest of the bench. The bench, so

carefully, lovingly made, where happiness had ended for me in one night. "Oh."

A nonanswer, but it came out in a soft, sustained note that told her everything. I had been safe. I had been busy. I had been fortunate, and successful.

She nodded, reached across our jumble of artifacts to touch my knee. "I'm sorry."

We sat quietly for a minute before I spoke. "But you have. And I'm glad."

She smiled. Picked up the leaf from Raptor Rock and examined its glossy chartreuse surface. "Two clues to go. Then, what? My mom shows up with a cake? Better be one hell of a cake."

"Good thing we're almost done or we'd need a bigger bag."

"Are you ready for? You know." She hitched her chin toward my house. "Clue 7?"

"Later. After the city."

"Sure," Casey said. "So I don't get ten. Why some tourist trap in San Francisco? You design their shirts, but still. It's such a long drive, and it's the only place on the list we never went together."

I knew Clue 10 by heart:

Once glass, this glorious place,
This human aquarium by the sea
Is now burned and abandoned, rubble and ruin
A tourist's curiosity
Truthful postcards the silly shop sells; buy one so I can tell

We had to get a postcard from a "silly shop" by the "rubble" of the "human aquarium by the sea." Goofy Foot was near the remains of the Sutro Baths. Alex had obviously Googled my address and seen that the shop was my biggest client.

"I've been thinking about that, too," I said. "My theory is she wants you to visit where I live, see my work?"

"Take this shindig out of Coeur-de-Lune, you mean?"

"Yeah. To make sure we stay friends. After."

"I guess that makes sense."

"Casey."

"Hmm?"

"I want to stay friends after."

She was working her left hand again, splaying and contracting her fingers, but she relaxed them and smiled. "Me, too."

"I shouldn't have stayed away so long. I didn't mean to."

"You're here now."

"I should've—"

"Don't. You should've come back sooner. My mom should've been a grown-up. I shouldn't have thrown the music box. It's never ending. Life's too short for if-onlys."

The words hung in the air, more piercing than if she'd spoken them: *especially for me.*

"It's rotten luck, Case."

"My odds weren't good. One in two."

"I thought it was super rare."

She shook her head. "There are two kinds of ALS. Random, that's the most common. And familial. I have that. I inherited the gene from my father. Nice of him to leave me something, huh? My mom found out I'd inherited it when I was eighteen."

"She's known that long? How?"

She spoke slowly, kindly, teacher to pupil. "My dad died of it, and it ran in his family. She'd known that since I was little, but when I was seventeen she learned that she could have me tested. Senior year, remember when she started losing it? She was sure the test would say I *didn't* have the gene, that I'd be on the lucky side. But…" She shrugged.

"So she brought you to the hospital for some DNA test and everyone lied about what it was for?"

Casey extended her left arm in front of her like a lazy ballerina. She turned her palm up, waited. And when I still didn't understand, she pointed her right index finger and poked the flesh of her upper arm.

She waited patiently for me to catch up, waited for the whirring and clicking in my brain to stop.

Alex's Blood Magick phase. Her kooky, random infatuation with the dark arts.

Not just another of Alex's hobbies. Not kooky, not random. It was her way of finding out about Casey.

"Magic with a *K*," I said.

"Magic with a *K*. It was just an excuse to test me without me realizing."

Casey ran through the details—Alex getting this wild idea one day, reading a book about Blood Magick in the Moonshadow occult store, a gene called SOD1, autosomal dominant inheritance patterns, a man working in a lab near Stanford who was infatuated with Alex, like so many were.

I let the specifics wash over me, needing no more proof of Alex's subterfuge than my memory of her attempts to get Casey's blood, her odd excitement in this same garden when Casey finally gave in.

"The lab guy who helped her... Remember him? Gary Summerland, no. Summerling. He drove up a bunch of times. The bald guy with the silver Audi? Serious, not her type? He's a genetic counselor she'd contacted to talk about my family history. She wasn't planning to test me at first. She says. And if the witchcraft thing didn't work she was going to try something else. Anyway, the lab guy still calls her, he's obsessed..."

I nodded. I could picture the silver Audi, a slender man paying calls all the way from Palo Alto. Our confusion over the fact that Alex let him stick around for so long. "It's so...extreme."

"My reaction exactly, when she told me. *There's no way*. But then I remembered. It's Alexandra Shepherd."

A vial secretly ferried from Coeur-de-Lune down to Palo Alto, Alex sweet-talking a smitten boyfriend in a lab coat.

It was extreme. But it was possible.

"She knew all this time and never said?"

Casey nodded.

"I can't imagine. Knowing and not being able to tell anyone."

"I'm glad she never told me. I'm glad I didn't know."

"But weren't you mad?"

"At first. But… It was brave of her. Would you want to know? Have that stalking you your whole life?"

I thought about it. Not even a question: no way. I shook my head.

"And I've had so much. Elle, girlfriends, the trips, the store. I'm glad I didn't know," she repeated. Though her voice caught at the end.

Would you want to know?

Would you want to know, if you were her?

"Casey," I said. And I almost couldn't get the rest out, because the realization was so awful. "Are you sure she never told anyone else?"

"No. I'm grateful to her. I wouldn't have been able to do it. Not in a million. I've thought about it, with Elle in my life now, how hard it would be…" She went on, saying all the things she'd wanted to share with me, everything she'd kept pent up.

I sat next to her, holding her hand, staring at the cutout of the mermaid and ocean waves in the faded wood. I listened.

But I was also outside the garden, just beyond the gate. Eavesdropping in the dark the night after my dad's funeral. And even over Casey's voice, and the roaring in my head, I could hear, clear as anything:

She can't find out.

Can't you see? She'll tell Casey. I have to protect Casey.

Would you want to know, if you were her?

46

May

Alexandra went with the group driving to the craft fair up the coast. They'd be gone Saturday night; they'd sleep in the truck bed, at the ocean under the stars. Daniel asked her to stay, to keep him company. She had a little cough he was worried about and he didn't think she should sleep outdoors. He was protective that way.

There was nobody else upstairs that night. They stayed up late, talking. He gave Katherine a pill with a star stamped on it.

It seemed the easiest, most natural thing in the world to sleep in Daniel's bed with him. She was so tired, and his caress on her shoulders was so warm and gentle. He didn't insist. She would focus on this detail, in the weeks to come. He didn't insist. His hands traveled down her shirt, and he leaned close to kiss her gently, whispering, "Only if you want to."

She woke in the night. It was dark, and Daniel slept soundly beside her. There was an ache between her legs, a sticky cold spot on the sheet under her thighs.

She looked up at the driftwood secured to the headboard. The good-luck horseshoe, just visible in the moonlight from the open window.

She pulled at it, fumbled with the wire coiled around the center, scraping her palm. She pulled again until it split into two pieces. The middle had always been more porous and weak than the ends, even before the wire had been wrapped tight around it. One half dropped behind the headboard to the floor.

She held the other piece in her hand, confused, running her hands on the splintered edge where it had broken off. She couldn't remember why she'd freed it from the wire, if she'd wanted it as a weapon or for luck. She cried out; she'd broken it, broken the moon itself, and couldn't remember why.

Daniel stirred, cradled her in his arms. He pulled the wood from her with one hand and let it drop to the floor with the other. "What've you done?" he said, laughing. "Don't worry. I'll take you to the beach tomorrow and you'll find one just like it."

Her tongue was swollen; the words wouldn't come. I won't. I never will.

"You're the only one," he whispered. "My special girl."

47

Fog

2016
Sunday, midday

I sat in the front passenger seat of J.B.'s truck, the goody bag on my lap. We'd be finished today. One postcard, one more picture. Done.

Casey had secured the goody bag with one of Elle's ponytail holders. Purple, with sparkly stars on the end. I squeezed the bag until the stars jabbed into my palm.

Casey sat in back, the oversized denim shirt she'd brought in lieu of a jacket bunched up against the window for her pillow. But she didn't nap. Nobody napped.

Nobody talked, either.

Not until we were half an hour out of Coeur-de-Lune and J.B. couldn't handle the silence anymore. "Everything okay?" he said, eyes darting from Casey's reflection in the rearview mirror to me.

"I told her," she said. "About me being sick. She's a little bummed out."

"Oh." J.B. glanced at me.

I twitched one side of my mouth sideways in a facsimile of a smile and stared out the window.

A little bummed out.

Yes. Just a little, Casey.

I concentrated on the shades of green whipping past the window. Trees that got blurrier as my eyes filled. I wiped them with my sleeve, trying to be discreet.

"Laur, don't," Casey said. "We're going to have a good day."

"I'm fine." I cleared my throat, flicked on the radio. News. Some guy analyzing Hillary Clinton's smile again. Maybe we could go to the same smile coach, a former pageant queen with a special protractor for measuring lip angles down to the arc second; I needed to work on my forced smile, too.

I flipped to a jazz station, turning it low so I could think.

She'll tell Casey. I have to protect Casey.

Would you want to know, if you were her?

J.B. tapped my knee. *You all right?* he mouthed.

I nodded, rested my cheek against the cold glass.

"I can't wait to see the beach," Casey yawned out, and after a few minutes I knew without turning that she was asleep.

Casey was sick. And I'd gotten something wrong in the garden years before.

Those two facts were clear. But nothing else was.

I stared out the window as the forested mountains of my childhood gave way to beige farmland, gray industrial towns, the blue of the bay. All the way to the foggy coast of San Francisco, I tried to knit images, clues, memories together into one piece that made sense.

We pulled up at the Ocean Beach scenic lookout after two. It was damp and cold; the sightseers on the narrow esplanade beside the highway were shivering in their shorts.

Refreshed from her nap, unburdened of her secret, Casey was in high spirits. She fed quarters into a coin-operated silver binocular stand, pivoting it back and forth eagerly. "I think I see a seal," she shouted. "Or maybe it's a rock, but let's pretend it's a seal."

We joined the tourists trudging up the hill toward the Cliff House, a boxy restaurant teetering on the edge of a rocky cliff. Sometimes Sam and I sat side by side at a window table there, sipping extra-spicy Bloody Marys. If you stared at the water long enough, hard enough, the murmurs and clinks of the bustling dining area receded until it almost felt like you were sailing out to sea.

"Lands End," Casey said thoughtfully, pausing by a sign. "What's that?"

"We're there," I said. "This whole place is called Lands End. You never came here that year you lived in the city?"

"Never. Poor, deprived me."

We wandered past the restaurant to the ruins of the Sutro Baths. I'd never thought the ruins were much to look at. Just some sad, burnt stone foundations, the eroded remains of stairwells in the sand. Puddles where there had once been massive saltwater swimming pools.

But Casey was entranced, marveling at how close we were to the ocean. She ran past the Keep Off, Dangerous Waves sign and climbed onto a broad rock, staring at the endless expanse of white-capped teal waves. Leaning into the wind, she pulled the flapping tails of her unbuttoned denim shirt taut around her stomach for warmth, revealing the too-lean curve of her back, her jutting shoulder blades.

I wondered if the stark beauty of this place made her sad, knowing what the future held. Was every second of happiness now a trap, ending in quick, devastating calculations? *How many more waves will I count? How many more rocks will I climb on?*

But when she turned from the sea her face was calm.

★ ★ ★

Casey led us from the rocks to a grassy area where a woman was singing for a knot of tourists.

"Sunshine, go away today..."

The busker grinned up at the leaden sky, hamming, and got a laugh from her audience. Casey pushed forward to drop a bill into her guitar case.

"She was a wreck at first," J.B. murmured. "Only got out of bed because of Elle."

"I'd still be in bed."

"It's moving slowly."

"So she said. I guess she's supposed to celebrate because of that?" My voice, though low, was cracked, ugly. "And that's why Alex wanted us to reunite now. Because Casey's sick?"

He paused before answering. "Yes."

I hesitated. Saying it out loud would make my mistake real. But I had to know. I spoke quickly, rushing to get my question out before Casey came back. "J.B. You and Alex never—"

Casey returned and we smiled wide. Too wide. "Nice try. I know you're talking about me. Laur, where's your friend's place?"

"That blue building up the road." I pointed. "You can't miss it."

"Good. I'm starving."

J.B. and I followed her out of the ruins and up the steep sidewalk toward Sam's until a woman asked us to take a picture of her family. Casey walked ahead while J.B. stopped and accepted the iPhone.

The family posed, the little girl in her dad's arms, the ocean behind them. J.B. framed the shot carefully. "Say...*beach*."

But the kid wouldn't cooperate. A curly-haired girl of about four in a tiny black *Star Wars* sweatshirt, she was red-faced, writhing and wailing. The parents gave up and apologized for holding us up. "Nap time," the dad said and laughed.

J.B. took my hand, rubbed it between his. "You're freezing. And Casey's way up there, we should catch up."

I walked up the hill backward. Slowly, taking one last look at the ruins from above. Sand, pools of mucky green water, rubbly outlines of foundation. Families posing for pictures.

Pictures.

"J.B., wait." I turned and grabbed his hand.

"Tired? I could use a coffee myself, and maybe—"

"That picture of Alex you used to stare at," I said. "From when she was a toddler. It was taken by the ruins. That's why she put this place on the list. I thought it was because of my work but that's not it, is it? This one is about Alex."

"You'll have to talk to Alex about that." He strode on, up the hill, breaking free of my grasp. Suddenly desperate for his espresso.

"And..." I chased after him. "And you never slept with her. Did you?"

That stopped him cold. I was aware of bodies passing us, aware that we were making a scene, blocking the sidewalk.

"I thought you didn't," I said softly, coming closer to where he stood. "I thought maybe I'd been wrong about that."

He turned, eyes wide with shock. "You actually—"

"I know it's not true. Now."

"Me and Alex? Why would you think that?"

"I heard you talking about keeping something from me. In the garden. The night after my dad's service. I was sure you were talking about how you'd been together. I thought you still wanted to be together. But that wasn't it. Was it?"

"Jesus." He closed his eyes, ran his hands through his hair, as if he could mess it up any more than the wind had already. So many filaments of silver in with the black now.

"You were talking about Casey," I said. "How she'd get sick."

He nodded. The weary pedestrians parted around us. When

J.B. opened his eyes they were so sad and disbelieving I had to look away.

It was the disbelief that hurt most. He couldn't believe how utterly foolish I'd been. Foolish, and vain, assuming their conversation had to be only about me. It disgusted me to see all that reflected in him.

I stared downhill at the ocean, at the distant line where the water disappeared into a wall of fog.

"Why didn't you tell me?" he said after a minute.

"I was a wreck." My eyes were streaming, the ocean before me a misty layer of color, grays over blues.

"But...to just leave. To leave, without... Look at me!" He shook my shoulder.

I turned to face him but still couldn't meet his eyes.

A panting older woman in a pink Ghirardelli Chocolate sweatshirt, the hood cinched tight around her face, glared at me behind J.B.'s back. Annoyed we were blocking the sidewalk. Realizing that I was crying, that J.B.'s arm on my shoulder wasn't an embrace, she softened her eyes in pity, locking her gaze on mine for a minute before ascending the hill.

"Hey, slowpokes!" Casey shouted into the wind from the crest of the hill. "No making out in the street!"

When I walked inside Goofy Foot Surf & Coffee Shack, setting off the tinkling bell over the door, Casey and Sam were already sitting together at a window table like old friends, Casey sipping a tall whipped-cream-topped drink.

"We thought you'd been carried off by a sneaker wave," Sam said.

I hugged him. He was so solid, so familiar, wearing the soft vintage Aloha shirt I'd given him for his sixty-fifth. He smelled like coffee and Big Red cinnamon gum.

When I finally let go he said to Casey, "What's gotten into this one?"

"My mom cooked up this game to keep us occupied," Casey said. "And we're a little worn-out from it. My mom can do that to you."

"I know what'll perk her up," Sam said. "Think she can handle one, Casey?"

"Maybe."

Casey nudged me, looking out the window at J.B. He was sitting on a bench across the street, unmoving. "What's up with him?"

"He wanted to see the view."

"Right." She scrutinized me. I'd made a hasty attempt to clean up outside, wiping my eyes and nose with my sleeve. But my face had to be a crumpled, blotchy mess. "What's going on?" she asked.

"Just tired."

Sam patted my shoulder only once, then entertained Casey with surfing stories as he made me a drink like Casey's, a new invention called a Gnarly Mocha. Three kinds of chocolate, cinnamon, and a little cayenne to give it a kick. I didn't touch it.

I stared blankly at the poster on the wall in front of me. It was a big emerald green print, art deco, showing the inside of the baths in their glory days. People in old-fashioned bathing costumes swimming, swinging on ropes, descending slides under a massive glass ceiling. I'd often admired the intricate design.

At the bottom it said, "When the Sutro Baths complex was completed in 1896, it was the largest indoor swimming center in the world… The structure, long vacant, burned down in 1966."

"Sam," I said. "Is this right? The baths burned in '66?"

"Yep. Must've been something to see."

1966.

Alex was born in 1959. She'd said it all the time, how she was one of the last children of the fifties. I calculated.

Truthful postcards the silly shop sells; buy one so I can tell.

"I like this guy," Casey said. "Guess you were right about

the clue, Laura. My mom must have wanted me to meet Sam. Searched online or whatever, saw you designed for him?"

I nodded, though I knew for sure now that she was wrong, that Alex had another reason for sending us here.

"Sam. You have a postcard with this Sutro print, right?"

"That rack over there. Top." He watched as I spun the post-card rack. "We only have one left."

Sam would never know this ordinarily. He was terribly lax about inventory. So I wasn't surprised when I flipped the card over and saw his handwriting:

Tucker, 8 p.m.
4 Ridge Farm Road.

I slapped the card on the table.

"Busted," he said.

Casey sighed. "So you've met my mom. Is she in the back room with champagne or what?"

He shook his head. "She called today and asked me to write that. That's all. Who's Tucker?"

"Not who," I said. "Where. A little town near where we grew up."

J.B. didn't speak on the drive back. Somewhere around Sacramento, Casey began snoring softly.

I had worked out one more fact:

The baths burned in 1966.

Alex was supposedly born in 1959.

But in the picture of her as a one-year-old the baths had already burned. If she was telling the truth about her age it would be way before 1966 in that picture. And the baths would still be standing.

So she'd lied about her age. *Truthful* postcards, Alex had written in the clue. I'd glossed over the word, thinking it was just filler, but *truthful* meant something here. And *so I can tell* didn't mean "so I can tell that you went there."

If my math was right, Alex couldn't have been older than sixteen when she'd had Casey, not twenty-two like she'd said. Was that what she wanted to tell us? That she'd been really young when she got pregnant? And she had been too ashamed to say it all these years?

J.B. stared straight ahead, driving carefully. His hands clutched the steering wheel a little too tight. When he felt me watching him he glanced over, pressed his lips together in a tight, wan smile.

I was grateful for it, but it was sadder than if he'd wept.

48

Spring/Summer

When Alexandra came back to the house Katherine didn't tell her about Daniel. She didn't tell anyone.

He didn't take her to the beach to replace the driftwood as he'd promised.

But he whispered that she was special, that he'd chosen her out of all the girls in the house. That it was beautiful, nothing to be ashamed of.

It became one more part of her new life, that secret hour at night. Sitting at the picnic table under the budding aspen tree, surrounded by her new family, she could almost forget it.

Katherine learned to carve. She practiced on soap until she could make simple items out of balsa wood: spoon rests, jewelry dishes with a graceful stalactite in the center for holding rings.

One day a girl stole a bag of music-box workings from a craft store in Humboldt. She stuffed it down the back of her jeans along with a pouch of imitation opals. Everyone pounced on the opals but nobody knew what to do with the music boxes. Sometimes they played games with them at the table, trying to get the music to start at exactly the same time.

They were cheap things, the kind that would go in a child's balle-rina jewelry box. Most played "Greensleeves" or "Beautiful Dreamer."

But one played another tune. Nobody at the table could identify it—a frustrating snippet that seemed to end too abruptly, on a down note. Long after the others got bored with the music boxes, Katherine played this one. She didn't know why she liked its song.

"Maybe you heard it before," Alexandra said one morning in June. She was covered in a lacy pattern of shade from the aspen tree's thin branches, on which green, spade-shaped leaves hung in delicate clusters. She was expertly wrapping wire around a piece of white sea glass for a pendant; these could fetch five or six dollars. They handed all the cash from the farmer's markets over to Daniel.

"I don't think so." When the music box finished playing, Katherine picked it up and examined the cylinder spiraled with Braille-like mark-ings, the miniature crank, then returned to her work. She'd learned to make earrings, though they were tedious compared with carving. She made one pair—imitation opals dangling from chains of cheap silver jump rings—before she put down the jewelry supplies and started to play the song again.

Everyone groaned; the pockmarked boy named Bryan snatched up the music box and pretended he might drop it down the umbrella hole in the table.

Seeing her alarm, he handed it back.

Katherine wandered away cradling it, as if it was a newborn she wanted to cuddle in private.

At night she would lie next to Alexandra waiting for the creak of Dan-iel's bathroom door. Her signal to come to him. He would give her one of the new pills, sometimes two, so what happened in the bed was soft-edged as a dream. He told her that he wouldn't let anyone take her from him. Everyone else had been stolen away, everyone he'd loved in his little hometown. But she'd never leave, would she? They were the same, he told her. Making a new family to replace what had been lost. He carried her back to bed after, tucked her in.

One morning in July, before the others woke, she retrieved the pieces of broken driftwood from beneath Daniel's bed and brought them to the picnic table. She cut and shaped and sanded them. Experimented with hinges and the jewelry glue that was so strong some of the kids sniffed it. Whittled out nooks so the tiny cranks could be turned. The driftwood became two cleverly concealed music boxes.

Her plan was to sell them at the farmer's market for ten dollars apiece.

She sat on the blanket with the open music boxes and two sea-glass pendants she'd made. A little boy of five or six with berry-stained lips picked up one of the music boxes, and she showed him how to turn the crank, to play the song she loved. His distracted mother, arms loaded down with a baby, tote bags spilling over with produce, tried to buy it.

"I'll give you five dollars," she said, digging in her purse.

But Katherine didn't like the way the boy handled the music box. He'd lose interest before he got home, and the case would soon be broken under a pile of abandoned action figures and trucks.

"I changed my mind," she said, handing the mom back her crumpled bills.

"I'm not giving you more money."

"I don't want more money."

Alexandra, sitting a few feet away selling candles, smiled at her, watching the woman stalk off with the wailing boy.

Alexandra didn't smile as much now, and when she did it only made her eyes look old, because they didn't match the smile. That was the only way Katherine could describe it.

Katherine returned the smile, grateful.

They didn't see each other as much as they used to, even though they lived in the same house. Alexandra didn't always sleep in the bed with her; she drifted to other rooms in the house, or slept during the day. She was no longer the bold girl who was going to act, sing, paint.

Katherine kept one music box for herself and gave the other to Alexandra, to make her smile again.

49

Weathr-All

I did Clue 7 alone.

J.B. and Casey waited in the truck, in the driveway of my old house.

I walked over to the little clearing in the side yard, up a slight hill. When I was a girl, it was my favorite place to sketch or stare out at the lake. I liked it because it was quiet, and far from the house, but I could still see my father working in his shed.

I was sure the bench would be ruined. I'd never asked anyone to take care of it.

But the lines were still true, the wood still pretty. Someone had cared for it. They'd rubbed every inch with varnish, on the schedule recommended on the Weathr-All or EvR-Seal can. They'd carried it inside in winter. It was almost as beautiful as when my dad first gave it to me.

I sat and gripped the armrest. "I miss you, Daddy," I whispered.

I wished, more than anything, that he was there. To wink at me, cheer me up. Even if he couldn't tell me what was going on.

I wished we could have another week together. I wasn't greedy—I wasn't asking for months or years.

I only wanted a week, a plain, uneventful, joking-around week, the way we always were together. To undo the last week we really got. Six days of shame and silence.

I'd forgiven myself for hiding the truth about the parties. But I hadn't forgiven myself for not trying harder to talk to him after that night. Maybe, if I hadn't given up so easily, I could have pushed through our mutual embarrassment and disappointment.

I took the photo quickly. A blurry, tilting shot with only my fingertip visible in the cutout of the moon, to prove I'd actually been sitting there.

When I returned to the truck J.B. held his finger to his lips; Casey was curled up on the back seat, asleep again.

Let's let her sleep, he mouthed.

Quietly, he opened the door and climbed out, and we both winced when it shut, fearing the *thunk* would wake Casey. But she only sighed and shifted a leg.

J.B. and I sat cross-legged under a cluster of pines by the driveway, looking up at my house. I'd had the shutters painted the previous summer. An inoffensive dove gray chosen by the property manager, a color that screamed *rental*. There was a pot of yellow-and-purple pansies by the front door, but even those felt too tidy, staged. The house needed a pile of shoes on the porch, a tacky kid's sticker in a window, to look like a family lived there.

"Who took care of the bench?"

"We all did," he said. "All three of us."

"Thank you."

"I might not have helped much the first few years." He smiled ruefully.

"You thought I just bailed. No goodbye, no real explanation."

"Alex said you only needed time. That you'd come back. Even when your mom moved, that October after you left, we all hoped..." He shook his head. "I didn't want to be mad at you. How can you be mad at someone when she's lost her father?"

"Because she broke up with you in a three-line email..." I pulled up a hank of grass, sifted it onto my knees. "And vanished. You must've hated me." I plucked at more grass, a habit from when I was a girl.

J.B. reached over and touched my cheek, waited for me to still my hands, meet his eyes.

"I didn't hate you," he said softly. "And I don't hate you now. I just wish you'd told me what was in your head."

He leaned closer, unblinking, not letting me look away even though he had to see that in a second I'd be crying again, at the waste of it.

"J.B., what's this game about?" I asked, barely able to form the words.

He sighed, shook his head.

"Is it something to do with Alex lying about her age? She had Casey young, really young. And she finally wants us to know?"

He hesitated, so I knew before he spoke what his answer would be: "Yes."

I grabbed his hand. "But that photo, you saw it years ago. Why didn't you tell us back then? Tell me what's going on."

I could sense by the pained way he squinted that he was torn. But then the words came, slowly at first. Halting, as he measured whatever loyalty he had to Alex, whatever promise he had made to keep her secrets, against my plea. And my desperate grip on his hand. "Her lying about her age, that old picture by the stairs...that was what first got me thinking. I knew she was hiding something."

And then he spoke more rapidly. "I watched her, the way she looked at you. You'd told me you fantasized that she was your mother, and I started to think maybe she could be. Or your sister, another relative."

"Is she, is that—"

"No. I was wrong about that. You're not related, Laur."

He paused, waiting for this to sink in.

"That summer they moved into The Shipwreck, when I was delivering for Ollie, I noticed a loose floorboard in her studio. I was trying to fix it so her sawhorses would sit level. And I saw something hidden under it. I thought it belonged to the Colliers, so I left it without saying anything. It felt wrong to disturb it."

"What was under there? Papers, pictures?"

"Something...small. Something...unusual. It wasn't a big deal. But I remembered it a few years later, when you showed me another one almost exactly like it. Something that opened. Something you'd always kept close—"

"My music box," I said softly.

He nodded a fraction of an inch.

I'd tried not to think about it over the years. It made me sad to picture it, silently drowning, disintegrating.

I had a small upright piano in the city, and I let myself pick out the notes to "Love is Blue" once a year, on the morning of my birthday. A ritual to help contain the sadness. Control it. At least, that's how I'd justified it to myself.

"I wish like hell I'd never pushed her to explain." He breathed deep, went on, the words pouring out now. "But I did push her. One night, that last summer, maybe a week after you showed me your music box, I got her alone and told her what I'd been thinking. How you fantasized she was your mother, even your crazy theory about your feet being identical. Except it didn't seem so crazy anymore... She tried to laugh it off. But something was off, I knew I'd rattled her. So a couple weeks later, when you and Casey were late getting back from Tahoe, I pulled up the floorboard in the studio again to show her the music box, forced her to talk. That's when she finally told me everything. And then your dad… And then you were gone, Laur."

Another music box.

J.B. had said my wildest fantasy wasn't true; Alex wasn't a relative. But she knew something about my birth mother.

"Tell me," I said. "What is the everything?"

J.B. flinched. I'd squeezed his hand so hard my fingernails had dug into his skin, almost piercing the flesh. I ran my finger along the chain of tiny red crescents on his wrist. "Please, J.B. I've been a good sport. I've gone along with everything. So has Casey. But we've had enough. What does Alex know?"

He pulled me to him. "I'm so sorry," he whispered, his lips humming against my temple. "The rest is for her to tell you. And she will soon, I promise." He kissed me near my hairline. Then again on my cheek, just as softly, but longer this time.

He hugged me tight until I relaxed for the first time in days, letting my body soften against his warm chest.

50

In August, Daniel dropped a glass. He ignored the shards on the kitchen floor and immediately poured another drink. When the bottle slipped and a lake of amber liquor spread on the counter, dripping over the edge, he threw the bottle at the wall.

A piece of glass struck Katherine's ankle, leaving two glistening dark commas of blood, but he pushed past her without noticing.

In September, Daniel's merchandise began to get more expensive, its palette more subdued—gray or dun-colored. His new customers didn't need pastels or stars or Hello Kitty faces.

Katherine didn't, either.

In October, Daniel began welcoming a new type of houseguest. Kids who hunched over spoons and slept next to needles. Katherine didn't bother to learn names anymore, people came and went so frequently.

The picnic table sat empty.

Katherine watched the aspen tree out her window change from emerald to moss green to yellow. Then to a gold so unearthly it seemed to be *on fire. One afternoon, her mind thick from a new pill, she imagined it was trying to warm her as she lay curled on her bed in the chilly house. The heat had been cut off.*

All winter, Daniel grew thinner. His guitar lay untouched under his window. He slept all day and gradually stopped opening the bathroom doors for her at night.

Something had happened to his feet. They'd flattened so it was difficult to walk, and someone whispered that he was probably using too much, that the changes in his body were from the new drugs.

Katherine's body changed, too.

It wasn't just that she was lethargic and weak, that every day she woke a little hungrier for the pale brown tabs Daniel hid, carelessly, under his mattress.

Her breasts felt tender, she couldn't remember her last period.

Her mother had been a nurse, so she knew what was happening, though she didn't tell anyone.

She wondered if her mother was still in Idaho. She imagined her living on a flat, endless farm. She couldn't picture her mother's face anymore; she saw only a stranger in a bonnet, her face hidden.

She wondered if her mother was happy, and if she would return if she knew.

But the thought, or maybe it was a wish, was too painful. Katherine swallowed whatever anyone would give her to keep the thought from coming back.

51

Treasure

2016
Sunday evening

J.B. drove us to the address on the postcard at sunset.

I held the purple goody bag. We'd had a hard time squeezing everything in, but by stacking the pictures in one corner and bending the mermaid over double we'd managed.

A little before eight we turned onto a long dirt road and pulled into the driveway of a shabby white house with a tilting for-sale placard out front. No sign of Alex, or anyone else. The lawn was all weeds and the place had obviously been broken into at least once; two smashed downstairs windows had been sloppily boarded up.

"Is she inside?" I asked.

"You're supposed to wait out back," J.B. said. "Under the tree." He gave my hand a reassuring touch.

Casey and I looked at each other. She raised one eyebrow a

fraction of a centimeter and we agreed, silently; we'd been obedient children long enough.

We scrambled out of the truck and ran up the porch steps.

"Guys, it looks pretty rickety, I don't think you should—"

"We'll be careful," I yelled back. I was already at the door, shaking the rusty Realtors' lockbox. It was ancient, but held fast to the key rattling inside.

"Over here," Casey said.

She was around the corner trying to wiggle into a window. "Give me a boost."

"Maybe I should be the one who—"

"Don't." *Don't treat me like an invalid.*

"Got it. Here." I clasped my hands to make a stirrup and she stepped into it so she could shimmy through the window.

"What do you see?" I called.

"I'm in the kitchen. I don't see anything. I smell plenty, though. This place needs some serious potpourri action. I'll try the back door."

A minute later she unbolted the wooden door and unlatched the rusty screen.

I glanced over my shoulder at our designated meeting spot— a picnic table under a single aspen tree. The leaves were green now but would turn gold-red by October.

No Alex yet.

I stepped inside and tried to breathe through my mouth, but the sharp scent of animal urine, and something humid and cloying, maybe rotting wood, was impossible to avoid. "You're right about the smell."

We walked through the empty rooms, staying close.

"What's she up to?" I whispered.

"Don't whisper. It freaks me out." Casey crooked a finger into my belt loop as we edged down the dark hallway.

"What are you up to, Alex?" I yelled.

"Mom! We've had enough of your juvenile horseshit!"

"You okay?" J.B. called from the porch. He was at the window, trying to peer in through the boards.

"We're fine," Casey called back.

Kitchen, den, front room, bath, dining room. The toilet had been stolen; all that was left was a filthy, gummy circle in the bathroom floor. In the dining room, the floral wallpaper had been ripped off in great, triangular strips. Except for a few mounds of crumpled newspaper pages, the rooms were empty.

I started to walk up the narrow staircase but Casey held me back by my belt loop.

"There could be rats," she said. "Waiting at the picnic table wouldn't kill us."

"Rats won't kill us. Stay here if you want. I'll check."

She followed me.

The upstairs was smellier and stuffier than downstairs, the floors covered in carpet that might have been blue once; it was so faded and stained it was hard to be sure.

Upstairs was empty, too. Just two bedrooms, a small, pink-tiled Jack-and-Jill bath between them.

I shoved a window open in the larger bedroom to let in some air, and spread my jacket on the floor so we could sit while we waited. We stared out back at the empty picnic table, just visible under the canopy of the big aspen.

"My mom." Casey sighed. "She drives me nuts. But she gets things done. Anyone else would've just called you. Told you I was sick, invited you for brunch."

"I would've come."

"Because you felt sorry for me. Like those Make-a-Wish people. This was better."

I nodded.

"But don't ever tell her I admitted it."

"You really don't know what the prize is?" I said.

"No. Unless she says, 'Ta-da, this is the prize.' This. Us. Being friends again."

"I thought that, too. Friday. But now I think there's more."

"You think she's giving us this house so we can be roomies at last?" Casey raked her fingers through the frayed carpet, tilted her head to inspect the brown bloom of a water stain on the ceiling. "It's kind of a dump."

"It's more."

"Why're you so sure?"

"Case. The reason I stayed away so long. The real reason. I made a mistake about something."

"What?"

I shook my head, looked outside. Still no Alex.

"What do you mean, mistake?"

"I heard your mom and J.B. talking. After my dad's funeral. They were talking about keeping a secret so I thought they were sleeping together."

"What the—"

I looked her in the eyes. "It's not true. They were talking about your gene."

"I don't get it. J.B. knew I'd get sick? She told him?"

"Yes. And there's more."

We sat facing each other by the window, our plastic bag of treasures between us.

"My sweet girls. There is more."

I stood and Alex hugged me, breathing out my name in one long, musical note. "Laura."

She kissed the top of Casey's head but Casey wouldn't stand. She kept her arms tight at her sides. "Where's Elle?"

"J.B. took her for a root beer float so we could talk."

"So start talking, fast," Casey said.

I handed Alex the purple goody bag. "We only got nine. Doctor Mona's closed."

"That's okay, sweetie. Nine is wonderful." She handed me a small white box.

I removed the lid and saw familiar silvery-gray; touched the soft, ridged texture of driftwood.

"Your mother made it for me," Alex said. "I know it can't replace the one you lost."

It was different from mine. Slightly bigger, the case more of a triangle than an oval. But the two stiff silver hinges holding the hollowed-out halves together were the same, and so was the cheap music box mechanism snugged inside.

"It used to play 'Greensleeves' but it doesn't work anymore, honey. I had it hidden away too long."

There was a photo taped to the inside cover. Small and faded, cut from a larger picture. Two girls in jeans sitting on a couch: one with long red hair, one with long brown hair. They weren't smiling or looking at the camera, and someone's elbow was marring the shot, floating above their heads.

"Mom, what is this? We've had enough games. Tell us what the hell's going on."

"Laura, look at me. Your mother's name was Katherine. I met her when we were thirteen, in 1979. We ran away and ended up in this house. Your father. Laura. He was here. He was…" She shook her head.

"Katherine had green eyes and brown hair, just like you. She liked strawberries. She didn't laugh much, but when she did it was the most gorgeous sound in the world.

"I wish I had a better picture for you. A diary. But this is all I have. Except memories of her. Stories."

She took a deep breath, shaking her head rapidly in frustration. "I'm screwing this up. I wanted to explain the right way, the perfect way."

I stared at the photo. "Just tell us, Alex."

52

The Visitor

April 1981

Katherine and Alexandra were sleeping upstairs when the visitor arrived. A tidy, silver-haired woman in a pale blue suit.

She knocked and knocked and finally pushed the front door open. She found strangers in the house. Filth. Daniel wasting away, curled up on the stained mattress in his bedroom.

And in the room attached to his, two young girls, pregnant with her grandchildren.

They had both been Daniel's special girls.

"He didn't," she said, sinking against the doorjamb and closing her eyes. Shaking her head, at what her son had done. "You poor children."

For months Katherine had kept to herself, sleeping, staring out the window, spending long hours in the bathroom monitoring the changes to her body. Her stomach was fuller, jutting forward between her hip bones.

She was tired all the time, but she didn't get sick like the women did in movies. She didn't tell anyone. She wore her loosest shirts.

Not that anybody would have noticed. Something had broken down in the house, and Alexandra rarely slept in their bedroom now.

But one day in early March, Katherine had heard retching behind the bathroom door.

She'd peeked in, and learned that Alexandra's body had changed, too.

Together, they'd stopped using. And they tried to plan their next escape. Alexandra had heard of a clinic in San Francisco, if they could find bus money to get there. One night they spoke of hitchhiking to Sacramento, where the perfect family in Eight is Enough *lived. There would be clinics there.*

But the house was too chaotic for plans; it was a jumble of immediate, individual wants.

Daniel stayed in his room all the time, listless and unreachable.

One afternoon when Katherine tiptoed in for the Gunsmoke *thermos, she found only a crumpled five-dollar bill. It smelled, faintly, like sour milk, and she had known then for sure that Daniel couldn't help.*

But the visitor said she would help. She seemed sure of what was best.

She lived in Boston and came to California rarely, though she owned two houses there. This one where her son had gone to waste, and another one nearby on the lake in Coeur-de-Lune, where he had grown up.

In the days to come, in the whirlwind of murmured phone calls and shopping and strangers coming and going, Daniel's mother explained that Daniel would not come back. He would not get well. He would get hospice care; he had what many in the Collier family had. Two of his siblings, seven cousins, an aunt, probably many more.

They had what ignorant people called a curse.

Daniel's father had died in the war, so it was impossible to know if he'd had it, too, but the doctors said it was likely.

Daniel had always thought he was the lucky one. He took risks that became increasingly disturbing, she told them. At seventeen, when one of his older brothers was long dead and another was sick, on a feeding tube, he drove his mother to the market in her car so fast, ignoring her pleas to slow down, that he made her weep.

At twenty-three, he skidded his motorcycle on a wet road, dislocating his shoulder, slashing his leg except for where two small metal fragments had already embedded in his flesh. It was a miracle he hadn't died.

It only made him feel more invincible.

"A way to hide his fear," she said one night, as Alexandra and Katherine listened, looking out the bedroom window at the rain, the dark silhouette of the aspen tree.

"His demons were his fear and his guilt. I'm his mother. I know. I spoiled him. I bought him this house, to get him out of my sight. And I moved away. I shouldn't have.

"Of course it does not excuse his unspeakable behavior."

That's what she called the acts that led to their canted bellies.

It was too late for a clinic, but she would pay for everything. She would make sure they got help so their babies were born healthy. When she asked if they had family they shook their heads, exchanging a look only after she'd turned her back. She seemed relieved about this.

She was efficient, certain, helping them pack their bags for a home she'd found.

Katherine almost left her music box behind. But at the last minute she slipped it in her bag.

She kept the music box on her nightstand in the group home in Oakland.

After her baby was born in June, she played the song for her, learned to bottle and bathe her. She went to meetings—Group and One-on-One and Drop-in. She stayed clean.

And it seemed things might turn out all right.

But when the baby was five weeks old she got a package from a charity called Wee Care. Clothes that wouldn't fit the little girl until she was six and twelve and thirty-six months. The numbers on the tags scared her; they looked like another trap.

Katherine decided to run away with a girl from the house. A hard girl nobody liked.

Alexandra, eight months along, begged her not to go.

But Katherine made Alexandra swear not to wake anyone, saying that it was better this way, the little girl was better off, she couldn't do it. "I just can't."

Her daughter was sleeping on her back, her impossibly small, pearlescent arms flung over her head. Katherine kissed her on the forehead, full of shame at what she was about to do.

She set the music box next to one open pink hand, so it seemed as if the girl was reaching for it.

She whispered, "I love you."

And then she left.

53

The Prize

2016
Sunday evening

By the time Alex finished talking it was nearly dark. The story
was sad, but then I'd always known my mother's story was sad.

"I'm sorry, honey," Alex said, wiping her face. "Sorry I
brought her here. Sorry I couldn't help her. I've wanted to say
that for so long."

She paused, but neither Casey nor I spoke so she went on.
"Your grandmother. Daniel's mother. She hadn't lived around
here for years, but her old church friend arranged for you to
be adopted by a nice older couple in Coeur-de-Lune. Private,
closed adoption."

Old church friend. Barbara Macon. My stork.

"Your parents didn't know anything. Your grandmother had
given me money over the years and when she died, when Casey
was eight, she left me more. And The Shipwreck. For years,

I stayed away. But I knew you were there, Laura. So close. I thought, if I could make sure you were happy, if we could make the house our own... And we did make it our own. The three of us. Didn't we?" Alex's voice cracked at the end, pleading.

Casey, sitting perfectly still, eyes closed and cheeks wet, didn't acknowledge Alex.

I was supposed to cry, too. To say something profound, heart-wrenching.

But I couldn't. I was remembering the strangest thing. "The lavender."

A word so odd, so apparently random that Alex looked alarmed, and even Casey opened her eyes.

"Lavender?" Alex crept close, cupped her hand around my cheek, clearly worried that her story had pushed me over the edge. "Honey?"

I pulled away from Alex, speaking only to Casey. "I'm not crazy. I was remembering that vase of lavender on the mantel. At The Shipwreck. It was always sliding in front of the picture my dad gave you of the Collier boys on the dock, and I could never figure out why. It was like...like a poltergeist kept moving it."

Casey nodded slowly, remembering this subtle haunting.

But the ghost was Alex. "You didn't want to look at the Colliers." I turned to Alex, challenging her.

Alex took a deep breath. "No. I couldn't."

Casey finally spoke. "Was he in the picture?"

"Daniel was the little one in front with the flag," Alex said. "The two-year-old, the one you thought was so sweet."

A sweet little boy, who'd grown up and done a monstrous thing to two sweet young girls.

Casey stood and paced around the room, settling by the window. She leaned against the wall, staring at the picnic table.

"I wanted you to know each other, even if I couldn't explain why," Alex said. Rushing now. "How could I have told you? What your father was like, that me and Katherine were so young.

I couldn't even say the word out loud until I was twenty-five. *Rape*." She said it clearly, not lowering her voice, so that Casey and I didn't have to say it first.

She went on more gently. "And the odds that one of you would get sick… But after they isolated the gene, and I read how families were getting tests, I thought, if I could only make sure you were okay, maybe I could tell you someday. When you were old enough. You were both seventeen when I found out I could test you. So I—"

"I told her," Casey said.

"I thought it was the answer to everything. So clever. I hoped you'd both get lucky."

She added quickly, touching my knee, "You don't have the gene, Laura. I got your results two months ago."

"But my blood spilled, I saw it."

"Then you needed blood. Now you can use other tissue. Like hair."

"Mom, what the hell?" Casey whirled from the window to face Alex.

I knew Casey was picturing a covert op, someone dispatched to pluck my hair on Market Street. It wasn't beyond imagining, after everything else Alex had pulled off.

"Your hairbrush," Alex said. She closed her eyes in shame, acknowledging the absurdity of what she'd done. "Elle was rooting around in a box of stuff from your drawer and asked who it belonged to. It was in winter, right around when Casey first got symptoms."

"Jesus," Casey said.

"And that's why you invited me now," I said. "Because you knew I was okay." *And because Casey knew she wasn't.*

"I didn't know what else to do," Alex said, opening her eyes. "It's as simple as that. As simple and complicated as that. I always thought you'd come back. I was… I'm sorry, Laura, but I was angry with you, for how you left Casey. I knew she'd need her best friend."

"I thought…" I said.

Alex looked at me, anxious, desperate.

"I'll tell you someday what I thought."

"It was your idea to foster Elle." Casey jumped in. "You're not going to say she's a Collier, too? Some goddamned orphaned Collier?"

"No. She's just a little girl whose mother was not so different from Katherine. Or me."

For a few minutes the three of us didn't speak. Casey paced, and Alex fiddled with the ponytail holder securing the goody bag, looking nervously from me to Casey.

I started to whisper something, then stopped myself.

Casey crossed the room, sat on the floor by my side, and touched my arm. "Laur wants to ask something else but she's scared."

"It's nothing," I said.

"Anything," Alex said. "Ask anything."

"The music box song," I said softly. "It's meaningless, then? She didn't even know what it was?"

Alex took a long time to respond, casting about for a gentle answer. So I knew before she spoke that I was right. "She loved it. Does it matter why?"

I shook my head. Though the tears came, finally. I'd wanted it to be a message from her. I'd wanted that more than anything.

I pulled my knees to my chest and hugged my elbows, resting my forehead on the bridge of my arms, letting the tears go inside this dark, private shelter. Neither of them spoke, but after a minute I felt someone's warmth on my back, a comforting weight that seemed barely heavier than the red wool blanket, and I knew it was Casey who had draped herself over my shoulders.

When I raised my head, the room was in shadows and Alex was gone. "Where's your mom?"

"Waiting downstairs."

"Well," I said, wiping my nose, looking up at her. "Some prize."

I couldn't say it out loud yet: a sister.

"I like the prize." Casey smiled, almost shyly, for her, eyes darting around the room before connecting with mine. Then her smile ebbed. "But Daniel. I always imagined…"

"Someone different. Someone good."

All those years of fantasizing about why my mother had given me up. "Poor Alex. The two of them, they were *kids*."

"She's still a kid," Casey whispered slowly. She shook her head slightly, disbelieving.

It explained so much. Part of Alex would be forever frozen at thirteen.

Casey tilted her head at the doorway to the hall. "So do we forgive her?"

We could punish Alex for her secrets. Refuse to speak to her. Add more hurt and wasted time to the pile, the tangled result of her good intentions. I knew that Casey wouldn't have posed the question if she wasn't going to at least try to forgive Alex. And I knew I would try, too. Alex had done her best in an impossible situation.

"It's not her fault I left, Case," I said. "Do you forgive me?"

"I will if you don't run away again."

I shook my head. *Never.* "Casey. I wish—"

A little girl's laughter floated up through the open window. J.B. was outside entertaining Elle, giving us time.

We rose and walked to the window, but couldn't see them. Their voices were coming from the front.

Together, we breathed in the night wind side by side, staring out at the swaying dark arms of the tree.

epilogue

September 2016
Coeur-de-Lune

I checked over the dining room table. Teapot, cups, saucers, lemon slices, chicken-tarragon sandwiches, apple-currant salad. Place settings for two: blue-rimmed china I'd bought specially, polished silver, the ecru cloth napkins my mother had embroidered with silver *C*s. She'd given them to me for my thirtieth birthday but I'd never used them.

The house was spotless. Even Jett, in her new run by the side of the house, was brushed to black satin.

But I'd almost forgotten the most important thing: the cakes Elle and I had baked yesterday afternoon while Casey was napping.

I pulled the white platter from the fridge, unpeeled the plastic. A dozen golden squares with shiny cobalt crescents of blueberry filling inside. Elle had arranged them with the crescents open to the right.

"So they look like the lake," she'd said.

There was way too much cake for two people.

Surveying the lunch spread for the hundredth time, I wished

I hadn't overdone it. The dated menu, my mother's signature cakes, the low September sun bouncing off the good silver: It all looked desperate. Anxiety spread out on a pretty blue tablecloth.

My mother was finally here.

I'd been asking her to visit for weeks. Ever since I rented my place in San Francisco to a twenty-three-year-old tech whiz girl from New York and moved into our old house on the lake with J.B.

My mother knew everything now. I'd told her one afternoon in July, after I'd dropped Casey off at UCSF for her monthly clinic visit. We'd sat on her tiny, sunny balcony and she'd listened quietly while I'd shared Alex's story. My story.

Then she'd gone into her bedroom, returning half an hour later looking tidy as always, but with a faint rosy shine rimming her eyes and nostrils.

Casey and I decided it was progress, that she hadn't powdered over the evidence of her tears.

But she'd resisted visiting Coeur-de-Lune. "Too many memories," she'd said brusquely, the first time I'd asked.

I knew a little about that.

So I'd worked on her, showing her photos of the house every time I'd visited. Pictures of Elle, gangly and laughing in purple shorts, throwing Jett's tattered tennis ball off the dock. Of the new white paint on the shutters, the pine out back at its most vivid jade green.

"It's such a long drive," she'd say, though I'd always offer to shuttle her both ways, that she could stay over, or not. Her choice.

"Soon," she began saying, sometime in August.

And now she was here for the night.

I'd given her a quick tour. She'd walked into each room silently, taking in the new furniture, the new counters in the kitchen and baths. When she'd seen everything, she nodded. "It fits. It's not trying to look too modern."

Then she'd disappeared into her room to rest after our long drive.

She'd been in there for almost an hour. I was considering hiding the Blue Moon cakes and serving store-bought oatmeal cookies instead when her door opened. She'd brushed her hair and changed from the pantsuit into a drapey cream blouse and green skirt.

"Isn't this a nice luncheon?" she said, inspecting the table. Her glance lingered on the cake platter for a long time, her smile not quite covering her surprise.

She made an effort to show an interest in my new life.

"How is she doing?" she said, meaning Casey.

"She gets tired, but she's managing. Her doctor even lets her swim if she takes it easy."

She glanced out the kitchen window at the lake, as if Casey would appear in the water on cue, showing off her slow but still-graceful sidestroke.

"I've missed it," she said, looking at the slash of blue out the window.

That was one thing we'd always had in common. We'd missed our lake.

She asked about Elle, who'd just started fifth grade and was obsessed with tetherball and her birthday party at the skating rink next Saturday.

As we were finishing up our cake she even said, "Your Julian did a marvelous job on the built-ins in the den."

Your Julian meant J.B.

She didn't ask about Alex, but I hadn't dared hope for that. Not yet.

As I was gathering the last of the dishes, congratulating myself on how well everything had gone, how much less awkward our "luncheon" had been than I'd feared, she said, "I have something to tell you."

The strain in her voice commanded me to sit.

After a long pause she shared a secret she'd been wanting to tell me for weeks, ever since I'd told her about Katherine and Alex.

The summer before she married my father, she had volunteered twice a week at the youth bible camp where my birth mother met Alex and Daniel. It was held on the same woody acres of church property, up by Buck's Peak, where she'd gone for her women's retreats when I was a girl.

She stared out across the lake, remembering. "I made felt cutouts with the youngest children. Bitty things. Lambs and crosses. I taught embroidery once or twice. And I drove the older girls to the beach."

She'd been forty-seven then, living alone in the house she'd grown up in in Coeur-de-Lune, and had long before accepted that she would never marry or have children. So that summer of her engagement to Bill Christie, licensed contractor, confirmed bachelor from Sacramento and fellow odd duck, was one of immense joy. He had worked on her house, replacing the dock with a fine new one, righting the foundation where it had subsided.

She had watched the kids at camp and thought, *Maybe.* Maybe there was a chance they could still have a child, though they were latecomers to the business of setting up a family.

"We called it a change-of-life baby, back then," she said. Formal as this expression was, I knew it was excruciatingly intimate for her to share. My mother did not discuss her bodily rhythms or functions; I had never seen her undressed, and when I visited her she slid her green plastic Mind-a-Pill, with its tiny square compartments stamped *Su-M-T-W-Th-F-Sa*, behind the toaster oven.

She said she'd noticed one girl in particular. A girl with bright red hair.

The girl stuck in her mind because after the church split up— the new, extreme branch splintering off, eventually heading to

Idaho, the rest staying behind in California, taking over the camp property—there had been whispers in the congregation about a girl in the Idaho-bound group who ran away. A redhead.

"What about my… Katherine?" I said.

She stiffened at the *my*.

But I couldn't help myself. I dashed over to the sideboard in the living room, grabbed the music box that Alex had given to me, and pressed the photo from the lid into her trembling hand.

She blinked rapidly, barely glancing at the small photo.

"You don't remember her, too?" I said, pointing at the girl with the brown hair. "Think back, someone who looked like this. Like me?"

She shook her head. Certain. Stubborn.

"Wait." I rushed to the den. Pulled my old "Love is Blue" record from the sleeve and set it on the turntable.

A swirling orchestra, a tune that had fallen out of fashion. *Lost to the cold and brutal judgment of time.*

Except it wasn't. Because Casey had kept the album for me, all these years.

I stared down at the 33 album cover in my hands, the woman on the front transformed into a butterfly with body paint. Ashamed that I was hurting my mother, even now, when I'd planned our day so carefully.

The last note rang out before I dared look at her. "Does it mean anything? Did they play it at the camp?"

She shook her head. "I only remember the red-haired girl. When Barbara called us about you being available for adoption, she said your mother had been a sad case, a runaway who over-dosed. Just like we told you. She didn't tell me your mother had been at the camp. But when Alexandra moved to town, I wondered if that redhead had possibly been the same girl. She was the right age. I wondered if…"

"If she wanted me back. You thought I was hers and she wanted me back."

Scratch-bump. Scratch-bump. The lonely static of the needle on the finished record.

Her head moved a degree, as if to shake away this idea, though her stillness after this barely perceptible gesture told me I was right. "The children did scavenger hunts at the camp, did Alexandra tell you that?" she said.

I nodded.

"On the beach." She traced the photo's jagged edges with a fingertip. "It was a game I'd played with my parents. We called it Flotsam and Jetsam. I thought the campers would enjoy it."

"Alex got the idea from you?"

She shrugged, handed me back the picture.

"I wish I'd known."

"It was a crazy thought, that she could be your birth mother."

"But it wasn't so crazy. Mother? It wasn't."

She shifted her eyes back to the lake again, toward the distant brown blur of The Shipwreck's dock. "The way she looked at you, at that church concert. As if she knew you were performing only for her. And the way you ran to her after! Ran."

She continued, more softly, "You never believed in God like I did, I know that. And now you'll say religion was to blame for what happened to those girls. But you worshipped just as blindly, as if she was the only one who could save you from me. And that decrepit old house…" She nodded at the window. "*That* was your church."

I couldn't answer. Couldn't even breathe.

Because she was right.

How much that must have hurt her, when she'd wanted me so badly. Casey had said—*Life's too short for if-onlys.* But if only I'd known.

I could try to explain to my mother that I was a lonely, confused child, that I didn't feel that way anymore, that no one person could save another—not a minister shouting from a pulpit and not a man playing guitar and not a woman passing out a list of clues.

In the end I simply said, "I'm sorry."

I clasped my mother's soft, cool hand and she didn't pull it away. Not at first.

Scratch-bump. Scratch-bump. I would not be the first to let go.

"I think I'll walk down to the water before it's too dark," she said, pulling her hand from mine and rising.

"Mother," I said to her broad back. "I wish…"

She stood, turned to face me.

When I didn't go on, because the list of things I wish I'd done differently was too endless to voice, she only nodded.

She wished, too.

So I have more answers now.

But I'll never know why Katherine left me the music box. The driftwood was the beginning of so much sadness for her, and the song might have been any song.

It was foolish to think it held a message for me, that I could ever understand it the way I do the objects Casey keeps on her nightstand: five blurry Polaroids, a blue tile, a cheap toy mermaid, a leaf, a napkin, a postcard.

Others would see it as junk, just household flotsam, but we know it's not, and it makes us smile.

The music box will always be part of the lake, and that seems right. It's lying there, keeping its secrets under the blue-black water.

California
1968

"This," Katherine says, one chubby finger punching the album cover. "Mama. This."

"What, Kathy? You want to hear the song?"

Her mother slips the record out and plays the song.

Katherine shakes her head. "This."

Finally, her mother realizes. The song is pretty, but it's not what her daughter wants.

They paint their faces like the lady in the picture.

Katherine is two, her small hand is clumsy. But she concentrates, trying her best to make orange-and-black wings on her mother's cheeks.

Her mother does a better job on Kathy's face, tickling her with the cold paintbrush.

They smile into the bathroom mirror together.

Two butterflies.

★ ★ ★ ★ ★

acknowledgments

Thank you to my brilliant agent, Stefanie Lieberman at Janklow & Nesbit. This book wouldn't exist without you.

Melanie Fried, my gifted and generous editor, loved these characters from day one and expertly wrestled with three narrative strands.

To everyone at Graydon House—I'm honored to be part of your launch. Thank you to Kathleen Carter, Lisa Wray, and Pamela Osti for working so hard to spread the word, and to Mary Luna and Gigi Lau for the beautiful cover.

Mike and Miranda, I love you beyond words. Mike, I don't know how you put up with all the angst and forced reads (consider this your second plaque). As Neil would say, you have a heart of gold.

Miranda, you fill our house with music and knock us over daily with your creativity and passion. Always follow your dreams.

To my sweet mom, Kay Doan, who's nothing like Ingrid (except for a few recipes). You're my ideal reader. Someday I'll write a book about our train trip.

To Dad. I miss you. E.T.

Carrie Higgins, the best big sister in the world, sent me a card saying, Never, Never, Never Give Up when I really wanted to. Sorry I called you "hisspiffy" when I was nine. Erin Higgins, you have so much soul; I'm proud to be your aunt.

To my aunt, Ann Kyle, whose spirit never wavered when her muscles gave. You taught me that life is too short for if-onlys; you are on every page of this book. You're my favorite teacher.

To my grandma, Alice Parker Wilson. Thanks for sending me to the library with a dollar for the used-book sale. You always said I'd be a writer. To my grandpa, Robert Storey Wilson. I'll always cherish your 1942 edition of *Jane Eyre*. You handled dining room walker battles with grace.

Love and gratitude to my Toronto family—Kelsey Mason, Wesley Mason, Tiffany Mason, David Mason, Natalie and Luke. Let's kayak at PKL soon.

Thank you, Linda Haderer, Paul Haderer, and Michael Kyle.

Mark Cunningham at Atelier26, your critique improved these pages immensely. David Biespiel, Jennifer Lauck, and everyone at The Attic took me seriously when I first shared my secret fiction habit.

Thank you, Judy Blume, Willamette Writers, Literary Arts, the Sterling Room for Writers, Broadway Books, Powell's, Tin House, A Children's Place, Rakestraw Books, the Multnomah County Library, Breitenbush Hot Springs, Grace Asuncion, Molly Steinblatt, Suzannah Bentley, Zuzana Sakova, Penny Lewis, Stacy Thomas, Gabriella Fiore, Sarah Shine, Leeann Lewis, Gail Caldwell, Jamie Pacton, Erin Gordon, Virginia La Forte, Jim Breithaupt, Erin Ferrell, Alisha Gorder, Pearl Griffin, Jennifer S. Brown, Meg Donohue, Polly Dugan, Lynda Cohen Loigman, Meg Mitchell Moore, Brian Jacobson, Theresa Griffin Kennedy, Kimberly Melton, Fletcher Reveley, Jessica Starr, Don Westlight, Cynthia Whitcomb, William Rader, Helen McDevitt, Lisa Towne, the TJ's Book Club, Pom-pom & Sparkle of the CCS, and my intrepid coworker, Leah Lilikoi McGonagall.

To everyone affected by amyotrophic lateral sclerosis: I'm in awe of your strength.

My family is so grateful to The ALS Association (alsa.org), the UCSF ALS Center, and the Stanford Neuromuscular Program for their work toward a cure.

THE
SUMMER LIST

AMY MASON DOAN

Reader's Guide

GRAYDON
HOUSE

1. What are your most cherished summer memories? Where did they take place? Have you been back to visit these spots? If so, what felt different or the same?

2. In *The Summer List*, the scavenger hunt leads Laura and Casey to the physical locations of their teenage summer memories. In what way does the scavenger hunt take on greater meaning in the novel?

3. Discuss these relationships: between Laura and Casey; Laura and Alex; Katherine and Alexandra; Katherine and Daniel. How are they similar or different?

4. Who is the Casey in your life? Are there friends you haven't spoken with in a long time with whom you'd like to reconnect? Is it ever best to leave a friendship in the past?

5. Why does Laura keep the music box in her pocket? What secrets did you keep from your family when you were a teenager? Why?

6. Did you understand Laura's decision to run away and attend school in Georgia, rather than in Los Angeles with Casey, following her father's death?

7. Did you agree with Alex's decision to keep the ALS gene a secret from Casey and Laura? If not, how would you have

approached the situation differently? Would you have wanted to know if it were you, or would you have preferred not to know, like Casey?

8. How did the dream-like quality of Katherine's chapters affect your reading experience and your understanding of Katherine's fate?

9. How did your feelings toward Ingrid Christie, Laura's mother, evolve throughout the novel, if at all?

10. Was the ending of the book uplifting or sad? What does the last scene suggest about the bonds between mothers and daughters?

11. Who was your favorite character in the novel? Who did you identify with most?

12. What was your favorite clue in the scavenger hunt?